# THE BROMELIAD TRILOGY

ALSO BY TERRY PRATCHETT

*The Wee Free Men*
*The Amazing Maurice and His Educated Rodents*
*The Carpet People*
*The Dark Side of the Sun*
*Strata*

THE JOHNNY MAXWELL TRILOGY
*Only You Can Save Mankind*
*Johnny and the Dead*
*Johnny and the Bomb*

*The Unadulterated Cat* (illustrated by Gray Jolliffe)
*Good Omens* (with Neil Gaiman)

THE DISCWORLD SERIES

# TERRY PRATCHETT

## the
## BROMELIAD TRILOGY

TRUCKERS

DIGGERS

WINGS

HarperCollins*Publishers*

Library of Congress Cataloging-in-Publication Data
Pratchett, Terry.
 The Bromeliad trilogy / by Terry Pratchett
  p.   cm.
 Summary: After generations of existing in the human-sized world, a group of four-inch-high nomes discover
their true nature and origin, with the help of a black square called the Thing.
 ISBN 0-06-009493-1.— 0-06-054855-X (lib. bdg.)
 [1. Science fiction. 2. Department stores—Fiction. 3. Quarries and quarrying—Fiction. 4. Computers—
Fiction.] I. Title.
PZ7.P8865 Br 2003
[Fic]—dc21                                                                    2002032944
                                                                                    CIP
                                                                                    AC

Typography by Nicole de las Heras
1  2  3  4  5  6  7  8  9  10

This collection first published in 1998 by Doubleday
a division of Transworld Publishers Ltd
First U.S. Edition, 2003

To Lyn and Rhianna
and the sandwich-eating alligator
at the Kennedy Space Center, Florida

# CONTENTS

# TRUCKERS

*The First Book of the Nomes*

───────○───────

## CONCERNING NOMES AND TIME

NOMES ARE SMALL. On the whole, small creatures don't live for a long time. But perhaps they do live *fast*.

Let me explain.

One of the shortest-lived creatures on the planet Earth is the adult common mayfly. It lasts for one day. The longest-living things are bristlecone pine trees, at 4,700 years and still counting.

This may seem tough on mayflies. But the important thing is not how long your life is but how long it seems.

To a mayfly, a single hour may last as long as a century. Perhaps old mayflies sit around complaining about how life this minute isn't a patch on the good old minutes of long ago, when the world was young and the sun seemed so much brighter and larvae showed you a bit of respect. Whereas the trees, which are not famous for their quick reactions, may just have time to notice the way the sky keeps flickering before the dry rot and woodworm set in.

It's all a sort of relativity. The faster you live, the more time stretches out. To a nome, a year lasts as long as ten years do to a human. Remember it. Don't let it concern you. They don't. They don't even know.

In the beginning . . .

    *I. There was the Site.*

    *II. And Arnold Bros (est. 1905) Moved upon the face of the Site, and Saw that it had Potential.*

    *III. For it was In the High Street.*

    *IV. Yea, it was also Handy for the Buses.*

    *V. And Arnold Bros (est. 1905) said, Let there be a Store, And Let it be a Store such as the World has not Seen hitherto;*

    *VI. Let the length of it be from Palmer Street even unto the Fish Market, and the Width of It, from the High Street right back to Disraeli Road;*

    *VII. Let it be High even Unto Five Stories plus Basement, And bright with Lifts; let there be the Eternal Fires of the Boiler Room in the subbasement and, above all other floors, let there be Customer Accounts to Order All Things;*

    *VIII. For this must be what all shall Know of Arnold Bros (est. 1905):* All Things Under One Roof. *And it shall be callèd: the Store of Arnold Bros (est. 1905).*

    *IX. And Thus it Was.*

    *X. And Arnold Bros (est. 1905) divided the Store into Departments, of Ironmongery, Corsetry, Modes and others After their Kind, and Created Humans to fill them with* All Things *saying, Yea,* All Things *Are Here. And Arnold Bros (est. 1905) said, Let there be Trucks, and Let their Colors be Red and Gold, and Let them Go Forth so that All May Know Arnold Bros (est. 1905), By Appointment, delivers* All Things;

*XI. Let there be Santa's Grottoes and Winter Sales and Summer Bargains and Back-to-School Week and All Commodities in their Season;*

*XII. And into the Store came the Nomes, that it would be their Place, for Ever and Ever.*

*From* The Book of Nome, Basements v. I–XII

# 1

THIS IS THE story of the Going Home.

This is the story of the Critical Path.

This is the story of the truck roaring through the sleeping city and out into the country lanes, smashing through streetlamps and swinging from side to side and shattering shop windows and rolling to a halt when the police chased it. And when the baffled men went back to their car to report *Listen, will you, listen? There isn't anyone driving it!*, it became the story of the truck that started up again, rolled away from the astonished men, and vanished into the night.

But the story didn't end there.

It didn't start there, either.

The sky rained dismal. It rained humdrum. It rained the kind of rain that is so much wetter than normal rain, the kind of rain that comes down in big drops and splats, the kind of rain that is merely an upright sea with slots in it.

It rained a tattoo on the old hamburger boxes and french fries wrappers in the wire basket that was giving Masklin a temporary hiding place.

Look at him. Wet. Cold. Extremely worried. And four inches high.

The litter bin was usually a good hunting ground, even in winter. There were often a few cold fries, sometimes even a chicken bone. Once or twice there had been a rat, too. It had been a really good day when there had last been a rat—it had kept them going for a week. The trouble was that you could get pretty fed up with rat by the third day. By the third mouthful, come to that.

Masklin scanned the parking lot.

And here it came, right on time, crashing through the puddles and pulling up with a hiss of brakes.

He'd watched this truck arrive every Tuesday and Thursday morning for the last four weeks. He timed the driver's stop carefully.

They had exactly three minutes. To someone the size of a nome, that's more than half an hour.

He scrambled down through the greasy paper, dropped out of the bottom of the bin, and ran for the bushes at the edge of the lot, where Grimma and the old folk were waiting.

"It's here!" he said. "Come on!"

They got to their feet, groaning and grumbling. He'd taken them through this dozens of times. He knew it wasn't any good shouting. They just got upset and confused, and then they'd grumble some more. They grumbled about cold fries, even when Grimma warmed them up. They moaned about rat. He'd seriously thought about leaving alone, but he couldn't bring himself to do it. They needed him. They needed someone to grumble at.

But they were too *slow*. He felt like bursting into tears.

He turned to Grimma instead.

"Come *on*," he said. "Give them a prod or something. They'll never get moving!"

She patted his hand.

"They're frightened," she said. "You go on. I'll bring them out."

There wasn't time to argue. Masklin ran back across the soaking mud of the lot, unslinging the rope and grapnel. It had taken him a week to make the hook out of a bit of wire teased off a fence, and he'd spent days practicing; he was already swinging it around his head as he reached the truck's wheel.

The hook caught the tarpaulin high above him at the second try. He tested it once or twice and then, his feet scrabbling for a grip on the tire, pulled himself up.

He'd done it before. Oh, he'd done it three or four times. He scrambled under the heavy tarpaulin and into the darkness beyond, pulling out more line and tying it as tightly as possible around one of the ropes that were as thick as his arm.

Then he slid back to the edge, and thank goodness, Grimma *was* herding the old people across the gravel. He could hear them complaining about the puddles.

Masklin jumped up and down with impatience.

It seemed to take hours. He explained it to them millions of times, but people hadn't been pulled up onto the backs of trucks when they were children and they didn't see why they should start now. Old Granny Morkie insisted that all the men look the other way so that they wouldn't see up her skirts, for example, and old Torrit whimpered so much that Masklin had to lower him again so that Grimma could blindfold him. It wasn't so bad after he'd hauled the first few up, because they were able to help on the rope, but time still stretched out.

He pulled Grimma up last. She was light. They were *all* light, if it came to that. You didn't get rat every day.

It was amazing. They were all on board. He'd worked with an ear cocked for the sound of footsteps on gravel and the slamming of the driver's door, and it hadn't happened.

"Right," he said, shaking with the effort. "That's it, then. Now if we just go—"

"I dropped the Thing," said old Torrit. "The Thing. I dropped it, d'you see? I dropped it down by the wheel when she was blindfoldin' me. You go and get it, boy."

Masklin looked at him in horror. Then he poked his head out from under the tarpaulin, and yes, there it was, far below. A tiny black cube on the ground.

The Thing.

It was lying in a puddle, although that wouldn't affect it. Nothing touched the Thing. It wouldn't even burn.

And then he heard the sound of slow footsteps on the gravel.

"There's no time," he whispered. "There really is no time."

"We can't go without it," said Grimma.

"Of course we can. It's just a, a thing. We won't need the wretched object where we're going."

He felt guilty as soon as he'd said it, amazed at his own lips for uttering such words. Grimma looked horrified. Granny Morkie drew herself up to her full, quivering height.

"May you be forgiven!" she barked. "What a terrible thing to say! You tell him, Torrit." She nudged Torrit in the ribs.

"If we ain't taking the Thing, I ain't going," said Torrit sulkily. "It's not—"

"That's your leader talkin' to you," interrupted Granny Morkie. "So you do what you're told. Leave it behind, indeed! It wouldn't be decent. It wouldn't be right. So you go and get it, this minute."

Masklin stared wordlessly down at the soaking mud and then, with a desperate motion, threw the line over the edge and slid down it.

It was raining harder now, with a touch of sleet. The wind

whipped at him as he dropped past the great arc of the wheel and landed heavily in the puddle. He reached out and scooped up the Thing—

And the truck started to move.

First there was a roar, so loud that it went beyond sound and became a solid wall of noise. Then there was a blast of stinking air and a vibration that shook the ground.

He pulled sharply on the line and yelled at them to pull him up, and realized that even he couldn't hear his own voice. But Grimma or someone must have got the idea because, just as the big wheel began to turn, the rope tightened and he felt his feet lifted off the mud.

He bounced and spun back and forth as, with painful slowness, they pulled him past the wheel. It turned only a few inches away from him, a black, chilly blur, and all the time the hammering sound battered at his head.

I'm not scared, he told himself. This is much worse than anything I've ever faced, and it's not frightening. It's too terrible to be frightening.

He felt as though he were in a tiny, warm cocoon, away from all the noise and the wind. I'm going to die, he thought, just because of this Thing that has never helped us at all, something that's just a lump of stuff, and now I'm going to die and go to the Heavens. I wonder if old Torrit is right about what happens when you die. It seems a bit severe to have to die to find out. I've looked at the sky every night for years, and I've never seen any nomes up there. . . .

But it didn't really matter, it was all outside him, it wasn't real—

Hands reached down and caught him under the arms and

dragged him into the booming space under the tarpaulin and, with some difficulty, pried the Thing out of his grip.

Behind the speeding truck, fresh curtains of gray rain dragged across the empty fields.

And, across the whole country, there were no more nomes.

There had been plenty of them, in the days when it didn't seem to rain so much. Masklin could remember at least forty. But then the highway had come; the stream was put in pipes underground, and the nearest hedges were dug up. Nomes had always lived in the corners of the world, and suddenly there weren't too many corners anymore.

The numbers started going down. A lot of this was due to natural causes, and when you're four inches high natural causes can be anything with teeth and speed and hunger. Then Pyrrince, who was by way of being the most adventurous, led a desperate expedition *across the highway* one night, to investigate the woods on the other side. They never came back. Some said it was hawks, some said it was a truck. Some even said they'd made it halfway and were marooned on the central reservation between endless swishing lines of cars.

Then the cafe had been built a little farther along the road. It had been a sort of improvement. It depended how you looked at it. If cold leftover fries and scraps of gray chicken were food, then there was suddenly enough for everyone.

And then it was spring, and Masklin looked around and found that there were just ten of them left, and eight of those were too old to get about much. Old Torrit was nearly ten.

It had been a dreadful summer. Grimma organized those who

could still get about into midnight raids on the litter bins, and Masklin tried to hunt.

Hunting by yourself was like dying a bit at a time. Most of the things you were hunting were also hunting *you*. And even if you were lucky and made a kill, how did you get it home? It had taken two days with the rat, including sitting out at night to fight off other creatures. Ten strong hunters could do anything—rob bees' nests, trap mice, catch moles, *anything*—but one hunter by himself, with no one to watch his back in the long grass, was simply the next meal for everything with talons and claws.

To get enough to eat, you needed lots of healthy hunters. But to get lots of healthy hunters, you needed enough to eat.

"It'll be all right in the autumn," said Grimma, bandaging his arm where a stoat had caught it. "There'll be mushrooms and berries and nuts and everything."

Well, there hadn't been any mushrooms, and it rained so much that most of the berries rotted before they ripened. There were plenty of nuts, though. The nearest hazel tree was half a day's journey away. Masklin could carry a dozen nuts if he smashed them out of their shells and dragged them back in a paper bag from the bin. It took a whole day to do it, risking hawks all the way, and it was just enough food for a day as well.

And then the back of the burrow fell in, because of all the rain. It was almost pleasant to get out, then. It was better than listening to the grumbling about him not doing essential repairs. Oh, and there was the fire. You needed a fire at the burrow mouth, both for cooking and for keeping away night prowlers. Granny Morkie went to sleep one day and let it go out. Even she had the decency to be embarrassed.

When Masklin came back that night, he looked at the heap of dead ashes for a long time and then stuck his spear in the ground and burst out laughing, and went on laughing until he started to cry. He couldn't face the rest of them. He had to go and sit outside where, presently, Grimma brought him a shellful of nettle tea. *Cold* nettle tea.

"They're all very upset about it," she volunteered.

Masklin gave a hollow laugh. "Oh, yes, I can tell," he said. "I've heard them: 'You ought to bring back another cigarette-end, boy, I'm right out of tobacco,' and 'We never have fish these days; you might find the time to go down to the river,' and 'Self, self, self, that's all you young people think about, in my day—'"

Grimma sighed. "They do their best," she said. "It's just that they don't realize. There were hundreds of us when they were young."

"It's going to take *days* to get that fire lit," said Masklin. They had a spectacle lens; it needed a very sunny day to work.

He poked aimlessly in the mud by his feet.

"I've had enough," he said quietly. "I'm going to leave."

"But we need you!"

"*I* need me, too. I mean, what kind of life is this?"

"But they'll die if you go away!"

"They'll die anyway," said Masklin.

"That's a wicked thing to say!"

"Well, it's true. Everyone dies anyway. *We'll* die anyway. Look at you. You spend your whole time washing and tidying up and cooking and chasing after them. You're nearly three! It's about time you had a life of your own."

"Granny Morkie was very kind to me when I was small," said Grimma defensively. "You'll be old one day."

"You think? And who will be working their fingers to the bone to look after me?"

Masklin found himself getting angrier and angrier. He was certain he was in the right. But it *felt* as if he was in the wrong, which made it worse.

He'd thought about this for a long time, and it had always left him feeling angry and awkward. All the clever ones and the bold ones and the brave ones had gone long ago, one way or the other. Good old Masklin, they'd said, stout chap, you look after the old folk and we'll be back before you know it, just as soon as we've found a better place. Every time good old Masklin thought about this, he got indignant with them for going and with himself for staying. He always gave in, that was his trouble. He knew it. Whatever he promised himself at the start, he always took the way of least resistance.

Grimma was glaring at him.

He shrugged.

"All right, all right, so they can come with us," he said.

"You know they won't go," she said. "They're too old. They all grew up around here. They like it here."

"They like it here when there's us around to wait on them," muttered Masklin.

They left it at that. There were nuts for dinner. Masklin's had a maggot in it.

He went out afterward and sat at the top of the bank with his chin in his hands, watching the highway again.

It was a stream of red and white lights. There were humans inside those boxes, going about whatever mysterious business humans spent their time on. They were always in a hurry to get to it, whatever it was.

He was prepared to bet they didn't eat rat. Humans had it really easy. They were big and slow, but they didn't have to live in damp burrows waiting for daft old women to let the fire go out. They never had maggots in their tea. They went wherever they wanted and they did whatever they liked. The whole world belonged to them.

And all night long they drove up and down in these little trucks with lights on. Didn't they ever go to sleep? There must be hundreds of them.

He'd dreamed of leaving on a truck. Trucks often stopped at the cafe. It would be easy—well, fairly easy—to find a way onto one. They were clean and shiny—they had to go somewhere better than this. And after all, what was the alternative? They'd never see winter through here, and setting out across the fields with the bad weather coming on didn't bear thinking about.

Of course, he'd never do it. You never actually did it, in the end. You just dreamed about following those swishing lights.

And above the rushing lights, the stars. Torrit said the stars were very important. Right at the moment, Masklin didn't agree. You couldn't eat them. They weren't even much good for seeing by. The stars were pretty useless, when you thought about it. . . .

Somebody screamed.

Masklin's body got to his feet almost before his mind had even thought about it, and sped silently through the scrubby bushes toward the burrow.

Where, its head entirely underground and its brush waving excitedly at the stars, there was a dog fox. He recognized it. He'd had a couple of close shaves with it in the past.

Somewhere inside Masklin's head the bit of him that was really him—old Torrit had a lot to say about this bit—was horrified to see him snatch up his spear, which was still in the ground where he had plunged it, and stab the fox as hard as he could in a hind leg.

There was a muffled yelp and the animal struggled backward, turning an evil, foaming mask to its tormentor. Two bright yellow eyes focused on Masklin, who leaned panting on his spear. This was one of those times when time itself slowed down and everything was suddenly more real. Perhaps, if you knew you were going to die, your senses crammed in as much detail as they could while they still had the chance. . . .

There were flecks of blood around the creature's muzzle.

Masklin felt himself become angry. It welled up inside him, like a huge bubble. He didn't have much, and this grinning *thing* was taking even that away from him.

As the red tongue lolled out, he knew that he had two choices. He could run, or he could die.

So he attacked instead. The spear soared from his hand like a bird, catching the fox in the lip. It screamed and pawed at the wound, and Masklin was running, running across the dirt, propelled by the engine of his anger, and then jumping and grabbing handfuls of rank red fur and hauling himself up the fox's flank to land astride its neck and drawing his stone knife and stabbing, stabbing, at everything that was wrong with the world. . . .

The fox screamed again and leaped away. If he had been capable of thinking, then Masklin would have known that his knife wasn't doing much more than annoying the creature, but it wasn't used to meals fighting back with such fury, and its only thought now was to get away. It breasted the embankment and rushed headlong down it, toward the lights of the highway.

Masklin started to think again. The rushing of the traffic filled his ears. He let go and threw himself into the long grass as the creature galloped out onto the asphalt.

He landed heavily and rolled over, all the breath knocked out of him.

But he remembered what happened next. It stayed in his memory for a long time, long after he'd seen so many strange things that there really should have been no room for it.

The fox, as still as a statue in a headlight's beam, snarled its defiance as it tried to outstare ten tons of metal hurtling toward it at seventy miles an hour.

There was a bump, a swish, and darkness.

Masklin lay facedown in the cool moss for a long time. Then, dreading what he was about to see, trying not to imagine it, he pulled himself to his feet and plodded back toward whatever was left of his home.

Grimma was waiting at the burrow's mouth, holding a twig like a club. She spun round and nearly brained Masklin as he staggered out of the darkness and leaned against the bank. He stuck out a weary hand and pushed the stick aside.

"We didn't know where you'd gone," she said, her voice on the edge of hysteria. "We just heard the noise and there it was you should have been here and it got Mr. Mert and Mrs. Coom and it was digging at the—"

She stopped and seemed to sag.

"Yes, thank you," said Masklin coldly, "I'm all right, thank you very much."

"What—what happened?"

He ignored her and trooped into the darkness of the burrow and lay down. He could hear the old ones whispering as he sank into a deep, chilly sleep.

I should have been here, he thought.

They depend on me.

We're going. All of us.

It had seemed a good idea, then.

It looked a bit different, now.

Now the nomes clustered at one end of the great dark space inside the truck. They were silent. There wasn't any *room* to be noisy. The roar of the engine filled the air from edge to edge. Sometimes it would falter and start again. Occasionally the whole truck lurched.

Grimma crawled across the trembling floor.

"How long is it going to take to get there?" she said.

"Where?" said Masklin.

"Wherever we're going."

"I don't know."

"They're hungry, you see."

They always were. Masklin looked hopelessly at the huddle of old ones. One or two of them were watching him expectantly.

"There isn't anything I can do," he said. "I'm hungry too, but there's nothing here. It's empty."

"Granny Morkie gets very upset when she's missed a meal," said Grimma.

Masklin gave her a long, blank stare. Then he crawled his way to the group and sat down between Torrit and the old woman.

He'd never really talked to them, he realized. When he was small, they were giants who were no concern of his, and then he'd been a hunter among hunters, and this year he'd either been out looking for food or deep in an exhausted sleep. But he knew why Torrit was the leader of the tribe. It stood to reason—he was the oldest nome. The oldest was always leader; that way there couldn't be any arguments. Not the oldest *woman*, of course, because everyone knew this was unthinkable; even Granny Morkie was quite firm about that. Which was a bit odd, because she treated him like an idiot and Torrit never made a decision without looking at her out of the corner of his eye. Masklin sighed. He stared at his knees.

"Look, I don't know how long—" he began.

"Don't you worry about me, boy," said Granny Morkie, who seemed to have quite recovered. "This is all rather excitin', ain't it?"

"But it might take ages," said Masklin. "I didn't know it was going to take this long. It was just a mad idea . . ."

She poked him with a bony finger. "Young man," she said, "I was alive in the Great Winter of 1999. Terrible, that was. You can't tell *me* anything about going hungry. Grimma's a good girl, but she worries."

"But I don't even know where we're going!" Masklin burst out. "I'm sorry!"

Torrit, who was sitting with the Thing on his skinny knees, peered shortsightedly at him.

"We have the Thing," he said. "It will show us the Way, it will."

Masklin nodded gloomily. Funny how Torrit always knew what the Thing wanted. It was just a black square thing, but it had some very definite ideas about the importance of regular meals and how you should always listen to what the old folk said. It seemed to have an answer for everything.

"And where does this Way take us?" said Masklin.

"You knows that well enough. To the Heavens."

"Oh. Yes," said Masklin. He glared at the Thing. He was pretty certain that it didn't tell old Torrit anything at all; he knew he had pretty good hearing, and he never heard it say anything. It never did anything, it never moved. The only thing it ever did was look black and square. It was *good* at that.

"Only by followin' the Thing closely in all particulars can we be sure of going to the Heavens," said Torrit uncertainly, as if he'd been told this a long time ago and hadn't understood it even then.

"Yes, well," said Masklin. He stood up on the swaying floor and made his way to the tarpaulin. Then he paused to screw up his courage and poked his head under the gap.

There was nothing but blurs and lights, and strange smells.

It was all going wrong. It had seemed so sensible that night, a week ago. Anything was better than here. That had seemed so obvious then. But it was odd. The old ones moaned like anything when things weren't exactly to their liking, but now, when everything was looking bad, they were almost cheerful.

People were a lot more complicated than they looked. Perhaps the Thing could tell you that, too, if you knew how to ask.

The truck turned a corner and rumbled down into blackness and then, without warning, stopped. He found himself looking into a huge lighted space, full of trucks, full of *humans*. . . .

He pulled his head back quickly and scuttled across the floor to Torrit.

"Er," he said.

"Yes, lad?"

"Heaven. Do humans go there?"

The old nome shook his head. "*The* Heavens," he said. "More than one of 'em, see? Only nomes go there."

"You're absolutely certain?"

"Oh, yes." Torrit beamed. "O' course, they may have heavens of their own," he said. "I don't know about that. But they ain't ours, you may depend upon it."

"Oh."

Torrit stared at the Thing again.

"We've stopped," he said. "Where are we?"

Masklin stared wearily into the darkness.

"I think I had better go and find out," he said.

There was whistling outside, and the distant rumble of human voices. The lights went out. There was a rattling noise, followed by a click, and then silence.

After a while there was a faint scrabbling around the back of one of the silent trucks. A length of line, no thicker than thread, dropped down until it touched the oily floor of the garage.

A minute went by. Then, lowering itself with great care hand over hand, a small, stumpy figure shinned down the line and dropped onto the floor. It stood rock still for a few seconds after landing, with only its eyes moving.

It was not entirely human. There were definitely the right number of arms and legs, and the additional bits like eyes and so on were in the usual places, but the figure that was now creeping across the darkened floor in its mouse skins looked like a brick wall on legs. Nomes are so stocky that a Japanese sumo wrestler would look half starved by comparison, and the way this one moved suggested that it was considerably tougher than old boots.

Masklin was, in fact, terrified out of his life. There was nothing here that he recognized, except for the smell of *oil*, which he had come to associate with humans and especially with trucks (Torrit had told him loftily that *all* was a burning water that trucks drank, at which point Masklin knew the old nome had gone mad. It stood to reason. Water didn't burn).

None of it made any sense. Vast cans loomed above him. There were huge pieces of metal that had a made look about them. This was definitely a part of a human heaven. Humans liked metal.

He did skirt warily around a cigarette end and made a mental note to take it back for Torrit.

There were other trucks in this place, all of them silent. It was, Masklin decided, a truck nest. Which meant that the only food in it was probably *all.*

He untensed a bit and prodded about under a bench that towered against one wall like a house. There were drifts of wastepaper there, and, led by a smell which here was even stronger than *all,* he found a whole apple core. It was going brown, but it was a pretty good find.

He slung it across one shoulder and turned around.

There was a rat watching him thoughtfully. It was considerably bigger and sleeker than the things that fought the nomes for the scraps from the litter bin. It dropped on all fours and trotted toward him.

Masklin felt that he was on firmer ground here. All these huge dark shapes and cans and ghastly smells were quite beyond him, but he knew what a rat was, all right, and what to do about one.

He dropped the core, brought his spear back slowly and carefully, aimed at a point just between the creature's eyes . . .

Two things happened at once.

Masklin noticed that the rat had a little red collar.

And a voice said: "Don't! He took a long time to train. Bargains Galore! Where did *you* come from?"

o  o  o

The stranger was a nome. At least Masklin had to assume so. He was certainly nome height and moved like a nome.

But his clothes . . .

The basic color for a practical nome's clothes is mud. That was common sense. Grimma knew fifty ways of making dyes from wild plants, and they all yielded a color that was, when you came right down to it, basically muddy. Sometimes yellow mud, sometimes brown mud, sometimes even greenish mud, but still, well, mud. Because any nome who ventured out wearing jolly reds and blues would have a life expectancy of perhaps half an hour before something digestive happened to him.

Whereas this nome looked like a rainbow. He wore brightly colored clothes of a material so fine, it looked like a fries wrapper, a belt studded with bits of glass, proper leather boots, and a hat with a feather in it. As he talked, he slapped his leg idly with a leather strap which, it turned out, was the leash for the rat.

"Well?" he snapped. "Answer me!"

"I came off the truck," said Masklin shortly, eyeing the rat. It stopped scratching its ears, gave him a look, and went and hid behind its master.

"What were you doing on there? Answer me!"

Masklin pulled himself up. "We were traveling," he said.

The nome glared at him. "What's traveling?" he snapped.

"Moving along," said Masklin. "You know? Coming from one place and going to another place."

This seemed to have a strange effect on the stranger. If it didn't actually make him polite, at least it took the edge off his tone.

"Are you trying to tell me you came from *Outside*?" he said.

"That's right."

"But that's impossible!"

"Is it?" Masklin looked worried.

"There's nothing Outside!"

"Is there? Sorry," said Masklin. "But we seem to have come in from it, anyway. Is this a problem?"

"You mean *really* Outside?" said the nome, sidling closer.

"I suppose I do. We never really thought about it. What's this pl—"

"What's it like?"

"What?"

"Outside! What's it like?"

Masklin looked blank. "Well," he said. "It's sort of big—"

"Yes?"

"And, er, there's a lot of it—"

"Yes? Yes?"

"With, you know, things in it—"

"Is it true the ceiling is so high you can't see it?" asked the nome, apparently beside himself with excitement.

"Don't know. What's a ceiling?" said Masklin.

"That is," said the nome, pointing up to a gloomy roof of girders and shadows.

"Oh, I haven't seen anything like that," said Masklin. "Outside it's blue or gray, with white things floating around in it."

"And, and, the walls are such a long way off, and there's a sort of green carpet thing that grows on the ground?" asked the nome, hopping from one foot to the other.

"Don't know," said Masklin, even more mystified. "What's a carpet?"

"Wow!" The nome got a grip on himself and extended a shaking hand. "My name's Angalo," he said. "Angalo de Haberdasheri. Haha. Of course, that won't mean anything to you! And this is Bobo."

The rat appeared to grin. Masklin had never heard a rat called anything, except perhaps, if you were driven to it, "dinner."

"I'm Masklin," he said. "Is it all right if the rest of us come down? It was a long journey."

"Gosh, yes! All from Outside? My father'll never believe it!"

"I'm sorry," said Masklin. "I don't understand. What's so special? We were outside. Now we're inside."

Angalo ignored him. He was staring at the others as they came stiffly down the line, grumbling.

"Old people, too!" said Angalo. "And they look just like us! Not even pointy heads or anything!"

"Saucy!" said Granny Morkie. Angalo stopped grinning.

"Madam," he said icily, "do you know who you're talking to?"

"Someone who's not too old for a smacked bottom," said Granny Morkie. "If I looked just like you, my lad, I'd look a great deal better. Pointy heads, indeed!"

Angalo's mouth opened and shut silently. Then he said: "It's amazing! I mean, Dorcas said that even if there was a possibility of life outside the Store, it wouldn't be life as we know it! Please, please, all follow me."

They exchanged glances as Angalo scurried away toward the edge of the truck nest, but followed him anyway. There wasn't much of an alternative.

"I remember when your old dad stayed out too long in the sun one day. He talked rubbish, too, just like this one," said Granny Morkie quietly.

Torrit appeared to be reaching a conclusion. They waited for it politely.

"I reckon," he said at last, "I reckon we ought to eat his rat."

"You shut up, you," said Granny, automatically.

"I'm leader, I am. You've got no right, talking like that to a leader," Torrit whined.

"O' course you're leader," snapped Granny Morkie. "Who said you weren't leader? I never said you weren't leader. You're leader."

"Right," sniffed Torrit.

"And now shut up," said Granny.

Masklin tapped Angalo on the shoulder. "Where *is* this place?" he said.

Angalo stopped by the wall, which towered up into the distance. "You don't know?" he said.

"We just thought, well, we just *hoped* that the trucks went to— to a good place to be," said Grimma.

"Well, you heard right," said Angalo proudly. "This is the best place to be. This is the Store!"

# 2

*XIII. And in the Store there was neither Night nor Day, only Opening Time and Closing Time. Rain fell not, neither was there Snow.*

*XIV. And the nomes grew fat and multiplied as the years passed, and spent their time in Rivalry and Small War, Department unto Department, and forgot all they knew of the Outside.*

*XV. For they said, Is it not so, Arnold Bros (est. 1905) has put* All Things *Under One Roof?*

*XVI. And those who said, Perhaps Not* All *Things, were cruelly laughed at, and prodded.*

*XVII. And other nomes said, Even if there were an Outside, What can it hold that we would need? For here we have the power of the Electric, the Food Hall, and All manner of Diversions.*

*XVIII. And thus the Seasons fell thicker than the cushions that are in Soft Furnishings (3rd Floor).*

*XIX. Until a Stranger came from afar, crying out in a loud voice, and he cried, Woe, woe.*

*From* The Book of Nome,
First Floor v. XIII–XIX

THEY TRIPPED OVER one another, they walked with their heads turned upward and their mouths open, they gawked. Angalo had stopped by a hole in the wall and waved them through hurriedly.

"In here," he said.

Granny Morkie sniffed.

"That's a rat hole," she said. "You're not asking me to go down a rat hole?" She turned to Torrit. "He's asking me to go down a rat hole! I'm not going down a rat hole!"

"Why not?" said Angalo.

"It's a rat hole!"

"That's just what it looks like," said Angalo. "It's a disguised entrance, that's all."

"Your rat just went through it," said Granny Morkie triumphantly. "I've got eyes. It's a rat hole."

Angalo gave Grimma a pleading look and ducked through the hole. She poked her head through after him.

"I don't *think* it's a rat hole, Granny," she said, in a slightly muffled voice.

"And why is that, pray?"

"Because there's stairs inside. Oh, and dear little lights."

It was a long climb. They had to stop and wait several times for the old ones to catch up, and Torrit had to be helped most of the way. At the top, the stairs went through a more dignified sort of door into—

Even when he was young, Masklin had never seen more than forty nomes all together at once.

There were more than that here. And there was food. It didn't look like anything he recognized, but it had to be food. After all, people were eating it.

A space about twice as high as he was stretched away into the distance. Food was stacked in neat piles with aisles between them, and these were thronged with nomes. No one paid much attention to the little group as it shuffled obediently behind Angalo, who had got some of his old swagger back.

Several nomes had sleek rats on leashes. Some of the ladies had mice, which trotted obediently behind them, and out of the corner of his ear Masklin could hear Granny Morkie tut-tutting her disapproval.

He also heard old Torrit say excitedly, "I know that stuff! That's cheese! There was a cheese sandwich in the bin once, back in the summer of ninety-seven, d'you remember—?" Granny Morkie nudged him hard in his skinny ribs.

"You shut up, you," she commanded. "You don't want to show us up in front of all these folk, do you? Be a leader. Act proud."

They weren't very good at it. They walked in stunned silence. Fruits and vegetables were stacked behind trestle tables, with nomes working industriously on them. There were other things, too, which he couldn't begin to recognize. Masklin didn't want to show his ignorance, but curiosity got the better of him.

"What's that thing over there?" he asked, pointing.

"It's a salami sausage," said Angalo. "Ever had it before?"

"Not lately," said Masklin truthfully.

"And they're dates," said Angalo. "And that's a banana. I expect you've never seen a banana before, have you?"

Masklin opened his mouth, but Granny Morkie beat him to it.

"Bit small, that one," she said, and sniffed. "Quite tiny, in fact, compared to the ones we got at home."

"It is, is it?" said Angalo, suspiciously.

"Oh, yes," said Granny, beginning to warm to her subject. "Very puny. Why, the ones we got at home"—she paused and looked at the banana, lying on a couple of trestles like a canoe, and her lips moved as she thought fast—"why," she added triumphantly, "we could hardly dig them out o' the ground!"

She stared victoriously at Angalo, who tried to outstare her and gave up.

"Well, whatever," he said vaguely, looking away. "You may all help yourselves. Tell the nomes in charge that it's to go on the Haberdasheri account, will you? But don't say you've come from Outside. I want that to be a surprise."

There was a general rush in the direction of the food. Even Granny Morkie just happened to wander toward it, and acted quite surprised to find her way blocked by a cake.

Only Masklin stayed where he was, despite the urgent complaints from his stomach. He wasn't sure he even began to understand how things worked in the Store, but he had an obscure feeling that if you didn't face them with dignity, you could end up doing things you weren't entirely happy about.

"You're not hungry?" said Angalo.

"I'm hungry," admitted Masklin. "I'm just not eating. Where does all the food *come* from?"

"Oh, we take it from the humans," said Angalo airily. "They're rather stupid, you know."

"And they don't mind?"

"They think it's rats," sniggered Angalo. "We take up rat doodahs with us. At least, the Food Hall families do," he corrected himself. "Sometimes they let other people go up with them. Then the humans just think it's rats."

Masklin's brow wrinkled.

"Doodahs?" he said.

"You know," said Angalo. "Droppings."

Masklin nodded. "They fall for that, do they?" he said doubtfully.

"They're very stupid, I told you." The boy walked around Masklin. "You must come and see my father," he said. "Of course, it's a foregone conclusion that you'll join the Haberdasheri."

Masklin looked at the tribe. They had spread out among the food stalls. Torrit had a lump of cheese as big as his head, Granny Morkie was investigating a banana as if it might explode, and even Grimma wasn't paying him any attention.

Masklin felt lost. What he was good at, he knew, was tracking a rat across several fields, bringing it down with a single spear throw, and dragging it home. He'd felt really good about that. People had said things like "Well done."

He had a feeling that you didn't have to track a banana.

"Your father?" he said.

"The Duke de Haberdasheri," said Angalo proudly. "Defender of the Mezzanine and Autocrat of the Staff Canteen."

"He's three people?" said Masklin, puzzled.

"Those are his titles. Some of them. He's nearly the most powerful nome in the Store. Do you have things like fathers Outside?"

Funny thing, Masklin thought. He's a rude little twerp except when he talks about the Outside; then he's like an eager little boy.

"I had one once," he said. He didn't want to dwell on the subject.

"I bet you had lots of adventures!"

Masklin thought about some of the things that had happened to him—or, more accurately, had *nearly* happened to him—recently.

"Yes," he said.

"I bet it was tremendous fun!"

Fun, Masklin thought. It wasn't a familiar word. Perhaps it referred to running through muddy ditches with hungry teeth chasing you. "Do you hunt?" he asked.

"Rats, sometimes. In the boiler-room. Of course, we have to keep them down." He scratched Bobo behind an ear.

"Do you eat them?"

Angalo looked horrified. "Eat *rat?*"

Masklin stared around at the piles of food. "No, I suppose not," he said. "You know, I never realized there were so many nomes in the world. How many live here?"

Angalo told him.

"Two what?" said Masklin.

Angalo repeated it.

"You don't look very impressed," he said, when Masklin's expression didn't change.

Masklin looked hard at the end of his spear. It was a piece of flint he'd found in a field one day, and he'd spent ages teasing a bit of twine out of the hay bale in order to tie it onto a stick. Right now it seemed about the one familiar thing in a bewildering world.

"I don't know," he said. "What *is* a thousand?"

Duke Cido de Haberdasheri, who was also Lord Protector of the Up Escalator, Defender of the Mezzanine, and Knight of the Counter, turned the Thing over in his hands, very slowly. Then he tossed it aside.

"Very amusing," he said.

The nomes stood in a confused group in the Duke's palace, which was currently under the floorboards in the Soft Furnishings Department. The Duke was still in armor, and not very amused.

"So," he said, "you're from Outside, are you? Do you really expect me to believe you?"

"Father, I—" Angalo began.

"Be quiet! You know the words of Arnold Bros (est. 1905)! Everything Under One Roof. *Everything!* Therefore, there can be no Outside. Therefore, you people are not from it. Therefore, you're from some other part of the Store. Corsetry. Or Young Fashions, maybe. We've never really explored there."

"No, we're—" Masklin began.

The Duke held up his hands.

"Listen to me," he said, glaring at Masklin. "I don't blame *you.* My son is an impressionable young lad. I have no doubt he talked you into it. He's altogether too fond of going to look at trucks, and he listens to silly stories and his brain gets overheated. Now I am not an unreasonable nome," he added, daring them to disagree, "and there is always room for a strong lad like yourself in the Haberdasheri guards. So let us forget this nonsense, shall we?"

"But we really do come from outside," Masklin persisted.

*"There is no Outside!"* said the Duke. "Except of course when a good nome dies, if he has led a proper life. *Then* there is an Outside, where he will live in splendor forever. Come now." He patted Masklin on the shoulder. "Give up this foolish chatter, and help us in our valiant task."

"Yes, but what *for?*" said Masklin.

"You wouldn't want the Ironmongri to take our department, would you?" said the Duke. Masklin glanced at Angalo, who shook his head urgently.

"I suppose not," he said, "but you're all nomes, aren't you? And there's masses for everyone. Spending all your time squabbling seems a bit silly."

Out of the corner of his eye he saw Angalo put his head in his hands.

The Duke went red.

"Silly, did you say?"

Masklin leaned backward to get out of his way, but he'd been brought up to be honest. He felt he wasn't bright enough to get away with lies.

"Well—" he began.

"Have you never heard of honor?" said the Duke.

Masklin thought for a while and then shook his head.

"The Ironmongri want to take over the whole Store," said Angalo hurriedly. "That would be a terrible thing. And the Millineri are nearly as bad."

"Why?" said Masklin.

"Why?" said the Duke. "Because they have always been our enemies. And now you may go," he added.

"Where?" said Masklin.

"To the Ironmongri, or the Millineri. Or the Stationeri—they're just the people for you. Or go back Outside, for all I care," said the Duke sarcastically.

"We want the Thing back," said Masklin stolidly. The Duke picked it up and threw it at him.

"Sorry," said Angalo when they had got away. "I should have told you Father has rather a temper."

"What did you go and upset him for?" asked Grimma irritably. "If we've got to join up with someone, why not with him? What happens to us now?"

"He was very rude," said Granny Morkie stoutly.

"He'd never heard of the Thing," said Torrit. "Terrible, that is. Or

Outside. Well, I was borned and bred outside. Ain't no dead people there. Not living in any splendor, anyway."

They started to squabble, which was fairly usual.

Masklin looked at them. Then he looked at his feet. They were walking on a sort of short dry grass that Angalo had said was called *carpet*. Something else stolen from the Store above.

He wanted to say: This is ridiculous. Why is it that as soon as a nome has all he needs to eat and drink, he starts to bicker with other nomes? There must be more to being a nome than this.

And he wanted to say: If humans are so stupid, how is it that they built this Store and all these trucks? If we're that clever, then *they* should be stealing from *us*, not the other way around. They might be big and slow, but they're quite bright, really.

And he wanted to add: I wouldn't be surprised if they're at least as intelligent as rats, say.

But he didn't say any of this, because while he was thinking, his eyes fell on the Thing, clasped in Torrit's arms.

He was aware that there was a thought he ought to be having. He made a space in his head politely and waited patiently to see what it was and then, just as it was about to arrive, Grimma said to Angalo: "What happens to nomes who aren't in a department?"

"They lead very sad lives," said Angalo. "They just have to get along as best they can."

He looked as if he were about to cry. "*I* believe you," he said. "My father says it's wrong to watch the trucks. They can lead you into wrong thoughts, he says. Well, I've watched them for months. Sometimes they come in wet. It's not all a dream Outside—things happen. Look, why don't you sort of hang around, and I'm sure he'll change his mind."

o    o    o

The Store was big. Masklin had thought the truck was big. The Store was bigger. It went on forever, a maze of floor and walls and long, tiring steps. Nomes hurried or sauntered past them on errands of their own, and there seemed to be no end of them. In fact the word "big" was too small. The Store needed a whole new word.

In a strange way it was even bigger than outside. Outside was so huge, you didn't really see it. It had no edges and no top, so you didn't think of it as having a size at all. It was just *there*. Whereas the Store did have edges and a top, and they were so far away they were, well, *big*.

As they followed Angalo, Masklin made up his mind and decided to tell Grimma first.

"I'm going back," he said.

She stared at him. "But we've only just arrived! Why on earth—?"

"I don't know. It's all wrong here. It just feels wrong. I keep thinking that if I stay here any longer, *I'll* stop believing there's anything outside, and I was *born* there. When I've got you all settled down, I'm going out again. You can come if you like," he added, "but you don't have to."

"But it's warm and there's all this food!"

"I said I couldn't explain. I just feel we're being, well, watched."

Instinctively she stared upward at the ceiling a few inches above them. Back home anything watching them usually meant something was thinking about lunch. Then she remembered herself and gave a nervous laugh.

"Don't be silly," she said.

"I just don't feel safe," he said wretchedly.

"You mean you don't feel wanted," said Grimma quietly.

"What?"

"Well, isn't that true? You spend all your time scrimping and scraping for everyone, and then you don't need to anymore. It's a funny feeling, isn't it."

She swept away.

Masklin stood and fiddled with the binding on his spear. Odd, he thought. I never thought anyone else would think like that. He had a few dim recollections of Grimma in the hole, always doing laundry or organizing the old women or trying to cook whatever it was he managed to drag home. Odd. Fancy missing something like that.

He became aware that the rest of them had stopped. The underfloor stretched away ahead of them, lit dimly by small lights fixed to the wood here and there. Ironmongri charged highly for the lights, Angalo said, and wouldn't let anyone else into the secret of controlling the electricity. It was one of the things that made the Ironmongri so powerful.

"This is the edge of Haberdasheri territory at the moment," he said. "Over there is Millineri country. We're a bit cool with them at the moment. Er. You're bound to find some department to take you in. . . ." He looked at Grimma.

"Er," he said.

"We're going to stay together," said Granny Morkie. She looked hard at Masklin, and then turned back imperiously and waved her hand at Angalo.

"Go away, young man," she said. "Masklin, stand up straight. Now . . . forward."

"Who're you, saying forward?" said Torrit. "I'm the leader, I am. It's my job, givin' orders."

"All right," said Granny Morkie. "Give 'em, then."

Torrit's mouth worked soundlessly. "Right," he managed. "Forward."

Masklin's jaw dropped.

"Where to?" he asked, as the old woman shooed them along the dim space.

"We will find somewhere. I lived through the Great Winter of 1999, I did," said Granny Morkie haughtily. "The cheek of that silly old Duke man! I nearly spoke up. He wouldn't of lasted long in the Great Winter, I can tell you."

"No 'arm can befall us if we obey the Thing," said Torrit, patting it carefully.

Masklin stopped. He had, he decided, had enough.

"What does the Thing say, then?" he said sharply. "Exactly? What does it actually tell us to do now? Come on, tell me what it says we should do now!"

Torrit looked a bit desperate.

"Er," he began, "it, er, is clear that if we pulls together and maintains a proper—"

"You're just making it up as you go along!"

"How dare you speak to him like that—" Grimma began. Masklin flung down his spear.

"Well, I'm fed up with it!" he muttered. "The Thing says this, the Thing says that, the Thing says every blessed thing except anything that might be useful!"

"The Thing has been handed down from nome to nome for hundreds of years," said Grimma. "It's very important."

"Why?"

Grimma looked at Torrit. He licked his lips.

"It shows us—" he began, white-faced.

*"Move me closer to the electricity."*

"The Thing seems to be more important than . . . what are you all looking like that for?" said Masklin.

*"Closer to the electricity."*

Torrit, his hands shaking, looked down at the Thing.

Where there had been smooth black surfaces there were now little dancing lights. Hundreds of them. In fact, Masklin thought, feeling slightly proud of knowing what the word meant, there were probably thousands of them.

"Who said that?" said Masklin.

The Thing dropped out of Torrit's grasp and landed on the floor, where its lights glittered like a thousand highways at night. The nomes watched it in horror.

"The Thing *does* tell you things . . . " said Masklin. "Gosh!"

Torrit waved his hands frantically. "Not like that! Not like that! It ain't supposed to talk out loud! It's ain't done that before!"

*"Closer to the electricity!"*

"It wants the electricity," said Masklin.

"Well, *I'm* not going to touch it!"

Masklin shrugged and then, using his spear gingerly, pushed the Thing across the floor until it was under the wires.

"How does it speak? It hasn't got a mouth," said Grimma.

The Thing whirred. Colored shapes flickered across its surfaces faster than Masklin's eyes could follow. Most of them were red.

Torrit sank to his knees. "It is angry," he moaned. "We shouldn't have eaten rat, we shouldn't have come here, we shouldn't—"

Masklin also knelt down. He touched the bright areas, gingerly at first, but they weren't hot.

He felt that strange feeling again, of his mind wanting to think certain thoughts without having the right words.

"When the Thing has told you things before," he said slowly, "you know, how we should live proper lives—"

Torrit gave him an agonized expression.

"It never has," he said.

"But you said—"

"It *used* to, it *used* to," moaned Torrit. "When old Voozel passed it on to me he said it *used* to, but he said that hundreds and hundreds of years ago it just stopped."

"What?" said Granny Morkie. "All these years, my good man, you've been telling us that the Thing says this and the Thing says that and the Thing says goodness knows what."

Now Torrit looked like a very frightened, trapped animal.

"Well?" said the old woman, menacingly.

"Ahem," said Torrit. "Er. What old Voozel said was, think about what the Thing *ought* to say, and then say it. Keep people on the right path, sort of thing. Help them get to the Heavens. Very important, getting to the Heavens. The Thing can help you get there, he said. Most important thing about it."

*"What?"* shouted Granny.

"That's what he told me to do. It worked, didn't it?"

Masklin ignored them. The colored lines moved over the Thing in hypnotic patterns. He felt that he ought to know what they meant. He was certain they meant *something.*

Sometimes, on fine days back in the times when he didn't have to hunt every day, he'd climb farther along the bank until he could look down on the place where the trucks parked. There was a big blue board there, with little shapes and pictures on it. And in the litter bins the boxes and papers had more shapes and pictures on them; he remembered the long argument they'd had about the chicken boxes with the pictures of the old man with the big whiskers on them. Several nomes had insisted that this was a picture of a chicken, but Masklin had rather felt that humans didn't go around eating old men. There had to be more to it than that. Perhaps old men *made* chicken.

The Thing hummed again.

*"Fifteen thousand years have passed,"* it said.

Masklin looked up at the others.

"You talk to it," Granny ordered Torrit. The old man backed away.

"Not me! Not me! I dunno what to say!" he said.

"Well, I ain't!" snapped Granny. "That's the leader's job, is that!"

*"Fifteen thousand years have passed,"* the Thing repeated.

Masklin shrugged. It seemed to be up to him.

"Passed what?" he said.

The Thing gave the impression that it was thinking busily. At last it said: *"Do you still know the meaning of the words Flight Navigation and Recording Computer?"*

"No," said Masklin earnestly. "None of them."

The light pattern moved.

*"Do you know anything about interstellar travel?"*

"No."

The box gave Masklin the distinct impression that it was very disappointed in him.

*"Do you know you came here from a place far away?"* it said.

"Oh, yes. We know that."

*"A place farther than the moon."*

"Er." Masklin hesitated. The journey had taken a long time. It was always possible that they had gone past the moon. He had often seen it on the horizon, and he was certain that the truck had gone farther than that.

"Yes," he said. "Probably."

*"Language changes over the years,"* said the Thing thoughtfully.

"Does it?" said Masklin politely.

*"What do you call this planet?"*

"I don't know what planet means, either," said Masklin.

*"An astronomical body."*

Masklin looked blank.

*"What is your name for this place?"*

"It's called . . . the Store."

*"Thestore."* The lights moved, as if the Thing were thinking again.

"Young man, I don't want to stand here all day exchanging nonsense with the Thing," said Granny Morkie. "What we need to do now is sort out where we're going and what we're going to do."

"That's right," said Torrit defiantly.

*"Do you even remember that you are shipwrecked?"*

"I'm Masklin," said Masklin. "I don't know who Shipwrecked is."

The lights changed again. Later, when he got to know the Thing better, Masklin always thought that particular pattern was its way of sighing deeply.

*"My purpose is to serve you and guide you,"* said the Thing.

"See?" said Torrit, who was feeling a bit out of things. "We was right about that!"

Masklin prodded the box. "You've been keeping a bit quiet about it lately, then," he said.

The Thing hummed. *"This was to maintain internal power. However, I can now use ambient electricity."*

"That's nice," said Grimma.

"You mean you sort of drink up the lights?" said Masklin.

*"That will suffice as an explanation for now."*

"Why didn't you talk before, then?" said Masklin.

*"I was listening."*

"Oh."

*"And now I await instructions."*

"In where?" said Grimma.

"I think it wants us to tell it what to do," said Masklin. He sat back on his heels and watched the lights.

"What *can* you do?" he said.

*"I can translate, calculate, triangulate, assimilate, correlate, and extrapolate."*

"I don't think we want anything like that," said Masklin. "Do we want anything like that?" he asked the others.

Granny Morkie appeared to think about it. "No," she said eventually, "I don't think we wants any of that stuff. Another banana'd be nice, mind."

"I think all we really want is to go home and be safe," said Masklin.

*"Go home."*

"That's right."

*"And be safe."*

"Yes."

Later on, those five words became one of the most famous quotations in nome history. They got taught in schools. They got carved in stone. And it's sad, therefore, that at the time no one thought they were particularly important.

All that happened was that the Thing said, *"Computing."*

Then all its lights died, except a small green one, which began to flash.

"Thank goodness for that," said Grimma. "What a horrible voice. What shall we do now?"

"According to that Angalo boy," said Granny, "we have to live very sad lives."

---
○
---

# 3

*I. For they did not know it, but they had brought with them the Thing, which awoke in the presence of Electricity, and it alone knew their History;*

*II. For nomes have memories of Flesh and Blood, while the Thing had a memory of Silicon, which is Stone and perisheth not, whereas the memory of nomes blows away like dust;*

*III. And they gave it Instructions, but knew it not.*

*IV. It is, they said, a Box with a Funny Voice.*

*V. But the Thing began to Compute the task of keeping all nomes safe.*

*VI. And the Thing also began to Compute the task of taking all nomes home.*

*VII. All the way Home.*

*From* The Book of Nome, Mezzanine v. I–VII

IT WAS EASY to get lost under the floor. It took no effort at all. It was a maze of walls and cables, with drifts of dust away from the paths. In fact, as Torrit said, they weren't exactly lost, more mislaid; there were paths all over the place, between the joists and walls, but no indication of where they led to. Sometimes a nome would hurry past on an errand of its own and pay them no attention.

They dozed in an alcove formed by two huge wooden walls and woke up to light as dim as ever. There didn't seem to be any night or day in the Store. It did seem noisier, though. There was a distant, all-pervading hubbub.

A few more lights were flashing on the Thing, and it had grown a little, cup-shaped, smaller thing that went round and round very slowly.

"Should we look for the Food Hall again?" asked Torrit hopefully.

"I think you have to be a member of a department," said Masklin. "But it can't be the only place with food, can it?"

"It wasn't as noisy as this when we came here," said Granny. "What a din!"

Masklin looked around. There was a space between the woodwork, and a distant gleam of very bright light. He edged toward it and stuck his eye to the crack.

"Oh," he said weakly.

"What is it?" Grimma called out.

"It's humans. More humans than you've ever seen before."

The crack was where the ceiling joined the wall of a room nearly as big as the truck nest and it was, indeed, full of humans. The Store had opened.

The nomes had always known that humans lived very slowly. Masklin had almost walked into humans once or twice, when he was hunting, and knew that even before one of their huge stupid faces could swivel its eyes, he could be off the path and hiding behind a clump of something.

The space below was crowded with them, walking their great slow clumping walk and booming at each other in their vague, deep voices.

The nomes watched, fascinated, for some time.

"What are those things they're holding?" said Grimma. "They look a bit like the Thing."

"Dunno," said Masklin.

"Look, they pick them up and then give something to the other human, and then it's put in a bag, and they go away. They almost look, well, as if they mean what they're doing."

"No, it's like ants," said Torrit authoritatively. "They *seems* intelligent, I'll grant you, but when you looks closely, there's nothing really clever about them."

"They build things," said Masklin vaguely.

"So do birds, my lad."

"Yes, but—"

"Humans are a bit like magpies, I've always said. They just want things that glitter."

"Hmm." Masklin decided not to argue. You couldn't argue with old Torrit, unless you were Granny Morkie, of course. He had room only for a certain number of ideas in his head, and once one had taken root, you couldn't budge it. But Masklin wanted to say: If they're so stupid, why isn't it *them* hiding from *us*?

An idea struck him. He lifted up the Thing.

"Thing?" he said.

There was a pause. Then the tinny little voice said: *"Operations on main task suspended. What is it that you require?"*

"Do you know what humans are?" said Masklin.

*"Yes. Resuming main task."*

Masklin looked blankly at the others.

"Thing?" he said.

*"Operations on main task suspended. What is it that you require?"*

"I asked you to tell me about humans," said Masklin.

*"This is not the case. You said: Do you know what humans are? My answer was correct in every respect."*

"Well, tell *me* what humans are!"

*"Humans are the indigenous inhabitants of the world you now call Thestore. Resuming main task."*

"There!" said Torrit, nodding wisely. "Told you, didn't I? They're indigenous. Clever, yes, but basically just indigenous. Just a lot of indigenouses." He hesitated. "Indigenice," he corrected himself.

"Are *we* indigenous?" said Masklin.

*"Main task interrupted. No. Main task resumed."*

"Course not," said Torrit witheringly. "We've got a bit of pride."

Masklin opened his mouth to ask what indigenous meant. He knew he didn't know, and he was *certain* that Torrit didn't. And after that, he wanted to ask a lot more questions, and before he asked them, he'd have to think about the words he used.

I don't know enough words, he thought. Some things you can't think unless you know the right words.

But he didn't get around to it, because a voice behind him said, "Powerful strange things, ain't they? And very busy just lately. I wonder what's got into them?"

It was an elderly, rather stocky nome. And drably dressed, which was unusual in the Store. Most of his clothing was a huge apron, its pockets bulging mysteriously.

"Have you been spying on us?" said Granny Morkie.

The stranger gave a shrug.

"I usually come here to watch humans," he said. "It's a good spot. There isn't usually anyone else here. What department are you?"

"We haven't got one," said Masklin.

"We're just people," said Granny.

"Not indigenous, either," Torrit added quickly.

The stranger grinned and slid off the wooden beam he'd been sitting on.

"Fancy that," he said. "You must be these new things I've heard about. *Outsiders?*"

He held out his hand. Masklin looked at it cautiously.

"Yes?" he said politely.

The stranger sighed. "You're supposed to shake it," he said.

"I am? Why?"

"It's traditional. My name's Dorcas del Icatessen." The stranger gave Masklin a lopsided grin. "Do you know yours?" he said.

Masklin ignored this. "What do you mean, you watch humans?" he said.

"I watch humans. Study them, you know. It's what I do. You can learn a lot about the future by watching humans."

"A bit like the weather, you mean?" said Masklin.

"Weather! Of course, weather!" The nome grinned hugely. "You'd know all about the weather. Powerful stuff, weather?"

"You've heard of it?" said Masklin.

"Only the old stories. Hmm." Dorcas looked him up and down. "I reckoned Outsiders'd have to be a different shape, though. Life, but not as we know it. You just come along with me. I'll show you what I mean."

Masklin looked slowly around the dusty space between the floors. This was just about it. He'd had just about enough of it. It was too warm and too dry and everyone treated him like a fool, and now they thought he was the wrong shape.

"Well—" he began, and under his arm the Thing said, *"We need this person."*

"My word," said Dorcas. "What a tiny radio. They get smaller all the time, don't they?"

· 49 ·

o     o     o

Where Dorcas led them was just a hole. Big, square, deep, and dark. A few cables, fatter than a nome, disappeared down into the depths.

"You live down here?" asked Grimma.

Dorcas fumbled in the darkness. There was a click. Far above, something went bang and there was a distant roaring sound.

"Hmm? Oh, no," he said. "Took me ages to sort out, did this. It's a sort of floor on a rope. It goes up and down, you know. With humans in it. So I thought, I'm not getting any younger, all those stairs were playing havoc with my legs, so I had a look at the way it worked. Perfectly simple. It'd have to be, o' course, otherwise humans wouldn't know how to use it. Stand back, please."

Something huge and black came down the shaft and stopped a few inches above their heads. There were clangs and thumps and the now-familiar sound of clumsy humans walking about.

There was also, slung under the elevator's floor, a small wire basket tied on with bits of string.

"If you think," said Granny Morkie, "that I'm going to get into a, a wire nest on a string, then you've got another—"

"Is it safe?" said Masklin.

"More or less, more or less," said Dorcas, stepping across the gap and fumbling with another little bundle of switches. "Hurry up, please. This way, madam."

"Er, how much more than less?" asked Masklin as Granny, astonished at being called madam, got aboard.

"Well, *my* bit I'm sure is safe," said Dorcas. "The bit above us was put together by humans, though, and you never can tell. Hold tight, please. Going *up!*"

There was a clang above them and a slight jerk as they began to rise.

"Good, isn't it," said Dorcas. "Took me ages to bypass all the switches. You'd have thought they'd notice, wouldn't you? They press the button to go down, but if I want to go up, we go up. I used to worry that the humans would think it odd that these lifts seemed to go up and down by themselves, but they seem powerful dense. Here we are."

The elevator stopped with another jerk, leaving the nome's basket level with another underfloor gap.

"Electrical and Domestic Appliances," said Dorcas. "Just a little place I call my own. No one bothers me here, not even the Abbot. I'm the only one who knows how things work, see."

It was a place of wires. They ran under the floor in every direction, great bundles of the things. A few young nomes were taking something to pieces in the middle of it all.

"Radio," said Dorcas. "Amazing thing. Trying to figure out how it talks." He rummaged among piles of thick paper, pulled out a sheet, and sheepishly passed it to Masklin.

It showed a small pinkish cone, with a little tuft of hair on top.

The nomes had never seen a limpet. If they had, they'd have known that this drawing looked exactly like one. Except for the hair.

"Very nice," said Masklin, uncertainly. "What is it?"

"Um. It was my idea of what an Outsider would look like, you see," said Dorcas.

"What, with pointy heads?"

"The Rain, you see. In the old legends of the time before the Store. Rain. Water dropping out of the sky all the time. It'd need to run off. And the sloping sides are so the Wind won't keep knocking it over. I only had the old stories to go on, you see."

"It hasn't even got any eyes!"

Dorcas pointed. "Yes, it has. Tiny ones. Tucked in under the hair so they won't get blinded by the Sun. That's a big bright light in the sky," Dorcas added helpfully.

"We've seen it," said Masklin.

"What's he sayin'?" said Torrit.

"He's saying you ought to of looked like that," said Granny Morkie sarcastically.

"My head ain't that sharp!"

"You're right there, you," said Granny.

"I think you've got it a bit wrong," said Masklin slowly. "It's not like that at all. Hasn't anyone been to *look*?"

"I saw the big door open once," said Dorcas. "The one down in the garage, I mean. But there was just a blinding white light outside."

"I expect it would seem like it, if you spend all your time in this gloom," said Masklin.

Dorcas pulled up an empty cotton reel. "You must tell me about it," he said. "Everything you can remember about the Outside."

In Torrit's lap, the Thing began to flash another green light.

One of the young nomes brought some food after a while. And they talked, and argued, and often contradicted one another, while Dorcas listened, and asked questions.

He was, he told them, an inventor. Especially of things to do with electricity. Back in the early days, when the nomes first began to tap into the Store's wiring, a good many had been killed. They'd found safer ways to do it now, but it was still a bit of a mystery and there weren't many who were keen to get close to it. That's why the leaders of the big families, and even the Abbot of the Stationeri himself, left him alone. It was always a good idea, he said, to be good at something other people couldn't or didn't want to do. So they put up with him sometimes wondering, out loud, about the Outside. Provided he wasn't *too* loud.

"I shan't remember it all," he sighed. "What was the other light, the one that you get at Closing Time? Sorry, I mean bite."

"Night," corrected Masklin. "It's called the moon."

"Moon," said Dorcas, rolling the word around his mouth. "But it's not as bright as the sun? Strange, really. It's be more sensible to have the brightest light at night, not during the day, when you can see anyway. I suppose you've no idea why, have you?"

"It just happens," said Masklin.

"I'd give anything to see for myself. I used to go and watch the trucks when I was a lad, but I never had the courage to get on one." He leaned closer.

"I reckon," he said, "that Arnold Bros (est. 1905) put us in the Store to find out things. To learn about it. Otherwise, why have we got brains? What do you think?"

Masklin was rather flattered at being asked, but he was interrupted as soon as he opened his mouth. "People keep talking about Arnold Bros (est. 1905)," said Grimma. "No one actually says who he is, though."

Dorcas leaned back. "Oh, he created the Store. In 1905, you know. The Bargain Basement, Consumer Accounts, and everything between. I can't deny it. I mean, *someone* must have done it. But I keep telling people, that doesn't mean we shouldn't think about—"

The green light on the Thing went off. Its little spinning cup vanished. It made a faint whirring sound, such as a machine would make to clear its throat.

*"I am monitoring telephonic communications,"* it said.

The nomes looked at one another.

"Well, that's nice," said Grimma. "Isn't that nice, Masklin?"

*"I have urgent information to impart to the leaders of this community. Are you aware that you are living in a constructed entity with a limited life?"*

"Fascinating," said Dorcas. "All those words. You could imagine you could almost understand what it's saying. There's things up there"— he jerked his thumb to the floorboards above them— "that're just like that. Radios, they're called. With pictures, too. Amazing."

*"Vitally important I communicate information of utmost significance to community leaders, concerning imminent destruction of this artifact,"* intoned the Thing.

"I'm sorry," said Masklin. "Could you try that again?"

*"You do not comprehend?"*

"I don't know what 'comprehend' means."

*"Evidently language has changed in ways I do not understand."*

Masklin tried to look helpful.

*"I will endeavor to clarify my statement,"* said the Thing. A few lights flashed.

"Jolly good," said Masklin.

*"Big-fella Store him go Bang along plenty soon enough chop-chop?"* said the Thing, hopefully.

The nomes watched one another's faces. There didn't seem to be any light dawning.

The Thing cleared its throat again. *"Do you know the meaning of the word 'destroyed'?"* it said.

"Oh, yes," said Dorcas.

*"That's what is going to happen to the Store. In twenty-one days."*

# 4

*I. Woe unto you, Ironmongri and Haberdasheri; woe unto you, Millineri and Del Icatessen; woe unto you, Young Fashions, and unto you, you bandits of Corsetry. And even unto to you, Stationeri.*

*II. For the Store is but a Place inside the Outside.*

*III. Woe unto you, for Arnold Bros (est. 1905) has opened the Last Sale.* Everything Must Go.

*IV. But they mocked him and said, You are an Outsider, You don't even Exist.*

*From* The Book of Nome, Goods Inward v. I–IV

OVERHEAD THE HUMANS plodded through their slow and incomprehensible lives. Below, so that that the din was muffled by carpet and floorboards into a distant rumbling, the nomes straggled hurriedly along their dusty passageways.

"It couldn't of meant it," said Granny Morkie. "This place is too big. Place as big as this can't be de-stroyed. Stands to reason."

"I *tole* you, dint I?" panted Torrit, who always cheered up immensely at any news of devastation and terror. "They always said the Thing knows things. And don't you go tellin' me to shut up, you."

"Why do we have to run?" said Masklin. "I mean, twenty-one days is a long time."

"Not in politics," said Dorcas grimly.

"I thought this was the Store?"

Dorcas stopped so suddenly that Granny Morkie cannoned into the back of him.

"Look," he said, with impatient patience, "what do you think nomes should do, eh, if the Store is destroyed?"

"Go outside, of—" Masklin began.

"But most of them don't even believe the Outside really exists! Even I'm not quite sure about it, and I have an extremely intelligent and questioning mind! *There isn't anywhere to go.* Do you understand me?"

"There's masses of outside—"

"Only if you believe in it!"

"No, it's really there!"

"I'm afraid people are more complicated than you think. But we ought to see the Abbot, anyway. Dreadful old tyrant, of course, but quite bright in his way. It's just a rather stuffy way." He looked hard at them.

"Possibly best if we don't draw attention to ourselves," he added. "People tend to leave me alone, but it's not a wise thing for people to wander around outside their department without good reason. And since you haven't got a department at all . . ."

He shrugged. He managed, in one shift of his shoulders, to hint at all the unpleasant things that could happen to departmentless wanderers.

It meant using the lift again. It led into a dusty underfloor area dimly lit by well-spaced, weak bulbs. No one seemed to be around.

After the bustle of the other departments, it was almost unpleasantly quiet. Even quieter, Masklin thought, than the big fields. After all, they were *meant* to be quiet. The underfloor spaces should have nomes in them.

They all sensed it. They drew closer to one another.

"What dear little lights," said Grimma, to break the silence. "Nome size. All different colors, look. And some of them flash on and off."

"We steal boxes of 'em every year, around Christmas Fayre," said Dorcas, without looking around. "Humans put them on trees."

"Why?"

"Search me. To see 'em better, I suppose. You can never tell, with humans," said Dorcas.

"But you know what trees are, then," said Masklin. "I didn't think you'd have them in the Store."

"Of course I know," said Dorcas. "Big green things with plastic prickles on. Some of 'em are made of tinsel. You can't move for the damn things every Christmas Fayre, I told you."

"The ones we have outside are huge," Masklin ventured. "And they have these leaves, which fall off every year."

Dorcas gave him an odd look.

"What do you mean, fall off?" he said.

"They just curl up and fall off," said Masklin. The other nomes nodded. There were a lot of things lately they weren't certain about, but they were experts on what happened to leaves every year.

"And this happens every year?" said Dorcas.

"Oh, yes."

"Really?" said Dorcas. "Fascinating. And who sticks them back on?"

"No one," said Masklin. "They just turn up again, eventually."

"All by themselves?"

They nodded. When there's one thing you're certain of, you hang on to it. "They seem to," said Masklin. "We've never really found out why. It just happens."

The Store nome scratched his head. "Well, I don't know," he said uncertainly. "It sounds like very sloppy management to me. Are you sure—"

There were suddenly figures surrounding them. One minute dust heaps, the next minute people. The one right in front of the party had a beard, a patch over one eye, and a knife clutched in his teeth. It somehow made his grin so much worse.

"Oh, dear," said Dorcas.

"Who're they?" hissed Masklin.

"Bandits. That's always a problem in Corsetry," said Dorcas, raising his hands.

"What's bandits?" said Masklin blankly.

"What's Corsetry?" said Grimma.

Dorcas pointed a finger at the floorboards overhead. "It's up there," he said. "A department. Only no one's really interested in it because there's nothing in it of any use. It's mainly pink," he added. "Sometimes the elastic—"

"Orr ossessionz orr orr ife," said the head bandit impatiently.

"Pardon?" said Grimma.

"I edd, orr ossessionz orr orr ife!"

"I think it's the knife," said Masklin. "I think we'd understand you if you took the knife out."

The bandit glared at them with his one good eye, but took the knife blade out of his mouth.

"I *said*, your possessions or your life!" he repeated.

Masklin gave Dorcas a questioning look. The old nome waved his hands.

"He wants you to give him everything you have," he said. "He won't kill you, of course, but they can be rather unpleasant."

The Outside nomes went into a huddle. This was something beyond their experience. The idea of stealing was a new one to them. Back home there had never been anyone to steal from. If it came to that, there had never been anything to steal.

"Don't they understand plain Nome?" said the bandit.

Dorcas gave him a sheepish grin. "You'll have to excuse them," he said. "They're new here."

Masklin turned around.

"We've decided," he said. "If it's the same to you, we'll keep what we have. Sorry."

He gave Dorcas and the bandit a bright smile.

The bandit returned it. At least, he opened his mouth and showed a lot of teeth.

"Er," said Dorcas, "you can't say that, you know. You can't say you don't want to be robbed!" He saw Masklin's look of complete bewilderment. "Robbed," he repeated. "It means having your things taken away from you. You just can't say you don't want it to happen!"

"Why not?" said Grimma.

"Because—" The old nome hesitated. "I don't know, really. Tradition, I suppose."

The bandit chief tossed his knife from one hand to the other. "Tell you what I'll do," he said, "you being new and everything. We'll hardly hurt you at all. Get them!"

Two bandits grabbed Granny Morkie.

This turned out to be a mistake. Her bony right hand flashed out and there were two ringing slaps.

"Cheeky!" she snapped as the nomes staggered sideways, clutching their ears.

A bandit who tried to hold old Torrit got a pointed elbow in his stomach. One waved a knife at Grimma, who caught his wrist; the knife dropped from his hand and he sank to his knees, making pathetic bubbling noises.

Masklin leaned down, grabbed a handful of the chief's shirt in one hand, and lifted him up to eye level.

"I'm not sure we fully understand this custom," he said. "But nomes shouldn't hurt other nomes, don't you think?"

"Ahahaha," said the chief, nervously.

"So I think perhaps it would be a good idea if you go away, don't you?"

He let go. The bandit scrabbled on the floor for his knife, gave Masklin another anxious grin, and ran for it. The rest of the band hurried after him, or at least limped fast.

Masklin turned to Dorcas, who was shaking with laughter.

"Well," he said, "what was that all about?"

Dorcas leaned against a wall for support.

"You really don't know, do you?" he said.

"No," said Masklin patiently. "That's why I asked, you see."

"The Corsetri are bandits. They take things that don't belong to them. They hide out in Corsetry because it's more trouble than it's worth to anyone to drag them out," said Dorcas. "Usually they just try to frighten people. They're really just a bit of a nuisance."

"Why'd that one have his knife in his mouth?" said Grimma.

"It's supposed to make him look tough and devil-may-care, I think."

"I think it makes him look silly," said Grimma flatly.

"He'll feel the back of my hand if he comes back here," said Granny Morkie.

"I don't think they'll be back. I think they were a bit shocked to have people hit them, in fact," said Dorcas. He laughed. "You know, I'm really looking forward to seeing what effect you lot have on the Abbot. I don't think we've ever seen anything like you. You'll be like a—a—what's that stuff you said there's a lot of Outside?"

"Fresh air?" said Masklin.

"That's right. Fresh air."

And so they came, eventually, to the Stationeri.

Go to the Stationeri or go Outside, the Duke had said, meaning that he didn't see a lot of difference between the two. And there was no doubt that the other great families distrusted the Stationeri, who they reckoned had strange and terrifying powers.

After all, they could read and write. Anyone who can tell you what a piece of paper is saying *must* be strange.

They also understood Arnold Bros (est. 1905)'s messages in the sky.

But it is very hard to meet someone who believes you don't exist.

Masklin had always thought that Torrit looked old, but the Abbot looked so old that he must have been around to give Time itself a bit of a push. He walked with the aid of two sticks, and a couple of younger nomes hovered behind him in case he needed support. His face was a bag of wrinkles, out of which his eyes stared like two sharp black holes.

The tribe clustered up behind Masklin, as they always did now when they were worried.

The Abbot's guest hall was an area walled with cardboard, near one of the lifts. Occasionally one went past, shaking down some dust.

The Abbot was helped to his chair and sat down slowly, while his assistants fussed around him. Then he leaned forward.

"Ah," he said, "del Icatessen, isn't it? Invented anything lately?"

"Not lately, my lord," said Dorcas. "My lord, I have the honor to present to you—"

"I can't see anyone," said the Abbot, smoothly.

"Must be blind," sniffed Granny.

"And I can't hear anyone, either," said the Abbot.

"Be quiet," Dorcas hissed. "Someone's told him about you! He won't let himself see you! My lord," he said loudly, turning back, "I bring strange news. The Store is going to be demolished!"

It didn't have quite the effect Masklin had expected. The Stationeri priests behind the Abbot sniggered to themselves, and the Abbot permitted himself a faint smile.

"Dear me." he said, "And when is this terrible event likely to occur?"

"In twenty-one days, my lord."

"Well, then," said the Abbot in a kindly voice. "You run along now and, afterward, tell us what it was like."

This time the priests grinned.

"My lord, this is no—"

The Abbot raised a gnarled hand. "I'm sure you know a great deal about electricity, Dorcas, but you must know that every time there is a Grand Final Sale, excitable people say, 'The end of the Store is nigh.' And, strangely enough, life goes on."

Masklin felt the Abbot's gaze on him. For someone who was invisible, he seemed to be attracting considerable attention.

"My lord, it is rather more than that," said Dorcas stiffly.

"Oh? Did the *electricity* tell you?" said the Abbot mockingly.

Dorcas nudged Masklin in the ribs. "Now," he said.

Masklin stepped forward and put the Thing down on the floor. "Now," he whispered.

*"Am I in the presence of community leaders?"* asked the Thing.

"About as much as you ever will be," said Dorcas. The Abbot stared at the box.

*"I will use small words,"* said the Thing. *"I am the Flight Recording and Navigation Computer. A computer is a machine that thinks. Think, computer, think. See the computer think. I use electricity. Sometimes elec-tricity can carry messages. I can hear the messages. I can under-stand the messages. Sometimes the messages go along wires called telephone wires. Sometimes they are in other computers. There is a computer in the Store. It pays humans their wages. I can hear it think. It thinks: No more Store soon, no more payroll, no more accounts. The telephone wires, they say, Is that Blackbury Demolition Co.? Can we discuss final arrangements for the demolition, all stock will be out by the twenty-first—"*

"Very amusing," said the Abbot. "How did you make it?"

"I didn't make it, my lord. These people brought it here—"

"Which people?" said the Abbot, looking straight through Masklin.

"What happens if I go and pull his nose?" whispered Granny, in a hoarse whisper.

"It would be extremely painful," said Dorcas.

"Good."

"I mean for you."

The Abbot rose hesitantly to his feet.

"I am a tolerant nome," he said. "You speculate about things Outside, and I do not mind, I say it is good mental exercise. We wouldn't be nomes if we didn't sometimes allow our minds to wander. But to insist that it is *real*, that is not to be tolerated. Little tricksy toys . . ." He hobbled forward and brought one stick down sharply on the Thing, which buzzed. "Intolerable! There is nothing Outside, and no one to live in it! Life in other Stores, pah! Audience concluded! Be off with you."

*"I can stand an impact of two thousand five hundred tons,"* said the Thing smugly, although no one took much notice.

"Away! Away!" shouted the Abbot, and Masklin saw that he was trembling.

That was the strange thing about the Store. Only a few days ago, there weren't that many things you needed to know, and they mainly involved big hungry creatures and how to avoid them. Fieldcraft, Torrit had called it. Now it was beginning to dawn on Masklin that there was a different sort of knowledge, and it consisted of the things you needed to understand in order to survive among other nomes. Things like: Be very careful when you tell people things they don't want to hear. And: The thought that they may be wrong makes people very angry.

Some of the lesser Stationeri ushered them hurriedly through the doorway. It was done quite expertly, without any of them actually touching Masklin's people or even looking them in the face. Several of them scattered hastily away from Torrit when he picked up the Thing and held it protectively.

Finally Granny Morkie's temper, which was never particularly long, shortened to vanishing point. She grabbed the nearest monk by his black robe and held him up inches in front of her nose. His eyes crossed frantically with the effort of not seeing her. She poked him violently in the chest.

"Do you feel my finger?" she demanded. "Do you feel it? Not here, am I?"

"Indigenous!" said Torrit.

The monk solved his immediate problem by giving a little whimper and fainting.

"Let's get away from here," said Dorcas hurriedly. "I suspect it's only a small step between not seeing people and making sure they don't exist."

"I don't understand," said Grimma. "How can people not see us?"

"Because they know we're from Outside," said Masklin.

"But other nomes can see us!" said Grimma, her voice rising. Masklin didn't blame her. He was beginning to feel a bit unsure too.

"I think that's because they don't know," he said, "or don't believe, we really *are* Outsiders!"

"I ain't an Outsider!" said Torrit. "They're all Insiders!"

"But that means that the Abbot really does think we're from Outside!" said Grimma. "That means he believes we're here and he can't see us! Where's the sense in that?"

"That's nomish nature for you," said Dorcas.

"Don't see that it matters much," said Granny grimly. "Come three weeks and they'll *all* be Outsiders. Serve them right. They'll have to go around not looking at themselves. See how they like that, eh?" She stuck her nose in the air. "Ho, hexcuse me, Mr. Abbot, went and tripped over hyou there, didn't see hyou hi'am sure. . . ."

"I'm sure they'd understand if only they'd listen," said Masklin.

"Shouldn't think so," said Dorcas, kicking at the dust. "Silly of me to think they would, really. The Stationeri never listen to new ideas."

"Excuse me," said a quiet voice behind them.

They turned and saw one of the Stationeri standing there. He was young, and quite plump, with curly hair and a worried expression. In fact he was nervously twisting the corner of his robe.

"You want me?" said Dorcas.

"Er. I was, er, I wanted to talk to the, er, Outsiders," said the little man carefully. He bobbed a curtsey in the direction of Torrit and Granny Morkie.

"You've got better eyesight than most, then," said Masklin.

"Er, yes," said the Stationeri. He looked back down the corridor. "Er, I'd like to talk to you. Somewhere private."

They shuffled around a floor joist.

"Well?" said Masklin.

"That, er, thing that spoke," said the Stationeri. "Do you believe it?"

"I think it can't actually tell lies," said Masklin.

"What is it, exactly? Some kind of radio?"

Masklin gave Dorcas a hopeful look.

"That's a thing for making noise," Dorcas explained loftily.

"Is it?" asked Masklin, and shrugged. "I don't know. We've just had it a long time. It says it came with nomes from a long way away, a long time ago. We've looked after it for generations, haven't we, Torrit?"

The old man nodded violently. "My dad had it before me, and his father before him, and his father before him, and his brother at the same time as him, and their uncle before them—" he began.

The Stationeri scratched his head.

"It's very worrying," he said. "The humans are acting very strangely. Things aren't being replaced in the Store. There's signs we've never seen before. Even the Abbot's worried—he can't work out what Arnold Bros (est. 1905) expects us to do. So, er . . ." He bunched up his robe, untwisted it hurriedly, and went on. "I'm the Abbot's assistant, you see. My name is Gurder. I have to do the things he can't do himself. So, er . . ."

"Well, what?" said Masklin.

"Could you come with me? Please?"

"Is there food?" said Granny Morkie, who could always put her finger on the important points.

"We'll certainly have some sent up," said Gurder hurriedly. He backed off through the maze of joists and wiring. "Please, follow me. Please."

# 5

*I. Yet there were some who said, We have seen Arnold Bros (est. 1905)'s new Signs in the Store, and we are Troubled for we Understand them not.*

*II. For this is the Season that should be Christmas Fayre, and yet the Signs are not the Signs of Christmas Fayre;*

*III. Nor are they January Sales, or Back-to-School Week, or Spring Into Spring Fashions, or Summer Bargains, or other Signs we know in their Season;*

*IV. For the Signs say Clearance Sale. We are sorely Troubled.*

*From* The Book of Nome, Complaints v. I–IV

GURDER, BOBBING AND curtseying, led them deeper into Stationeri territory. It had a musty smell. Here and there were stacks of what Masklin was told were books. He didn't fully understand what they were for, but Dorcas obviously thought they were important.

"Look at 'em," he said. "Powerful lot of stuff in there that we could find useful, and the Stationeri guard it like, like—"

"Like something well guarded?" said Masklin.

"Right. Right. That's exactly right. They keep looking hard at 'em. Reading, they call it. But they don't understand any of it."

There was a whirr from the Thing in Torrit's arms, and a few lights lit up.

*"Books are repositories of knowledge?"* it said.

"There's said to be a lot in them," said Dorcas.

*"It is vital that you obtain books,"* said the Thing.

"Stationeri hold on to 'em," said Dorcas. "Unless you know how to read books properly, they inflame the brain, they say."

"In here, please," said Gurder, shifting a cardboard barrier.

Someone was waiting for them, sitting stiffly on a pile of cushions with his back to them.

"Ah. Gurder," he said. "Come in. Good."

It was the Abbot. He didn't turn around.

Masklin prodded Gurder. "It was bad enough just now," he said. "Why are we doing this again?"

Gurder gave him a look that seemed to say: Trust me, this is the only way.

"Have you arranged for some food, Gurder?" said the Abbot.

"My lord, I was just—"

"Go and do it now."

"Yes, my lord."

Gurder gave Masklin another desperate look and scurried away.

The nomes stood sheepishly, wondering what was going to happen next.

The Abbot spoke.

"I am nearly fifteen years old," he said. "I am older even than some departments in the Store. I have seen many strange things, and soon I am going to meet Arnold Bros (est. 1905) in the hope that I have been a good and dutiful nome. I am so old that there are nomes who think that in some way I *am* the Store, and fear that when I am gone, the Store will end. Now you tell me this is so. Who is in charge?"

Masklin looked at Torrit. But everyone else looked at him.

"Well, er," he said. "Me. I suppose. Just for the moment."

"That's right," said Torrit, relieved. "Just for the moment I'm puttin' him in charge, see. Because I'm the leader."

The Abbot nodded.

"A very wise decision," he said. Torrit beamed.

"Stay here with the talking box," said the Abbot to Masklin. "The rest of you, please go. There will be food brought to you. Please go and wait."

"Um," said Masklin, "no."

There was a pause.

Then the Abbot said, quite softly, "Why not?"

"Because, you see, um, we're all together," said Masklin. "We've never been split up."

"A very commendable sentiment. You'll find, however, that life doesn't work like that. Come, now. I can hardly harm you, can I?"

"You talk to him, Masklin," said Grimma. "We won't be far away. It's not important."

He nodded reluctantly.

When they had left, the Abbot turned around. Close to, he was even older than he had looked before. His face wasn't just wrinkled, it was one big wrinkle. He was middle-aged when old Torrit was born, Masklin told himself. He's old enough to be Granny Morkie's grandfather!

The Abbot smiled. It was a difficult smile. It was as if he'd had smiling explained to him but had never had the chance to practice.

"Your name, I believe, is Masklin," he said.

Masklin couldn't deny it.

"I don't understand!" he said. "You can see me! Ten minutes ago you said I didn't even exist, and now you're talking to me!"

"There is nothing strange about it," said the Abbot. "Ten minutes ago it was official. Goodness me, I can't go around letting people believe that I've been wrong all along, can I? The Abbots have been denying there is anything Outside for generations. I can't suddenly say they were all wrong. People would think I've gone mad."

"Would they?" said Masklin.

"Oh, yes. Politics, you see. Abbots can't go changing their minds all the time. You'll find this out. The important thing about being a leader is not being right or wrong, but being *certain*. Otherwise people wouldn't know what to think. Of course, it helps to be right as well," the Abbot conceded. He leaned back.

"There were terrible wars in the Store once," he said. "Terrible wars. A terrible time. Nome against nome. Decades ago, of course. It seemed that there was always some nome who thought his family should rule the Store. The Battle of the Freight Elevator, the Goods Inward Campaign, the dreadful Mezzanine Wars . . . But that's past, now. And do you know why?"

"No," said Masklin.

"*We* stopped it. The Stationeri. By cunning and common sense and diplomacy. We made them see that Arnold Bros (est. 1905) expects nomes to be at peace with one another. *Now* then. Supposing that I, in there, had said I believed you. People would have thought, The old boy has gone off his head." The Abbot chuckled. "And then they'd have said, Have the Stationeri been wrong all this time? They would have panicked. Well, of course, that would never do. We must hold the nomes together. You know how they bicker at every opportunity."

"That's true," said Masklin. "And they always blame you for everything and say, What're you going to do about it?"

"You've noticed, have you?" said the Abbot, smiling. "It seems to me that you have exactly the right qualification for being a leader."

"I don't think so!"

"That's what I mean. You don't want to be one. *I* didn't want to be Abbot." He drummed his fingers on his walking stick and then looked sharply at Masklin.

"People are always a lot more complicated than you think," he said. "It's very important to remember that."

"I will," said Masklin, not knowing what else to say.

"You don't believe in Arnold Bros (est. 1905), do you?" said the Abbot. It was more a statement than a question.

"Well, er—"

"I've seen him, you know. When I was a boy. I climbed all the way up to Consumer Accounts, by myself, and hid, and I saw him at his desk writing."

"Oh?"

"He had a beard."

"Oh."

The Abbot drummed his fingers on his stick. He seemed to be making up his mind about something. Then he said, "Hmm. Where was your home?"

Masklin told him. Funnily, it seemed a lot better now that he looked back on it. More summers than winters, more nuts than rat. No bananas or electric or carpets, but plenty of fresh air. And in memory there didn't seem to be as much drizzle and frost. The Stationeri listened politely.

"It was a lot better when we had more people," Masklin finished. He glanced at his feet. "You could come and stay. When the Store is demo-thinged."

The Abbot laughed. "I'm not sure I'd fit in," he said. "I'm not sure I want to believe in your *Outside*. It sounds cold and dangerous.

Anyway, I shall be going on a rather more mysterious journey. And now, please excuse me, I must rest." He thumped on the floor with his stick. Gurder appeared as if by magic.

"Take Masklin away and educate him a little," said the Abbot, "and then the both of you come back here. But leave that black box, please. I wish to learn more about it. Put it on the floor."

Masklin did so. The Abbot poked it with his stick.

"Black box," he said, "what are you, and what is your purpose?"

"*I am the Flight Recorder and Navigation Computer of the starship Swan. I have many functions. My current major function is to guide and advise those nomes shipwrecked when their scout ship crashed here fifteen thousand years ago.*"

"It talks like this all the time," said Masklin apologetically.

"Who are these nomes of which you speak?" said the Abbot.

"*All nomes.*"

"Is that your only purpose?"

"*I have also been given the task of keeping nomes safe and taking them Home.*"

"Very commendable," said the Abbot. He looked up at the other two.

"Run along, then," he commanded. "Show him a little of the world, Gurder. And then I shall have a task for both of you."

Educate him a little, the Abbot had said.

That meant starting with *The Book of Nome*, which consisted of pieces of paper sewn together with marks on them.

"Humans use it for cigarettes," said Gurder, and read the first dozen verses. They listened in silence, and then Granny Morkie said, "So this Arnold Bros—"

"—(est. 1905)—" said Gurder primly.

"Whatever," said Granny. "He built the Store just for nomes?"

"Er. Ye-ess," said Gurder, uncertainly.

"What was here before, then?" said Granny.

"The Site." Gurder looked uncomfortable. "You see, the Abbot says there is nothing outside the Store. Um."

"But we've *come*—"

"He says that tales of Outside are just dreams."

"So when I said all that about where we lived, he was just laughing at me?" said Masklin.

"It is often very hard to know what the Abbot really believes," said Gurder. "I think most of all he believes in Abbots."

"*You* believe us, don't you?" said Grimma. Gurder nodded, half hesitantly.

"I've often wondered where the trucks go, and where the humans come from," he said. "The Abbot gets very angry when you mention it, though. The other thing is there's been a new season. That means something. Some of us have been watching humans, and when there's a new season, something unusual is happening."

"How can you have seasons when you don't know about weather?" said Masklin.

"Weather has got nothing to do with seasons. Look, someone can take the old people down to the Food Hall, and I'll show you two. It's all very odd. But"— and now Gurder's face was a picture of misery—"Arnold Bros (est. 1905) wouldn't destroy the Store, would he?"

# 6

*III. And Arnold Bros (est. 1905) said, Let there be Signs, so that All within shall know the Proper Running of the Store.*

*IV. On the Moving Stairs, let the Sign Be: Dogs and Strollers* Must *be Carried;*

*V. And Arnold Bros (est. 1905) waxed wroth, for many carried neither dog nor stroller;*

*VI. On the Lifts, let the Sign Be: This Elevator to Carry Ten Persons;*

*VII. And Arnold Bros (est. 1905) waxed wroth, for oftimes the Lifts carried only two or three;*

*VIII. And Arnold Bros (est. 1905) said, Truly Humans* are *Stupid, who do not understand plain language.*

*From* The Book of Nome, Regulations v. III–VIII

IT WAS A long walk through the busy underfloor world.

They found that Stationeri could go where they liked. The other departments didn't fear them, because the Stationeri weren't a true department. There were no women and children, for one thing.

"So people have to *join?*" said Masklin.

"We are selected," Gurder corrected. "Several intelligent boys from each department every year. But when you're a Stationeri, you have to forget about your department and serve the whole Store."

"Why can't women be Stationeri, then?" asked Grimma.

"It's a well-known fact that women can't read," said Gurder. "It's not their fault, of course. Apparently their brains get too hot. With the strain, you know. It's just one of those things."

"Fancy," said Grimma. Masklin glanced sideways at her. He'd heard her use that sweet, innocent tone of voice before. It meant that pretty soon there was going to be trouble.

Trouble or not, it was amazing the effect that Gurder had on people. They would stand aside and bow slightly as he went past, and one or two of them held small children up and pointed him out. Even the guards at the border crossings touched their helmets respectfully.

All around them was the bustle of the Store moving through time. Thousands of nomes, Masklin thought. I didn't even think there were any *numbers* that big. A world made up of people.

He remembered hunting alone, running along the deep furrows in the big field behind the highway. There was nothing around but earth and flints, stretching into the distance. The whole sky was an upturned bowl with him at the center.

Here, he felt that if he turned around suddenly, he would knock someone over. He wondered what it would be like, living here and never knowing anywhere else. Never being cold, never being wet, never being afraid.

You might start thinking it was never possible to be anything else. . . .

He was vaguely aware that they'd gone up a slope and out through another gap into the big emptiness of the Store itself. It was night—Closing Time—but there were bright lights in the sky, except that he'd have to start learning to call it the ceiling.

"This is the Haberdashery Department," said Gurder. "Now, do you see the sign hanging up there?"

Masklin peered into the misty distance and nodded. He could see it. It had huge red letter shapes on a white banner.

"It should say *Christmas Fayre*," said the Stationeri. "That's the right season, it comes after *Summer Bonanza* and before *Spring Into Spring Fashions*. But instead it says"—Gurder narrowed his eyes, and his lips moved soundlessly for a moment—"*Final Reductions*. We've been wondering what that means."

"This is just a thought," said Grimma, sarcastically, "it's only a small idea, you understand. I expect big ideas would make my head explode. But doesn't it mean, well, everything is finally being reduced?"

"Oh, it can't mean anything as simple as that. You have to interpret these signs," said Gurder. "Once they had one saying *Fire Sale*, and we didn't see them sell any fire."

"What do all the other things say?" said Masklin. Everything being Finally Reduced was too horrible to think about.

"Well, that one over there says *Everything Must Go*," said Gurder. "But that turns up every year. It's Arnold Bros (est. 1905)'s way of telling us that we must lead good lives because we all die eventually. And those two over there, they're always there too." He looked solemn. "No one really believes them anymore. There were wars over them, years ago. Silly superstition, really. I mean, I don't think there is a monster called Prices Slashed who walks around the Store at night, seeking out bad people. It's just something to frighten naughty children with."

Gurder bit his lip. "There's another odd thing," he said. "See those things against the wall? They're called shelves. Sometimes humans take things off them, sometimes they put things on them. But just lately . . . well, they just take things away."

Some of the shelves were empty.

Masklin wasn't too familiar with the subtleties of human behavior. Humans were humans, in the same way that cows were just cows. Obviously there was some way that other cows or humans told them apart, but he'd never been able to spot it. If there was any sense in anything they did, he'd never been able to work it out.

*"Everything Must Go,"* he said.

"Yes, but not go," said Gurder. "Not actually *go*. You don't really think it means actually go, do you? I'm sure Arnold Bros (est. 1905) wouldn't allow it. Would he?"

"Couldn't rightly say," said Masklin. "Never heard of him till we came here."

"Oh, yes," said Gurder in a meek voice. "From Outside, you said. It sounded . . . very interesting. And nice."

Grimma took Masklin's hand and squeezed it gently.

"It's nice here, too," she said. He looked surprised.

"Well, it is," she said defiantly. "You know the others think so, too. It's warm and there's amazing food, even if they have funny ideas about women's brains." She turned back to Gurder. "Why can't you ask Arnold Bros (est. 1905) what is going on?"

"Oh, I don't think we should do that!" said Gurder hurriedly.

"Why not? Makes sense, if he's in charge," said Masklin. "Have you ever even *seen* Arnold Bros (est. 1905)?"

"The Abbot did, once. When he was young he climbed all the way up to Consumer Accounts. He doesn't talk about it, though."

Masklin thought hard about this as they walked back. There had never been any religion or politics back home. The world was just too *big* to worry about things like that. But he had serious doubts about Arnold Bros (est. 1905). After all, if he had built the Store for nomes, why hadn't he made it nome sized? But, he thought, it was probably not the time to ask questions like that.

If you thought hard enough, he'd always considered, you could work out everything. The wind, for example. It had always puzzled him until the day he'd realized that it was caused by all the trees waving about.

They found the rest of the group near the Abbot's quarters. Food had been brought up for them. Granny Morkie was explaining to a couple of baffled Stationeri that the pineapples were nothing like as good as the ones she used to catch at home.

Torrit looked up from a hunk of bread.

"Everyone's been looking for you two," he said. "The Abbot fellow wants you. This bread's *soft.* You don't have to spit on it like the bread we had at ho—"

"Never you mind going on about that!" snapped Granny, suddenly full of loyalty for the old hole.

"Well, it's true," muttered Torrit. "We never had stuff like this. I mean, all these sausages and meat in big lumps, not stuff you have to kill, no ferreting around in dirty bins . . ."

He saw the others glaring at him and lapsed into shamefaced muttering.

"Shut up, you daft old fool," said Granny.

"Well, we dint have no foxes, I expect?" said Torrit. "Like Mrs. Coom and my old mate Mert, they never—"

Her furious glare finally worked. His face went white.

"It just wasn't all sunshine," he whispered, shaking his head. "Not all sunshine, that's all I'm saying."

"What does he mean?" asked Gurder brightly.

"He don't mean nothing," snapped Granny.

"Oh." Gurder turned to Masklin. "I know what a fox is," he said. "I can read Human books, you know. Quite well. I read a book called"—he hesitated—"*Our Furry Friends*, I think it was. A handsome and agile hunter, the red fox scavenges carrion, fruit, and small rodents. It—I'm sorry, is something wrong?"

Torrit was choking on his bread while the others slapped him hurriedly on the back. Masklin took the young Stationeri by the arm and quickly walked him away.

"Was it something I said?" said Gurder.

"In a way," said Masklin. "And now I think the Abbot wants to see us, doesn't he?"

The old man was sitting very still, with the Thing on his lap, staring at nothing.

He paid them no attention when they came in. Once or twice his fingers drummed on the Thing's black surface.

"Sir?" said Gurder after a while.

"Hmm?"

"You wanted to see us, sir?"

"Ah," said the Abbot vaguely. "Young Gurder, isn't it?"

"Yes, sir!"

"Oh. Good."

There was silence. Gurder coughed politely.

"You wanted to see us, sir?" he repeated.

"Ah." The Abbot nodded gently. "Oh. Yes. You, there. The young man with the spear."

"Me?" said Masklin.

"Yes. Have you spoken to this, this thing?"

"The Thing? Well, in a way. It talks funny, though. It's hard to understand."

"It has talked to me. It has told me it was made by nomes, a long time ago. It eats electric. It says it can hear electric things. It has said"—he glared at the thing in his lap—"it has said that it has heard Arnold Bros (est. 1905) plans to demolish the Store. It is a mad thing, it talks about stars, it says we came from a star, flying. But . . . there is talk of strange events. I wonder to myself, is this a messenger from the Management, sent to warn us? Or is it a trap set by Prices Slashed? So!" He thumped the Thing with a wrinkled hand. "We must *ask* Arnold Bros (est 1905). We will learn his truth."

"But, sir!" Gurder burst out. "You're far too—I mean, it wouldn't be right for you to go all the way to the Top again—it's a terrible dangerous journey!"

"Quite so, boy. So you will go instead. You can read Human, and your boisterous friend with the spear can go with you."

Gurder sagged to his knees. "Sir? All the way to the Top? But I am not worthy . . . " His voice faded away.

The Abbot nodded. "None of us are," he said. "We are all Shop soiled. Everything Must Go. Now be off, and may Bargains Galore go with you."

"Who's Bargains Galore?" said Masklin, as they went out.

"She's a servant of the Store," said Gurder, who was still trembling. "She's the enemy of the dreadful Prices Slashed, who wanders the corridors at night with his terrible shining light, to catch evil nomes!"

"It's a good thing you don't believe in him, then," said Masklin.

"Of course I don't," agreed Gurder.

"Your teeth are chattering, though."

"That's because my *teeth* believe in him. And so do my knees. And my stomach. It's only my head that doesn't, and it's being carried around by a load of superstitious cowards. Excuse me—I'll go and collect my things. It's very important that we set out at once."

"Why?" said Masklin.

"Because if we wait any longer, I'll be too scared to go."


The Abbot sat back in his chair.

"Tell me again," he said, "about how we came here. You mentioned a color. Mauve, wasn't it?"

*"Marooned,"* said the Thing.

"Ah, yes. From something that flew."

*"A galactic survey ship,"* said the Thing.

"But it got broken, you said."

*"There was a fault in one of the everywhere engines. It meant we could not return to the main ship. Can it be that this is forgotten? In the early days, we managed to communicate with humans, but the different metabolic rates and time sense eventually made this impossible. It was hoped originally that humans could be taught enough science to build us a new ship, but they were too slow. In the end, we had to teach them the very basic skills, such as metallurgy, in the hope that they might eventually stop fighting one another long enough to take an interest in space travel."*

"Metal Urgy." The Abbot turned the word over and over. Metal urgy. The urge to use metals. That was humans, all right. He nodded. "What was that other thing you said we taught them? Began with a G."

The Thing appeared to hesitate, but it was learning how to talk to nomes now. *"Agriculture?"* it said.

"That's right. A Griculture. Important, is it?"

*"It is the basis of civilization."*

"What does that mean?"

*"It means 'yes.'"*

The Abbot sat back while the Thing went on talking. Strange words washed over him, like *planets* and *electronics.* He didn't know what they meant, but they sounded *right.* Nomes had taught humans. Nomes came from a long way away. From a distant star, apparently.

The Abbot didn't find this astonishing. He didn't get about much these days, but he had seen the stars in his youth. Every year, around the season of Christmas Fayre, stars would appear in most of the departments. Big ones, with lots of pointy bits and glitter on them, and lots of lights. He'd always been very impressed by them. It was quite fitting that they should have belonged to nomes, once. Of course, they weren't out all the time, so presumably there was a big storeroom somewhere where the stars were kept.

The Thing seemed to agree with this. The big room was called the galaxy. It was somewhere above Consumer Accounts.

And then there were these "light years." The Abbot had seen nearly fifteen years go past, and they had seemed quite heavy at the time—full of problems, swollen with responsibilities. Lighter ones would have been better.

And so he smiled, and nodded, and listened, and fell asleep as the Thing talked and talked and talked. . . .

# 7

*XXI. But Arnold Bros (est. 1905) said, This is the Sign I give you:*
*XXII. If You Do Not See What You Require, Please Ask.*

*From* The Book of Nome, Regulations v. XXI–XXII

"SHE CAN'T COME," said Gurder.

"Why not?" said Masklin.

"Well, it's dangerous."

"So?" Masklin looked at Grimma, who was wearing a defiant expression.

"You shouldn't take girls anywhere dangerous," said Gurder virtuously.

Once again Masklin got the feeling he'd come to recognize often since he'd arrived in the Store. They were talking, their mouths were opening and shutting, every word by itself was perfectly understandable, but when they were all put together, they made no sense at all. The best thing to do was ignore them. Back home, if women weren't to go anywhere dangerous, they wouldn't go anywhere.

"I'm coming," said Grimma. "What danger is there, anyway? Only this Price Slasher, and—"

"And Arnold Bros (est. 1905) himself," said Gurder nervously.

"Well, I'm going to come anyway. People don't need me, and there's nothing to do," said Grimma. "What can happen, anyway? It's not as if something terrible could happen," she added sarcastically, "like me reading something and my brain overheating, for example."

"Now, I'm sure I didn't say—" said Gurder weakly.

"I bet the Stationeri don't do their own washing," said Grimma. "Or darn their own socks. I bet—"

"All right, all right," said Gurder, backing away. "But you mustn't lag behind, and you mustn't get in the way. We'll make the decisions, all right?"

He gave Masklin a desperate look.

"You tell her she mustn't get in the way," he said.

"Me?" said Masklin. "I've never told her anything."

The journey was less impressive than he'd expected. The old Abbot had told of staircases that moved, fire in buckets, long empty corridors with nowhere to hide.

But since then, of course, Dorcas had put the lifts in. They only went as far as Kiddies Klothes and Toys, but the Klothians were a friendly people who had adapted well to life on a high floor and always welcomed the rare travelers who came with tales of the world below.

"They don't even come down to use the Food Hall," said Gurder. "They get everything they want from the Staff restroom. They live on tea and biscuits, mainly. And yogurt."

"How strange," said Grimma.

"They're very gentle," said Gurder. "Very thoughtful. Very quiet. A little bit *mystical*, though. It must be all that yogurt and tea."

"I don't understand about the fire in buckets, though," said Masklin.

"Er," said Gurder, "we think that the old Abbot might, er, we think his memory . . . after all, he *is* extremely old . . ."

"You don't have to explain," said Grimma. "Old Torrit can be a bit like that."

"It's just that his mind is not as sharp as it was," said Gurder.

Masklin said nothing. It just seemed to him that if the Abbot's mind was a bit blunt now, it must once have been sharp enough to cut the breeze.

The Klothians gave them a guide to take them through the outlying regions of the underfloor. There were few nomes this high up. Most of them preferred the busy floors below.

It was almost like being outside. Faint breezes blew the dust into gray drifts; there was no light except what filtered through from odd cracks. In the darkest places the guide had to light matches. He was a very small nome who smiled a lot in a shy way and said nothing at all when Grimma tried to talk to him.

"Where are we going?" said Masklin, looking back at their deep footprints.

"To the moving stairs," said Gurder.

"Move? How do they move? Bits of the Store move *around*?"

Gurder chuckled patronizingly.

"Of course, all this is new to you. You mustn't worry if you don't understand everything," he said.

"Do they move or don't they?" said Grimma.

"You'll see. It's the only one we use, you know. It's a bit dangerous. You have to be topsides, you see. It's not like the lifts."

The little Klothian pointed forward, bowed, and hurried away.

Gurder led them up through a narrow crack in the ancient floorboards, into the bright emptiness of a passageway, and there—

—the moving stair.

Masklin watched it hypnotically. Stairs rose out of the floor, squeaking eerily as they did so, and whirred up into the distant heights.

"Wow," he said. It wasn't much, but it was all that he could think of.

"The Klothians won't go near it," said Gurder. "They think it is haunted by spirits."

"I don't blame them," said Grimma, shivering.

"Oh, it's just superstition," said Gurder. His face was white and there was a tremble in his voice. "There's nothing to be frightened of," he squeaked.

Masklin peered at him.

"Have you ever been here before?" he asked.

"Oh, yes. Millions of times. Often," said Gurder, picking up a fold of his robe and twisting it between his fingers.

"So what do we do now?"

Gurder tried to speak slowly, but his voice began to go faster and faster of its own accord: "You know, the Klothians say that Arnold Bros (est. 1905) waits at the Top, you know, and when nomes die—"

Grimma looked reflectively at the rising stairs and shivered again. Then she ran forward.

"What're you doing?" said Masklin.

"Seeing if they're right!" she snapped. "Otherwise we'll be here all day!"

Masklin ran after her. Gurder gulped, looked behind him, and scurried after both of them.

Masklin saw her run toward the rising bulk of a stair, and then the floor below her came up and she was suddenly rising, wobbling as she fought for balance. The floor below him pushed against his feet and he rose after her, one step below.

"Jump down!" he shouted. "You can't trust ground that moves by itself!"

Her pale face peered over the edge of her stair.

"What good will that do?" she said.

"Then we can go and talk about it!"

She laughed. "Go where? Have you looked down lately?"

Masklin looked down.

He was already several stairs up. The distant figure of Gurder, his face just a blob, screwed up his courage and jumped onto a step of his own. . . .

Arnold Bros (est. 1905) was not waiting at the Top.

It was simply a long brown corridor lined with doors. There were words painted on some of them.

But Grimma was waiting. Masklin waved a finger at her as he staggered off his stair, which mysteriously folded itself into the floor.

"Never, *ever*, do anything like that again!" he shouted.

"If I hadn't, you'd still be at the bottom. You could see Gurder was scared out of his wits!" she snapped.

"But there could have been all sorts of dangers up here!"

"Like what?" said Grimma haughtily.

"Well, there could be . . ." Masklin hesitated. "That's not the point, the point is—"

At this point Gurder's stair rolled him almost to their feet. They picked him up.

"There," said Grimma brightly. "We're all here, and everything's perfectly all right, isn't it."

Gurder stared around him. Then he coughed and adjusted his clothes.

"I lost my balance there," he said. "Tricky, these moving stairs. But you get used to them eventually." He coughed again and looked along the corridor. "Well, we'd better get a move on," he said.

The three nomes crept forward, past the rows of doors.

"Does one of these belong to Prices Slashed?" asked Grimma. Somehow the name sounded far worse up here.

"Um, no," said Gurder. "He dwells among the furnaces in the basement." He squinted up at the nearest door. "This one is called Salaries," he said.

"Is that good or bad?" asked Grimma, staring at the word on the varnished wood.

"Don't know."

Masklin brought up the rear, turning slowly to keep all the corridor in view. It was too open. There was no cover, nothing to hide behind.

He pointed to a row of giant red things hanging halfway up the opposite wall. Gurder whispered that they were buckets.

"There's pictures of them in *Colin and Susan Go to the Seaside*," he confided.

"What's that written on them?"

Gurder squinted. "'Fire,'" he said. "Oh, my. The Abbot was right. Buckets of fire!"

"Fire in buckets?" said Masklin. "Buckets of *fire*? I can't see any flames."

"They must be inside. Perhaps there's a lid. There's beans in bean tins, and jam in jam jars. There should be fire in fire buckets," said Gurder vaguely. "Come on."

Grimma stared at this word, too. Her lips moved silently as she repeated it to herself. Then she hurried after the other two.

Eventually they reached the end of the corridor. There was another door there, with glass in the top half.

Gurder stared up at it.

"I can see there's words," said Grimma. "Read them out. I'd better not look at them," she added sweetly, "in case my brain goes bang."

Gurder swallowed. "They say 'Arnold Bros (est. 1905). D.H.K. Butterthwaite, General Manager.' Er."

"He's in there?" she said.

"Well, there's beans in bean tins and fire in fire buckets," said Masklin helpfully. "The door's not shut—look. Want me to go and see?"

Gurder nodded wretchedly. Masklin walked over to the door, leaned against it, and pushed it until his arms ached. Eventually it swung in a little way.

There was no light inside, but by the faint glow from the corridor through the glass he could see he was entering a large room. The carpet was much thicker—it was like wading through grass. Several yards away was a large rectangular wooden thing; as he walked around it, he saw a chair behind it. Perhaps this was where Arnold Bros (est. 1905) sat.

"Where are you, Arnold Bros (est. 1905)?" he whispered.

Some minutes later the other two heard him calling softly. They peered around the door.

"Where are you?" hissed Grimma.

"Up here," came Masklin's voice. "This big wooden thing. There's sticking-out bits you can climb on. There's all kinds of things up here. Careful of the carpet—there could be wild animals in it. If you wait a minute, I can help you up."

They waded through the deep pile of the carpet and waited anxiously by the wooden cliff.

"It's a desk," said Gurder, loftily. "There's lots of them in Furnishing. Amazing Value In Genuine One Hundred Percent Oak Veneer."

"What's he doing up there?" said Grimma. "I can hear clinking noises."

"A Must In Every Home," said Gurder, as if saying the words gave him some comfort. "Wide Choice Of Styles To Suit Every Pocket."

"What are you talking about?"

"Sorry. It's the sort of thing Arnold Bros (est. 1905) writes on the signs. I just feel better for saying it."

"What's that other thing up there?"

He looked where she was pointing.

"That? It's a chair. Swiveled Finish For That Executive Look."

"It looks big enough for humans," she said thoughtfully.

"I expect humans sit there when Arnold Bros (est. 1905) is giving them their instructions."

"Hmm," she said.

There was a clinking noise by her head.

"Sorry," Masklin called down. "It took me a while to hook them together."

Gurder looked up at the heights, and the gleaming chain that now hung down.

"Paper clips," he said, amazed. "I never would have thought it."

When they clambered to the top, they found Masklin wandering across the shiny surface, prodding things with his spear. This was paper, Gurder explained airily, and things for making marks.

"Well, Arnold Bros (est. 1905) doesn't seem to be around," Masklin said. "Perhaps he's gone to bed, or whatever."

"The Abbot said he saw him here one night, sitting at the desk right here," said Gurder. "Watching over the Store."

"What, sitting on that chair?" said Grimma.

"I suppose so."

"So he's big, then, is he?" Grimma pressed on relentlessly. "Sort of human sized?"

"Sort of," Gurder agreed reluctantly.

"Hmm."

Masklin found a cable as thick as his arm winding off across the top of the desk. He followed it.

"If he's human shaped and human sized," said Grimma, "then perhaps he's a—"

"Let's just see what we can find up here, shall we?" said Gurder hurriedly. He walked over to a pile of paper and started reading the top sheet by the dim light coming in from the corridor. He read slowly, in a very loud voice.

"'The Arnco Group,'" he read, "'incorporating Arnco Developments (UK), United Television, Arnco-Schultz (Hamburg) AG, Arnco Airlines, Arnco Recording, the Arnco Organization (Cinemas) Ltd., Arnco Petroleum Holdings, Arnco Publishing, and Arnco UK Retailing Ltd.'"

"Gosh," said Grimma flatly.

"There's more," said Gurder excitedly, "in much smaller letters— perhaps they're meant to be right for *us*. Listen to all these names: 'Arnco UK Retailing Ltd. includes Bonded Outlets Ltd., the Blackbury Dye and Paint Company, Kwik-Kleen Mechanical Sweepers Ltd., and—and—and—'"

"Something wrong?"

"'—Arnold Bros (est. 1905).'" Gurder looked up. "What do you think it all means? *Bargains Galore preserve us!*"

There was a light. It skewered down on the two of them, white and searing, so that they stood over a black pool of their own shadows.

Gurder looked up in terror at the brilliant globe that had appeared above them.

"Sorry, I think that was me," said Masklin's voice from the shadows. "I found this sort of lever thing, and when I pushed it, it went click. Sorry."

"Ahaha," said Gurder mirthlessly. "An electric light. Of course. Ahaha. Gave me quite a start for a moment."

Masklin appeared in the circle of brightness and looked at the paper.

"I heard you reading," he said. "Anything interesting?"

Gurder pored over the print again.

"'Notice to all Staff,'" he read. "'I am sure we are all aware of the increasingly poor financial performance of the store in recent years. This rambling old building, while quite suitable for the leisured shopper of 1905, is not appropriate in the exciting world of the twenty-first century, and as we all know, there have unfortunately been marked stock losses and a general loss of custom following the opening of newer major outlets in the town. I am sure our sorrow at the closure of Arnold Bros, which as you know was the foundation of the Arnco fortunes, will be lessened by the news of plans by the Group to replace it with an Arnco Super Saverstore in the Neil Armstrong Shopping Mall. To this end, the store will close at the end of the month, and will shortly be demolished to make way for an exciting new Arnco Leisure Complex. . . .'"

Gurder fell silent, and put his head in his hands.

"There's those words again," said Masklin slowly. "Closure. Demolished."

"What's leisure?" said Grimma.

The Stationeri ignored her.

Masklin took her gently by the arm.

"I think he wants to be alone for a while," he said. He pulled the tip of his spear across the broad sheet of paper, creasing it, and folded it up until it was small enough to carry.

"I expect the Abbot will want to see it," he said. "He'll never believe us if we—"

He stopped. Grimma was staring over his shoulder. He turned and looked out through the glass part of the great door into the corridor beyond. There was a shadow out there. Human shaped. And growing bigger.

"What *is* it?" she said.

Masklin gripped the spear. "I think," he said, "it may be Prices Slashed."

They turned and hurried over to Gurder.

"There's someone coming," Masklin whispered. "Get down to the floor, quickly!"

"Demolished!" moaned Gurder, hugging himself and rocking from side to side. "Everything Must Go! Final Reductions! We're all doomed!"

"Yes, but do you think you could go and be doomed on the floor?" said Masklin.

"He's not himself—you can see that," said Grimma. "Come on," she added in a horribly cheerful voice. "Upsy-daisy."

She lifted him up bodily and helped him toward the rope of clips. Masklin followed them, walking backward with his eye on the door.

He thought: He has seen the light. It should be dark in here now, and he has seen the light. But I'll never get it off in time, and anyway it won't make any difference. I don't believe in any demon called Prices Slashed, and now here he comes. What a strange world.

He sidled into the shade of a pile of paper and waited.

He could hear Gurder's feeble protests, down around floor level, suddenly stop. Perhaps Grimma had hit him with something. She had a way of taking obvious action in a crisis.

The door drifted open, very slowly. There *was* a figure there. It looked like a human in a blue suit. Masklin wasn't much of a judge of human expressions, but the man didn't look very happy. In one hand he held a metal tube. Light shone out of one end. *His terrible flashlight*, Masklin thought.

The figure came closer, in that slow-motion, sleepwalking way that humans had. Masklin peered around the paper, fascinated despite himself. He looked up into a round, red face, felt the breath, saw the peaked hat.

He'd learned that humans in the Store had their names on little badges, because—he'd been told—they were so stupid they wouldn't remember them otherwise. This man had his name on his hat. Masklin squinted and made out the shape of the letters: S . . . E . . . C . . . . U . . . R . . . I . . . T . . . Y. He had a white mustache.

The man straightened up and started to walk around the room. They're not stupid, Masklin told himself. He's bright enough to know there shouldn't be a light on, and he wants to find out why. He's bound to see the others if he just looks in the right place. Even a human could see them.

He gripped his spear. The eyes, he thought, I'd have to go for the eyes. . . .

Security drifted dreamily around the room, examining cupboards and looking in corners. Then he headed back toward the door.

Masklin dared to breathe, and at that moment, Gurder's hysterical voice came from somewhere below him.

"It *is* Prices Slashed! Oh, Bargains Galore, save us! We're all mmphmmphmmph—"

Security stopped. He turned back, a look of puzzlement spreading across his face as slowly as treacle.

Masklin shrank farther back into the shadows. This is it, then, he thought. If I can get a good run at him . . .

Something outside the door started to roar. It was almost a truck noise. It didn't seem to worry the man, who just pulled the door open and looked out.

There was a human woman in the passage. She looked quite elderly, as far as Masklin was any judge, with a pink apron with flowers on it and carpet slippers on her feet. She held a duster in one hand, and with the other she was . . .

Well, it looked as though she was holding back a sort of roaring thing, like a bag on wheels. It kept rushing forward across the carpet, but she kept one hand on its stick and kept pulling it back.

While Masklin watched, she gave the thing a kick. The roaring died away as Security started to talk to her. To Masklin the conversation sounded like a couple of foghorns having a fight.

Masklin ran to the edge of the desk and half climbed, half fell down the chain of clips. The other two were waiting in the shadow of the desk. Gurder's eyes were rolling; Grimma had one hand clamped firmly over his mouth.

"Let's get out of here while he's not looking!" said Masklin.

"How?" said Grimma. "There's only the doorway."

"Mmphmmph."

"Well, let's at least get somewhere better than this." Masklin stared around across the rolling acres of dark carpet. "There's a cupboard thing over there," he said.

"Mmphmmph!"

"What are we going to do with *him?*"

"Look," said Masklin to Gurder's frightened face, "you're not going to go on about doom, doom again, are you? Otherwise we'll have to gag you. Sorry."

"Mmph."

"Promise?"

"Mmph."

"Okay, you can take your hand away."

"It was Bargains Galore!" hissed Gurder excitedly.

Grimma looked up at Masklin. "Shall I shut him up again?" she said.

"He can say what he likes as long as he keeps quiet," said Masklin. "It probably makes him feel better. He's had a bit of a shock."

"Bargains Galore came to protect us! With her great roaring Soul Sucker . . ." Gurder's brow wrinkled in puzzlement.

"It was a carpet cleaner, wasn't it?" he said slowly. "I always thought it was something magical, and it was just a carpet cleaner. There's lots of them in Household Appliances. With Extra Suction For Deep-Down Carpet Freshness."

"Good. That's nice. Now, how do we get out of here?"

Some searching behind the filing cabinets found a crack in the floorboards just big enough to squeeze through with difficulty. Getting back took half a day, partly because Gurder would occasionally sit down and burst into tears, but mainly because they had to climb down inside the wall itself. It was hollow and had wires and odd bits of wood in it, tied into place by the Klothians, but it was still a tedious job. They came out under Kiddies Klothes. Gurder had pulled himself together by then and haughtily ordered food and an escort.

And so at last they came back to the Stationery Department.

Just in time.

Granny Morkie looked up as they were ushered into the Abbot's bedroom. She was sitting by the bed with her hands on her knees.

"Don't make any loud noises," she ordered. "He's very ill. He says he's dyin'. I suppose he should know."

"Dying of what?" said Masklin.

"Dyin' of bein' alive for such a long time," said Granny.

The Abbot lay, wrinkled and even smaller than Masklin remembered him, among his pillows. He was clutching the Thing in two thin, clawlike hands.

He looked at Masklin and, with a great effort, beckoned him to come closer.

"You'll have to lean over," Granny ordered. "He can't talk above a croak, poor old soul."

The Abbot gently grabbed Masklin's ear and pulled it down to his mouth.

"A sterling woman," he whispered. "Many fine qualities, I am sure. But please send her away before she gives me any more medicine."

Masklin nodded. Granny's remedies, made from simple, honest, and generally nearly poisonous herbs and roots, were amazing things. After one dose of stomachache jollop, you made sure you never complained of stomachache ever again. In its way, it was a sort of cure.

"I can't *send*," he said, "but I can ask."

She went out, shouting instructions to mix up another batch.

Gurder knelt down by the bed.

"You're not going to die, are you, sir?" he said.

"Of course I am. Everyone is. That's what being alive is all about," whispered the Abbot. "Did you see Arnold Bros (est. 1905)?"

"Well. Er." Gurder hesitated. "We found some Writing, sir. It's true, it says the Store will be demolished. That means the end of everything, sir—whatever shall we do?"

"You will have to leave," said the Abbot.

Gurder looked horrified.

"But you've always said that everything outside the Store could only be a dream!"

"And you never believed me, boy. And maybe I was wrong. That young man with the spear, is he still here? I can't see very well."

Masklin stepped forward.

"Oh, there you are," said the old nome. "This box of yours."

"Yes?" said Masklin.

"Told me things. Showed me pictures. Store's a lot bigger than I thought. There's this room they keep the stars in, not just the glittery ones they hang from the ceiling at Christmas Fayre, but hundreds of the damn things. It's called the universe. We used to live in it, it nearly all belonged to us, it was our *home*. We didn't live under anyone's floor. I think Arnold Bros (est. 1905) is telling us to go back there."

He reached out, and his cold white fingers gripped Masklin's arm with surprising strength.

"I don't say you're blessed with brains," he said. "In fact, I reckon

· 99 ·

you're the stupid but dutiful kind who gets to be leader when there's no glory in it. You're the kind who sees things through. Take them Home. Take them all Home."

He slumped back onto the pillows and shut his eyes.

"But—leave the Store, sir?" said Gurder. "There's thousands of us, old people and babies and everyone. Where can we go? There's foxes out there, Masklin says, and wind and hunger and water that drops out of the sky in bits! Sir? Sir?"

Grimma leaned over and felt the old nome's wrist.

"Can he hear me?" said Gurder.

"Maybe," said Grimma. "Perhaps. But he won't be able to answer you, because he's dead."

"But he can't die! He's always been here!" said Gurder, aghast. "You've got it wrong. Sir? Sir!"

Masklin took the Thing out of the Abbot's unresisting hands as other Stationeri, hearing Gurder's voice, hurried in.

"Thing?" he said quietly, walking away from the crowd around the bed.

*"I hear you."*

"Is he dead?"

*"I detect no life functions."*

"What does that mean?"

*"It means 'yes.'"*

"Oh." Masklin considered this. "I thought you had to be eaten or squashed first. I didn't think you just sort of stopped."

The Thing didn't volunteer any information.

"Any idea what I should do now?" said Masklin. "Gurder was right. They are not going to leave all this warmth and food. I mean, some of the youngsters might, for a lark. But if we're going to survive outside, we'll need lots of people. Believe me, I know what I'm talking about. And what am I supposed to say to them: Sorry, you've all got to leave it all behind?"

The Thing spoke.

*"No,"* it said.

Masklin had never seen a funeral before. Come to that, he'd never seen a nome die from being alive too long. Oh, people had been eaten, or had never come back, but no one had simply come to an end.

"Where do you bury your dead?" Gurder had asked.

"Inside badgers and foxes, often," he'd replied, and hadn't been able to resist adding, "You know. The handsome and agile hunters?"

This was how the nomes said farewell to their dead:

The body of the old Abbot was ceremoniously dressed in a green coat and a pointy red hat. His long white beard was carefully combed out, and then he lay, peacefully, on his bed as Gurder read the service.

"Now that it has pleased you, Arnold Bros (est. 1905), to take our brother to your great Gardening Department beyond Consumer Accounts, where there is Ideal Lawn Edging and an Amazing Floral Display and the pool of eternal life in Easy-To-Lay Polythene With Real-Crazy-Paving Edging, we will give him the gifts a nome must take on his journey."

The Count de Ironmongri stepped forward. "I give him," he said, laying an object beside the nome, "the Spade Of Honest Toil."

"And I," said the Duke de Haberdasheri, "lay beside him the Fishing Rod Of Hope."

Other leading nomes brought other things: the Wheelbarrow Of

Leadership, the Shopping Basket Of Life. Dying in the Store was quite complicated, Masklin gathered.

Grimma blew her nose as Gurder completed the service and the body was ceremoniously carried away.

To the subbasement, they later learned, and the incinerator. Down in the realms of Prices Slashed, the Security, where he sat at nighttimes, legend said, and drank his horrible tea.

"That's a bit dreadful, I reckon," said Granny Morkie as they stood around aimlessly afterward. "In my young day, if a person died, we buried 'em. In the ground."

"Ground?" said Gurder.

"Sort of floor," explained Granny.

"Then what happened?" said Gurder.

Granny looked blank. "What?" she said.

"Where did they go after that?" said the Stationeri patiently.

"Go? I don't reckon they went anywhere. Dead people don't get about much."

"In the Store," said Gurder slowly, as if he were explaining things to a rather backward child, "when a nome dies, if he has been a *good* nome, Arnold Bros (est. 1905) sends them back to see us before they go to a Better Place."

"How can—" Granny began.

"The inner bit of them, I mean," said Gurder. "The bit inside you that's really you."

They looked at him politely, waiting for him to make any sort of sense.

Gurder sighed. "All right," he said, "I'll get someone to show you."

o    o    o

They were taken to the Gardening Department. It was a strange place, Masklin thought. It was like the world outside but with all the difficult bits taken away. The only light was the faint glow of indoor suns, which stayed on all night. There was no wind, no rain, and there never would be. There was grass, but it was just painted green sacking with bits sticking out of it. There were mountainous cliffs of nothing but seeds in packets, each one with a picture that Masklin suspected was quite unreal. They showed flowers, but flowers unlike any he'd ever seen before.

"Is the Outside like this?" said the young priest who was guiding them. "They say, they say, er, they say you've been there. They say you've *seen* it." He sounded hopeful.

"There was more green and brown," said Masklin flatly.

"And flowers?" said the priest.

"*Some* flowers," Masklin agreed. "But not like these."

"I seed flowers like these once," said Torrit and then, unusually for him, fell silent.

They were led around the bulk of a giant lawn mower and there—

—were nomes. Tall, chubby-faced gnomes. Pink-cheeked painted gnomes. Some of them held fishing rods or spades. Some of them were pushing painted wheelbarrows. And every single one of them was grinning.

The tribe stood in silence for some time.

Then Grimma said, very softly, "How horrible."

"Oh, no!" said the priest, horrified. "It's marvelous! Arnold Bros (est. 1905) sends you back smart and new, and then you leave the Store and go to a wonderful place!"

"There's no women," said Granny. "That's a mercy, anyway."

"Ah, well," said the priest, looking a bit embarrassed. "That's always been a bit of a debatable question. We're not sure why, but we think—"

"And they don't look like anyone," said Granny. "They all look the same."

"Well, you see—"

"Catch me coming back like that," said Granny. "If you come back like that, I don't want to go."

The priest was almost in tears.

"No, but—"

"I saw one like these once." It was old Torrit again. He looked very gray in the face and was trembling.

"You shut up, you," said Granny. "You never saw nothing."

"I did too," said Torrit. "When I was a little lad. Grandpa Dimpo took some of us across the fields, through the wood, and there was all these big stone houses where humans lived, and they had little fields in front full of flowers like what they got here, and grass all short, and ponds with orange fish, and we saw one of these. It was sitting on a stone toadstool by one of these ponds."

"It never was," said Granny automatically.

"It was an' all," said Torrit levelly. "And I mind Grandpa sayin', 'That ain't no life, out there in all weathers, birds doing their woss-name on your hat and dogs widdlin' all over you.' He tole us it was a giant nome who got turned to stone on account of sitting there for so long and never catching no fish. And he said, 'Wot a way to go. That ain't for me, lads—I want to go sudden like,' and then a cat jumped out on him. Talk about a laugh."

"What happened?" said Masklin.

"Oh, we gave it a good seeing-to with our spears and picked him up, and we all run like bu—run very fast," said Torrit, watching Granny's stern expression.

"No, no!" wailed the priest. "It's not like that at all!" and then he started to sob.

Granny hesitated for a moment and then patted him gently on the back.

"There, there," she said. "Don't you worry about it. Daft old fool says any old thing that comes into his head."

"I don't—" Torrit began. Granny's warning look stopped him.

They went back slowly, trying to put the terrible stone images out of their minds. Torrit trailed along behind, grumbling like a worn-out thunderstorm.

"I did see it, I'm telling you," he whispered. "Damn great grinning thing, it were, sitting on a spotty stone mushroom. I did see it. Never went back there, though. Better safe than sorry, I always said. But I did see it."

It seemed taken for granted by everyone that Gurder was going to be the new Abbot. The old Abbot had left strict instructions. There didn't seem to be any argument.

The only one against the idea, in fact, was Gurder.

"Why me?" he said. "I never wanted to lead anyone! Anyway . . . you know . . ." He lowered his voice. "I have Doubts, sometimes. The old Abbot knew it, I'm sure. I can't imagine why he'd think I'd be any good."

Masklin said nothing. It occurred to him that the Abbot might have had a very definite aim in mind. Perhaps it was time for a little doubt. Perhaps it was time to look at Arnold Bros (est. 1905) in a different way.

· 105 ·

They were off to one side in the big underfloor area the Stationeri used for important meetings; it was the one place in the Store, apart from the Food Hall, where fighting was strictly forbidden. The heads of the families, rulers of departments and subdepartments, were milling around out there. They might not be allowed to bear weapons, but they were cutting one another dead at every opportunity.

Getting them to even think of working together would be impossible without the Stationeri. It was odd, really. The Stationeri had no real power at all, but all the families needed them and none of them feared them, and so they survived and, in a strange sort of way, led. A Haberdasheri wouldn't listen even to common sense from an Ironmongri, on general principles, but he would if the speaker was a Stationeri because everyone knew the Stationeri didn't take sides.

Masklin turned to Gurder.

"We need to talk to someone in the Ironmongri. They control the electric, don't they? And the truck nest."

"That's the Count de Ironmongri over there," said Gurder, pointing. "Thin fellow with the mustache. Not very religious. Doesn't know much about electric, though."

"I thought you told me—"

"Oh, the *Ironmongri* do. The underlings and servants and whatnot. But not people like the Count. Good heavens." Gurder smiled. "You don't think the Duke de Haberdasheri ever touches a pair of scissors, do you, or Baroness del Icatessen goes and cuts up food her actual self?"

He looked sideways at Masklin. "You've got a plan, haven't you?" he said.

"Yes. Sort of."

"What are you going to tell them, then?"

Masklin picked absently at the tip of his spear.

"The truth. I'm going to tell them they can leave the Store and take it all with them. I think it should be possible."

Gurder rubbed his chin. "Hmm," he said. "I *suppose* it's possible. If everyone carries as much food and stuff as they can. But it'll soon run out, and anyway, you can't carry electric. It lives in wires, you know."

"How many Stationeri can read Human?" said Masklin, ignoring him.

"All of us can read a bit, of course," said Gurder. "But only four of us are any real good at it, if you must know."

"I don't think that's going to be enough," said Masklin.

"Well, there's a trick to it, and not everyone can get the hang of it. What *are* you planning?"

"A way to get everyone, *everyone*, out. Carrying everything we'll ever need, ever," said Masklin.

"They'll be squashed under the weight!"

"Not really. Most of what they'll be carrying doesn't weigh anything at all."

Gurder looked worried.

"This isn't some mad scheme of Dorcas's, is it?" he said.

"No."

Masklin felt that he might explode. His head wasn't big enough to hold all the things the Thing had told him.

And he was the only one. Oh, the Abbot had known, and died with his eyes full of stars, but even he didn't understand. The galaxy! The old man thought it was just a great big room outside the Store, just the biggest department ever. Perhaps Gurder wouldn't comprehend either. He'd lived all his life under a roof. He had no idea of the sort of distances involved.

Masklin felt a slight surge of pride at this. The Store nomes *couldn't* understand what the Thing was saying, because they had no experiences to draw on. To them, from one end of the Store to the other was the biggest possible distance in the world.

They wouldn't be able to come to grips with the fact that the stars, fr'instance, were much farther away. Even if you ran all the way, it'd probably take *weeks* to reach them.

He'd have to lead up to it gently.

The stars! And a long, long time ago, nomes had traveled between them on things that made trucks look tiny—and had been built by nomes. And one of the great ships, exploring around a little star on the edge of nowhere, had sent out a smaller ship to land on the world of the humans.

But something had gone wrong. Masklin hadn't understood that bit, except that the thing that moved the ships was very, very powerful. Hundreds of nomes had survived, though. One of them, searching through the wreckage, had found the Thing. It wasn't any good without electricity to eat, but the nomes had kept it nevertheless, because it had been the machine that steered the Ship.

And the generations passed by, and the nomes forgot everything except that the Thing was very important.

That was enough for one head to carry, Masklin thought. But it wasn't the most important bit, it wasn't the bit that made his blood fizz and his fingers tingle.

*This* was the important bit. The big Ship, the one that could fly between stars, was still up there somewhere. It was tended by machines like the Thing, patiently waiting for the nomes to come back. Time meant nothing to them. There were machines to sweep the long corridors, and machines that made food and watched the stars and patiently counted the hours and minutes in the long, dark emptiness of the Ship.

And they'd wait forever. They didn't know what Time was, except something to be counted and filed away. They'd wait until the sun went cold and the moon died, carefully repairing the Ship and keeping it ready for the nomes to come back.

To take them Home.

And while they waited, Masklin thought, we forgot all about them, we forgot everything about ourselves, and lived in holes in the ground.

He knew what he had to do. It was, of course, an impossible task. But he was used to impossible tasks. Dragging a rat all the way from the woods to the hole had been an impossible task. But it wasn't impossible to drag it a little way, so you did that, and then you had a rest, and then you dragged it a little way again. . . . The way to deal with an impossible task was to chop it down into a number of merely very difficult tasks, and break each one of *them* into a group of horribly hard tasks, and each one of *them* into tricky jobs, and each one of them . . .

Probably the hardest job of all was to make nomes understand what they once were and could be again.

He did have a plan. Well, it had started off as the Thing's plan, but he'd turned it over and over in his mind so much, he felt it belonged to him. It was probably an impossible plan. But he'd never know unless he tried it.

Gurder was still watching him cautiously.

"Er," Masklin said. "This plan . . ."

"Yes?" said Gurder.

"The Abbot told me that the Stationeri have always tried to make nomes work together and stop squabbling," said Masklin.

"That has always been our desire, yes."

"*This* plan will mean they'll *have* to work together."

"Good."

"Only I don't think you're going to like it much," said Masklin.

"That's unfair! How can you make assumptions like that?"

"I think you'll laugh at it," said Masklin.

"The only way to find out is to tell me," said Gurder.

Masklin told him. When Gurder was over the shock, he laughed and laughed.

And then he looked at Masklin's face, and stopped.

"You're not serious?" he said.

"Let me put it like this," said Masklin. "Have you got a better plan? Will you support me?"

"But how will you—how can nomes—is it even possible that we can—?" Gurder began.

"We'll find a way," said Masklin. "With Arnold Bros (est. 1905)'s help, of course," he added diplomatically.

"Oh. Of course," said Gurder weakly. He pulled himself together. "Anyway, if I'm to be the new Abbot, I have to make a speech," he said. "It's expected. General messages of goodwill and so on. We can talk about this later. Reflect upon it at leisure in the sober surroundings of—"

Masklin shook his head. Gurder swallowed.

"You mean *now*?" he said.

"Yes. Now. We tell them *now*."

# 8

*I. And the leaders of the nomes were Assembled,* and *the Abbot Gurder said unto them, Harken to the Words of the Outsider;*

*II. And some waxed wroth, saying, He is an Outsider, wherefor then shall we harken to him?*

*III. The Abbot Gurder said, Because the old Abbot wished it so. Yea, and because I wish it so, also.*

*IV. Whereupon they grumbled, but were silent.*

*V. The Outsider said, Concerning the Rumors of Demolition, I have a Plan.*

*VI. Let us not go like Woodlice fleeing from an overturned log, but like Brave Free People, at a time of our choosing.*

*VII. And they interrupted him, saying, What's Woodlice? Whereupon the Outsider said, All right, Rats.*

*VIII. Let us take with us the things that we need to begin our life anew Outside, not in some other Store, but under the sky. Let us take all nomes, the aged and the young, and all the food and materials and information that we need.*

*IX. And they said, All? And he said, All. And they said unto him, We cannot do this thing. . . .*

*From* The Book of Nome, Third Floor v. I–IX

"YES, WE CAN," said Masklin. "If we steal a truck."

There was a dead silence.

The Count de Ironmongri raised an eyebrow.

"The big smelly things with wheels at each corner?" he asked.

"Yes," said Masklin. All eyes were on him. He felt himself beginning to blush.

"The nome's a fool!" snapped the Duke de Haberdasheri. "Even if the Store were in danger, and I see no reason, no reason I say, to believe it, the idea is quite preposterous."

"You see," said Masklin, blushing even more, "there's plenty of room, we can take everyone, we can steal books that tell us how to do things—"

"The mouth moves, the tongue waggles, but no sense comes out," said the Duke. There was nervous laughter from some of the nomes around him. Out of the corner of his eye Masklin saw Angalo standing by his father, his face shining.

"No offense to the late Abbot," said one of the lesser lords hesitantly, "but I've heard there are other Stores Out There. I mean to say, we must have lived somewhere before the Store." He swallowed. "What I'm getting at, if the Store was built in 1905, where did we live in 1904? No offense meant."

"I'm not talking about going to another Store," said Masklin. "I'm talking about living free."

"And I'm listening to no more of this nonsense. The old Abbot was a sound man, but he must have gone a little funny in the head at the finish," snapped the Duke. He turned and stormed out noisily. Most of the other lords followed him. Some of them quite reluctantly, Masklin noticed; in fact, a few hung around at the back, so that if asked they could say that they were just about to leave.

Those left were the Count, a small fat woman whom Gurder had identified as the Baroness del Icatessen, and a handful of lesser lords from the subdepartments.

The Count looked around theatrically.

"Ah," he said. "Room to breathe. Carry on, young man."

"Well, that's about it," Masklin admitted. "I can't plan anything more until I've found out more things. For example, can you make electric? Not steal it from the Store but make it?"

The Count stroked his chin.

"You are asking me to give you departmental secrets?" he said.

"My lord," said Gurder sharply, "if we take this desperate step, it is vital that we be open with one another and share our knowledge."

"That's true," said Masklin.

"Quite," said Gurder sternly. "We must all act for the good of all nomes."

"Well said," said Masklin. "And that's why the Stationeri, for their part, will teach all nomes who request it—to read."

There was a pause. It was broken by the faint wheezing noise of Gurder trying not to choke.

"To read—!" he began.

Masklin hesitated. Well, he'd gone this far. Might as well get it over with. He saw Grimma staring at him.

"Women too," he said.

This time it was the Count who looked surprised. The Baroness, on the other hand, was smiling. Gurder was still making little mewling noises.

"There's all kinds of books on the shelves in the Stationery Department," Masklin plunged on. "Anything we want to do, there's a book that tells us how! But we're going to need lots of people to read them, so we can find out what we need."

"I think our Stationeri friend would like a drink of water," observed the Count. "I think he may be overcome by the new spirit of sharing and cooperation."

"Young man," said the Baroness, "what you say might be true, but do these precious books tell us how one may control one of these truck things?"

Masklin nodded. He had been ready for this one. Grimma came up behind him, dragging a thin book that was nearly as big as she was. Masklin helped her prop it up so they could all see it.

"See, it's got words on it," he said proudly. "I've learned them already. They say . . ." He pointed each one out with his spear as he said it. ". . . The . . . High . . . Way . . . Code. High Way Code. It's got pictures inside. When you learn The High Way Code, you can drive. It says so. High Way Code," he added uncertainly.

"And I've been working out what some of the words mean," said Grimma.

"And she's been reading some of the words," Masklin agreed. He couldn't help noticing that this fact interested the Baroness.

"And that is all there is to it?" said the Count.

"Er," said Masklin. He'd been worrying about this himself. He had an obscure feeling that it couldn't be as easy as that, but this was no time to worry about details that could be sorted out later. What was it the Abbot had said? The important thing about being a leader was not so much being right or wrong as being certain. Being right helped, of course.

"Well, I went and looked in the truck nest, I mean the garage, this morning," he said. "You can see inside them if you climb up. There's levers and wheels and things, but I suppose we can find out what they do." He took a deep breath. "It can't be very difficult— otherwise humans wouldn't be able to do it."

The nomes had to concede this.

"Most intriguing," said the Count. "May I ask what it is you require from us now?"

"People," said Masklin simply. "As many as you can spare. *Especially* the ones you can't spare. And they'll need to be fed."

The Baroness glanced at the Count. He nodded, so she nodded.

"I'd just like to ask the young girl," she said, "whether she feels all right. With this reading, I mean."

"I can only do some words," said Grimma quickly. "Like Left and Right and Bicycle."

"And you haven't experienced any feelings of pressure in the head?" asked the Baroness carefully.

"Not really, ma'am."

"Hmm. That's extremely interesting," said the Baroness, staring fixedly at Gurder.

The new Abbot was sitting down now. "I—I—" he began.

Masklin groaned inwardly. He'd thought it would be difficult, learning to drive, learning how a truck worked, learning to *read*, but they were, well, just tasks. You could see all the difficulties before you started. If you worked at them for long enough, then you were bound to succeed. He'd been right. The difficult thing was going to be all the people.

There turned out to be twenty-eight.

"Not enough," said Grimma.

"It's a start," said Masklin. "I think there will be more by and by. They all need to be taught to read. Not well, but enough. And then five of the best of them must be taught how to teach people to read."

"How did you work that out?" said Grimma.

"The Thing told me," said Masklin. "It's something called *critical path analysis*. It means there's always something you should have done first. For example, if you want to build a house, you need to know how to make bricks, and before you can make bricks you need to know what kind of clay to use. And so on."

"What's clay?"

"Don't know."

"What're bricks?"

"Not sure."

"Well, what's a house?" she demanded.

"Haven't quite worked it out," said Masklin. "But anyway, it's all very important. Critical path analysis. And there's something else called *progress chasing*."

"What's *that*?"

"I think it means shouting at people, 'Why haven't you done it yet?'" Masklin looked down at his feet. "I think we can get Granny Morkie to do that," he said. "I don't reckon she will be interested in learning to read, but she knows how to shout."

"What about me?"

"I want you to learn to read even more."

"Why?"

"Because we need to learn how to think," said Masklin.

"I know how to think!"

"Dunno," said Masklin. "I mean, yes, you do, but there's some things we can't think because we don't know the words. Like the Store nomes. They don't even know what the wind and rain are really like!"

"I know, and I tried to tell the Baroness about snow and—"

Masklin nodded. "There you are, then. They don't know, and

they don't even *know* they don't know. What is it that *we* don't know? We ought to read everything that we can. Gurder doesn't like it. He says only the Stationeri should read. But the trouble is they don't try to understand things."

Gurder had been furious.

*"Reading,"* he'd said. "Every stupid nome coming up here and wearing all the printing out with looking at it! Why don't you give away all our skills while you're about it? Why don't we teach everyone to write, eh?"

"We can do that later," said Masklin mildly.

*"What!"*

"It isn't so important, you see."

Gurder thumped the wall. "Why in the name of Arnold Bros (est. 1905) didn't you ask my permission first?"

"Would you have given it?"

"No!"

"That's why, you see," said Masklin.

"When I said I'd help you, I didn't expect this!" shouted Gurder.

"Nor did I!" snapped Masklin.

The new Abbot paused.

"What do you mean?" he said.

"I thought you'd help," said Masklin, simply.

Gurder sagged. "All right, all right," he said. "You know I can't forbid it now, not in front of everyone. Do whatever is necessary. Take whatever people you must."

"Good," said Masklin. "When can you start?"

"Me? But—"

"You said yourself that you're the best reader."

"Well, yes, of course, this is the case, but—"

"Good."

They grew used to that word, later. Masklin developed a way of saying it that indicated that everything was all sorted out, and there was no point in saying anything more.

Gurder waved his hands wildly.

"What do you want me to do?" he said.

"How many books are there?" said Masklin.

"Hundreds! Thousands!"

"Do you know what they're all about?"

Gurder looked at him blankly. "Do you know what you're saying?" he said.

"No. But I want to find out."

"They're about everything! You'd never believe it! They're full of words even I don't understand!"

"Can you find a book that tells you how to understand words you don't understand?" said Masklin. This is critical path analysis, he thought. Gosh, I'm doing it without thinking.

Gurder hesitated. "It's an intriguing thought," he said.

"I want to find out everything about trucks, and electric, and food," said Masklin. "And then I want you to find a book about, about . . ."

"Well?"

Masklin looked desperate. "Is there a book that tells you how nomes can drive a truck built for humans?" he said.

"Don't you know?"

"Not . . . exactly. I was sort of hoping we could work it out as we went along."

"But you said all we needed to do was learn *The High Way Code*!"

"Ye-ss," said Masklin uncertainly, "and it *says* you have to know *The High Way Code* before you can drive. But somehow I get the feeling that it might not be as simple as that."

"Bargains Galore preserve us!"

"I hope so," said Masklin. "I really do."

And then it was time to put it all to the test.

It was cold in the truck nest, and stank of *oil*. It was also a long way to the ground if they fell off the girder. Masklin tried not to look down.

There was a truck below them. It looked much bigger indoors. Huge, red, and terrible in the gloom.

"This is about far enough," he said. "We're right over the sticking-out bit where the driver sits."

"The cab," said Angalo.

"Right. The cab."

Angalo had been a surprise. He'd turned up in the Stationery Department breathing heavily, his face red, and demanding to be taught to read.

So he could learn about trucks.

They fascinated him.

"But your father objects to the whole idea," Masklin had said.

"That doesn't matter," said Angalo shortly. "It's all right for you, you've *been* there! I want to see all those things, I want to go Outside, I want to know if it's real!"

He hadn't been very good at reading, but he'd tried until his brain hurt when the Stationeri found him some books with trucks on the front. Now he probably knew more about them than any other nome. Which wasn't a lot, Masklin had to admit.

He listened to Angalo muttering to himself as he struggled into the straps.

"Gear," he said. "Shift. Steering Wheel. Wipers. Auto Transmission. Breaker Break Good Buddy. Smoky. Truckers." He looked up and smiled thinly at Masklin. "Ready," he said.

"Now remember," said Masklin, "they don't always leave the windows open, so if they're closed, one pull on the rope and we'll pull you back up, okay?"

"Ten-four."

"What?"

"It's Trucker for 'yes,'" explained Angalo.

"Oh. Fine. Now, when you're in, find somewhere to hide so you can watch the driver—"

"Yes, yes. You explained it all before," said Angalo impatiently.

"Yes. Well. Have you got your sandwiches?"

Angalo patted the package at his waist. "And my notebook," he said. "Ready to go. Put the Pedal to the Metal."

"What?"

"It means 'go' in Truck."

Masklin looked puzzled. "Do we have to know all this to drive one?"

"Negatory," said Angalo proudly.

"Oh? Well, so long as you understand yourself, that's the main thing."

Dorcas, who was in charge of the rope detail, tapped Angalo on the shoulder.

"You sure you won't take the Outside suit?" he said hopefully.

It was cone shaped, made out of heavy cloth over a sort of umbrella frame of sticks so that it folded up, and had a little window to look out of. Dorcas had insisted on building it, to protect Outsidegoers.

"After all," he'd said to Masklin, "*you* might be used to the Rain and the Wind—perhaps your heads have grown specially hard. Can't be too careful."

"I don't think so, thank you," said Angalo politely. "It's so heavy, and I don't expect I'll go outside the truck this trip."

"Good," said Masklin. "Well, let's not hang about. Except for you, Angalo. Haha. Ready to take the strain, lads? Over you go, Angalo," he said, and then, because it paid to be on the safe side and you never knew, it might help, he added, "May Arnold Bros (est. 1905) watch over you."

Angalo eased himself over the edge and slowly became a small spinning shape in the gloom as the team carefully let the thread out. Masklin prayed that they'd brought enough of it; there hadn't been time to come and measure.

There was a desperate tugging on the thread. Masklin peered down. Angalo was a small shape a yard or so below him.

"If anything should happen to me, no one is to eat Bobo," he called up.

"Don't you worry," said Masklin. "You're going to be all right."

"Yes, I know. But if I'm not, Bobo is to go to a good home," said Angalo.

"Right you are. A good home. Yes."

"Where they don't eat rat. Promise?"

"No rat eating. Fine," said Masklin.

Angalo nodded. The gang started to pay out the thread again.

Then Angalo was down and hurrying across the sloping roof to the side of the cab. It made Masklin dizzy just to look down at him.

The figure disappeared. After a while came two tugs, meaning "pay out more thread." They let it slip past gradually. And then there were three tugs, faint but—well, three. And a few seconds later they came again.

Masklin let out his breath in a whoosh.

"Angalo has landed," he said. "Pull the thread back up. We'll leave it here, in case—I mean, for when he comes back."

He risked another look at the forbidding bulk of the truck. The trucks went out, the trucks came back, and it was the considered opinion of nomes like Dorcas that they were the same trucks. They went out loaded with goods, and they came back loaded with goods, and why Arnold Bros (est. 1905) felt the need to let goods out for the day was beyond anyone's understanding. All that was known with any certainty was that they were always back within a day, or two at the outside.

Masklin looked down at the truck that now contained the explorer. Where would it go, what would happen to it? What would Angalo *see*, before he came back again? If he didn't come back, what would Masklin tell his parents? That someone had to go, that he'd *begged* to go, that they had to see how a truck was driven, that everything depended on him? Somehow, he knew, it wouldn't sound very convincing in those circumstances.

Dorcas leaned over next to him.

"It'll be a job and a half getting everyone down this way," he said.

"I know. We'll have to think of some better way."

The inventor pointed down toward one of the other silent trucks. "There's a little step there," he said, "just by the driver's door, look. If we could get to that and get a rope around the handle—"

Masklin shook his head.

"It's too far up," he said. "It's a small step for a man, but a giant leap for nomekind."

# 9

*V. Thus the Outsider said, Those who believe* not *in the Outside,* see, *one will be sent Outside to Prove This Thing; VI. And one went upon a Truck, and went Outside, to see where there may be a new Home; VII. And there was much waiting, for he did not return.*

*From* The Book of Nome, Goods Outward v. V–VII

MASKLIN HAD TAKEN to sleeping in an old shoebox in the Stationery Department, where he could find a little peace. But when he got back, there was a small deputation of nomes waiting for him. They were holding a book between them.

Masklin was getting a bit disillusioned with the books. Maybe all the things he wanted to know were written down somewhere, but the real problem was to find them. The books might have been put together especially to make it difficult to find things out. There seemed to be no sense in them. Or, rather, there was sense, but in nonsensical ways.

He recognized Vinto Pimmie, a very young Ironmongri. He sighed. Vinto was one of the keenest and fastest readers, just not a particularly good one, and he tended to get carried away.

"I've cracked it," said the boy proudly.

"Can you repair it?" said Masklin.

"I *mean*, I know how we can get a human to drive the truck for us!"

Masklin sighed. "We've thought about this, but it really won't work. If we show ourselves to a human—"

"Don't matter! Don't matter! He won't do anything, the reason being, we'll have—you'll like this—we'll have a gnu!"

Vinto beamed at him, like a dog who's just done a difficult trick.

"A gnu," repeated Masklin weakly.

"Yes! It's in this book!" Vinto proudly displayed it. Masklin craned to see. He was picking reading up as he went along, a little bit at a time, but as far as he could make out the book was about *Host Age at 10,000 Feet.*

"It's got something to do with lots of shoes?" he said hopefully.

"No, no, no, what you do is, you get a gnu, then you point it at the driver and someone says, 'Look out, he's got a gnu!' and you say, 'Take us where we want to go or I'll fire this gnu at you!' and then he—"

"Right, right. Fine," said Masklin, backing away. "Jolly good. Splendid idea. We'll definitely give it some thought. Well done."

"That was clever of me, wasn't it?" said Vinto, jumping from one foot to the other.

"Yes. Certainly. Er. You don't think you might be better reading a more *practical* kind of—" Masklin hesitated. Who knew what kind of books were best?

He staggered inside his box and pulled the cardboard over the door and leaned against it.

"Thing?" he said.

*"I hear you, Masklin,"* said the Thing, from the heap of rags that was Masklin's bed.

"What's a gnu?"

There was a brief pause. Then the Thing said: *"The gnu, a member of the genus* Connochaetes *and the family Bovidae, is an African antelope with down-curving horns. Body length is up to 6.5 ft. The shoulder height is about 4.5 ft., and weight is up to 600 lb. Gnus inhabit grassy plains in central and southern Africa."*

"Oh. Could you threaten someone with one?"

*"Quite possibly."*

"Would there be one in the Store?"

There was another pause. *"Is there a Pet Department?"*

Masklin knew what that was. The subject had come up yesterday, when Vinto had suggested taking a herd of guinea pigs to raise for meat.

"No," he said.

*"Then I should think the chance is remote."*

"Oh. Just as well, really." Masklin sagged down on his bed. "You see," he said, "we've got to be able to control where we're going. We need to find somewhere a little way from humans. But not too far. Somewhere safe."

*"You must look for an atlas or map."*

"What do they look like?"

*"They may have the words 'atlas' or 'map' written on them."*

"I'll ask the Abbot to have a search made." Masklin yawned.

*"You must sleep,"* said the Thing.

"People always want me to do things. Anyway, you don't sleep."

*"It's different for me."*

"What I need," said Masklin, "is a way. We can't use a gnu. They all think I know the way to do it, and I don't know the way. We know what we need, but we'll never get it all into a truck in one night. They all think I know all the answers, but I don't. And I don't know the way . . ."

He fell asleep and dreamed of being human sized. Everything was so easy, if you were human sized.

Two days went past. The nomes kept watch from the girder over the garage. A small plastic telescope was rolled down from the Toy Department, and with its help the news came back that the big metal doors to the garage opened themselves when a human pressed a red button next to them. How could you press a button ten times higher than your head? It went down on Masklin's list of problems to solve.

Gurder found a map. It was in quite a small book.

"That was *no* trouble," he said. "We have dozens of these every year. It's called"—he read the gold lettering slowly—"Pocket Diary. And it has this map all at the back, look."

Masklin stared down at the small pages of blue and red blobs. Some of the blobs had names, like Africa and Asia.

"We-ell," he said, and "Ye-ss. I suppose so. Well done. Where are we, exactly?"

"In the middle," said Gurder promptly. "That's logical."

And then the truck returned.

Angalo didn't.

Masklin ran along the girder without thinking of the drop on either side. The little knot of figures told him everything he didn't want to know. A young nome who had just been lowered over the edge was sitting down and getting his breath back.

"I tried all the windows," he said. "They're all shut. Couldn't see anyone in there. It's very dark."

"Are you sure it's the right truck?" said Masklin to the head watcher.

"They've all got numbers on the front of them," he was told. "I was particularly sure to remember the one he went out on, so when it came back this afternoon, I—"

"We've got to get inside to have a look," said Masklin firmly. "Someone go and get . . . no, it'll take too long. Lower me down."

"What?"

"Lower me down," Masklin repeated. "All the way to the floor."

"It's a long way down," said one of them doubtfully.

"I know! Far too long to go all the way around by the stairs." Masklin handed the end of the thread to a couple of nomes. "He could be in there hurt, or anything."

"'Tisn't our fault," said a nome. "There were humans all over the place when it came in. We had to wait."

"It's no one's fault. Some of you, go around the long way and meet me down there. Don't look so upset—it's no one's fault."

Except perhaps mine, he thought, as he spun around in the darkness. He watched the huge shadowy bulk of the truck slide past him. Somehow, they'd looked smaller outside.

The floor was greasy with *all*. He ran under the truck into a world roofed with wires and pipes, far too high to reach, but he poked around near one of the benches and came back dragging a length of wire and, with great difficulty, bent it into a hook at one end.

A moment later he was crawling among the pipes. It wasn't hard. Most of the underneath of the truck seemed to be pipes or wires, and after a minute or two he found a metal wall ahead of him, with holes in it to take even more bundles of wires. It was possible, with a certain amount of pain, to squeeze through. Inside—

There was carpet. Odd thing to find in a truck. Here and there a candy wrapper lay, large as a newspaper to a nome. Huge pedal-shaped things stuck out of greasy holes in the floor. In the distance was a seat, behind a huge wheel. Presumably it was something for the human in the truck to hold on to, Masklin thought.

"Angalo?" he called out softly.

There was no answer. He poked around aimlessly for a while, and had nearly given up when he spotted something in the drifts of fluff and paper under the seat. A human would have thought it was just another scrap of rubbish. Masklin recognized Angalo's coat.

He looked carefully at the rubbish. It was just possible to imagine someone had been lying there, watching. He rummaged among it and found a small sandwich wrapper.

He took the coat back out with him; there didn't seem to be much else to do.

A dozen nomes were waiting anxiously on the *all*-soaked floor under the engine. Masklin held out the coat and shrugged.

"No sign," he said. "He's been there, but he's not there now."

"What could have happened to him?" said one of the older nomes.

Someone behind him said darkly: "Perhaps the Rain squashed him. Or he was blown away by the fierce Wind."

"That's right," said one of the others. "There could be dreadful things, Outside."

"No!" said Masklin. "I mean, there *are* dreadful things—"

"Ah," said the nomes, nodding.

"—but not like that! He should have been perfectly all right if he stayed in the truck! I told him not to go exploring—"

He was aware of a sudden silence. The nomes weren't looking at him but past him, at something behind him.

The Duke de Haberdasheri was standing there, with some of his soldiers. He stared woodenly at Masklin and then held out his hands without saying a word.

Masklin gave him the coat. The Duke turned it over and over, staring at it. The silence stretched out thinner and thinner, until it almost hummed.

"I forbade him to go," said the Duke softly. "I told him it would be dangerous. You know, that was foolish of me. It just made him more determined." He looked back up at Masklin.

"Well?" he said.

"Er?" said Masklin.

"Is my son still alive?"

"Um. He could be. There's no reason why not."

The Duke nodded vaguely.

This is it, thought Masklin. It's all going to end here.

The Duke stared up at the truck and then looked around at his guards.

"And these things go Outside, do they?" he said.

"Oh, yes. All the time," said Masklin.

The Duke made an odd noise in the back of his throat.

"There is nothing Outside," he said. "I know this. But my son knew differently. You think we should go Out. Will I see my son then?"

Masklin looked into the old man's eyes. They were like two eggs that weren't quite cooked yet. And he thought about the size of everything outside, and the size of a nome. And then he thought: A leader should know all about truth and honesty, and when to see the difference. Honestly, the chance of finding Angalo out there is greater than the whole Store taking wings and flying, but the *truth* is that—

"It's possible," he said, and felt terrible. But it *was* possible.

"Very well," said the Duke, his expression unchanged. "What do you need?"

"What?" said Masklin, his mouth dropping open.

"I said what do you need? To make the truck go Outside?" said the Duke.

Masklin floundered. "Well, er, at the moment, I suppose, we need people—"

"How many?" snapped the Duke.

Masklin's mind raced.

"Fifty?" he ventured.

"You shall have them."

"But—" Masklin began. The Duke's expression changed now. He no longer looked totally lost and alone. Now he looked his usual angry self.

"*Succeed,*" he hissed, and spun on his heel and stalked off.

That evening fifty Haberdasheri turned up, gawping at the garage and acting generally bewildered. Gurder protested, but Masklin put all those who looked even vaguely capable onto the reading scheme.

"There's too many!" said Gurder. "And they're common soldiers, for Arnold Bros (est. 1905)'s sake!"

"I expected him to say fifty was too many and beat me down to twenty or so," said Masklin. "But I think we will need them all, soon."

The reading program wasn't going the way he expected. There *were* useful things in books, it was true, but it was a hard job to find them among all the strange stuff.

Like the girl in the rabbit hole.

It was Vinto who came up with *that* one.

". . . and she fell down this hole and there was a white rabbit with a watch, I know about rabbits, and then she found this little bottle of stuff that made her BIG, I mean really huge, and then she found some more stuff which made her really small," he'd said breathlessly, his face glowing with enthusiasm, "so all we need do *is* we just find some more of the BIG stuff and then one of us can drive the truck."

Masklin didn't dare ignore it. If just one nome could be made the size of a human, it would be *easy*. He'd told himself that dozens of times. It had to be worth an effort.

So they'd spent nearly all the night searching the Store for any bottles labeled "Drink Me." Either the Store didn't have it—and Gurder wasn't prepared to accept that, because the Store had Everything Under One Roof—or it just wasn't real. There seemed to be lots of things in books that weren't real. It was hard to see why Arnold Bros (est. 1905) had put so many unreal things in books.

"So the faithful can tell the difference," Gurder had said.

Masklin had taken one book himself. It just fitted his box. It was called *A Child's Guide to the Stars*, and most of it was pictures of the sky at night. He knew that was real.

He liked to look at it when he had too much to think about. He looked at it now.

They had names, like Sirius and Rigel or Wolf 359 or Ross 154. He tried a few on the Thing.

*"I do not know the names,"* it said.

"I thought we came from one of them," said Masklin. "You said—"

*"They are different names. Currently I cannot identify them."*

"What was the name of the star that nomes came from?" said Masklin, lying back in the darkness.

*"It was called: The Sun."*

"But the sun's here!"

*"All stars are called The Sun by the people who live nearby. It is because they believe them to be important."*

"Did they—I mean, did we visit many?"

*"I have 94,563 registered as having been visited by nomes."*

Masklin stared up at the darkness. Big numbers gave him trouble, but he could see that this number was one of the biggest. Bargains Galore! he thought, and then felt embarrassed and corrected it to Gosh! All those suns, miles apart, and all I have to do is move one truck!

Put like that, it seemed ridiculous.

# 10

*X. When Lo! One returned, saying, I have Gone upon*
*Wheels, and I have Seen the Outside.*
*XI. And they said to him, What is the Outside?*
*XII. And he said, It is Big.*

*From* The Book of Nome, Accounts v. X–XII

ON THE FOURTH day, Angalo returned, wild-eyed and grinning like
a maniac.

The nome on guard came running into the department, with
Angalo swaggering behind him and a gaggle of younger nomes trail-
ing, fascinated, in his wake. He was grimy, and ragged, and looked
as though he hadn't slept for hours—but he walked proudly, with a
strange swaying motion, like a nome who has boldly gone where no
nome has gone before and can't wait to be asked about it.

"Where've I been?" he said. "Where've I *been*? Where haven't I
been, more like. You should see what's out there!"

"What?" they asked.

"Everywhere!" he said, his eyes glowing. "And you know what?"

"What?" they chorused.

"I've seen the Store from the outside! It's . . ." He lowered his voice.
"It's beautiful. All columns and big glass windows full of color!"

Now he was the center of a growing crowd as the news spread.

"Did you see all the departments?" said a Stationeri.

"No!"

"What?"

"You can't see the departments from outside! It's just one big thing! And, and . . ." In the sudden silence he fumbled in his pouch for his notebook, which was now a lot fatter, and thumbed through the pages. "It's got a great big sign outside it, and I copied it down because it's not Trucker language and I didn't understand it but this is what it was."

He held it up.

The silence got deeper. Quite a few nomes could read by now.

The words said *CLOSING DOWN SALE.*

Then he went to bed, still babbling excitedly about trucks and hills and cities, whatever they were, and slept for two hours.

Later on, Masklin went to see him.

Angalo was sitting up in bed, his eyes still shining like bright marbles in the paleness of his face.

"Don't you get him tired," warned Granny Morkie, who always nursed anyone too ill to prevent it. "He's very weak and feverish. It's all that rattling around in those great noisy things; it's not natural. I've just had his dad in here, and I had to toss him out after five minutes."

"You got rid of the Duke?" said Masklin. "But how? He doesn't listen to anyone!"

"He might be a big nome in the Store," said Granny in a self-satisfied tone of voice, "but he's just an awkward nuisance in a sick-room."

"I need to talk to Angalo," said Masklin.

"And I want to talk!" said Angalo, sitting up. "I want to tell every-one! There's everything out there! Some of the things I've seen—"

"You just settle down," said Granny, gently pushing him back into the pillows. "And I'm not too happy about rats in here, either." Bobo's whiskers could just be seen under the end of the blankets.

"But he's very clean and he's my friend," said Angalo. "And you said you like rats."

"*Rat.* I said *rat.* Not rats," said Granny. She prodded Masklin. "Don't you let him get overexcited," she commanded.

Masklin sat down by the bed while Angalo talked with wild enthusiasm about the world outside, like someone who had spent his life with a blindfold on and had just been allowed to see. He talked about the big light in the sky, and roads full of trucks, and big things sticking out of the floor that had green things all over them—

"Trees," said Masklin.

—and great buildings where things went on the truck or came off it. It was at one of these that Angalo got lost. He'd climbed out when it stopped for a while, to go to the lavatory, and hadn't been able to get back before the driver returned and drove away. So he'd climbed onto another one, and some time after it had driven away it stopped at a big park with other trucks in it. He started looking for another Arnold Bros (est. 1905) truck.

"It must have been a cafe on a highway," said Masklin. "We used to live near one."

"Is that what it's called?" said Angalo, hardly listening. "There was this big blue sign with pictures of cups and knives and forks on it. Anyway—"

—there weren't any Store trucks. Or perhaps there were, but

there were so many other types, he couldn't find one. Eventually he'd camped out on the edge of a parking lot, living on scraps, until by sheer luck one had turned up. He hadn't been able to get into the cab, but he had managed to climb up a tire and find a dark place where he had to hold on to cables with his hands and knees to stop himself from falling off onto the rushing road, far below.

Angalo produced his notebook. It was stained almost black.

"Nearly lost it," he said. "Nearly *ate* it once, I was so hungry."

"Yes, but the actual driving," Masklin said insistently, with one eye on the impatient Granny Morkie. "How do they do the actual driving?"

Angalo flicked through the book. "I made a note somewhere," he said. "Ah, here." He passed it over.

Masklin looked at a complicated sketch of levers and arrows and numbers. "'Turn the key . . . one, two . . . press the red button . . . one, two . . . push pedal number one down with the left foot, push big lever left and up . . . one, two . . . let pedal one up gently, push pedal number two down . . .'" He gave up. "What does it all mean?" he said, dreading the answer. He knew what it was going to be.

"It's how you drive a truck," said Angalo.

"Oh. But, er, all these pedals and buttons and levers and things," said Masklin weakly.

"You need 'em all," said Angalo, proudly. "And then you go rushing along, and you change up the gears, and—"

"Yes. Oh. I see," said Masklin, staring at the piece of paper.

How? he thought.

Angalo had been very thorough. Once, when he'd been alone in the cab, he'd measured the height of what he called the Gear Lever, which seemed very important. It was five times the height of a nome. And the big wheel that moved and seemed to be very important was as wide as eight nomes standing side by side.

And you had to have keys. Masklin hadn't known about the keys. He hadn't known about *anything*.

"I did well, didn't I?" said Angalo. "It's all in there."

"Yes. Yes. You did very well."

"You have a good look—it's all in there. All about the going-around-corners flasher and the horn," Angalo went on enthusiastically.

"Yes. Yes, I'm sure it is."

"And the go-faster pedal and the go-slower pedal and everything! Only you don't look very pleased."

"You've given me a lot to think about, I'm sure."

Angalo grabbed him by the sleeve. "They said there was only one Store," he said urgently. "There isn't—there's so much outside, so much. There's other Stores. I saw some. There could be nomes living in 'em! Life in other Stores! Of course, *you* know."

"You get some more sleep," said Masklin as kindly as he could manage.

"When are we going to go?"

"There's plenty of time," said Masklin. "Don't worry about it. Get some sleep."

He wandered out of the sickroom and straight into an argument. The Duke had returned, with some followers, and wanted to take Angalo up to the Stationery Department. He was arguing with Granny Morkie. Or trying to, anyway.

"Madam, I assure you he'll be well looked after!" he was saying.

"Humph! Wot do you people know about doctorin'? You hardly ever have anything go wrong here! Where *I* come from," said Granny, proudly, "it's sick, sick, sick all year round. Colds and sprains and bellyache and bites the whole time. That's what you call *experience*. I reckon I've seen more ill people that you've had hot dinners and"— she prodded the Duke in the stomach—"you've had a few of those."

"Madam, I could have you imprisoned!" roared the Duke.

Granny sniffed. "And what has that got to do with it?" she said.

The Duke opened his mouth to roar back and then caught sight of Masklin. He shut it again.

"Very well," he said. "You are, in fact, quite right. But I will visit him every day."

"No longer than two minutes, mind," said Granny, sniffing.

"Five!" said the Duke.

"Three," said Granny.

"Four," they agreed.

The Duke nodded and beckoned Masklin toward him.

"You have spoken to my son," he said.

"Yes, sir," said Masklin.

"And he told you what he saw."

"Yes, sir."

The Duke looked quite small. Masklin had always thought of him as a big nome, but now he realized that most of the size was a sort of inward inflation, as if the nome were pumped up with importance and authority. It had gone now. The Duke looked worried and uncertain.

"Ah," he said, looking approximately at Masklin's left ear. "I think I sent you some people, didn't I?"

"Yes."

"Satisfactory, are they?"

"Yes, sir."

"Let me know if you need any more help, won't you? Any help

at all." The Duke's voice faded to a mumble. He patted Masklin vaguely on the shoulder and wandered away.

"What's up with him?" asked Masklin.

Granny Morkie started to roll bandages in a businesslike way. No one needed them, but she believed in having a good supply. Enough for the whole world, apparently.

"He's having to think," she said. "That always worries people."

"I just never thought it would be as hard as this!" Masklin wailed.

"You mean you didn't have any idea how we can drive one?" said Gurder.

"None at all?" said Grimma.

"I . . . well, I suppose I thought the trucks sort of went where you wanted," said Masklin. "I thought if they did it for humans, they'd do it for us. I didn't expect all this go-one-two-pull stuff! Those wheels and pedals are huge—I've seen them!"

He stared distractedly at their faces.

"I've thought about it for ages," he said. He felt they were the only two he could trust.

The cardboard door slid open and a small, cheerful face appeared.

"You'll like this one, Mr. Masklin," he said. "I've been doing some more reading."

"Not now, Vinto. We're a bit busy," said Masklin. Vinto's face fell.

"Oh, you might as well listen to him," said Grimma. "It's not as if we've got anything more important to do *now*."

Masklin hung his head.

"Well, lad," said Gurder with forced cheerfulness, "what idea have you come with this time, eh? Pulling the truck with wild hamsters, eh?"

"No, sir," said Vinto.

"Maybe you think we could make it grow wings and fly away in the sky?"

"No, sir. I found this book, it's how to capture humans, sir. And then we can get a gnu—"

Masklin gave the others a sick little smile.

"I explained to him that we can't use humans," he said. "I told you, Vinto. And I'm really not certain about threatening people with antelopes—"

With a grunt of effort, the boy swung the book open.

"It's got a picture in it, sir."

They looked at the picture. It showed a human lying down. He was surrounded by nomes and covered with ropes.

"Gosh," said Grimma, "they've got books with pictures of us!"

"Oh, I know this one," said Gurder dismissively. "It's *Gulliver's Travels*. It's just stories, it's not real."

"Pictures of us in a book," said Grimma. "Imagine that. You see it, Masklin?"

Masklin stared.

"Yes, you're a good boy, well done," said Gurder, his voice sounding far off. "Thank you very much, Vinto, and now please go away."

Masklin stared. His mouth dropped open. He felt the ideas fizz up inside him and slosh into his head.

"The ropes," he said.

"It's just a picture," said Gurder.

"The ropes! Grimma, the ropes!"

"The ropes?"

Masklin raised his fists and stared up at the ceiling. At times like this, it was almost possible to believe that there *was* someone up there, above Kiddies Klothes.

"I can see the way!" he shouted, while the three of them watched in astonishment. "I can see the way! Arnold Bros (est. 1905), *I can see the way!*"

After Closing Time that evening, several dozen small and stealthy figures crept across the garage floor and disappeared under one of the parked trucks. Anyone listening would have heard the occasional tiny clink, thud, or swear word. After ten minutes they were in the cab.

They stood in wonder, looking around.

Masklin wandered over to one of the pedals, which was taller than he was, and gave it an experimental push. It didn't so much as wobble. Several of the others came over and helped, and managed to get it to move a little.

One nome stood and watched them thoughtfully. It was Dorcas, wearing a belt from which hung a variety of homemade tools, and he was idly twiddling the pencil lead that was kept permanently behind one ear when it wasn't being used.

Masklin walked back to him.

"What d'you think?" he said.

Dorcas rubbed his nose. "It's all down to levers and pulleys," he said. "Amazing things, levers. Give me a lever long enough, and a firm enough place to stand, and I could move the Store."

"Just one of these pedals would be enough for now," said Masklin politely.

Dorcas nodded. "We'll give it a try," he said. "All right, lads. Bring it up."

A length of wood, carried all the way down from the Home Handyman Department, was nomehandled into the cab. Dorcas ambled around, measuring distances with a piece of thread, and finally had them wedge one end into a crack in the metal floor. Four nomes lined up at the other end and hauled the wood across until it was resting on the pedal.

"Right, lads," said Dorcas again.

They pushed down. The pedal went all the way to the floor. There was a ragged cheer.

"How did you *do* that?" said Masklin.

"That's levers for you," said Dorcas. "*O*-kay." He looked around, scratching his chin. "So we'll need three levers." He looked up at the great circle of the steering wheel. "You have any ideas about that?" he said.

"I thought ropes," said Masklin.

"How d'you mean?"

"It's got those spokes in it, so if we tie ropes to them and have teams of nomes on the ropes, they could pull it one way or the other, and that'll make the truck go the way we want," said Masklin.

Dorcas squinted at the wheel. He paced the floor. He looked up. He looked down. His lips moved as he worked things out.

"They won't see where they're going," he said finally.

"I thought someone could stand right up there, by the big window in the front, and sort of tell them what to do?" said Masklin, looking hopefully at the old nome.

"These're powerful noisy things, young Angalo said," said Dorcas. He scratched his chin again. "I reckon I can do something about that. Then there's this big lever here, the Beer Lever—"

"Gear Lever," said Masklin.

"Ah. Ropes again?"

"I thought so," said Masklin earnestly. "What do *you* think?"

Dorcas sucked in his breath. "We-ell," he said. "What with teams pulling the wheel, and teams shifting the Gear Lever, and people working the pedals with levers, and someone up there telling them all what to do, it's going to take a powerful lot of practicing. Supposing I rig up all the tackle, all the ropes and such: How many nights will we have to practice? You know, get the hang of it?"

"Including the night we, er, leave?"

"Yes," said Dorcas.

"One," said Masklin.

Dorcas sniffed. He stared upward for a while, humming under his breath.

"It's impossible," he said.

"We'll only have one chance, you see," said Masklin. "If it's a problem with all the equipment—"

"Oh, no problem there," said Dorcas. "That's just bits of wood and string—I can have that ready by tomorrow. I was thinking of the people, see. You're going to need a powerful lot of nomes to do all this. And *they're* going to need training."

"But—but all that they'll have to do is pull and push when they're told, won't they?"

Dorcas hummed under his breath again. Masklin got the impression that he always did that if he was going to break some bad news.

"Well, laddie," he said, "I'm six; I've seen a lot of people, and I've got to tell you, if you lined up ten nomes and shouted 'Pull!,' four of them would push and two of them would say 'Pardon?' That's how people are. It's just nomish nature."

He grinned at Masklin's crestfallen expression.

"What you ought to do," he said, "is find us a little truck. To practice on."

Masklin nodded gloomily.

"And," said Dorcas, "have you thought again about how you're going to get everyone on? Two thousand nomes, mind. Plus all this stuff we're taking. You can't have old grannies and little babies shinning up ropes or crawling through holes, can you?"

Masklin shook his head. Dorcas was watching him with his normal mild grin.

This nome, Masklin thought, knows his stuff. But if I say to him *Leave it all to me*, he'll leave it all to me, just to serve me right. Oh, critical path analysis! Why is it always people?

"Have you got any ideas?" he said. "I really would appreciate your help."

Dorcas gave him a long, thoughtful look and then patted him on the shoulder.

"I've been looking around this place," he said. "Maybe there's a way we can practice *and* solve the other problem. You come down here again tomorrow night and we'll see, shall we?"

Masklin nodded.

The trouble was, he thought as he walked back, that there weren't enough people. A lot of the Ironmongri were helping, and some of the other departments, and quite a few young nomes were sneaking off to help because it was all exciting and unusual. As far as the rest of them were concerned, though, life was going on as normal.

In fact the Store was, if anything, busier than usual.

Of all the family heads, only the Count seemed at all willing to take an interest, and Masklin suspected that even he didn't really think the Store was going to end. It just meant that the Ironmongri could learn to read, and that annoyed the Haberdasheri, which amused the Count. Even Gurder didn't seem so sure as he had been.

Masklin went back to his box and slept, and woke up an hour later.

The terror had started.

# 11

*I. Run to the Lifts*
*Lifts, won't you carry me?*
*Run to the Walls,*
*Walls, won't you hide me?*
*Run to the Truck,*
*Truck, won't you take me?*
*All on that Day.*

*From* The Book of Nome, Exits Chap. 1, v. I.

IT STARTED WITH silence when there should have been noise. All the nomes were used to the distant thumping and murmuring of the humans during the long daylight hours, so they didn't notice it. Now that it was gone, they could hear the strange, oppressive silence. There were days, of course, when humans didn't come into the Store—for instance, Arnold Bros (est. 1905) sometimes allowed them almost a week off between the excitement of Christmas Fayre and the hurly-burly of Winter Sale Starts Today! But the nomes were used to this; it was part of the gentle rhythm of Store life. This wasn't the right day.

After several hours of silence, they just stopped telling one another not to worry, it was probably just some special day or something, like that time when the Store had shut for a week for redecoration, and one or two of the braver or more inquisitive ones risked a quick glance above floor level.

Emptiness stretched away between the familiar counters. And there didn't seem to be much stock around.

"It's always like this after a Sale," they said. "And then, before you know where you are, all the shelves are filled up again. Nothing to get upset about at all. It's all part of Arnold Bros (est. 1905)'s great plan."

And they sat in silence, or hummed a little tune, or found something to occupy their minds, to stop thinking unpleasant thoughts. It didn't work.

And then, when the humans came in and started taking the few things that *were* left off the shelves and counters, and piling them in great boxes and taking them down to the garage and loading them onto the trucks . . .

And started taking up the floorboards . . .

Masklin awoke. People were prodding him. Somewhere in the distance, other people were shouting. It was somehow familiar.

"Get up, quickly!" said Gurder.

"What's happening?" asked Masklin, yawning.

"Humans are taking the Store to bits!"

Masklin sat bolt upright.

"They can't be! It's not time!" he said.

"They're doing it just the same!"

Masklin stood up, struggling into his clothes. He jigged sideways across the floor, one leg out of his trousers, and thumped the Thing.

"Hey!" he said. "You said the demolition wasn't for ages yet!"

*"Fourteen days,"* said the Thing.

"It's starting *now!*"

*"This is probably the removal of remaining stock to new premises, and preliminary works,"* said the Thing.

"Oh, good. That should make everyone feel a lot better. Why didn't you tell us?"

*"I was not aware you did not know."*

"Well, we didn't. So what do you suggest we do now?"

*"Leave as soon as possible."*

Masklin snarled. He had expected two more weeks to solve all the problems. They could have stockpiled stuff to take with them. They could have made proper plans. Even two weeks was hardly long enough. Now the thought of even one week was a luxury.

He went out into the milling, disorganized crowd. Fortunately the boards hadn't been taken up in an inhabited area—some of the more sensible refugees said that only a few had been taken up in the far end of the Gardening Department, so the humans could get at the water pipes—but nomes living nearby were taking no chances.

There was a thump overhead. A few minutes later, a breathless nome arrived and reported that the carpets were being rolled up and taken away.

That caused a terrified silence. Masklin realized that they were all looking at him.

"Er," he said.

Then he said, "I think everyone ought to get as much food as they can carry and go down to the basement, near to the garage."

"You mean you still think we should do *it*?" said Gurder.

"We haven't much choice, have we?"

"But we were—you said we should take as much as we could from the Store, all the wire and tools and things. And books," said Gurder.

"We'll be lucky if we can just take ourselves. There's no *time!*"

Another messenger came running up. It was one of Dorcas's group. He whispered something to Masklin, who gave a strange smile.

"Can it be that Arnold Bros (est. 1905) has abandoned us in our hour of need?" said Gurder.

"I don't think so. He may be helping us," said Masklin. "Because, well, you'll never guess where the humans are putting all this stuff. . . ."

# 12

*I. And the Outsider said, Glory to the Name of Arnold Bros (est. 1905).*

*II. For he hath sent us a Truck, and the Humans are loading it now with all manner of Things needful to nomes. It is a Sign. Everything* Must *Go. Including us.*

*From* The Book of Nome, Exits Chap. 2, v. I–II

HALF AN HOUR later Masklin lay on the girder with Dorcas, looking down at the garage.

He had never seen it so busy. Humans sleepwalked across the floor, carrying bundles of carpet into the backs of some of the trucks. Yellow things, like a cross between a very small truck and a very large armchair, inched around them, stacking boxes.

Dorcas passed him the telescope.

"Busy little things, ain't they," he said conversationally. "Been at it all morning, they have. A couple of trucks have already gone out and come back, so they can't be going very far."

"The letter we saw said something about a new Store," said Masklin. "Perhaps they're taking the stuff there."

"Could be. It's mostly carpets at the moment, and some of the big frozen humans from Fashions."

Masklin made a face. According to Gurder, the big pink humans that stood in Fashions, and Kiddies Klothes, and Young Living, and never moved at all, were those who had incurred Arnold Bros (est. 1905)'s displeasure. They had been turned into horrible pink stuff, and some said they could even be taken apart. But certain Klothian philosophers said no, they were particularly *good* humans, who had been allowed to stay in the Store forever and not made to disappear at Closing Time. Religion was very hard to understand.

As Masklin watched, the big roller door creaked upward and a truck nearby started with a roar and ground slowly out into the blinding daylight.

"What we need," he said, "is a truck with a lot of stuff from the Ironmongery Department. Wire, you know, and tools and things. Have you seen any food?"

"Looked like a lot of stuff from the Food Hall on the first truck out," said Dorcas.

"We'll have to make do, then."

"What'll I do," said Dorcas slowly, "if they load it all up on a truck and drive it away? They're working powerful fast, for humans."

"Surely they can't empty the Store in one day?" said Masklin.

Dorcas shrugged.

"Who knows?" he said.

"You'll have to stop the truck from leaving," said Masklin.

"How? By throwing myself under it?"

"Any way you can think of," said Masklin.

Dorcas grinned. "I'll find a way. The lads are getting used to this place."

Refugees were flowing into the Ironmongery Department from all over the Store, filling all the space under the floor with a frightened buzz of whispered conversation. Many of them looked up as Masklin walked past, and what he saw in their faces terrified him.

They believe I can help, he thought. They're looking at me as if I'm their only hope.

And I don't know what to do. Probably none of it will work—we should have had more *time*. He forced himself to look brimful of confidence, and it seemed to satisfy people. All they wanted to know was that someone, somewhere, knew what he was doing. Masklin wondered who it was; it certainly wasn't him.

The news was bad from everywhere. A lot of the Gardening Department had been cleared. Most of the Clothes departments were empty. The counters were being ripped out of Cosmetics, although fortunately not many nomes lived there. Masklin could hear, even here, the thud and crunch of the work going on.

Finally he could stand it no longer. Too many people kept staring at him. He went back down to the garage, where Dorcas was still watching from his spy post on top of the girder.

"What's happened?" said Masklin.

The old nome pointed to the truck immediately below them.

"That's the one we want," he said. "It's got all sorts in it. Lots of stuff from the Do-It-Yourself Department. There's even some Haberdashery things, needles and whatnot. All the stuff you told me to look out for."

"We've got to stop them from driving it out!" said Masklin.

Dorcas grinned. "The machinery that raises the door won't work," he said. "The fuse has gone."

"What's a fuse?" said Masklin.

Dorcas picked up a long, thick red bar lying by his feet. "This is," he said.

"You took it?"

"Tricky job—we had to tie a bit of string round it. Made a powerful big spark when we pulled it out."

"But I expect they can put another one in," said Masklin.

"Oh, they did," said Dorcas, with a self-satisfied expression. "They're not daft. Didn't work, though, because after we took the fuse out, the lads went and cut the wires inside the wall in a couple of places. Very dangerous, but it'll take the humans forever to find it."

"Hmm. But supposing they lever the door up?"

"Won't do them any good. It's not as if the truck will go, anyway."

"Why not?"

Dorcas pointed downward. Masklin watched, and after a moment he saw a couple of small figures scurry out from under the truck and dive into the shadows by the wall. They were carrying a pair of pliers.

A moment later a solitary figure hurried after them, dragging a length of wire.

"Powerful lot of wire them trucks need," said Dorcas. "This one ain't got so much, now. Funny, isn't it? Take away a tiny spark and the truck won't go. Don't worry, though—I reckon we'll know where to put it all back later."

There was a clang down below. One of the humans had given the door a kick.

"Temper, temper," said Dorcas mildly.

"You've thought of just about everything," said Masklin admiringly.

"I hope so," said Dorcas. "But we'd better make sure, hadn't we." He stood up and produced a large white flag, which he waved over his head. There was an answering flicker of white from the shadows on the far side of the garage.

And then the lights went out.

"Useful thing, electricity," said Dorcas in the darkness. There was a rumble of annoyance from the humans below, and then a jangling noise as one of them walked into something. After some grunting and a few more thuds, one of the humans found a doorway out into the basement, and the rest of them followed it.

"Don't you think they'll suspect something?" said Masklin.

"There's other humans working in the Store. They'll probably think they caused it," said Dorcas.

"That electricity is amazing stuff," said Masklin. "Can you make it? The Count de Ironmongri was very mysterious about it."

"That's because the Ironmongri don't know anything." Dorcas sniffed. "Just how to steal it. I can't seem to get the hang of the reading business, but young Vinto has been looking at books for me. He says making electricity is very simple. You just need to get hold of some stuff called you-ranium. I think it's a kind of metal."

"Is there some in the Ironmongery Department?" said Masklin hopefully.

"Apparently not," said Dorcas.

The Thing wasn't very helpful, either.

"*I doubt if you are ready for nuclear power yet,*" it said. "*Try windmills.*"

Masklin finished putting his possessions, such as they were, in a bag.

"When we leave," he said, "you won't be able to talk, will you? You need electricity to drink."

"*That is the case, yes.*"

"Can't you tell us which way we should go?"

"*No. However, I detect radio traffic indicative of airline activity to the north of here.*"

Masklin hesitated. "That's good, is it?"

"*It means there are flying machines.*"

"And we can fly all the way Home?" said Masklin.

*"No. But they may be the next step. It may be possible to communicate with the starship. But first, you must ride the truck."*

"After that, I should think anything is possible," said Masklin gloomily. He looked expectantly at the Thing, and then noticed with horror that its lights were going off, one by one.

"Thing!"

*"When you are successful, we will talk again,"* said the Thing.

"But you're supposed to *help* us!" said Masklin.

*"I suggest you consider deeply the proper meaning of the word 'help,'"* said the box. *"You are either intelligent nomes or just clever animals. It's up to you to find out which."*

"What?"

The last light went off.

"Thing?"

The lights stayed off. The little black box contrived to look extremely dead and silent.

"But I relied on you to help us sort out the driving and everything! You're just going to leave me like this?"

If anything, the box got darker. Masklin stared at it.

Then he thought: It's all very well for *it*. Everyone's relying on me. I've got no one to rely on. I wonder if the old Abbot felt like this. I wonder how he stood it for so long. It's always me who has to do everything—no one ever thinks about me or what I want. . . .

The shabby cardboard door swung aside and Grimma stepped in.

She looked from the darkened Thing to Masklin.

"They're asking for you out there," she said quietly. "Why is the Thing all dark?"

"It just said good-bye! It said it won't help anymore!" Masklin wailed. "It just said we have to prove we can do things for ourselves and it will speak to us when we're successful! What shall I do?"

I know what I could do, he thought. I could do with a cool washcloth. I could do with a bit of understanding. I could do with a bit of sympathy. Good old Grimma. You can rely on her.

"What you'll do," she said sharply, "is jolly well stop moping and get up and go out there and *get things organized!*"

"Wha—"

"Sort things out! Make new plans! Give people orders! *Get on with it!*"

"But—"

*"Do it now!"* she snapped.

Masklin stood up.

"You shouldn't talk to me like that," he said plaintively. "I'm the leader, you know."

She stood arms akimbo, glaring at him.

"Of course you're the leader," she said. "Did I say you weren't the leader? Everyone knows you're the leader! Now get out there and lead!"

He lurched past. She tapped him on the shoulder.

"And learn to listen," she added.

"Eh? What do you mean?"

"The Thing's a sort of thinking machine, isn't it? That's what Dorcas said. Well, machines say exactly what they mean, don't they?"

"Yes, I suppose so, but—"

Grimma gave him a bright, triumphant smile.

"Well, it said 'When,'" she said. "*Think* about it. It could have said 'If.'"

o     o     o

Night came. Masklin thought the humans were never going to leave. One of them, with a flashlight and a box of tools, spent a long time examining fuse boxes and peering at the wiring in the basement. Now at last even it was gone, grumbling and slamming the door behind it.

After a little while, the lights came on in the garage.

There was a rustling in the walls, and then a dark tide flowed out from under benches. Some of the young nomes in the lead carried hooks on the ends of thread lines, which they swung up to the truck's covers. They caught, one after another, and the nomes swarmed up them.

Other nomes brought thicker string, which was tied to the ends of the thread and gradually dragged upward. . . .

Masklin ran along, under the endless shadow of the truck, to the oily darkness under the engine where Dorcas's teams were already dragging their equipment into position. Dorcas himself was in the cab, rooting around among the thick wires. There was a sizzling noise, and then the light in the cab came on.

"There," said Dorcas. "Now we can see what we're at. Come on, lads! Let's have a bit of effort!"

When he turned around and saw Masklin, he made as if to hide his hands behind his back, then thought better of it. Both of them were thrust into what Masklin could now see were the fingers cut out of rubber gloves.

"Ah," said Dorcas, "didn't know you were there. Bit of a trade secret, see? Electricity can't abide rubber. It stops the stuff from biting you." He ducked as a team of nomes swung a long wooden beam across the cab and started to fasten it to the gear lever.

"How long's it going to take?" shouted Masklin, as another team ran past dragging a ball of string. There was quite a din in the cab now, and threads and bits of wood were moving in every direction in what he hoped was an organized way.

"Could be an hour, maybe," said Dorcas, and added, not unkindly, "We'd get on quicker without people in the way."

Masklin nodded, and explored the rear of the cab. The truck was old, and he found another hole for a bundle of wires which, at a squeeze, would take a nome as well. He crawled out into the open air and then found another gap that let him into the rear of the truck.

The first nomes aboard had dragged up one end of a thin piece of wood, which was acting as a gangplank. The rest were scrambling up it now.

Masklin had put Granny Morkie in charge of this. The old woman had a natural talent for making frightened people do things.

"Steep?" she was shouting at a fat nome, who had got halfway up and was clinging there in fright. "Call this steep? It ain't steep, it's a stroll! Want me to come down there and help you?"

The mere threat budged him from his perch and he nearly ran the rest of the way, ducking gratefully into the shadows of the cargo.

"Everyone had better try to find somewhere soft to lie down," said Masklin. "It could be a rough journey. And you must send all the strongest nomes up toward the cab. We're going to need everyone we can get, believe me."

She nodded, and then shouted at a family that was blocking the gangway.

Masklin looked down at the endless stream of people climbing into the truck, many of them staggering under the weight of possessions.

Funny, but now he felt he'd done everything he could. Everything was ticking along like a, like a, like something that went tick. Either all the plans would work or they wouldn't. Either the nomes could act together or they couldn't.

He recalled the picture of Gulliver. It probably wasn't real, Gurder had said. Books often had things in them that weren't really real. But it would be nice to think that nomes could agree on something long enough to be like the little people in the book. . . .

"Well, it's all going well, then," he said vaguely.

"Well enough." Granny nodded.

"It would be a good idea if we found out exactly what was in all these boxes and things," Masklin ventured, "because we might have to get out quickly when we stop and—"

"I tole Torrit to see to it," said Granny. "Don't you worry about it."

"Oh," said Masklin weakly. "Good."

He hadn't left himself anything to do.

He went back to the cab out of sheer—well, not boredom, because his heart was pounding like a drum—but out of restlessness.

Dorcas's nomes had already built a wooden platform above the steering wheel and right in front of the big window. Dorcas himself was back down on the floor of the cab, drilling the driving teams.

"Right!" he shouted. "Give me . . . First Gear!"

"Pedal Down . . . two, three . . ." chorused the team on the clutch pedal.

"Pedal Up . . . two, three . . ." shouted the accelerator team.

"Lever Up . . . two, three . . ." echoed the nomes by the gear lever.

"Pedal Up . . . two, three, four!" The leader of the clutch team threw Dorcas a salute. "Gear all changed, sir!" he shouted.

"That was terrible. Really terrible," said Dorcas. "What's happened to the accelerator team, eh? Get that pedal down!"

"Sorry, Dorcas."

Masklin tapped Dorcas on the shoulder.

"Keep doing it!" Dorcas commanded. "I want you dead smooth all the way up to fourth. Yes? What? Oh, it's you."

"Yes, it's me. Everyone's nearly on," said Masklin. "When will you be ready?"

"This lot won't be ready *ever*."

"Oh."

"So we might as well start whenever you like and pick it up as we go along. We can't even *try* steering until it's moving, of course."

"We're going to send a lot more people to help you," said Masklin.

"Oh, good," said Dorcas. "Just what I need, lots more people who don't know their right from their left."

"How are you going to know which way to steer?"

"Semaphore," said Dorcas firmly.

"Semaphore?"

"Signaling with flags. You just tell my lad up on the platform what you want done, and I'll watch the signals. If we'd had one more week, I reckon I could have rigged up some sort of telephone."

"Flags," said Masklin. "Will that work?"

"It'd better, hadn't it. We can give it a try later on."

And now it was later on. The last nome scouts had climbed aboard. In the back of the truck most of the people made themselves as comfortable as possible and lay, wide awake, in the darkness.

Masklin was up on the platform with Angalo, Gurder, and the Thing. Gurder knew even less about trucks than Masklin, but it was felt best to have him there, just in case. After all, they were stealing Arnold Bros (est. 1905)'s truck. Someone might have to do some explaining. But he'd drawn the line about having Bobo in the cab. The rat was back with everyone else.

Grimma was there, too. Gurder asked her what she was doing there. She asked him what *he* was doing there. They both looked at Masklin.

"She can help me with the reading," he said, secretly relieved. He wasn't, despite lots of effort, all that good at it. There seemed to be a knack he couldn't get the hang of. Grimma, on the other hand, seemed to do it now without thinking. If her brain was exploding, it was doing it in unnoticeable ways.

She nodded smugly and propped *The High Way Code* open in front of him.

"There's things you've got to do," he said uncertainly. "Before you start, you've got to look in a mur—"

"—mirror—" said Grimma.

"—mirror. That's what it says here. Mirror," said Masklin, firmly.

He looked inquiringly at Angalo, who shrugged.

"I don't know anything about that," he said. "My driver used to look at it, but I don't know why."

"Do you have to look for anything special? I mean, perhaps you have to make a face in it or something," said Masklin.

"Whatever it is, we'd better do things properly," said Gurder firmly. He pointed. "There's a mirror up there, near the ceiling."

"Daft place to put it," said Masklin. He managed to hook it with a grapnel and, after some effort, pulled himself up to it.

"Can you see anything?" Gurder called out.

"Just me."

"Well, come on back down. You've done it, that's the main thing."

Masklin slid back down to the decking, which wobbled under him.

Grimma peered at the *Code.*

"Then you've got to signal your intentions," she said. "That's clear, anyway. Signaler?"

One of Dorcas's assistants stepped forward a bit uncertainly, holding his two white flags carefully downward.

"Yes, sir ma'am?" he said.

"Tell Dorcas—" Grimma looked at the others. "Tell him we're ready to start."

"Excuse *me*," said Gurder. "If it's anyone's job to tell them when we're ready to start, it's *my* job to tell them we're ready to start. I want it to be quite clear that I'm the person who tells people to start." He looked sheepishly at Grimma. "Er. We're ready to start," he said.

"Right you are, ma'am." The signaler waved his arms briefly. From far below, the engineer's voice boomed back: "Ready!"

"Well, then," said Masklin. "This is it, then."

"Yes," said Gurder, glaring at Grimma. "Is there anything we've forgotten?"

"Lots of things, probably," said Masklin.

"Too late now, at any rate," said Gurder.

"Yes."

"Yes."

"Right then."

"Right."

They stood in silence for a moment.

"Shall you give the order, or shall I?" asked Masklin.

"I was wondering whether to ask Arnold Bros (est. 1905) to watch over us and keep us safe," said Gurder. "After all, we may be leaving the Store, but this is still his truck." He grinned wretchedly and sighed. "I wish he'd give us some sort of sign," he said, "to show he approved."

"Ready when you are, up there!" shouted Dorcas.

Masklin went to the edge of the platform and leaned on the flimsy rail.

The whole of the floor of the cab was covered in nomes, holding ropes in readiness or waiting by their levers and pulleys. They stood in absolute silence in the shadows, but every face was turned upward, so Masklin was looking down at a sea of frightened and excited blobs.

He waved his hand.

"Start the engine," he said, and his voice sounded unnaturally loud in the expectant silence.

He walked back and looked out into the bright emptiness of the garage. There were a few other trucks parked against the opposite wall, and one or two of the small yellow loading trucks stood where the humans had left them. To think he'd once called it a truck nest! Garage, that was the word. It was amazing, the feeling you got from knowing the right names. You felt in control. It was as if knowing what the right name was gave you a sort of lever.

There was a whirring noise from somewhere in front of them, and then the platform shook to a thunder roll. Unlike thunder, it didn't die away. The engine had started.

Masklin grabbed hold of the rail before he was shaken off and felt Angalo tug on his sleeve.

"It always sounds like this!" he shouted above the din. "You get used to it after a while!"

"Good!" It wasn't a noise. It was too loud to be called a noise. It was more like solid air.

"I think we'd better practice a bit! To get the hang of it! Shall I tell the signaler that we want to move forward very slowly?"

Masklin nodded grimly. The signaler thought for a moment and then waved his flags.

Masklin could distantly hear Dorcas yelling orders. There was a grinding noise, followed by a jolt that knocked him over. He managed to land on his hands and knees and looked into Gurder's frightened face.

"We're moving!" shouted the Stationeri.

Masklin stared out of the windshield.

"Yes, and you know what?" he yelled, springing up. "We're moving *backward*!"

Angalo staggered over to the signaler, who had dropped one of his flags.

"Forward slowly, I said! Forward slowly! Not backward! Forward!"

"I signaled Forward!"

"But we're *going* backward! Signal them to go forward!"

The signaler scrabbled for his other flag and waved frantically at the teams below.

"No, don't signal forward, just signal them to sto—" Masklin began.

There was a sound from the far end of the truck. The only word to describe it was "crunch," but that's far too short and simple a word to describe the nasty, complicated, metallic noise and the jolt that threw Masklin onto his stomach again. The engine stopped.

The echoes died away.

"Sorree!" Dorcas called out, in the distance. They heard him talking in a low, menacing voice to the teams: "Satisfied? Satisfied, are we? When I said move the Gear Lever up and left and up, I meant up and left and up, not up and right and up! Right?"

"Your right or our right, Dorcas?"

"Any right!"

"No, but—"

"Don't you 'but' me!"

"Yes, but—"

Masklin and the others sat down as the argument skidded back and forth below them. Gurder was still lying on the planks.

"We actually moved!" he was whispering. "Arnold Bros (est. 1905) *was* right. Everything *Must* Go!"

"I'd like it to go a little farther, if it's all right by him," said Angalo grimly.

"Hello up there!" Dorcas's voice boomed with mad cheerfulness. "Little bit of teething trouble down here. All sorted out now. Ready when you are!"

"Should I look in the mirror again, what do you think?" said Masklin to Grimma. She shrugged.

"I shouldn't bother," said Angalo. "Let's just go forward. And as soon as possible, I think. I can smell dies-all. We must have knocked over some drums of it or something."

"That's bad, is it?" said Masklin.

"It burns," said Angalo. "It just needs a spark or something to set it off."

The engine roared into life again. This time they did inch forward, after some grinding noises, and rolled across the floor until the truck was in front of the big steel door. It stopped with a slight jerk.

"Like to try a few practice turns," shouted Dorcas. "Smooth out a few rough edges!"

"I really think it would be a very bad idea to stay here," said Angalo urgently.

"You're right," said Masklin. "The sooner we get out of here the better. Signal Dorcas to open the door."

The signaler hesitated. "I don't think we've got a signal for that," he said. Masklin leaned over the rail.

"Dorcas!"

"Yes?"

"Open the door! We've got to get out *now*!"

The distant figure cupped his hand to its ear.

"What?"

"I said open the door! It's urgent!"

Dorcas appeared to consider this for a while and then raised his megaphone.

"You'll laugh when I tell you this," he said.

"What was that?" said Grimma.

"He said we're going to laugh," said Angalo.

"Oh. Good."

"Come *on*!" shouted Masklin. Dorcas's reply was lost in the din from the engine.

"What?" shouted Masklin.

"What?"

"What did you *say*?"

*"I said, in all this rush I clean forgot about the door!"*

"What'd he say?" said Gurder.

Masklin turned and looked at the door. Dorcas had been very proud of the way he'd stopped it opening. Now it had an extremely closed look. If something with no face could look smug, the door had managed it.

He turned back in exasperation, and also in time to see the small door to the rest of the Store swing slowly open. There was a figure there, behind a little circle of sharp white light.

*His terrible flashlight*, Masklin thought again.

It was Prices Slashed.

Masklin felt his mind begin to think very clearly and slowly.

It's just a human, it said. It's nothing scary. Just a human, with its name on it in case it forgets who it is, like all those female humans in the Store with names like "Tracy" and "Sharon" and "Mrs. J. E. Williams, Supervisor." This is just old "Security" again. He lives down in the boiler room and drinks tea. He's heard the noise.

He's come to find out what made it.

That is, us.

"Oh, no," whispered Angalo, as the figure lurched across the floor. "Do you see what it's got in its mouth?"

"It's a cigarette. I've seen humans with it before. What about it?" said Masklin.

"It's alight," said Angalo. "Do you think it can't even *smell* the dies-all?"

"What happens if it catches alight, then?" said Masklin, suspecting that he knew the answer.

"It goes *whoomph*," said Angalo.

"Just *whoomph*?"

"*Whoomph* is enough."

The human came nearer. Masklin could see its eyes now. Humans weren't very good at seeing nomes even when they were standing still, but even a human would wonder why a truck was driving itself around its garage in the middle of the night.

Security arrived at the cab and reached out slowly for the door handle. His light shone in through the side window, and at that moment Gurder reared up, trembling with rage.

"Begone, foul fiend!" he yelled, illuminated as by a spotlight. "Heed ye the Signs of Arnold Bros (est. 1905)! *No Smoking! Exit This Way!*"

The human's face wrinkled in ponderous astonishment and then, as slowly as the drift of clouds, became an expression of panic. It let go of the door handle, turned, and began to head for the little door at what, for a human, was high speed. As it did so, the glowing cigarette fell from its mouth and, turning over and over, dropped slowly toward the floor.

Masklin and Angalo looked at each other, and then at the signaler. "Go fast!" they shouted.

A moment later the entire truck shuddered as the teams tackled the complicated process of changing gear. Then it rolled forward.

"Fast! I said fast!" Masklin shouted.

"What's going on?" shouted Dorcas. "What about the door?"

"We'll open the door! We'll open the door!" shouted Masklin.

"How?"

"Well, it didn't look very thick, did it?"

The world of nomes is, to humans, a rapid world. They live so fast that the things that happen around them seem quite slow, so the truck seemed to drift across the floor, drive up the ramp, and hit the door in a leisurely way. There was a long-drawn-out boom and the noise of bits of metal being torn apart, a scraping noise across the roof of the cab, and then there was no door at all, only darkness studded with lights.

"Left! Go left!" Angalo screamed.

The truck skidded around slowly, bounced lazily off a wall, and rolled a little way down the street.

"Keep going! Keep going! Now straighten up!"

A bright light shone briefly on the wall outside the cab.

And then, behind them, a sound like *whoomph*.

# 13

*I. Arnold Bros (est. 1905) said, All is now Finished;*
*II. All Curtains, Carpeting, Bedding, Lingerie, Toys,*
*Millinery, Haberdashery, Ironmongery, Electrical;*
*III. All walls, floors, ceilings, lifts, moving stairs;*
*IV. Everything Must Go.*

*From* The Book of Nome, Exits Chap. 3, v. I–IV

LATER ON, WHEN the next chapters of *The Book of Nome* came to be written, they said the end of the Store started with a bang. This wasn't true but was put in because "bang" sounded more impressive. In fact, the ball of yellow and orange fire that rolled out of the garage, carrying the remains of the door with it, just made a noise like a giant dog gently clearing its throat.

*Whoomph.*

The nomes weren't in a position to take much notice of it at the time. They were more concerned with the noise made by other things nearly hitting them.

Masklin had been prepared for other vehicles on the road. *The High Way Code* had a lot to say about it. It was important not to drive into them. What was worrying him was the way they seemed determined to run into the truck. They emitted long blaring noises, like sick cows.

"Left a bit!" Angalo shouted. "Then right just a smidgen, then go straight!"

"Smidgen?" said the signaler slowly. "I don't think I know a code for smidgen. Could we—"

"Slow! Now left a bit! We've got to get on the right side of the road!"

Grimma peered over the top of *The High Way Code*.

"We *are* on the right side," she said.

"Yes, but the right side should be the left side!"

Masklin jabbed at the page in front of them. "It says here we've got to show cons—consy—"

"Consideration," murmured Grimma.

"—consideration for other road users," he said. A jolt threw him forward. "What was that?" he said.

"Us going onto the sidewalk! Right! *Right!*"

Masklin caught a brief glimpse of a brightly lit shop window before the truck hit it sideways on and bounced back onto the road in a shower of glass.

"Now left, now left, now right, right! Straight! Left, I said *left!*" Angalo peered at the bewildering pattern of lights and shapes in front of them.

"There's another road here," he said. "Left! Give me left! Lots and lots of left! More left than that!"

"There's a sign," said Masklin helpfully.

"Left!" shrieked Angalo. "Now right. Right! Right!"

"You wanted left," said the signaler accusingly.

"And now I want right! Lots of right! Duck!"

"We haven't got a signal for—"

This time *whoomph* wouldn't have done. It was definitely *bang*. The truck hit a wall, ground along it in a spray of sparks, rolled into a pile of litter bins, and stopped.

There was silence, except for the hissing sounds and *pink, pink* noises from the engine.

Then Dorcas's voice came up from the darkness, slow and full of menace.

"Would you mind telling us down here," it said, "what you're doing up there?"

"We'll have to think of a better way of steering," Angalo called down. "And lights. There should be a switch somewhere for lights."

Masklin struggled to his feet. The truck appeared to be stuck in a dark, narrow road. There were no lights anywhere.

He helped Gurder stand up and brushed him down. The Stationeri looked bewildered.

"We're there?" he said.

"Not quite," said Masklin. "We've stopped to, er, sort out a few things. While they're doing that, I think we'd better go back and check that everyone's all right. They must be getting pretty worried. You come too, Grimma."

They climbed down and left Angalo and Dorcas deep in argument about steering, lights, clear instructions, and the need for a proper supply of all three.

There was a gabble of voices in the back of the truck, mixed with the crying of babies. Quite a few nomes had been bruised by the throwing about, and Granny Morkie was tying a splint to the broken leg of a nome who had been caught by a falling box when they hit the wall.

"Wee bit rougher than the last time," she commented dryly, tying a knot in the bandage. "Why've we stopped?"

"Just to sort out a few things," said Masklin, trying to sound more cheerful than he felt. "We'll be moving again soon. Now that everyone knows what to expect." He gazed down at the dark shadowy length of the truck, and inquisitiveness overcame him.

"While we're waiting, I'm going to take a look outside," he said.

"What on earth for?" said Grimma.

"Just to, you know, look around," said Masklin awkwardly. He nudged Gurder. "Want to come?" he said.

"What? Outside? Me?" The Stationeri looked terrified.

"You'll have to sooner or later. Why not now?"

Gurder hesitated for a moment and then shrugged.

"Will we be able to see the Store"—he licked his dry lips—"from the *Outside?*" he said.

"Probably. We haven't really gone very far," said Masklin, as diplomatically as he could.

A team of nomes helped them over the end of the truck, and they swung down onto what Gurder would almost certainly have called the floor. It was damp, and a fine spray hung in the air. Masklin breathed deeply. This was outside, all right. Real air, with a slight chill to it. It smelled fresh, not as though it had been breathed by thousands of nomes before him.

"The sprinklers have come on," said Gurder.

"The what?"

"The sprinklers," said Gurder. "They're in the ceiling, you know, in case of f . . ." He stopped and looked up. "Oh, my," he said.

"I think you mean the rain," said Masklin.

"Oh, my."

"It's just water coming out of the sky," said Masklin. He felt something more was expected of him. "It's wet," he added, "and you can drink it. Rain. You don't have to have pointy heads. It just rolls off anyway."

"Oh, my."

"Are you all right?"

Gurder was trembling. "There's no roof!" he moaned. "And it's so big!"

Masklin patted him on the shoulder.

"Of course, all this is new to you," he said. "You mustn't worry if you don't understand everything."

"You're secretly laughing at me, aren't you?" said Gurder.

"Not really. I know what it's like to feel frightened."

Gurder pulled himself together. "Frightened? Me? Don't be foolish. I'm quite all right," he said. "Just a little, er, surprised. I, er, wasn't expecting it to be quite so, quite so, quite so *Outside*. Now I've had time to come to terms with it, I feel much better. Well, well. So this is what it's like"—he turned the word around his tongue, like a new candy—"Outside. So, er, big. Is this all of it, or is there any more?"

"Lots," said Masklin. "Where we lived, there was nothing but outside from one edge of the world to the other."

"Oh," said Gurder weakly. "Well, I think this will be enough Outside for now. Very good."

Masklin turned and looked up at the truck. It was almost wedged into an alleyway littered with rubbish. There was a large dent in the end of it.

The opening at the far end of the alley was bright with streetlights in the drizzle. As he watched, a vehicle swished by with a blue light flashing. It was singing. He couldn't think of any other word to describe it.

"How odd," said Gurder.

"It used to happen sometimes at home," said Masklin. It was secretly rather pleasing, after all this time, to be the one who knew things. "You'd hear ones go along the highway like that. Dee-dah dee-dah DEE-DAH DEE-DAH dee-dah. I think it's just to get people to get out of the way."

They crept along the gutter and craned to look over the pavement at the corner, just as another bawling car hurtled past.

"Oh, Bargains Galore!" said Gurder, and put his hands over his mouth.

The Store was on fire.

Flames fluttered at some of the upper windows like curtains in a breeze. A pall of smoke rose gently from the roof and made a darker column against the rainy sky.

The Store was having its last sale. It was holding a Grand Final Clearance of specially selected sparks, and flames to suit every pocket.

Humans bustled around in the street below it. There were a couple of trucks with ladders on them. It looked as though they were spraying water into the building.

Masklin looked sidelong at Gurder, wondering what the nome was going to do. In fact he took it a lot better than Masklin would have believed, but when he spoke, it was in a wound-up way, as if he were trying to keep his voice level.

"It's . . . it's not how I imagined it," he croaked.

"No," said Masklin.

"We . . . we got out just in time."

"Yes."

Gurder coughed. It was as if he'd just had a long debate with himself and had reached a decision. "Thanks to Arnold Bros (est. 1905)," he said firmly.

"Pardon?"

Gurder stared at Masklin's face. "If he hadn't called you to the Store, we'd all still be in there," he said, sounding more confident with every word.

"But—" Masklin paused. That didn't make any sense. If they hadn't left, there wouldn't have been a fire. Would there? Hard to be sure. Maybe some fire had got out of a fire bucket. Best not to argue. There were some things people weren't happy to argue about, he thought. It was all very puzzling.

"Funny he's letting the Store burn," he said.

"He needn't," said Gurder. "There's the sprinklers, and there's these special things, to make the fire go out. Fire Exits, they're called. But he let the Store burn because we don't need it anymore."

There was a crash as the entire top floor fell in on itself.

"There goes Consumer Accounts," said Masklin. "I hope all the humans got out."

"Who?"

"You know. We saw their names on the doors. Salaries. Accounts. Personnel. General Manager," said Masklin.

"I'm sure Arnold Bros (est. 1905) made arrangements," said Gurder.

Masklin shrugged. And then he saw, outlined against the fire-light, the figure of Prices Slashed. There was no mistaking that hat. He was even holding his flashlight, and he was deep in conversation with some other humans. When he half turned, Masklin saw his face. He looked very angry.

He also looked very human. Without the terrible light, without the shadows of the Store at night, Prices Slashed was just another human.

On the other hand . . .

No, it was too complicated. And there were more important things to do.

"Come on," he said. "Let's get back. I think we should get as far away as possible as quickly as we can."

"I shall ask Arnold Bros (est. 1905) to guide us and lead us," said Gurder firmly.

"Yes, good," said Masklin. "Good idea. And why not? But now we really must—"

"Has his Sign not said *If You Do Not See What You Require, Please Ask?*" said Gurder.

Masklin took him firmly by the arm. Everyone needs something, he thought. And you never know.


"I pull this string," said Angalo, indicating the thread over his shoulder and the way it disappeared down into the depths of the cab, "and the leader of the steering wheel left-pulling team will know I want to turn left. Because it's tied to his arm. And this other one goes to the right-pulling team. So we won't need so many signals, and Dorcas can concentrate on the gears and things. And the brakes. After all," he added, "we can't always rely on a wall to run into when we want to stop."

"What about lights?" said Masklin. Angalo beamed.

"Signal for the lights," he said to the nome with flags. "What we did was, we tied threads to switches—"

There was a click. A big metal arm moved across the windshield, clearing away the raindrops. They watched it for a while.

"Doesn't really *illuminate* much, does it?" said Grimma.

"Wrong switch," muttered Angalo. "Signal to leave the wipers on but put on the *lights*."

There was some muffled argument below them, and then another click. Instantly the cab was filled with the dull throbbing sound of a human voice.

"It's all right," said Angalo. "It's only the radio. But it's not the *lights*, tell Dorcas."

"I know what a radio is," said Gurder. "You don't have to tell me what a radio is."

"What is it, then?" said Masklin, who didn't know.

"Twenty-Nine Ninety-Five, Batteries Extra," said Gurder. "With AM, FM, And Auto-Reverse Cassette. Bargain Offer, Not To Be Repeated."

"Am and Fum?" said Masklin.

"Yes."

The radio voice droned on.

"*—ggest fire in the town's history, with firemen coming in from as far afield as Newtown. Meanwhile, police are searching for one of the store's trucks, last seen leaving the building just before—*"

"The lights. The *lights*. Third switch along," said Angalo. There was a few seconds' pause, and then the alley in front of the truck was bathed in white light.

"There should be two, but one got broken when we left the Store," said Angalo. "Well, then, are we ready?"

"*—Anyone seeing the vehicle should contact Blackbury police on—*"

"And turn off the radio," said Angalo. "That mooing gets on my nerves."

"I wish we could understand it," said Masklin. "I'm sure they're fairly intelligent, if only we could understand it."

He nodded at Angalo. "Okay," he said. "Let's go."

It seemed much better this time. The truck scraped along the wall for a moment, then came free and moved gently down the narrow alley toward the lights at the far end. As the truck came out from between the dark walls, Angalo called for the brakes, and it stopped with only a mild jolt.

"Which way?" he said. Masklin looked blank.

Gurder fumbled through the pages of the diary. "It depends on which way we're going," he said. "Look for signs saying, er, Africa. Or Canada, perhaps."

"There's a sign," said Angalo, peering through the rain. "It says Town Center. And then there's an arrow and it says—" He squinted. "Onny—"

"One Way Street," murmured Grimma.

"Town Center doesn't sound like a good idea," said Masklin.

"Can't seem to find it on the map, either," said Gurder.

"We'll go the other way, then," said Angalo, hauling on a thread.

"And I'm not sure about One Way Street," said Masklin. "I think you should only go along it one way."

"Well, we are," said Angalo smugly. "We're going *this* way."

The truck rolled out of the side road and bumped neatly onto the pavement.

"Let's have second gear," said Angalo. "And a bit more go-faster pedal." A car swerved slowly out of the truck's way, its horn sounding—to nome ears—like the lost wail of a foghorn.

"Shouldn't be allowed on the road, drivers like that," said Angalo. There was a thump, and the remains of a streetlight bounced away. "And they put all this stupid stuff in the roadway, too," he added.

"Remember to show consideration for other road users," said Masklin severely.

"Well, I am, aren't I? I'm not running into them, am I?" said Angalo. "What was that thump?"

"Some bushes, I think," said Masklin.

"See what I mean? Why do they put things like that in the road?"

"I think the road is more sort of over to your right," said Gurder.

"And it moves around, as well," said Angalo sullenly, pulling the right-hand string slightly.

It was nearly midnight, and Blackbury was not a busy town after dark. Therefore there was no one rushing to run into the truck as it slid out of Alderman Surley Way and roared up John Lennon Avenue, a huge and rather battered shape under the yellow sodium glare. The rain had stopped, but there were wisps of mist coiling across the road.

It was almost peaceful.

"Right, third gear," said Angalo, "and a bit faster. Now, what's that sign coming up?"

Grimma and Masklin craned to see.

"Looks like *Road Works Ahead*," said Grimma in a puzzled voice.

"Sounds good. Let's have some more fast, down there."

"Yes, but," said Masklin, "why say it? I mean, you could understand *Road* Doesn't *Work Ahead*. Why tell us it works?"

"Maybe it means they've stopped putting curbs and lights and bushes in it," said Angalo. "Maybe—"

Masklin leaned over the edge of the platform.

"Stop!" he shouted. "Lots and lots of stop!"

The brake-pedal team looked up in astonishment but obeyed. There was a scream from the tires, yells from the nomes who were thrown forward, and then a lot of crunching and clanging from the front of the truck as it skidded through an assortment of barriers and cones.

"There had better," said Angalo, when it had finally stopped, "be a very good reason for that."

"I've hurt my *knee*," said Gurder.

"There isn't any more road," said Masklin, simply.

"Of course there's road," snapped Angalo. "We're on it, aren't we?"

"Look down. That's all. Just look down," said Masklin.

Angalo peered down at the road ahead. The most interesting thing about it was that it wasn't there. Then he turned to the signaler.

"Can we please have just a wee bit of backward," he said quietly.

"A smidgen?" said the signaler.

"And none of your cheek," said Angalo.

Grimma was also staring at the hole in the road. It was big. It was deep. A few pipes lurked in the depths.

"Sometimes," she said, "I think humans really don't understand anything about the proper use of language."

She leafed through the *Code* as the truck was reversed carefully away from the pit and, after crushing various things, driven onto the grass until the road was clear.

"It's time we were sensible about this," she said. "We can't assume anything means what it says. So go slow."

"I was driving perfectly safely," said Angalo sulkily. "It's not my fault if things are all wrong."

"So go slow, then."

They stared in silence at the rolling road.

Another sign loomed up.

"*Roundabout*," said Angalo. "And a picture of a circle? Well. Any ideas?"

Grimma leafed desperately through the *Code*.

"I saw a picture of a roundabout once," said Gurder. "If it's any help. It was in *We Go to the Fair*. It's a big shiny thing with lots of gold and horses on it."

"I'm sure that's not it," muttered Grimma, turning the pages hurriedly. "I'm sure there's something in here some—"

"Gold, eh?" said Angalo. "Should be easy to spot, anyway. I think"—he glared at Grimma—"that we can have a little third gear."

"Right you are, Mr. Angalo sir," said the signaler.

"Can't see any golden horses," said Masklin. "You know, I'm not entirely certain—"

"And there should be cheerful music," said Gurder, pleased to be making a contribution.

"Can't hear any cheer—" Masklin began.

There was the long-drawn-out blast of a car horn. The road stopped and was replaced by a mound covered in bushes. The truck roared up it, all wheels leaving the ground for a moment, then thumped down on the other side of the roundabout and continued a little way, rocking from side to side, on the opposite road. It rolled to a halt.

There was silence in the cab again. Then someone groaned.

Masklin crawled to the edge of the platform and looked down into the frightened face of Gurder, who was hanging on to the edge.

"What happened?" he groaned.

Masklin hauled him back up to safety and dusted him off.

"I think," he said, "that although the signs mean what they say, what they say isn't what they mean."

Grimma pulled herself out from underneath the *Code*. Angalo untangled himself from the lengths of string and found himself looking into her furious scowl.

"You," she said, "are a total idiot. And speed mad! Why don't you *listen*?"

"You can't speak to me like that!" said Angalo, cowering back. "Gurder, tell her she can't call me names like that!"

Gurder sat trembling on the edge of the platform.

"As far as I am concerned right now," he said, "she can call you what she likes. Go to it, young woman."

Angalo glowered. "Hang *on*! You were the one who went on about golden horses! I didn't see any golden horses! Did anyone see any golden horses? He confused me, going on about golden horses—"

Gurder waved a finger at him. "Don't you 'he' me—" he began.

"And don't you 'young woman' me in that tone of voice!" screamed Grimma.

Dorcas's voice came up from the depths.

"I don't want to interrupt anything," it said, "but if this happens one more time, there are people down here who will be getting very angry. Is that understood?"

"Just a minor steering problem," Masklin called down cheerfully. He turned back to the others.

"Now you all look here," he said quietly. "This arguing has got to stop. Every time we hit a problem, we start bickering. It's not sensible."

Angalo sniffed. "We were doing perfectly all right until he—"

"*Shut up!*"

They stared at him. He was shaking with anger.

"I've had just about enough of all of you!" he shouted. "You make me ashamed! We were doing so well! I haven't spent ages trying to make all this happen just for a, a, a *steering committee* to ruin it all! Now you can all get up and get this thing moving again! There's a whole truckload of nomes back there! They're depending on you! Understand?"

They looked at one another. They stood up sheepishly. Angalo pulled up the steering strings. The signaler untangled his flags.

"Ahem," said Angalo quietly. "I think . . . yes, I think a little bit of first gear might be in order here, if it's all the same to everybody?"

"Good idea. Go ahead," said Gurder.

"But carefully," said Grimma.

"Thank you," said Angalo politely. "Is that all right by you, Masklin?" he added.

"Hmm? Yes. Yes. Fine. Go."

At least there were no more buildings. The truck purred along the lonely road, its one remaining headlight making a white glow in the mist. One or two vehicles passed them on the other side of the road.

Masklin knew that soon they should be looking for somewhere to stop. It would have to be somewhere sheltered, away from humans—but not too far away, because he was pretty certain there were still plenty of things the nomes were going to need. Perhaps they were going north, but if they were, it would be sheer luck.

It was at that moment—tired, angry, with his mind not entirely on what was in front of him—that he saw Prices Slashed.

There was no doubt about it. The human was standing in the road, waving its flashlight. There was a car beside him, with a blue flashing light on top.

The others had seen it, too.

"Prices Slashed!" moaned Gurder. "He's got here in front of us!"

"More speed," said Angalo grimly.

"What are you going to do?" said Masklin.

"We'll see how his light can stand up to a truck!" muttered Angalo.

"You can't do that! You can't drive trucks into people!"

"It's Prices Slashed!" said Angalo. "It's not people!"

"He's right," said Grimma. "*You* said we mustn't stop now!"

Masklin grabbed the steering strings and gave one a yank. The truck skewed around just as Prices Slashed dropped his flashlight and, with respectable speed, jumped into the hedge. There was a bang as the rear of the truck hit the car, and then Angalo had the threads again and was guiding them back into something like a straight line.

"You didn't have to do that," he said sullenly. "It's all right to run into Prices Slashed, isn't it, Gurder?"

"Well. Er," said Gurder. He gave Masklin an embarrassed look. "I'm not sure it *was* Prices Slashed, in fact. He had darker clothes, for one thing. And the car with the light on it."

"Yes, but he had the peaked hat and the terrible light!"

The truck bumped off a bank, taking away a large chunk of soil, and lurched back onto the road.

"Anyway," said Angalo in a satisfied voice, "that's all behind now. We left Arnold Bros (est. 1905) behind in the Store. We don't need that stuff. Not Outside."

Noisy though it was in the cab, the words created their own sort of silence.

"Well, it's true," said Angalo defensively. "And Dorcas thinks the same thing. And a lot of younger nomes."

"We shall see," said Gurder. "However, I suspect that if Arnold Bros (est. 1905) was ever anywhere, then he's everywhere."

"What do you mean by that?"

"I'm not sure myself. I need to think about it."

Angalo sniffed. "Well, think about it, then. But I don't believe it. It doesn't matter anymore. May Bargains Galore turn against me if I'm wrong," he added.

Masklin saw a blue light out of the corner of his eye. There were mirrors over the wheels of the truck and, although one of them was smashed and the other one was bent, they still worked after a fashion. The light was behind the truck.

"He's coming after us, whoever it is," he said mildly.

"And there's that dee-dah, dee-dah noise," said Gurder.

"I think," Masklin went on, "that it might be a good idea to get off this road."

Angalo glanced from side to side.

"Too many hedges," he said.

"No, I meant onto another road. Can you do that?"

"Ten-four. No problem. Hey, he's trying to pass! What a nerve! Ha!" The truck swerved violently.

"I wish we could open the windows," he added. "One of the drivers I watched, if anyone behind him honked, he'd wave his hand out of the window and shout things. I think that's what you're supposed to do." He waved his arm up and shouted, *"Yahgerronyerr!"*

"Don't worry about that. Just find another road, a small road," said Masklin soothingly. "I'll be back in a minute."

He lowered himself down the swaying ladder to Dorcas and his people. There wasn't too much going on at the moment, just little tugs on the big wheel from the steering groups and a steady pressure on the go-faster pedal. Many of the nomes were sitting down and trying to relax. There was a ragged cheer when Masklin joined them.

Dorcas was sitting by himself, scribbling things on a piece of paper.

"Oh, it's you," he said. "Everything working now? Have we run out of things to bump into?"

"We're being followed by someone who wants to make us stop," said Masklin.

"Another truck?"

"A car, I think. With humans in it."

Dorcas scratched his chin.

"What do you want me to do about it?"

"You used things to cut the truck wires when you didn't want it to go," said Masklin.

"Pliers. What about them?"

"Have you still got them?"

"Oh, yes. But you need two nomes to use them."

"Then I shall need another nome." Masklin told Dorcas what he had in mind.

The old nome looked at him with something like admiration and then shook his head.

"It'll never work," he said. "We won't have the time. Nice idea, though."

"But we're so much faster than humans! We *could* do it and be back at the truck before they know!"

"Hmm." Dorcas grinned nastily. "You going to come?"

"Yes. I, er, I'm not sure nomes who've never been outside the Store will be able to cope."

Dorcas stood and yawned. "Well, I'd like to try some of this 'fresh air' stuff," he said. "I'm told it's very good for you."

If there had been watchers, peering over the hedge into that mist-wreathed country lane, they would have seen a truck come thundering along at quite an unsafe speed.

They might have thought: That's an unusual vehicle—it seems to have lost quite a few things it should have, like one headlight, a bumper, and most of the paint down one side, and picked up a number of things it shouldn't have, like some bits of bush and more dents than a sheet of corrugated iron.

They might have wondered why it had a *Road Works Ahead* sign hanging from one door handle.

And they would have certainly have wondered why it rolled to a stop.

The police car behind it stopped rather more impressively, in a shower of gravel. Two men almost fell out of it and ran to the truck, wrenching open the doors.

If the watchers had been able to understand Human, they'd have heard someone say, *All right, chummy, that's it for it tonight* and then say, *Where's he gone? There's just a load of string in here!* And then someone else would say, *I bet he's slipped out and has legged it over the fields.*

And while this was going on, and while the policemen poked vaguely in the hedge and shone their flashlights into the mist, the watchers might have noticed a couple of very small shadows run from under the rear of the truck and disappear under the car. They moved very fast, like mice. Like mice, their voices were high-pitched, fast, and squeaky.

They were carrying a pair of pliers.

A few seconds later, they scurried back again. And almost as soon as they'd disappeared under the truck, it started up.

The men shouted and ran back to their car.

But instead of roaring into life, it went *whirr, whirr, whirr* in the misty night.

After a while one of them got out and lifted the hood.

As the truck vanished into the mist, its single rear light a fading glow, he knelt down, reached under the car, and held up a handful of neatly cut wires. . . .

This is what the watchers would have seen. In fact, the only watchers were a couple of cows, and they didn't understand any of it.

Perhaps it nearly ends there.

A couple of days later the truck was found in a ditch some way outside the town. What was stranger was this: The battery, and every wire, light bulb, and switch had been taken out of it. So had the radio.

The cab was full of bits of string.

# 14

*XV. And the nomes said, Here is a New Place, to be ours
for Ever and Ever.*
*XVI. And the Outsider said Nothing.*

*From* The Book of Nome, Exits Chap. 4, v. XV–XVI

IT HAD BEEN a quarry. The nomes knew this because the gate had a
rusty sign on it: *Quarry. Dangerous. Do Not Enter.*

They found it after a mad panicking run across the fields. By
luck, if you listened to Angalo. Because of Arnold Bros (est. 1905),
if you believed Gurder.

It doesn't matter how they settled in, found the few old tumbledown buildings, explored the caves and rock heaps, cleared out the
rats. That wasn't too difficult. The harder part was persuading most
of the older nomes to go outside; they felt happier with a floor over
their heads. Granny Morkie came in useful there. She made them
watch her walk up and down outside, braving the terrible Fresh Air.

Besides, the food taken from the Store didn't last forever. There
was hunger, and there were rabbits in the fields above. Vegetables,
too. Not nice and clean, of course, as Arnold Bros (est. 1905) had
intended they should be, but just sticking in the ground covered
with dirt. There were complaints about this. The molehills that

appeared in a nearby field were simply the result of the first experimental potato mine. . . .

After a couple of nasty experiences, foxes learned to keep away.

And then there was Dorcas's discovery of electricity, still in wires leading to a box in one of the deserted sheds. Getting at it while staying alive seemed to need nearly as much planning as the Great Drive, with a lot of broom handles and rubber gloves involved.

After a lot of thought, Masklin had pushed the Thing near one of the electric wires. It had flashed a few lights but had kept silent. He felt it was listening. He could *hear* it listening.

He'd taken it away again and tucked it into a gap in one of the walls. He had an obscure feeling that it wasn't time to use the Thing yet. The longer they left it, he thought, the longer they'd have to work out for themselves what it was they were doing. He'd like to wake it up later and say, "Look, this is what we've done, all by ourselves."

Gurder had already worked out that they were probably somewhere in China.

And so the winter became spring, and spring became summer. . . .

But it wasn't finished, Masklin felt.

He sat on the rocks above the quarry, on guard. They always kept a guard on duty, just in case. One of Dorcas's inventions, a switch that was connected to a wire that would light a bulb down under one of the sheds, was hidden under a stone by his side. He'd been promised radio, one of these days. One of these days might be quite soon, because Dorcas had pupils now. They seemed to spend a lot of time in one of the tumbledown sheds, surrounded by bits of wire and looking very serious.

Guard duty was quite popular, at least on sunny days.

This was home, now. The nomes were settling in, filling in the corners, planning, spreading out, starting to *belong*.

Especially Bobo. He'd disappeared on the first day, and turned up again, scruffy and proud, as the leader of the quarry rats and father of a lot of little ratlings. Perhaps it was because of this that the rats and the nomes seemed to be getting along okay, politely avoiding each other whenever possible and not eating one another.

They belong here more than we do, thought Masklin. This isn't really our place. This belongs to humans. They've just forgotten about it for a while, but one day they'll remember it. They'll come back here and we'll have to move on. We'll always have to move on. We'll always try to create our own little worlds inside the big world. We used to have it all, and now we think we're lucky to have a little bit.

He looked down at the quarry below him. He could just make out Grimma sitting in the sun with some of the young nomes, teaching them to read.

That was a good thing, anyway. He'd never be that good at it, but the kids seemed to pick it up easily enough.

But there were still problems. The departmental families, for example. They had no departments to rule, and they spent a lot of time squabbling. There seemed to be arguments going on the whole time, and everyone expected *him* to sort them out. It seemed the only time nomes acted together was when they had something to occupy their minds. . . .

Beyond the moon, the Thing had said. You used to live in the stars.

Masklin lay back and listened to the bees.

One day we'll go back. We'll find a way to get to the big Ship in the sky, and we'll go back. But not yet. It'll take some doing, and the hard part again will be getting people to understand. Every time we climb up a step, we settle down and think we've got to the top of the stairs, and start bickering about things.

Still, even *knowing* that the stairs are there is a pretty good start.

From here, he could see for miles across the countryside. For instance, he could see the airport.

It had been quite frightening, the day they'd seen the first jet go over, but a few of the nomes had recalled pictures from books they'd read, and it turned out to be nothing more than a sort of truck built to drive in the sky.

Masklin hadn't told anyone why he thought that knowing more about the airport would be a good idea. Some of the others suspected, he knew, but there was so much to do that they weren't thinking about it now.

He'd led up to it carefully. He'd just said that it was important to find out as much about this new world as possible, just in case. He'd put it in such a way that no one had said, "In case of what?" and, anyway, there were people to spare and the weather was good.

He'd led a team of nomes across the fields to it; it had been a long journey, but there were thirty of them and there had been no problems. They'd even had to cross a highway, but they'd found a tunnel built for badgers, and a badger coming along it the other way turned around and hurried off when they approached. Bad news like armed nomes spreads quickly.

And then they'd found the wire fence, and climbed up it a little way, and spent hours watching the planes landing and taking off.

Masklin had felt, just as he had done once or twice before, that here was something very important. The jets looked big and terrible, but once he'd thought that about trucks. You just had to know about them. Once you had the name, you had something you could handle, like a sort of lever. One day, they could be useful. One day, the nomes might need them.

To take another step.

Funnily enough, he felt quite optimistic about it. He'd had one glorious moment of feeling that, although they argued and bickered and got things wrong and tripped over themselves, nomes would come through in the end. Because Dorcas had been watching the planes, too, clinging to the wire with a calculating look in his eyes. And Masklin had said:

"Just supposing—for the sake of argument, you understand—we need to steal one of *those*, do you think it could be done?"

And Dorcas had rubbed his chin thoughtfully.

"Shouldn't be too hard to drive," he said, and grinned. "They've only got three wheels."

# DIGGERS
*The Second Book of the Nomes*

And so the nomes settled down in their new home, quite certain that everything was going to be All Right.

The months passed. . . .

This is the story of the Winter.

This is the Great Battle.

This is the story of the awakening of Big John, the Dragon in the Hill, with eyes like great eyes and a voice like a great voice and teeth like great teeth.

But the story didn't end there.

It didn't start there, either.

The sky blew a gale. The sky blew a fury. The wind became a wall sweeping across the country, a giant stamping on the land. Small trees bent, big trees broke. The last leaves of autumn whirred through the air like lost bullets.

The trash heap by the gravel pits was deserted. The seagulls that patrolled it had found shelter somewhere, but it was still full of movement.

The wind tore into the heap as though it had something particular against old detergent boxes and leftover shoes. Cans rolled into the ruts and clanked miserably, while lighter bits of rubbish flew up and joined the riot in the sky.

Still the wind burrowed. Papers rustled for a while, then got caught and blasted away.

Finally, one piece that had been flapping for hours tore free and flew up into the booming air. It looked like a large white bird with oblong wings.

Watch it tumble. . . .

It gets caught on a fence, but very briefly. Half of it tears off and now, that much lighter, it pinwheels across the furrows of the field beyond. . . .

It is just gathering speed when a hedge looms up and snaps it out of the air like a fly.

# 1

*I. And in that time were Strange Happenings: the Air moved harshly, the Warmth of the Sky grew Less, on some mornings the tops of puddles grew Hard and Cold.*

*II. And the nomes said unto one another, What is this Thing?*

*From* The Book of Nome, Quarries Chap. 1, v. I–II

"WINTER," SAID MASKLIN firmly. "It's called winter."

Abbot Gurder frowned at him.

"You never said it would be like *this*," he said. "It's so *cold*."

"Call this cold?" said Granny Morkie. "Cold? This ain't cold. You think this is cold? You wait till it gets really cold!" She was enjoying this, Masklin noticed; Granny Morkie always enjoyed doom—it was what kept her going. "It'll be really cold then, when it gets cold. You get *real* frosts and, and water comes down out of the sky in frozen bits!" She leaned back triumphantly. "What d'you think to that, then? Eh?"

"You don't have to use baby talk to us." Gurder sighed. "We *can* read, you know. We know what snow is."

"Yes," said Dorcas. "There used to be cards with pictures on, back in the Store. Every time Christmas Fayre came around. We know about snow. It's glittery."

"You get robins," agreed Gurder.

"There's, er, actually there's a bit more to it than that," Masklin began.

Dorcas waved him into silence. "I don't think we need to worry," he said. "We're well dug in, the food stores are looking satisfactory, and we know where to go to get more if we need it. Unless anyone's got anything else to raise, why don't we close the meeting?"

Everything was going well. Or, at least, not very badly.

Oh, there was still plenty of squabbling and rows between the various families, but that was nomish nature for you. That's why they'd set up the Council, which seemed to be working.

Nomes liked arguing. At least the Council of Drivers meant they could argue without hitting one another—or hardly ever.

Funny thing, though. Back in the Store, the great departmental families had run things. But now all the families were mixed up and, anyway, there were no departments in a quarry. But by instinct, almost, nomes liked hierarchies. The world had always been neatly divided between those who told people what to do and those who did it. So, in a strange way, a new set of leaders was emerging.

The Drivers.

It depended on where you had been during the Long Drive. If you were one of the ones who had been in the truck cab, then you were a Driver. All the rest were just Passengers. No one talked about it much. It wasn't official or anything. It was just that the bulk of nomekind felt that anyone who could get the Truck all the way here was the sort of person who knew what they were doing.

Being a Driver wasn't necessarily much fun.

Last year, before they'd found the Store, Masklin had to hunt all day. Now he hunted only when he felt like it; the younger Store nomes liked hunting, and apparently it wasn't *right* for a Driver to do it. They mined potatoes, and there'd been a big harvest of corn from a nearby field, even after the machines had been round. Masklin would have preferred them to grow their own food, but the nomes didn't seem to have the knack of making seeds grow in the rock-hard ground of the quarry. But they were getting fed, that was the main thing.

Around him he could feel thousands of nomes living their lives. Raising families. *Settling down.*

He wandered back to his own burrow, down under one of the derelict quarry sheds. After a while he reached a decision and pulled the Thing out of its own hole in the wall.

None of its lights were on. They wouldn't go on until it was close to electricity wires, when it would light up and be able to talk. There were some in the quarry, and Dorcas had got them working. Masklin hadn't taken the Thing to them, though. The solid black box had a way of talking that always made him unsettled.

He was pretty certain it could hear, though.

"Old Torrit died last week," he said after a while. "We were a bit sad but, after all, he was very old and he just died. I mean, nothing ate him first or ran him over or anything."

Masklin's little tribe had once lived in a highway embankment beside rolling countryside that was full of things that were hungry for fresh nome. The idea that you could die simply of not being alive anymore was a new one to them.

"So we buried him up on the edge of the potato field, too deep for the plow. The Store nomes haven't got the hang of burial yet, I think. They think he's going to sprout, or something. I think they're mixing it up with what you do with seeds. Of course, they don't know about growing things. Because of living in the Store, you see. It's all new to them. They're always complaining about eating food that comes out of the ground; they think it's not natural. And they think the rain is a sprinkler system. I think *they* think the whole world is just a bigger store. Um."

He stared at the unresponsive cube for a while, scraping his mind for other things to say.

"Anyway, that means Granny Morkie is the oldest nome," he said eventually. "And *that* means she's entitled to a place on the Council even though she's a woman. Abbot Gurder objected to that, but we said, All right, you tell her, and he wouldn't, so she is. Um."

He looked at his fingernails. The Thing had a way of listening that was quite off-putting.

"Everyone's worried about the winter. Um. But we've got masses of potatoes stored up, and it's quite warm down here. They've got some funny ideas, though. In the Store they said that when it was Christmas Fayre time, there was this thing that came called Santer Claws. I just hope it hasn't followed us, that's all. Um."

He scratched an ear.

"All in all, everything's going right. Um."

He leaned closer.

"You know what that means? If you think everything's going right, something's going wrong that you haven't heard about yet. That's what I say. Um."

The black cube managed to look sympathetic.

"Everyone says I worry too much. I don't think it's *possible* to worry too much. Um."

He thought some more.

"Um. I think that's about all the news for now." He lifted the Thing up and put it back in its hole.

He'd wondered whether to tell it about his argument with Grimma, but that was, well, personal.

It was all that reading books, that was what it was. He shouldn't have let her learn to read, filling her head with stuff she didn't need to know. Gurder was right—women's brains *did* overheat. Grimma's seemed to be boiling hot the whole time, these days.

He'd gone and said, Look, now everything was settled down more, it was time they got married like the Store nomes did, with the Abbot muttering words and everything.

And she'd said she wasn't sure.

So he'd said, It doesn't work like that—you get told, you get married, that's how it's done.

And she'd said, Not anymore.

He'd complained to Granny Morkie. You'd have expected some support there, he thought. She was a great one for tradition, was Granny. He'd said: Granny, Grimma isn't doing what I tell her.

And *she'd* said: Good luck to her. Wish I'd thought of not doin' what I was told when I was a girl.

Then he'd complained to Gurder, who'd said, Yes, it was very wrong, girls should do what they were instructed. And Masklin had said, Right then, you tell her. And Gurder had said, Well, er, she's got a real temper on her, perhaps it would be better to leave it a bit and these were, after all, changing times. . . .

Changing times. Well, that was true enough. Masklin had done most of the changing. He'd had to make people think in different ways to leave the Store. Changing was necessary. Change was right. He was all in favor of change.

What he was dead set against was things not staying the same.

His spear was leaning in the corner. What a pathetic thing it was . . . now. Just a bit of flint held onto the shaft with a twist of binder twine. They'd brought saws and things from the Store. They could use metal these days.

He stared at the spear for some time. Then he picked it up and went out for a long, serious think about things and his position in them. Or, as other people would have put it, a good sulk.

The old quarry was about halfway up the hillside. There was a steep turf slope above it, which in turn became a riot of bramble and hawthorn thicket. There were fields beyond.

Below the quarry, a lane wound down through scrubby hedges and joined the main road. Beyond that there was the railway, another name for two long lines of metal on big wooden blocks. Things like very long trucks went along it sometimes, all joined together.

The nomes had not got the railway fully worked out yet. But it was obviously dangerous, because they could see a lane that crossed it, and whenever the railway moving thing was coming, two gates came down over the road.

The nomes knew what gates were for. You saw them on fields, to stop things getting out. It stood to reason, therefore, that the gates were to stop the railway from escaping from its rails and rushing around on the roads.

Then there were more fields, some gravel pits—good for fishing, for the nomes who wanted fish—and then there was the airport.

Masklin had spent hours in the summer watching the planes. They drove along the ground, he noticed, and then went up sharply, like birds, and got smaller and smaller and disappeared.

That was the *big* worry. Masklin sat on his favorite stone, in the rain that was starting to fall, and started to worry about it. So many things were worrying him these days, he had to stack them up, but below all of them was this big one.

They should be going where the planes went. That was what the Thing had told him, when it was still speaking to him. The nomes had come from the sky. Up above the sky, in fact, which was a bit hard to understand, because surely the only thing above the sky was more sky. And they should go back. It was their . . . something beginning with D. Density. Their density. Worlds of their own, they once had. And somehow they'd got stuck here. But—this was the worrying part—the Ship thing, the airplane that flew through the really high sky, between the stars, was still up there somewhere. The first nomes had left it behind when they came down here in a smaller ship, and it had crashed, and they hadn't been able to get back.

And he was the only one who knew.

The old Abbot, the one before Gurder, he had known. Grimma and Dorcas and Gurder all knew some of it, but they had busy minds and they were practical people, and there was so much to organize these days.

It was just that everyone was settling down. We're going to turn this into our little world, just like in the Store, Masklin realized. They thought the roof was the sky, and we think the sky is the roof.

We'll just stay and . . .

There was a truck coming up the quarry road. It was such an unusual sight that Masklin realized he had been watching it for a while without really seeing it at all.

o    o    o

"There was no one on watch! Why wasn't there anyone on watch? I said there should always be someone on watch!"

Half a dozen nomes scurried through the dying bracken toward the quarry gate.

"It was Sacco's turn," muttered Angalo.

"No, it wasn't!" hissed Sacco. "You remember, yesterday you asked me to swap because—"

"I don't care whose turn it was!" shouted Masklin. "There was no one there! And there should have been! Right?"

"Sorry, Masklin."

"Yeah. Sorry, Masklin."

They scrambled up a bank and flattened themselves behind a tuft of dried grass.

It was a small truck, as far as trucks went. A human had already climbed out of it and was doing something to the gates leading into the quarry.

"It's a Land Rover," said Angalo smugly. He'd spent a long time in the Store reading everything he could about vehicles, before the Long Drive. He liked them. "It's not really a truck, it's more to carry humans over—"

"That human is sticking something on the gate," said Masklin.

"On *our* gate," said Sacco disapprovingly.

"Bit odd," said Angalo. The man sleepwalked, in the slow, ponderous way that humans did, back to the vehicle. Eventually it backed around and roared off.

"All the way up here just to stick a bit of paper on the gate," said Angalo, as the nomes stood up. "That's humans for you."

Masklin frowned. Humans were big and stupid, that was true enough, but there was something unstoppable about them, and they seemed to be controlled by bits of paper. Back in the Store, a piece of paper had said the Store was going to be demolished and, sure enough, it *had* been demolished. You couldn't trust humans with bits of paper.

He pointed to the rusty wire netting, an easy climb for an agile nome.

"Sacco," he said, "you'd better fetch it down."

Miles away, *another* piece of paper fluttered on the hedge. Spots of rain pattered across its sun-bleached words, soaking the paper until it was heavy and soggy and . . .

. . . tore.

It flopped onto the grass, free. A breeze made it rustle.

# 2

*III. But there came a Sign, and people said, What is it that this means?*

*IV. And it was not good.*

*From* The Book of Nome, Signs Chap. 1, v. III–IV

GURDER SHUFFLED ON hands and knees across the paper that had been taken down from the gate.

"Of course I can read it," he said. "I know what every word means."

"Well, then?" said Masklin.

Gurder looked embarrassed. "It's what every sentence means that's giving me trouble," he said. "It says here . . . where was it . . . yes, it says here the quarry is going to be reopened. What does that mean? It's open already—any fool knows that. You can see for miles."

The other nomes crowded around. You certainly could see for miles. That was the terrible part. On three sides the quarry had decent high cliff walls, but on the fourth side . . . well, you got into the habit of not looking in that direction. There was too much of nothing, which made you feel even smaller and more vulnerable than you were already.

Even if the meaning of the paper wasn't clear, it certainly looked unpleasant.

"The quarry's a hole in the ground," said Dorcas. "You can't open a hole unless it's been filled in. Stands to reason."

"A quarry's a place you get stone from," said Grimma. "Humans do it. They dig a hole and they use the stone for making, well, roads and things."

"I expect you read that, did you?" said Gurder sourly. He suspected Grimma of lack of respect for authority. It was also incredibly annoying that, against all the obvious deficiencies of her sex, she was better at reading than he was.

"I did, actually," said Grimma, tossing her head.

"But, you see," said Masklin patiently, "there aren't any more stones here, Grimma. That's why there's a hole."

"Good point," said Gurder sternly.

"*Then he'll make the hole bigger!*" snapped Grimma. "Look at those cliffs up there"—they obediently looked—"they're made of stone! Look here"—every head swiveled down to where her foot was tapping impatiently at the paper—"it says it's for a highway extension! That's a road! He's going to make the quarry bigger! Our quarry! That's what it says he's going to do!"

There was a long silence.

Then Dorcas said: "Who is?"

"Order! He's put his name on it," said Grimma.

"She's right, you know," said Masklin. "Look. It says: 'To be reopened, by Order.'"

The nomes shuffled their feet. Order. It didn't sound like a promising name. Anyone called Order would probably be capable of anything.

Gurder stood up and brushed the dust off his robe.

"It's only a piece of paper, when all's said and done," he said sullenly.

"But the human came up here," said Masklin. "They've never come up here before."

"Dunno about that," said Dorcas. "I mean, all the quarry buildings. The old workshops. The doorways and so on. I mean, they're for humans. Always worried me, that has. Where humans have been before, they tend to go again. They're rascals for that."

There was another crowded silence, the kind that gets made by lots of people thinking unhappy thoughts.

"Do you mean," said a nome slowly, "that we've come all this way, we've worked so hard to make a place to live in, and now it's going to be taken away?"

"I don't think we should get too disturbed right at this time—" Gurder began.

"We've got families here," said another nome. Masklin realized that it was Angalo. He'd been married in the spring to a young lady from the del Icatessen family, and they'd already got a fine pair of youngsters, two months old and talking already.

"And we were going to have another go at planting seeds," said another nome. "We've spent ages clearing that ground behind the big sheds. You *know* that."

Gurder raised his hand imploringly.

"We don't know anything," he said. "We mustn't start getting upset until we've found out what's going on."

"And *then* can we get upset?" said another nome sourly. Masklin recognized Nisodemus, one of the Stationeri and Gurder's own assistant. He'd never liked the young nome, and the young nome had never liked anyone, as far as Masklin could see.

"I've never, um, been happy with the *feel* of this place, um, I *knew* there was going to be trouble—" Nisodemus complained.

"Now, now, Nisodemus," said Gurder. "There's no cause to go talking like that. We'll have another meeting of the Council," he added. "That's what we'll do."

The crumpled newspaper lay beside the road. Occasionally a breeze would blow it randomly along the shoulder while, a few inches away, the traffic thundered past.

A stronger gust hit it at the same time as a particularly large truck roared by, dragging a tail of whirling air. The paper shot up over the road, spread out like a sail, and rose on the wind.

The Quarry Council was in session, in the space under the floor of the old quarry office.

Other nomes had crowded in, and the rest of the tribe milled around outside.

"Look," said Angalo, "there's a big old barn up on the hill, the other side of the potato field. It wouldn't hurt to take some stores up there. Make it ready, you know. Just in case. Then if anything *does* happen, we've got somewhere to go."

"The quarry buildings don't have spaces under the floors, except in the canteen and the office," said Dorcas gloomily. "It's not like the Store. There aren't many places to hide. We need the sheds. If humans come here, we'll have to leave."

"So the barn will be a good idea, won't it?" repeated Angalo.

"There's a man on a tractor who goes up there sometimes," said Masklin.

"We could keep out of his way. Anyway," said Angalo, looking around at the rows of faces, "maybe the humans will go away again. Perhaps they'll just take their stone and go. And we can come back. We could send someone to spy on them every day."

"It seems to me you've been thinking about this barn for some time," said Dorcas.

"Me and Masklin talked about it one day when we were hunting up there," said Angalo. "Didn't we, Masklin?"

"Hmm?" said Masklin, who was staring into space.

"You remember, we went up there and I said that'd be a useful place if ever we needed it, and you said yes."

"Hmm," said Masklin.

"Yes, but there's this Winter thing coming," said one of the nomes. "You know. Cold. Glitter on everythin'."

"Robins," another nome put in.

"Yeah," said the first nome uncertainly. "Them, too. Not a good time to go movin' around, with robins zoomin' about."

"Nothing wrong with robins," said Granny Morkie, who had nodded off for a moment. "My dad used to say there's good eatin' on a robin, if you catched one." She beamed at them proudly.

This comment had the same effect on everyone's train of thought as a brick wall built across the line. Eventually Gurder said: "I still say we shouldn't get too excited right at this moment. We should wait and trust in Arnold Bros (est. 1905)'s guidance."

There was more silence. Then Angalo said, very quietly: "Fat lot of good that'll do us."

There was silence again. But this time it was a thick, heavy silence, and it got thicker and heavier and more menacing, like a storm cloud building up over a mountain, until the first flash of lightning would come as a relief.

It came.

"What did you say?" said Gurder, slowly.

"Only what everyone's been thinking," said Angalo. Many of the nomes started to stare at their feet.

"And what do you mean by that?" said Gurder.

"Where *is* Arnold Bros (est. 1905), then?" said Angalo. "*How* did he help us get out of the Store? Exactly, I mean? He didn't, did he?" Angalo's voice shook a bit, as if even he was terrified to hear himself talking like this. "*We* did it. By learning things. We did it all ourselves. We learned to read books, *your* books, and we found things out and we did things for ourselves. . . ."

Gurder jumped to his feet, white with fury. Beside him Nisodemus put his hand over his mouth and looked too shocked to speak.

"Arnold Bros (est. 1905) goes wherever nomes go!" Gurder shouted.

Angalo swayed backward, but his father had been one of the toughest nomes in the Store, and he didn't give in easily.

"You just made that up!" he snorted. "I'm not saying that there wasn't, well, *something* in the Store, but that was the Store and this is here, and all we've got is *us*! The trouble is, you Stationeri were so powerful in the Store, you just can't bear to give it up!"

Now Masklin stood up.

"Just a moment, you two—" he began.

"So that's all it is, is it?" growled Gurder, ignoring him. "That's the Haberdasheri for you! You always were too proud! Too arrogant by half! Drive a truck a little way and we think we know it all, do we? Perhaps we're getting what we deserve, eh?"

"—this isn't the time or place for this sort of thing—" Masklin went on.

"That's just a silly threat! Why can't you accept it, you old fool. Arnold Bros doesn't exist! Use the brains Arnold Bros gave you, why don't you?"

*"If you don't both shut up I'll bang your heads together!"*

That seemed to work.

"Right," said Masklin, in a more normal voice. "Now, I think it would be a very good idea if everyone went and got on with—with whatever it was they were getting on with. Because this is no way to make complicated decisions. We all need to think for a bit."

The nomes filed out, relieved that it was over. Masklin could hear Gurder and Angalo still arguing.

"Not you two," he warned.

"Now *look*—" said Gurder.

"No, you look, the pair of you!" said Masklin. "Here we are, maybe a big problem looming up, and you start arguing! You both ought to know better! Can't you see you're upsetting people?"

"Well, it's important," muttered Angalo.

*"What we should do now,"* said Masklin sharply, "is have another look at this barn. Can't say I'm happy with the idea, but it might be useful to have a bolt-hole. Anyway, it'll keep people occupied, and that'll stop them worrying. How about it?"

"I suppose so," said Gurder, with bad grace. "But—"

"No more buts," said Masklin. "You're acting like idiots. People look up to the pair of you, so you'll set an example, do you hear?"

They glowered at each other, but they both nodded.

"Right, then," said Masklin. "Now, we'll all go out, and people'll see you've made up, and that'll stop them fretting. *Then* we can start planning."

"But Arnold Bros (est. 1905) *is* important," said Gurder.

"I daresay," said Masklin, as they came out into the daylight of the quarry. The wind was dropping again, leaving the sky a deep cold blue.

"There's no 'daresay' about it," said Gurder.

"Listen," said Masklin, "I don't know whether Arnold Bros exists, or was in the Store, or just lives in our heads or whatever. What I *do* know is that he isn't just going to drop out of the sky."

All three of them glanced up when he said this. The Store nomes shuddered just a bit. It still took a certain courage to look up at the endless sky when you'd been used to nice friendly floorboards, but it was traditional, when you referred to Arnold Bros, to look up. Up was where Management and Accounts had been, back in the Store.

"Funny you should say that. There's something up there," said Angalo.

Something white and vaguely rectangular was drifting gently through the air, and growing bigger.

"It's just a bit of paper," said Gurder. "Something the wind's blown off the dump."

It was definitely a lot bigger now, and turned gently in the air as it tumbled into the quarry.

"I think," said Masklin slowly, as its shadow raced toward him across the ground, "that we'd better stand back a bit—"

It dropped on him.

It was, of course, only paper. But nomes are small and it had fallen quite some way, so the force was enough to knock him over.

What was more surprising were the words he saw as he fell backward. They were: Arnold Bros.

# 3

*I. And they Sought for a Better Sign from Arnold Bros
(est. 1905), and there was a Sign;*

*II. And some spake up saying, Well, all right, but it is
really nothing but a Co incidence;*

*III. But others said, Even a Co incidence can be a Sign.*

*From* The Book of Nome, Signs Chap. 2, v. I–III

MASKLIN HAD ALWAYS kept an open mind on the subject of Arnold Bros (est. 1905). When you thought about it, the Store had been pretty impressive, what with the moving staircases and so on, and if Arnold Bros (est. 1905) hadn't created it, who had? After all, that left only humans. Not that he considered humans to be as stupid as most nomes thought. They might be big and slow, but there was a sort of unstoppability about them. They could certainly be taught to do simple tasks.

On the other hand, the world was *miles* across and full of complicated things. It seemed to be asking a lot of Arnold Bros (est. 1905) to create the whole thing.

So Masklin had decided not to decide anything about Arnold Bros (est. 1905), in the hope that if there *was* an Arnold Bros (est. 1905) and he found out about Masklin, he wouldn't mind much.

The trouble with having an open mind, of course, is that people will insist on coming along and trying to put things in it.

The faded newspaper from the sky had been carefully spread out on the floor of one of the old sheds.

It was covered with words. Most of them even Masklin could understand, but even Grimma had to admit she couldn't guess at what they were supposed to mean when you read them all in one go. SCHOOL SLAMS SHOCK PROBE, for example, was a bit of a mystery. So was FURY OVER RATES REBEL. So was PLAY SUPER BINGO IN YOUR SOARAWAY BLACKBURY EVENING POST & GAZETTE. But they were mysteries that would have to wait.

What all eyes were staring at was the quite small area of words, about nome sized, under the word PEOPLE.

"That means people," said Grimma.

"Really?" said Masklin.

"And the lettering underneath it says: 'Fun-loving, globe-trotting millionaire playboy Richard Arnold will be jetting to the Florida sunshine next week to witness the launch of Arnsat 1, the first communi'"—she hesitated—"'cations sat . . . ellite built by Arnco Inter . . . national Group. This leap into the future comes only a few months after the dest . . . ruction by fire of—'"

The nomes, who'd been silently reading along with her, shivered.

"Arnold Bros, the store here in Blackbury that was the first of the Arnold chain and the basis of the multimillion trad . . . ing group. It was founded in 1905 by Alderman Frank W. Arnold and his brother Arthur. Grand . . . son Richard, 39, who will—" Her voice faded to a whisper.

"Grandson Richard, 39," repeated Gurder, his face bright with triumph. "What d'you think of *that*, eh?"

"What does globe-trotting mean?" said Masklin.

"Well, globe means ball, and trotting is a sort of slow running," said Grimma. "So he runs slowly on a ball. Globe-trotting."

"This is a message from Arnold Bros," said Gurder ponderously. "It's been sent to us. A message."

"A message meant, um, for us!" said Nisodemus, who was standing just behind Gurder. He held up his hands. "Yea, all the way from—"

"Yes, yes, Nisodemus," said Gurder. "Do be quiet, there's a good chap." He gave Masklin an embarrassed look.

"Doesn't sound very likely, running slowly. I mean, you'd fall off. If it was a ball, is what I'm saying," said Masklin.

They stared at The Picture again. It was made up of tiny dots. They showed a smiling face. It had teeth and a beard.

"It stands to reason," said Gurder, more confidently. "Arnold Bros (est. 1905) has sent Grandson Richard, 39, to—to—"

"And these two names who founded the Store," said Masklin. "I don't understand that. I thought Arnold Bros (est. 1905) created the Store."

"Then these two people founded it," said Gurder. "That makes sense. It was a big Store. It'd be easy to find, even if you weren't looking for it." He looked slightly uneasy. "Losted and founded," he said, half to himself. "That makes sense. Yes."

"O-kay," said Dorcas. "So let's just see where we've got to. The message is, isn't it, that Grandson Richard, 39, is in Florida, wherever that is—"

"Going to *be* in Florida," said Grimma.

"It's a type of colored juice," volunteered a nome. "I know, 'cause one day when we went over to the dump, there was this old carton, and it said 'Florida Orange Juice.' I read it," he added proudly.

"Going to *be* in this orange-colored juice, so I'm given to understand," said Dorcas doubtfully, "running slowly on a ball and jetting, whatever that is. And liking it, apparently."

The nomes fell silent while they thought about this.

"Holy utterances are often difficult to understand," said Gurder gravely.

"This must be a *powerful* holy one," said Dorcas.

"I think it's just a coincidence," said Angalo loftily. "This is just a story about a human being, like in some of the books we read."

"And how many humans could even stand on a ball, let alone run slowly on it?" demanded Gurder.

"All *right*," said Angalo, "but what are we going to *do*, then?"

Gurder's mouth opened and shut a few times. "Why, it's obvious," he said uncertainly.

"Tell us, then," said Angalo sourly.

"Well, er. It's, er, obvious. We must go to, er, the place where the orange juice is—"

"Yes?" said Angalo.

"And, er, and find Grandson Richard, 39, which should be easy, you see, because we've got this picture—"

"Yes?" said Angalo.

Gurder gave him a haughty look. "Remember the commandment that Arnold Bros (est. 1905) put up in the Store," he said. "Did it not say, *If You Do Not See What You Require, Please Ask?*"

The nomes nodded. Many of them had seen it. And the other commandments: *Everything Must Go*, and, by the Moving Stairs, *Dogs and Strollers Must be Carried*. They were the words of Arnold Bros (est. 1905). You couldn't really argue with them. . . . But on the other hand, well, that had been the Store, and this was here.

"And?" said Angalo.

Gurder began to sweat. "Well, er, and then we ask him to let us be left alone in the quarry."

There was an awkward silence.

Then Angalo said, "That sounds like about the most half-baked—"

"What does jetting mean?" said Grimma. "Is it anything to do with jet?"

"A jet is a kind of aircraft," said Angalo, the transport expert.

"So jetting means to go like an aircraft. Or in an aircraft?" said Grimma.

Everyone turned to Masklin, whose fascination with the airport was well known to one and all.

He wasn't there.

Masklin pulled the Thing from its niche in the wall and padded back out into the open. The Thing didn't have to be attached to any wires. It was enough to put it near them.

There was electricity in the old manager's office. He ran across the empty alley between the tumbledown buildings and squeezed his way in through a crack in the sagging door.

Then he placed the box in the middle of the floor and waited.

It took some time for the Thing to wake up. Its lights flickered at random and it made odd beeping noises. Masklin supposed it was the machine's equivalent of a nome getting up in the morning.

Eventually it said, *"Who is there?"*

"It's me," said Masklin, "Masklin. Look, I need to know what the words 'communications satellite' mean. I've heard you use the word 'satellite' before. You said the moon is one, didn't you?"

"*Yes. But communications satellites are artificial moons. They are used for communications. Communications means the transferring of information. In this case, by radio and television.*"

"What's television?" said Masklin.

"*A means of sending pictures through the air.*"

"Does this happen a lot?"

"*All the time.*"

Masklin made a mental note to look out for any pictures in the air.

"I see," he lied. "So these satellites—where are they, exactly?"

"*In the sky.*"

"I don't think I've ever seen one," said Masklin doubtfully. There was an idea forming in his mind. He wasn't quite sure yet. Bits and pieces of things he'd read and heard were coming together. The important thing was to let them take their own time, and not frighten them away.

"*They are in orbit, many miles up. There are a great many above this planet,*" said the Thing.

"How do you know that?"

"*I can detect them.*"

"Oh."

Masklin stared at the flickering lights.

"If they are artificial, does that mean they're not real?" he said.

"*They are machines. They are usually built on the planet and then launched into space.*"

The idea was nearly there now. It was rising like a bubble. . . .

"Space is where our Ship is, you said."

"*That is correct.*"

Masklin felt the idea explode quietly, like a dandelion. "If we knew where one of these things was going to be flown into space," he said, speaking quickly before the words had time to escape, "and we could sort of hang on to the sides or whatever, or maybe drive it like the Truck, and we took you with us, then we could jump off when we got up there and go and find this Ship of ours, couldn't we?"

The lights on top of the Thing moved oddly, into patterns Masklin had never seen before. This went on for quite a while before it spoke again. When it did, it sounded almost sad.

*"Do you know how big space is?"* it said.

"No," said Masklin politely. "It's pretty big, is it?"

*"Yes. However, it might be possible for me to detect and summon the Ship if I were taken above the atmosphere. But do you know what the words 'oxygen supply' mean?"*

"No."

*"'Space suit'?"*

"No."

*"It is very cold in space."*

"Well, couldn't we sort of jump around a bit to keep warm?" said Masklin desperately.

*"I think you do not appreciate what it is that space contains."*

"What's that, then?"

*"Nothing. It contains nothing. And everything. But there is very little everything and more nothing than you could imagine."*

"It's still worth a try, though, isn't it?"

*"What you are proposing is an extremely unwise endeavor,"* said the Thing.

"Yes, but, you see," said Masklin firmly, "if I don't try, then it's always going to be like this. We're always going to escape, and find somewhere new, and just when we're getting the hang of it all, we'll have to go again. Sooner or later we must find somewhere that we can know really belongs to us. Dorcas is right. Humans get everywhere. Anyway, you were the one who told me that our Home was . . . up there somewhere."

*"This is not the right time. You are ill prepared."*

Masklin clenched his fists. "I'll never be well prepared! I was born in a hole, Thing! A muddy hole in the ground! How can I ever be well prepared for anything? That's what being alive *is*, Thing! It's being badly prepared for everything! Because you only get one chance, Thing! You only get one chance and then you die and they don't let you go round again after you've got the hang of it! Do you understand, Thing! So we'll try it *now*! I *order* you to help! You're a machine and you must do what you're told!"

The lights formed a spiral.

*"You're learning fast,"* said the Thing.

# 4

*III. And in a voice like Thunder, the Great Masklin said
unto the Thing, Now is the Time to go back to our Home
in the Sky;*

*IV. Or we will Forever be Running from Place to Place.*

*V. But None must know what I Intend, or they will say,
Ridiculous, Why go to the Sky when we Have Problems
Right Here?*

*VI. Because that is how People are.*

*From* The Book of Nome, Quarries Chap. 2, v. III–VI

GURDER AND ANGALO were having a blazing row when Masklin got
back.

He didn't try to interrupt. He just put the Thing down on the
floor and sat down next to it, and watched them.

Funny how people needed to argue. The whole secret was not to
listen to what the other person was saying, Masklin had noticed.

Gurder and Angalo had really got the hang of *that*. The trouble was
that neither of them was entirely certain he was right, and the funny
thing was that people who weren't *entirely* certain they were right
always argued much louder than other people, as if the main person
they were trying to convince were themselves. Gurder was not certain,

not *entirely* certain, that Arnold Bros (est. 1905) really existed, and Angalo wasn't entirely certain that he didn't.

Eventually Angalo noticed Masklin.

"You tell him, Masklin," he said. "He wants to go and find Grandson Richard, 39!"

"Do you? Where do you think we should look?" Masklin asked Gurder.

"The airport," said Gurder. "You know that. Jetting. In a jet. That's what he'll do."

"But we *know* the airport!" said Angalo. "I've been right up to the fence several times! Humans go in and out of it all day! Grandson Richard, 39, looks just like them! He could have gone already. He could be in the juice by now! You can't believe words that just drop out of the sky!" He turned to Masklin again. "Masklin's a steady lad," he said. "He'll tell you. You tell him, Masklin," he said. "You listen to him, Gurder. He thinks about things, Masklin does. At a time like this—"

"Let's go to the airport," said Masklin.

"There," said Angalo, "I told you, Masklin isn't the kind of nome—what?"

"Let's go to the airport and watch."

Angalo's mouth opened and shut silently.

"But . . . but . . ." he managed.

"It must be worth a try," said Masklin.

"But it's all just a coincidence!" said Angalo.

Masklin shrugged. "Then we'll come back. I'm not suggesting we *all* go. Just a few of us."

"But supposing something happens while we're gone?"

"It'll happen anyway, then. There's thousands of us. Getting people to the old barn won't be difficult, if we need to do it. It's not like the Long Drive."

Angalo hesitated. "Then *I'll* go," he said. "Just to prove to you how, how superstitious you're being."

"Good," said Masklin.

"Provided Gurder comes, of course," Angalo added.

"What?" said Gurder.

"Well, you *are* the Abbot," said Angalo sarcastically. "If we're going to talk to Grandson Richard, 39, then it'd better be you who does it. I mean, he probably won't want to listen to anyone else."

"Aha!" shouted Gurder. "You think I won't come! It'd be worth it just to see your face—"

"That's settled, then," said Masklin calmly. "And now, I think we'd better see about keeping a special watch on the road. And some teams had better go to the old barn. And it would be a good idea to see what people can carry. Just in case, you know."

Grimma was waiting for him outside. She didn't look happy.

"I know you," she said. "I know the kind of expression you have when you're getting people to do things they don't want to do. What are you planning?"

They strolled into the shadow of a rusting sheet of corrugated iron. Masklin occasionally squinted upward. This morning he'd thought the sky was just a blue thing with clouds. Now it was something that was full of words and invisible pictures and machines whizzing around. Why was it that the more you found out, the less you really *knew*?

Eventually he said, "I can't tell you. I'm not quite sure myself."

"It's to do with the Thing, isn't it?"

"Yes. Look, if I'm away for, er, a little bit longer than—"

She stuck her hands on her hips. "I'm not stupid, you know," she said. "Orange-colored juice indeed! I've read nearly every book we brought out of the Store. Florida is a, a *place*. Just like the quarry. Probably even bigger. And it's a long way away. You have to go across a lot of water to get there."

"I think it might even be farther away than we came on the Long Drive," said Masklin quietly. "I know, because one day when we went to look at the airport, I saw water on the other side, by the road. It looked as though it went on forever."

"I told you," said Grimma smugly. "It was probably an ocean."

"There was a sign by it," said Masklin. "Can't remember everything on it—I'm not as good at the reading as you. One of the words was res . . . er . . . voir, I think."

"There you are, then."

"But it must be worth a try." Masklin scowled. "There's only one place where we can ever be safe, and that's where we belong," he said. "Otherwise we'll always have to keep running away."

"Well, I don't like it," said Grimma.

"But *you* said you didn't like running away," said Masklin. "There isn't an alternative, is there? Let me just try something. If it doesn't work, then we'll come back."

"But supposing something goes wrong? Supposing you don't come back? I'll . . ." Grimma hesitated.

"Yes?" said Masklin hopefully.

"I'll have a terrible time explaining things to people," she said firmly. "It's a silly idea. I don't want to have anything to do with it."

"Oh." Masklin looked disappointed but defiant. "Well, I'm going to try anyway. Sorry."

# 5

*V. And he said, What are these frogs of which you speak?*
*VI. And she said, You wouldn't understand.*
*VII. And he said, You are right.*

*From* The Book of Nome, Strange Frogs Chap. 1, v. V–VII

THERE WAS A busy night. . . .

It would be a journey of several hours to the barn. Parties went on to mark the path and generally prepare the way, besides watching out for foxes. Not that they were often seen, these days; a fox might be quite happy to attack a solitary nome, but thirty well-armed, enthusiastic hunters were a different proposition, and it would be a very stupid fox indeed that even showed an interest. The few that did live near the quarry tended to wander off hurriedly in the opposite direction whenever they saw a nome. They'd learned that nomes meant trouble.

It had been a hard lesson for some of them. Not long after the nomes moved into the quarry, a fox was surprised and delighted to come across a couple of unwary berry gatherers, which it ate. It was even more surprised that night when two hundred grim-faced nomes tracked it to its lair, lit a fire in the entrance, and speared it to death when it ran out, eyes streaming.

There are a lot of animals that would like to dine off nome, Masklin had said. They'd better learn: It's us or them. And they'd better learn right now that it's going to be *them*. No animal is going to get a taste for nome. Not anymore.

Cats were a lot brighter. No cats came anywhere near the quarry.

"Of course, it might all be nothing to worry about," said Angalo nervously, around dawn. "We might never have to do it."

"Just when we were beginning to get settled down, too," said Dorcas. "Still, I reckon that if we keep a proper lookout, we can have everyone on the move in five minutes. And we'll start moving some food stores up there this morning. No harm in that. Then they'll be there if we need them."

Nomes sometimes went as far as the airport. There was a trash dump on the way, which was a prime source of bits of cloth and wire, and the flooded gravel pits farther on were handy if anyone had the patience to fish. It was a pleasant enough journey, largely along badger tracks. There was a main road to be crossed, or rather, to be burrowed under; for some reason pipes had been carefully put underneath it just where the track needed to cross it. Presumably the badgers had done it. They certainly used it a lot.

Masklin found Grimma in her school hole under one of the old sheds, supervising a class in writing. She glared at him, told the children to get on with it—and would Nicco Haberdasheri like to share the joke with the rest of the class? No? Then he could jolly well get on with things—and came out into the passage.

"I've just come to say we're off," said Masklin, twiddling his hat in his hands. "There's a load of nomes going over to the dump, so we'll have company the rest of the way. Er."

"Electricity," said Grimma, vaguely.

"What?"

"There's no electricity at the old barn," said Grimma. "You remember what that meant? On moonless nights, there was nothing to do but stay in the burrow. I don't want to go back to that."

"Well, maybe we were better nomes for it," mumbled Masklin. "We didn't have all the things we've got today, but we were—"

"Cold, frightened, ignorant, and hungry!" snapped Grimma. "You know that. You try telling Granny Morkie about the Good Old Days and see what she says."

"We had each other," said Masklin.

Grimma examined her hands.

"We were just the same age and living in the same hole," she said vaguely. She looked up. "But it's all different now! There's . . . well, there's the frogs, for one thing."

Masklin looked blank. And, for once, Grimma looked unsure.

"I read about them in a book," she said. "There's this place, you see. Called Southamerica. And there's these hills where it's hot and rains all the time, and in the rainforests there are these very tall trees and right in the top branches of the trees there are these like great big flowers called bromeliads and water gets into the flowers and makes little pools and there's a type of frog that lays eggs in the pools and tadpoles hatch and grow into new frogs and these little frogs live their whole lives in the flowers right at the top of the trees and don't even know about the ground and the world is full of things like that and now I know about them and I'm never ever going to be able to see them and then *you*," she gulped for breath, "want me to come and live with you in a hole and wash your socks!"

Masklin ran this sentence through his head again, in case it made any sense when you listened to it a second time.

"But I don't wear socks," he pointed out.

This was apparently not the right thing to say. Grimma prodded him in the stomach.

"Masklin," she said, "you're a good nome and bright enough in your way, but there aren't any answers up in the sky. You need to have your feet on the ground, not your head in the air!"

She swept away and shut the door behind her.

Masklin felt his ears growing hot.

"I can do both!" Masklin shouted after her. "At the same time!"

He thought about it and added, "So can everyone!"

He stamped off along the tunnel. Bright enough in his way! Gurder *was* right, universal education was not a good idea. He'd never understand women, he thought. Even if he lived to be ten.

Gurder had turned over the leadership of the Stationeri to Nisodemus. Masklin felt less than happy about this. It wasn't that Nisodemus was stupid. Quite the reverse. He was clever in a bubbling, sideways way that Masklin distrusted; he always seemed to be bottling up excitement about something, and when he spoke, the words always rushed out, with Nisodemus putting "ums" in the flow of words so that he could catch his breath without anyone having the chance to interrupt him. He made Masklin uneasy. He mentioned this to Gurder.

"Nisodemus might be a bit overenthusiastic," said Gurder, "but his heart's in the right place."

"What about his head?"

"Listen," said Gurder. "We know each other well enough, don't we? We understand one another, wouldn't you say?"

"Yes. Why?"

"Then I'll let you make the decisions that affect all nomes' bodies," said Gurder, his voice just one step away from being threatening, "and you'll let me make the decisions that affect all nomes' souls. Fair enough?"

And so they set off.

The good-byes, the last-minute messages, the organization, and, because they were nomes, the hundred little arguments, are not important.

They set off.

Life at the quarry began to get back to something like normal. No more trucks came up to the gate. Dorcas sent a couple of his more agile young assistant engineers up the wire netting, just in case, to stuff the rusty padlock full of mud. He also ordered a team of nomes to twist wire round and round the gates as well.

"Not that it'd hold them very long," he said. "Not if they were determined."

The Council, or what was left of it now, nodded wisely although frankly none of them understood or cared much about mechanical things.

The truck came back the same afternoon. The two nomes watching the lane hurried back into the quarry to report. The driver had fiddled with the padlock for a while, pulled at the wire, and then driven off.

"And it said something," said Sacco.

"Yes, it said something. Sacco heard it," said his partner, Nooty Kiddies Klothes. She was a plump young nome who wore trousers and was good at engineering and had actually volunteered to be a guard instead of staying at home learning how to cook; things were really changing in the quarry.

"I heard it say something," said Sacco helpfully, in case the point hadn't sunk in.

"That's right," said Nooty. "We both heard it, didn't we, Sacco?"

"And what was it?" said Dorcas encouragingly. I don't really deserve this sort of thing, he thought. Not at my time of life. I'd rather be in my workshop, trying to invent radio.

"It said"—Sacco took a deep breath, his eyes bulged, and he attempted the foghorn mooing that was human sound—"'Bbbllllooooooooodddyyyee kkiiiddddddssss!'"

Dorcas looked at the others.

"Anyone got any ideas?" he said. "It almost seems to mean something, doesn't it? I tell you, if only we could understand them. . . .

"This must have been one of the stupid ones," said Nooty. "It was trying to get in!"

"Then it'll come back," said Dorcas gloomily. He shook his head.

"All right, you two," he said. "Well done. Get back on watch. Thank you."

He watched them go off hand in hand, and then he wandered away across the quarry, heading for the old manager's office.

I've seen Christmas Fayre come around six times, he thought. Six whatd'youcallems—years. And almost one more, I think, although it's hard to be sure out here. No one puts up any signs to say what's happening, and the heating just gets turned down. Seven years old. Just about the time when a nome ought to be taking it easy. And I'm out here, where there aren't any proper walls to the world, and the water goes cold and hard as glass some mornings, and the ventilation and heating systems are quite shockingly out of control. Of course— he pulled himself together a bit—as a scientist I find all these phenomena extremely interesting. It would just be nicer to find them extremely interesting from somewhere nice and snug, inside.

Ah, inside. That was the place to be. Most of the older nomes suffered from the fear of the Outside, but no one liked to talk about it much. It wasn't too bad in the quarry, with its great walls of rock. If you didn't look up too much, and avoided the fourth side with its terribly huge views across the countryside, you could almost believe you were back in the Store. Even so, most of the older nomes preferred to stay in the sheds, or in the cozy gloom under the floorboards. That way you avoided this horrible *exposed* feeling, the dreadful sensation that the sky was watching you.

The children seemed to quite like the Outside, though. They weren't really used to anything else. They could just about remember the Store, but it didn't mean much to them. They belonged Outside. They were used to it. And the young men who went out hunting and gathering . . . well, young men liked to show how brave they were, didn't they? Especially in front of other young men. And young women.

Of course, Dorcas thought, as a scientist and rational-thinking nome, I know we weren't really intended to live under floorboards the whole time. It's just that, as a nome who is probably seven years old and feeling a bit creaky, I've got to admit I'd find it sort of comforting to have a few of the good old signs around the place. *Amazing Reductions*, perhaps, or just a little sign saying *Mammoth Sale Starts Tomorrow*. It wouldn't hurt, and I'm sure I'd feel happier. Which is, of course, totally ridiculous, when you look at it rationally.

It's just like Arnold Bros (est. 1905), he thought sadly. I'm pretty sure he doesn't exist in the way I was taught he did, when I was young. But when you saw things like *If You Do Not See What You Require, Please Ask* on the walls, you felt that everything was somehow All Right.

He thought: These are very wrong thoughts for a rational-thinking nome.

There was a crack in the woodwork by the door of the manager's office. Dorcas slipped into the familiar gloom under the floor and padded along until he found the switch.

He was rather proud of this idea. There was a big red bell on the outside wall of the office, presumably so that humans could hear the telephone ring when the quarry was noisy. Dorcas had changed the wiring so that he could make it ring whenever he liked.

He pressed the switch.

Nomes came running from all corners of the quarry. Dorcas waited as the underfloor space filled up and then dragged up an empty matchbox to stand on.

"The human has been back," he announced. "It didn't get in, but it'll keep trying."

"What about your wire?" said one of the nomes.

"I'm afraid there are such things as wire cutters."

"So much for your theory about, um, humans being intelligent. An *intelligent* human would know enough not to go, um, where it wasn't wanted," said Nisodemus sourly.

Dorcas liked to see eagerness in a young nome, but Nisodemus vibrated with a peculiarly hungry kind of eagerness that was unpleasant to see. He gave him as sharp a look as he dared.

"Humans out here might be different from the ones in the Store," he snapped. "Anyway—"

"Order must have sent it," said Nisodemus. "It's a judgment, um, on us!"

"None of that. It's just a human," said Dorcas. Nisodemus glared at him as he went on. "Now, we really should be sending some of the women and children to the—"

There was the sound of running feet outside, and the gate guards piled in through the crack.

"It's back! It's back!" panted Sacco. "The human's back!"

"All right, all right," said Dorcas. "Don't worry about it, it can't—"

"No! No! No!" yelled Sacco, jumping up and down. "It's got a pair of cutter things! It's cut the wire *and* the chain that holds the gates shut, and it—!"

They didn't hear the rest of it.

They didn't need to.

The sound of an engine coming closer said it all.

It grew so loud that the shed shook, and then it stopped suddenly, leaving a nasty kind of silence that was worse than the noise. There was the crump of a metal door slamming. Then the rattle and squeak of the shed door.

Then footsteps. The boards overhead buckled and dropped little clouds of dust as great thumping steps wandered around the office.

The nomes stood in absolute silence. They moved nothing except their eyes, but *they* moved in perfect time to the footsteps, marking the position, flicking backward and forward as the human crossed the room above. A baby started to whimper.

There was some clicking, and then the muffled sound of a human voice making its usual incomprehensible noises. This went on for some time.

Then the footsteps left the office again. The nomes could hear them crunching around outside, and then more noises. Nasty, clinking metal noises.

A small nome said, "Mum, I want the lavatory, Mum—"

"Shh!"

"I really *mean* it, Mum!"

"Will you be quiet!"

All the nomes stood stock-still as the noises went on around them. Well, nearly all. One small nome hopped from one foot to the other, going very red in the face.

Eventually the noise stopped. There was the thunk of a truck door closing, the growl of its engine, and the motor noise died away.

Dorcas said, very quietly, "I think perhaps we can relax now."

Hundreds of nomes breathed a sigh of relief.

"*Mum!*"

"Yes, all right, off you go."

And after the sigh of relief, the outbreak of babble. One voice rose above the rest.

"It was never like this in the Store!" said Nisodemus, climbing onto a half brick. "I ask you, fellow nomes, is this what we were led, um, to expect?"

There was a mumble chorus of "noes" and "yeses" as Nisodemus went on: "A year ago we were safe in the Store. Do you remember what it was like at Christmas Fayre? Do you remember what it was like in the Food Hall? Anyone remember, um, roast beef and turkey?"

There were one or two embarrassed cheers. Nisodemus looked triumphant. "And here we are at the same time of year—well, *they* tell us it's the same time of year," he said, sarcastically, "—and what we're expected to eat are knobbly things actually grown in *dirt*! Um. And the meat isn't proper meat at all, it's just dead animals cut up! Actual dead animals, actually cut up! Is this what you want your, um, children to get used to? Digging up their food? And *now* they tell us we might even have to go to some barn that hasn't even got proper floorboards for us to live under as Arnold Bros (est. 1905) intended. Where next, we ask ourselves? Out in a field somewhere? Um. And do you know what is the worst thing about all of this? I'll tell you." He pointed a finger at Dorcas. "The people who seem to be giving us all the orders now are the very people who, um, got us into this trouble in the first place!"

"Now just you hold on—" Dorcas began.

"You all know I'm right!" shouted Nisodemus. "Think about it, nomes! Why in the name of Arnold Bros (est. 1905) did we have to leave the Store?"

There were a few more vague cheers, and several arguments broke out among the audience.

"Don't be stupid," said Dorcas. "The Store was going to be demolished!"

"We don't know that!" shouted Nisodemus.

"Of course we do!" roared Dorcas. "Masklin and Gurder saw—"

*"And where are they now, eh?"*

"They've gone to—well, they've gone to—" Dorcas began. He wasn't much good at this, he knew. Why did it have to be him? He preferred messing around with wires and bolts and things. Bolts didn't keep shouting at you.

"Yes, they've gone!" Nisodemus lowered his voice to a sort of angry hiss. "Think about it, you nomes! Use your, um, brains! In the Store, we knew where we were, things worked, everything was exactly as Arnold Bros (est. 1905) decreed. And suddenly we're out here. Remember how you used to despise Outsiders? Well, the Outsiders are us! Um. And now it's all panic again, and it always will be—until we mend our ways and Arnold Bros (est. 1905) graciously allows us back into the Store as better, wiser nomes!"

"Let's just get this clear," said a nome. "Are you saying that the Abbot *lied* to us?"

"I'm not saying anything like that," said Nisodemus, sniffing. "I'm just presenting you with the facts. Um. That's all I'm doing."

"But, but, but the Abbot has gone to get help," said a lady nome uncertainly. "And, and, after all, I'm *sure* the Store was demolished.

I mean, we wouldn't have gone to all this trouble otherwise, would we? Er." She looked desperate.

"I know this, though," said the nome beside her. "Say what you like, but I don't fancy this old barn everyone's talking about. There's not even any electricity there."

"Yes, and it's in the middle of"—another nome began, and then lowered his voice—"you know. Things. You know what I'm talking about."

"Yeah," said an elderly nome. "*Things.* I've seen 'em. My lad took me blackberryin' a month or two back, up above the quarry, and I seen 'em."

"I don't mind seeing them a long way off," said the worried lady nome. "It's the thought of being in the middle of them that makes me come over all shaky."

They don't even like to say the words *open fields*, thought Dorcas. I know how they feel.

"It's snug enough here, I'll grant you," said the first nome, "but all this stuff you get outside, what d'you call it, begins with an N—"

"Nature?" said Dorcas weakly. Nisodemus was smiling madly, his eyes sparkling.

"That's right," said the nome. "Well, it's not natural. And there's a sight too much of it. 'S not like a proper world at all. You've only got to look at it. The floor's all rough, 'n' it should be flat. There's hardly any walls. All them little starry lights that comes out at night, well, they're not much help, are they? And now these humans go where they please, and there's no proper Regulations like there was in the Store."

"That's why Arnold Bros Established the Store in 1905," said Nisodemus. "A *proper* place for, um, nomes to live."

Dorcas gently grabbed Sacco's ear and pulled the young nome toward him.

"Do you know where Grimma is?" he whispered.

"Isn't she here?"

"I'm quite sure she isn't," said Dorcas. "She'd have had something very sharp to say by now if she was. She may have stayed in the school hole with the children when the bell went. It's just as well."

Nisodemus has got something on his mind, he thought. I'm not certain what it is, but it smells bad.

And it got worse as the day wore on, especially since it began to rain. A nasty, freezing sort of rain. Sleet, according to Granny Morkie. It was soggy, not really water but not quite ice. Rain with bones.

Somehow it seemed to find its way into places where ordinary rain hadn't managed to get. Dorcas organized younger nomes to digging drainage trenches and rigged up a few of the big light bulbs for heat. The older nomes sat hunched around them, sneezing and grumbling.

Granny Morkie did her best to cheer them up. Dorcas began to really wish the old woman wouldn't do that.

"This ain't nothing," she said. "I remember the Great Flood. Made our hole cave right in—we was cold and drenched for days!" She cackled and rocked backward and forward. "Like drownded rats, we was! Not a dry stitch on, you know, and no fire for a week. Talk about a laugh!"

The Store nomes stared at her and shivered.

"And you don't want to go worrying about crossing them open fields," she went on, conversationally. "Nine times out o' ten you don't get et by anything."

"Oh, dear," said a lady nome, faintly.

"Yes, I've been out in fields hundreds o' times. It's a doddle if you stay close to the hedge and keep your eyes open. You hardly ever have to run very much," said Granny.

No one's temper was improved when they learned that the Land Rover had parked right on the patch of ground they were going to plant things in. The nomes had spent ages during the summer hacking the hard ground into something resembling soil. They'd even planted seeds, which hadn't grown. Now there were two great ruts in it, and a new padlock and chain on the gate.

The sleet was already filling the ruts. Oil had leaked in and formed a rainbow sheen on the surface.

And all the time, Nisodemus was reminding people how much better it had been in the Store. They didn't really need much persuading. After all, it *had* been better. Much better.

I mean, thought Dorcas, we can keep warm and there's plenty of food, although there is a limit to the number of ways you can cook rabbit and potatoes. The trouble is, Masklin thought that once we got outside the Store, we'd all be digging and building and hunting and facing the future with strong chins and bright smiles. Some of the youngsters are doing well enough, I'll grant you. But us old 'uns are too set in our ways. It's all right for me, I like tinkering with things, I can be useful, but the rest of them, well . . . all they've really got to occupy themselves is grumbling, and they've become really *good* at that.

I wonder what Nisodemus's game is. He's too keen, if you ask me.

I wish Masklin would come back.

Even young Gurder wasn't too bad.

It's been three days now.

At a time like this, he knew he'd feel better if he went and looked at Big John.

# 6

*I. For in the Hill was a Dragon, from the days when the World was made.*
*II. But it was old and broken and dying.*
*III. And the Mark of the Dragon was on it.*
*IV. And the Mark was Big John.*

*From* The Book of Nome, Big John Chap. 1, v. I–IV

BIG JOHN.

Big John was his. His little secret. His *big* secret, really. No one else knew about Big John, not even Dorcas's assistants.

He'd been pottering around in the big old half-ruined sheds on the other side of the quarry, one day back in the summer. He hadn't really had any aim in mind, except perhaps the possibility of finding a useful bit of wire or something.

So he'd rummaged around in the shadows, straightened up, glanced above him *and there Big John was.*

*With his mouth open.*

It had been a terrible few seconds until Dorcas's eyes adjusted to the distance.

After that, he'd spent a lot of time with Big John, poking around, finding out about it. Or *him.* Big John was definitely a him. A terrible him, perhaps, and old and wounded, like a dragon that had come here for one last final sleep. Or perhaps it was like one of those big animals Grimma had showed him in a book once. Diner soars.

But Big John didn't grumble, and he didn't keep on asking Dorcas why he hadn't got around to inventing radio *yet*. Dorcas had spent many a peaceful hour getting to know Big John. He was someone to talk to. He was the best kind of person to talk to, in fact, because you didn't have to listen to him back.

Dorcas shook his head. There was no time for that sort of thing now. Everything was going wrong.

Instead, he went to find Grimma. She seemed to have her head screwed on right, even if she was a girl.

The school hole was under the floor of the old shed with *Canteen* on the door. It was Grimma's personal world. She'd invented schools for children, on the basis that since reading and writing were quite difficult, it was best to get them over with early.

The library was also kept there.

In those last hectic hours, the nomes had managed to rescue about thirty books from the Store. Some were very useful—*Gardening All the Year Round* was well thumbed, and Dorcas knew *Essential Theory for the Amateur Engineer* almost by heart—but some were, well, difficult, and not opened much.

Grimma was standing in front of one of these when he wandered in. She was biting her thumb, which she always did when she was concentrating.

He had to admire the way she read. Not only was Grimma the best reader among the nomes, she also had an amazing ability to understand what she was reading.

"Nisodemus is causing trouble," he said, sitting down on a bench.

"I know," said Grimma vaguely. "I've heard." She grabbed the edge of the page in both hands and turned it over with a grunt of effort.

"I don't know what he's got to gain," said Dorcas.

"Power," said Grimma. "We've got a *power vacuum*, you see."

"I don't think we have," said Dorcas uncertainly. "I've never seen one here. There were plenty in the Store. *Sixty-Nine Ninety-Five With Range Of Attachments For Round-The-House Cleanliness*," he added, remembering with a sigh the familiar signs.

"No, it's not a thing like that," said Grimma. "It's what you get when no one's in charge. I've been reading about them."

"*I'm* in charge, aren't I?" said Dorcas plaintively.

"No," said Grimma, "because no one really listens to you."

"Oh. Thank you very much."

"It's not your fault. People like Masklin and Angalo and Gurder can make people listen to them, but you don't seem to keep their attention."

"Oh."

"But you can make nuts and bolts listen to you. Not everyone can do that."

Dorcas thought about this. He would never have put it like that himself. Was it a compliment? He decided it probably was.

"When people are faced with lots of troubles and they don't know what to do, there's always someone ready to say anything, just to get some power," said Grimma.

"Never mind. When the others get back, I'm sure they'll sort it all out," said Dorcas, more cheerfully than he felt.

"Yes, they'll—" Grimma began, and then stopped. After a while Dorcas realized that her shoulders were shaking.

"Is there anything the matter?" he said.

"It's been more than three whole days!" sobbed Grimma. "*No one's* ever been away that long before! Something must have happened to them!"

"Er," said Dorcas, "well, they *were* going to look for Grandson Richard, 39, and we can't be sure that—"

"And I was so nasty to him before he went! I told him about the frogs and all he could think of was socks!"

Dorcas couldn't quite see how frogs had got involved. When he sat and talked to Big John, frogs were never dragged into the conversation.

"Er?" he said.

Grimma, in between sobs, told him about the frogs.

"And I'm sure he didn't even begin to understand what I meant," she mumbled. "And you won't either."

"Oh, I don't know," said Dorcas. "You mean that the world was once so simple, and suddenly it's full of amazingly interesting things that you'll never ever get to the end of as long as you live. Like biology. Or climatology. I mean, before all you Outsiders came, I was just tinkering with things and I really didn't know anything about the world."

He stared at his feet. "I'm still very ignorant," he said, "but at least I'm ignorant about really important things. Like what the sun is, and why it rains. That's what you're talking about."

She sniffed and smiled a bit, but not too much, because if there is one thing worse than someone who doesn't understand you, it's someone who understands perfectly, before you've had a chance to have a good pout about not being understood.

"The thing *is*," she said, "that he still thinks I'm the person he used to know when we all lived in the old hole in the bank. You know, running around. Cooking things. Bandaging up people when they'd been hur-hur-hur—"

"Now then, now then," said Dorcas. He was always at a loss when people acted like this. When machines went funny, you just oiled them or prodded them or, if nothing else worked, hit them with a hammer. Nomes didn't respond well to this treatment.

"Supposing he never comes back?" she said, dabbing at her eyes.

"Of course he'll come back," said Dorcas reassuringly. "What could have happened to him, after all?"

"He could have been eaten or run over or trodden on or blown away or fallen down a hole or trapped," said Grimma.

"Er, yes," said Dorcas. "Apart from that, I meant."

"But I shall pull myself together," said Grimma, sticking out her chin. "When he *does* come back, he won't be able to say, 'Oh, I see everything's gone to pieces while I've been away.'"

"Jolly good," said Dorcas. "That's the spirit. Keep yourself occupied, that's what I always say. What's the book called?"

"It's *A Treasury of Proverbs and Quotations*," said Grimma.

"Oh. Anything useful in it?"

"That," said Grimma distantly, "depends."

"Oh. What's 'Proverbs' mean?"

"Not sure. Some of them don't make much sense. Do you know, humans think the world was made by a sort of big human?"

"Get out!"

"It took a week."

"I expect it had some help, then," said Dorcas. "You know. With the heavy stuff." Dorcas thought of Big John. You could do a lot in a week, with Big John helping.

"No. All by himself, apparently."

"Hmm." Dorcas considered this. Certainly bits of the world were rough, and things like grass seemed simple enough. But from what he'd heard, it all broke down every year and had to be started up again in the spring, and—"I don't know," he said. "Only humans could believe something like that. There's a good few months' work, if I'm any judge."

Grimma turned the page. "Masklin used to believe—I mean, Masklin *believes*—that humans are much brighter than we think." She looked thoughtful. "I really wish we could study them properly," she said. "I'm sure we could learn a—"

For the second time, the alarm bell rang out across the quarry.

This time, the hand on the switch belonged to Nisodemus.

# 7

II. *And Nisodemus said, You are betrayed, People of the Store;*

III. *Falsely you were led into This Outside of Rain and Cold and Sleet and Humans and Order, and Yet it Will become Worse;*

IV. *For there will be Sleet and Snow, and Hunger in the Land;*

V. *And There will come Robins;*

VI. *Um.*

VII. *Yet those who brought you here, where are they Now?*

VIII. *They said, We go to seek Grandson Richard, 39, but tribulation abounds on every side and no help comes. You are betrayed into the hands of Winter.*

IX. *It is time to put aside things of the Outside. . . .*

*From* The Book of Nome, Complaints v. II–IX

"YES. WELL. THAT'S hard to do, isn't it?" said a nome uneasily. "I mean, we *are* Outside."

"But I have a *plan*," said Nisodemus.

"Ah," said the nomes in unison. Plans were the thing. Plans were what was needed. You knew where you were, with a plan.

Grimma and Dorcas, almost the last to arrive, sidled their way into the crowd. The old engineer was going to push his way to the front, but Grimma restrained him.

"Look at the others up there," she whispered.

There were quite a few nomes behind Nisodemus. Many of them Dorcas recognized as Stationeri, but there were a few others from some of the great departmental families. They weren't looking at Nisodemus as he spoke, but at the crowd. Their eyes flickered back and forth, as though they were searching for something.

"I don't like the look of this," said Grimma quietly. "The big families never used to get on too well with the Stationeri, so why are they up there now?"

"Grubby pieces of work, some of them," said Dorcas.

Some of the Stationeri had been particularly upset about common, everyday nomes learning to read. They said it gave people ideas, Dorcas gathered, which were not a good thing unless they were the right kind of ideas. And some of the great families hadn't been too happy about nomes being able to go where they pleased, without having to ask permission.

They're all up there, he thought. The nomes who haven't done so well since the Drive. They all lost a little power.

Nisodemus was explaining his plan.

As he listened, Dorcas's mouth slowly dropped open.

It was magnificent in its way, that plan. It was like a machine where every single bit was perfectly made, but which had been put together by a one-handed nome in the dark. It was crammed full of good ideas that you couldn't sensibly argue with, but they had been turned upside down. The trouble was, they were *still* ones you couldn't sensibly argue with, because the basically good idea was still in there somewhere. . . .

Nisodemus wanted to rebuild the Store.

The nomes stood in horrified admiration as the Stationeri explained that yes, Abbot Gurder *had* been right: When they left the Store, they had taken Arnold Bros (est. 1905) with them *inside their heads.* And if they could show him that they really *cared* about the Store, he would come out again and put a stop to all these problems and reestablish the Store here, in this green unpleasant land.

That was how it all arrived in Dorcas's head, anyway. He'd long ago decided that if you spent all your time listening to what people actually *said,* you'd never have time to work out what they *meant.*

But it wouldn't mean building the whole Store, said Nisodemus, his eyes shining like two bright black marbles. They could change the quarry in other ways. Go back to living in proper departments instead of any old how all over the place. Put up some signs. Get back to the Good Old Ways. Make Arnold Bros (est. 1905) feel at home. Build the Store *inside their heads.*

Nomes didn't often go mad. Dorcas vaguely recalled an elderly nome who had once decided that he was a teapot, but he'd changed his mind after a few days.

Nisodemus, though, had definitely been getting too much fresh air.

It was obvious that one or two other nomes thought so too.

"I don't quite see," said one of them, "how Arnold Bros (est. 1905) is going to stop these humans. No offense meant."

"Did humans interfere with us when we were in the Store?" demanded Nisodemus.

"Well, no, because—"

"Then trust in Arnold Bros (est. 1905)!"

"But that didn't stop the Store being demolished, did it?" said a voice. "When it came to it, you all trusted Masklin and Gurder and the Truck. And yourselves! Nisodemus is always telling you how clever you are. Try and *be* clever, then!"

Dorcas realized it was Grimma. He'd never seen anyone so angry.

She pushed her way through the apprehensive nomes until she was face to face, or at least, since Nisodemus was standing on something and she wasn't, face to chest. He was one of those people who liked standing on things.

"What will actually *happen*, then?" she shouted. "When you've built the Store, what will *happen*? Humans came into the Store, you know!"

Nisodemus's mouth opened and shut for a while. Then he said, "But they obeyed the Regulations! Yes! Um! That's what they did! And things were better then!"

She glared at him.

"You don't really think people are going to accept that, do you?" she said.

There was silence.

"You've got to admit," said an elderly nome, very slowly, "things *were* better then."

The nomes shuffled their feet.

That was all you could hear.

Just people, shuffling their feet.

"They just accepted it!" said Grimma. "Just like that! No one's bothered about the Council anymore! They just do what he tells them!"

Now she was in Dorcas's workspace under a bench in the old quarry garage. My little sanctuary, he always called it. My little nook. Bits of wire and tin were scattered everywhere. The wall was covered with scrawls done with a bit of pencil lead.

Dorcas sat and twiddled a bit of wire aimlessly.

"You're being hard on people," he said quietly. "You shouldn't yell at them like that. They've been through a lot. They get all confused if you shout at them. The Council was all right for when times were good—" He shrugged. "And without Masklin and Gurder and Angalo, well, it hardly seems worthwhile."

"But after all that's happened!" She waved her arms. "To act so *stupidly*, just because he's offered them—"

"A bit of comfort," said Dorcas. He shook his head. You couldn't explain things like this to people like Grimma. Nice girl, bright head on her, but she kept thinking that everyone else was as passionate about things as she was. All people *really* wanted, Dorcas considered, was to be left alone. The world was quite difficult enough as it was without people going around trying to make it better all the time.

Masklin had understood that. He knew the way to make people do what you wanted was to make them think it was their idea. If there was one thing that got right up a nome's nose, it was someone saying, "Here is a really sensible idea. Why are you too *stupid* to understand?"

It wasn't that people *were* stupid. It was just that people were people.

"Come on," he said wearily. "Let's go and see how the signs are getting on."

The whole of the floor of one of the big sheds had been turned over to the making of the signs. Or rather, the Signs. Another thing Nisodemus was good at was giving words capital letters. You could *hear* him doing it.

Dorcas had to admit that the Signs were a pretty good idea, though. He felt guilty about thinking this.

He'd thought that when Nisodemus had summoned him and asked if there was any paint in the quarry, only now the quarry was being called the New Store.

"Um," Dorcas had said, "there's some old cans. White and red, mainly. Under one of the benches. We might be able to lever the tops off."

"Then do it. It is very important. Um. We must make Signs," said the Stationeri.

"Signs. Right," said Dorcas. "Cheer the place up a bit, you mean?"

"No!"

"Sorry, sorry, I just thought—"

"Signs for the gate!"

Dorcas scratched his chin. "The gate?" he said.

"Humans obey Signs," said Nisodemus, calming down. "We know that. Did they not obey the Signs in the Store?"

"Most of 'em," agreed Dorcas. *Dogs and Strollers Must Be Carried* had always puzzled him. Lots of humans didn't carry either of them.

"Signs make humans do things," said Nisodemus, "or stop doing things. So get to work, good Dorcas. Signs. Um. Signs that say *No.*"

Dorcas had given this a lot of thought as teams of nomes sweated to pry the lids off the paint-streaked cans. They still had *The High Way Code* from the Truck, and there were plenty of signs in there. And he could remember some of the signs from the Store.

Then there was a stroke of luck. Normally the nomes stayed at floor level, but Dorcas had taken to sending his young assistants onto the big desk in the manager's office occasionally, where there were useful scraps of paper. Now he needed to work out what the signs should say.

Sacco and Nooty came back with the news.

They'd found more signs. A great big grubby notice pinned to the wall, covered with signs.

"Masses of them," Sacco said, coming back out of breath. "And you know what, sir? You know what? I read what it said on the notice, and it said, *Health And Safety At Work*, it said, *Obey These Signs*, it said, and it said, *They Are There For Your Protection.*"

"That's what it said?" said Dorcas.

*"For Your Protection,"* Sacco repeated.

"Can you get it down?"

"There's a coat hook next to it," said Nooty enthusiastically. "I bet we could sling a hook up and then pull it over toward the window, and then—"

"Yes, yes, you're good at that sort of thing," said Dorcas. Nooty could climb like a squirrel. "I expect Nisodemus will be very pleased," he added.

Nisodemus was, especially with the bit that said *For Your Protection*. It showed, he said, that, um, Arnold Bros (est. 1905) was on their side.

Every bit of board and rusty sheet of metal had to be pressed into service. The nomes went at it cheerfully enough, though, happy to be doing something.

Next morning the sun rose to see a variety of signs hanging, not always squarely, on the battered quarry gate.

They had been very thorough. The signs said: *No Etnry. Exit This Way. Dagner—Hard Hat Area. Blastign In Progres. All Trucks Report To Wieghbridge. Slipery When Wet. This Till Closed. Lift Out Fo Order. Beware Of Flaling Rocks. Road Floooded.*

And one that Dorcas had found in a book and was rather proud of: *Unexploded Bom.*

Just to be on the safe side, though, and without telling Nisodemus, he found some more chain and, in one of the greasy old toolboxes in Big John's shed, a padlock nearly as big as he was. It took four nomes to carry it.

The chain was massive. Some of the nomes found Dorcas painstakingly levering it along across the quarry floor, one link at a time. He didn't seem to want to tell them where he had found it.

The truck turned up around noon. The nomes waiting in the hedge by the side of the lane saw the driver get out, look at the signs, and . . .

No, that wasn't right. Humans couldn't do that sort of thing. It couldn't be true. But twenty nomes, peering out from the undergrowth, saw it happen.

The human disobeyed the signs.

Not only that, it pulled some of them off the gate and threw them away.

They watched in astonishment. Even *Unexploded Bom* was whirled into the bushes, nearly knocking young Sacco from his perch.

The new chain, though, caused the human a few problems. It rattled it once or twice, peered in through the wire mesh of the gate, stamped around for a bit, and then drove off.

The nomes in the bushes cheered, but not too happily.

If humans weren't going to do what was expected of them, nothing was right in the world.

"I reckon that's it," said Dorcas when they got back. "I don't like the idea any more than anyone else, but we've got to move. I know humans. That chain won't stop them if they really want to get in."

"I absolutely forbid anyone to leave!" said Nisodemus.

"But you see, metal can be cut through—" Dorcas began, in a reasonable tone of voice.

"Silence!" shouted Nisodemus. "It's your fault, you old fool! Um! You put the chain on the gate!"

"Well, you see, it was to stop the—pardon?" said Dorcas.

"If you *hadn't* put the chain on the gate, the signs *would* have stopped the human," said Nisodemus. "But you can't expect Arnold Bros (est. 1905) to help us if we show we don't trust him!"

"Um," said Dorcas. What he was thinking was: Mad. A mad nome. A dangerously mad nome. We're not talking about teapots here. He backed out of Nisodemus's presence and was glad to get out into the bitingly cold air.

Everything's going wrong, he thought. I was left in charge, and now it's all going wrong. We haven't got any proper plans, Masklin hasn't come back, and it's all going wrong.

If humans come into the quarry, they'll find us.

Something cold landed on his head. He brushed at it irritably.

I'll have a word with some of the younger nomes, he thought. Maybe going to the barn isn't such a bad idea; we could keep our eyes shut on the way. Or something.

Something else, cold and soft, settled on his neck.

Oh, why are people so *complicated*?

He looked up and realized that he couldn't see the other side of the quarry. The air was full of white specks that got thicker as he watched.

He stared at it in horror.

It was snowing.

# 8

*VII. And Grimma said, We have two choices.*
*VIII. We can run, or we can hide.*
*IX. And they said, Which shall we do?*
*X. She said, We shall Fight.*

*From* The Book of Nome, Quarries Chap. 3, v. VII–X

IT WASN'T MUCH of a fall, just one of those nippy little sprinklings that come early in the winter to make it absolutely clear that it is, well, the winter. That's what Granny Morkie said.

She'd never been very interested in the Council anyway. She liked to spend her time with the other old people, exchanging grumbles and, as she put it, cheerin' them up and takin' them out o' themselves.

She strutted around in the snow as if it belonged to her.

The other old nomes watched her in horrified silence.

"Course, this is nothing to some of 'em," she said. "I mind we've had snow, we couldn't walk round in it, we had to dig tunnels! Talk about a laugh!"

"Er, madam," said a very old nome, gravely, "does it always drop out of the sky like this?"

"Course! Sometimes it gets blown along by the wind. You get great big heaps!"

"We thought it—you see, on the cards—that is, in the Store—well, we thought it just sort of appeared on things," said the old nome. "In a rather jolly and festive way," he added, looking embarrassed.

They watched it pile up. Over the quarry, the clouds hung like overstuffed mattresses.

"At least it means we won't have to go to that horrid barn place," said a nome.

"That's right," said Granny Morkie. "You could catch your death, going out in this." She looked cheerful.

The old nomes grumbled among themselves and scanned the sky anxiously for the first signs of robins or reindeer.

The snow closed the quarry in. You couldn't see out across the fields.

Dorcas sat in his workshop and stared at the snow piling up against the grubby window, giving the shed a dull gray light.

"Well," he said quietly, "we wanted to be shut away. And now we are. We can't run away, and we can't hide. We ought to have gone when Masklin left."

He heard footsteps behind him. It was Grimma. She spent a long time near the gate these days, but the snow had driven her indoors at last.

"He wouldn't be able to come," she said. "Not in the snow."

"Yeah. Right," said Dorcas uncertainly.

"It's been eight days now."

"Yes. Quite a long time."

"What were you saying when I came in?" she said.

"I was just talking to myself. Does this snow stuff stay for a long time?"

"Granny says it does, sometimes. Weeks and weeks, she says."

"Oh."

"When the humans come back, they'll be here for good," said Grimma.

"Yes," said Dorcas sadly. "Yes, I think you're right."

"How many of us would be able to . . . you know . . . go on living here?"

"A couple of dozen, perhaps. If they don't eat much, and lie low during the day. There's no Food Hall, you see." He sighed. "And there won't be much hunting. Not with humans around the quarry the whole time. All the game up in the thickets will run away."

"But there's thousands of us!"

Dorcas shrugged.

"It's hard enough for me to walk through this snow," he said. "There's hundreds of older nomes who'll never do it. And young ones, come to that."

"So we've got to stay, just like Nisodemus wants," said Grimma.

"Yes. Stay and hope. Perhaps the snow will be gone. We could make a run for the thickets or something," he said vaguely.

"We could stay and fight," said Grimma.

Dorcas growled. "Oh, that's easy. We fight all the time. Bicker, bicker, bicker. That's nomish nature for you."

"I mean, fight the humans. Fight for the quarry."

There was a long pause.

Then Dorcas said, "What, us? Fight *humans*?"

"Yes."

"But they're *humans*!"

"Yes."

"But they're so much bigger than we are!" said Dorcas desperately.

"Then they'll make better targets," said Grimma, her eyes alight. "And we're faster than them, and smarter than them, and we know they exist—and we have," she added, "the element of surprise."

"The what?" said Dorcas, totally lost.

"The element of surprise. They don't know we're here," she explained.

He gave her a sidelong glance.

"You've been reading strange books again," he said.

"Well, it's better than sitting around wringing our hands and saying, 'Oh dear, oh dear, the humans are coming and we shall all be squashed.'"

"That's all very well," said Dorcas, "but what are you suggesting? Bashing them over the head would be really tricky—take it from me."

"Not their heads," said Grimma.

Dorcas stared at her. Fight humans? It was such a novel idea, it was hard to get your mind around it.

But . . . well, there was that book, wasn't there? The one Masklin had found in the Store, the one that had given him the idea for driving the Truck. What was it? *Gulliver's Travels*? And there'd been this picture of a human lying down, with what looked like nomes tying it up with hundreds of ropes. Not even the oldest nomes could remember it ever happening. It must have been a long time ago.

A snag struck him.

"Hang on a minute, he said. "If we start fighting humans . . ." His voice trailed off.

"Yes?" said Grimma impatiently.

"They'll start fighting us, won't they? I know they're not very bright, but it'll dawn on them that something's happening and they'll fight back. Retaliation, that's called."

"That's right," said Grimma. "And that's why it's vitally important we retaliate right at the start."

Dorcas thought about this. It seemed a logical idea.

"But only in self-defense," he said. "Only in self-defense. Even with humans. I don't want there to be any unnecessary suffering."

"I suppose so," she said.

"You really think we could fight humans?"

"Oh, yes."

"So . . . how?"

Grimma bit her lip. "Hmm," she said. "Young Sacco and his friends. Can you trust them?"

"They're keen lads. And lasses, one or two of them." He smiled. "Always ready for something new."

"Right. Then we shall need some nails. . . ."

"You've really been thinking hard, haven't you?" said Dorcas. He was almost in awe. Grimma was often bad-tempered. He thought perhaps it was because her mind worked very fast, sometimes, and she was impatient with people who weren't keeping up. But now she was furious. You could begin to feel sorry for any humans who got in her way.

"I've been doing a lot of reading," she said.

"Er, yes. Yes, I can see," said Dorcas. "But, er, I wonder if it wouldn't be more sensible to—"

"We're not going to run away again," she said flatly. "We shall fight them in the lane. We shall fight them at the gates. We shall fight them in the quarry. And we shall never surrender."

"What does 'surrender' mean?" said Dorcas, desperately.

"We don't know the meaning of surrender," said Grimma.

"Well, *I* don't," said Dorcas.

Grimma leaned against the wall.

"Do you want to hear something strange?" she said.

Dorcas thought about it.

"I don't mind," he said.

"There's books about us."

"Like *Gulliver*, you mean?"

"No. That was about a human. About us, I mean. Ordinary-sized people, like us. But wearing all green suits and with little knobbly stalks on their heads. Sometimes humans put out bowls of milk for us, and we do all the housework for them. And they have wings, like bees. That's what gets put in books about us. They call us pixies. It's in a book called *Fairy Tales for Little Folk*."

"I don't think the wings would work," said Dorcas doubtfully. "I don't think you could get the lifting power."

"And they think we live in mushrooms," Grimma finished.

"Hmm? Doesn't sound very practical to me," said Dorcas.

"And they think we repair shoes."

"That's a bit more like it," said Dorcas. "Good solid work."

"And the book said we paint the flowers to make them pretty colors," said Grimma.

Dorcas stared at her.

"Nah," he said eventually. "I've looked at the colors on flowers. They're definitely built-in."

"We're real," said Grimma. "We do real things. Why do you think that sort of thing goes in books?"

"Search me," said Dorcas. "I only read manuals. It's not a proper book, I've always said, unless it's got lists and part numbers in it."

"If ever humans do catch us, that's what we'll become," said Grimma. "Sweet little people, painting flowers. They won't let us be anything else. They'll turn us into *little* people." She sighed. "Do you ever get the feeling you'll never know everything you ought to know?"

"Oh, yes. All the time."

Grimma frowned.

"*I* know one thing," she said. "When Masklin comes back, he's going to have somewhere to come back to."

"Oh," said Dorcas.

"Oh," he repeated. "Oh. I see."


It was bitterly cold in Big John's lair. Other nomes never came in, because it was drafty and stank unpleasantly. That suited Dorcas fine.

He padded across the floor and under the huge tarpaulin where Big John lived. It took quite a long time to climb up to his preferred perch on the monster, even using the bits of wood and string he'd painstakingly tied to it . . . *him*.

He sat down and waited until he got his breath back.

"I only want to help people," he said quietly. "Like giving them things like electricity and making their lives better. But they never say thank you, you know. They wanted me to paint signs, so I painted signs. Now Grimma wants to fight humans. She's got lots of ideas out of books. I know she's doing it to help forget about Masklin, but no good will come of it, you mark my words. But if I don't help, things will only be even worse. I don't want *anybody* to get hurt. People like us can't be repaired as easily as people like you."

He drummed his heels on Big John's—what would it be?—Big John's neck, probably.

"It's all right for you," he said. "Sleeping quietly here all the time. Having a nice rest . . ."

He stared at Big John for a long while.

Then, very quietly, he said, "I wonder . . . ?"

Five long minutes went past. Dorcas appeared and reappeared among the complicated shadows, muttering to himself, saying things like "That's dead, that's no good, we need a new battery," and "Seems okay, nothing that a good clean couldn't put right," and "Hmm, not much in your tank. . . ."

Finally he walked out from under the dusty cloth and rubbed his hands together.

Everyone has a purpose in life, he thought. It's what keeps them going.

Nisodemus wants things to be as they were. Grimma wants Masklin back. And Masklin . . . no one knows exactly what it is that Masklin wants, except that it's very big.

But they all have this *purpose*. If you have a purpose in life, you can feel six inches tall.

And now I've found one.

Gosh.

The human came back later, and he did not come alone. There was the small truck and a much larger one, with the words *Blackbury Stone & Gravel Ltd* painted on the side. Its tires turned the thin coating of snow into glistening mud.

It jolted up the lane, slowed down as it came out into the space in front of the quarry gates, and stopped.

It wasn't a very good stop. The back of the vehicle swung around and nearly hit the hedge. The engine coughed into silence. There was the sound of hissing. And, very slowly, the truck sank.

Two humans got out. They walked around the truck, looking at each tire in turn.

"They're only flat at the bottom," whispered Grimma, in their hiding place in the bushes.

"Don't worry about it," whispered Dorcas. "The thing about tires is, the flat bit always sinks to the bottom. Amazing what you can do with a few nails, isn't it?"

The smaller truck came to a stop. Two humans got out of that, too, and joined the others. One of them was holding the longest pair of pliers Dorcas had ever seen. While the rest of the humans bent down by one of the flat tires, it strolled up to the gate, fiddled the teeth of the pliers onto the padlock, and squeezed.

It was an effort, even for a human. But there was a snap loud enough to be heard in the bushes, and then a long-drawn-out clinking noise as the chain fell away.

Dorcas groaned. He'd had great hopes for that chain. It was Big John's; at least, it was in a big yellow box bolted to part of Big John, so presumably it had belonged to Big John. But it had been the padlock that had broken, not the chain. Dorcas felt oddly proud about that.

"I don't understand it," Grimma muttered. "They can see they're not wanted, so why are they so stupid?"

"It's not as if there aren't masses of stone around," agreed Sacco.

The human pulled at the gate and swung it enough to allow itself inside.

"It's going to the manager's office," said Sacco. "It's going to make noises in the telephone."

"No, it's not," Dorcas prophesied.

"But it will be ringing up Order," said Sacco. "It'll be saying—in Human, I mean—it'll be saying, 'Some Of Our Wheels Have Gone Flat.'"

"No," said Dorcas, "it'll be saying, 'Why Doesn't the Telephone Work?'"

"Why doesn't the telephone work?" said Nooty.

"Because I know what wires to cut," said Dorcas. "Look, it's coming back out."

They watched it walk around the sheds. The snow had covered the nomes' sad attempts at cultivation. There were plenty of nome tracks, though, like little bird trails in the snow. The human didn't notice them. Humans hardly ever noticed anything.

"Trip wires," said Grimma.

"What?" said Dorcas.

"Trip wires. We should put trip wires down. The bigger they are," said Grimma, "the harder they fall."

"Not on us, I hope," said Dorcas.

"No. We could put more nails down," said Grimma.

"Good grief."

The humans clustered around the stricken truck. Then they appeared to reach a decision and walked back to the Land Rover. They got in. It couldn't go forward but reversed slowly down the lane, turned around in a field gateway, and headed back to the main road. The truck was left alone.

Dorcas breathed out.

"I was afraid one of them would stay," he said.

"They'll come back," said Grimma. "You've always said it. Humans'll come back and mend the wheels or whatever it is they do."

"Then we'd better get on with it," said Dorcas. "Come on, you lot."

He stood up and trotted toward the lane. To Sacco's surprise, Dorcas was whistling under his breath.

"Now, the important thing is to make sure they can't move it," he said as they ran to keep up. "If they can't move it, it means it stays blocking the lane. And if it stays blocking the lane, they can't get any more machines in."

"Good thinking," said Grimma in a slightly puzzled voice.

"We must immobilize it," said Dorcas. "We'll take out the battery first. No electricity, no go."

"Right," said Sacco.

"It's a big square thing," said Dorcas. "It'll need eight of you at least. Don't drop it, whatever you do."

"Why not?" said Grimma. "We want to smash it, don't we?"

"Er. Er. Er," said Dorcas urgently, like a motor trying to get started. "No, because, because, because it could be dangerous. Yes. Dangerous. Yes. Because, because, because of the acid and whatnot. You must take it out very carefully, and I'll find somewhere safe to put it. Yes. Very safe. Off you go now. Two nomes to a wrench."

They trotted off.

"What else can we do?" said Grimma.

"We'd better drain the fuel out," said Dorcas firmly, as they walked under the shadow of the truck. It was much smaller than the one that had brought them out of the Store, but still quite big enough. He wandered around until he was under the enormous swelling bulk of the fuel tank.

Four of the young nomes had dragged an empty can out of the bushes. Dorcas called them over and pointed to the tank above them.

"There'll be a nut on there somewhere," he said. "It'll be to let the fuel out. Get a wrench round it. Make sure the can's underneath it first!"

They nodded enthusiastically and got to work. Nomes are good climbers and remarkably strong for their size.

"And try not to spill any, please!" Dorcas shouted up after them.

"I don't see why that matters," said Grimma, behind him. "All we want to do is get it out of the truck. Where it *goes* doesn't matter, does it?"

She gave him another thoughtful look. Dorcas blinked back at her, his mind racing.

"Ah," he said. "Ah. Ah. Because. Becausebecausebecause. Ah. Because it's dangerous stuff. We don't want it polluting things, do we? Best to put it carefully in a can and—"

"Keep it safe?" said Grimma suspiciously.

"Right! Right," said Dorcas, who was starting to sweat. "Good idea. Now let's just go over here—"

There was sudden rush of air and a thump from right behind them. The truck's battery landed where they had been standing.

"Sorry, Dorcas," Sacco called down. "It was a lot heavier than we thought. It got away from us."

"You idiots!" Grimma shouted.

"Yes, you idiots!" shouted Dorcas. "You might have damaged it! Just you come down here right now and get it into the hedge, quickly!"

"He might have damaged *us*!" said Grimma.

"Yes. Yes. Yes, that's what I meant, of course," said Dorcas vaguely. "You wouldn't mind organizing them a bit, would you? They're good boys, but always a bit too enthusiastic, if you know what I mean."

He wandered off into the shadow, his head tilted backward.

"Well!" said Grimma. She looked around at Sacco and his friends, who were sheepishly climbing down again.

"Don't just stand there," she said. "Get it into the hedge. Hasn't Dorcas told you about using levers? Very important things. It's amazing what you can do with levers. We used them a lot on the Long Drive—"

Her voice trailed off. She turned and looked at the distant figure of Dorcas and her eyes narrowed.

*The cunning old devil is up to something,* she thought.

"Oh, just get on with it," she said, and ran after Dorcas.

He was standing under the truck's engine, staring intently into the masses of rusting pipework. As she came up, she distinctly heard him say, "Now, what else do we need?"

"How do you mean, need?" said Grimma quietly.

"Oh, to help Big—" Dorcas stopped and turned around slowly. "I mean, what else do we need to *do* to make the thing totally immobile," he said stonily. "That was what I meant."

"You're not planning to drive this truck, are you?" said Grimma.

"Don't be silly. Where'd we go? It'd never get across the fields to the barn."

"Well. All right, then."

"I just want to have a look around it. Time spent collecting knowledge is never wasted," said Dorcas primly. He stepped out into the light on the other side of the truck and looked up.

"Well, well," he said.

"What is it?"

"They left the door open. I suppose they thought it was all right because they'd be coming back."

Grimma followed his gaze. The truck's door *was* slightly ajar.

Dorcas looked around at the hedge behind them.

"Help me find a big enough stick," he said. "I reckon we could climb up there and have a look around."

"A look around? What do you expect to find?"

"You never know till you've looked," said Dorcas philosophically. He peered back underneath the truck.

"How are you all doing under there? We need a hand here."

Sacco staggered up. "We managed to get the battery thing behind the hedge," he said, "and the can's nearly full. Smells horrible. There's still lots coming out."

"Can you get the screw back in?"

"Nooty tried and she got all covered in yuk."

"Let it go on the road, then," said Dorcas.

"Hang on, you said that would be dangerous," said Grimma. "It's dangerous until you've filled the can up, is it, and then not dangerous at all?"

"Look, you wanted me to stop the truck, and I've stopped the truck," said Dorcas. "So just shut up, will you?"

Grimma looked at him in horror.

"What did you say?" she said.

Dorcas swallowed. Oh, well. If you were going to get shouted at, you might as well get your money's worth.

"I said just shut up," he said quietly. "I don't want to be rude, but you do go on at people. I'm sorry, but that's how it is. I'm helping you. I'm not asking you to help me, but at least you can let me get on with things instead of badgering me the whole time. And you never say please or thank you, either. People are a bit like machines," he added solemnly, while her face went redder, "and words like please and thank you are just like grease. They make them work better. Is that all right?" He turned to the boys, who were looking very embarrassed.

"Find a stick long enough to reach up to the cab," he said. "Please."

They fell over themselves to obey.

# 9

*III. The younger nomes spoke, saying, Would that we were the nomes our fathers were, to ride upon the Truck, and what was it like?*

*IV. And Dorcas said, It was scary.*

*V. That was what it was like.*

*From* The Book of Nome, Strange Frogs Chap. 2, v. III–V

IT WAS PRETTY much like the cab of the truck that had brought them from the Store. It brought back old memories.

"Wow!" said Sacco. "And we all drove one of these?"

"Seven hundred of us," said Dorcas proudly. "Your dad was one of them. You were in the back with your mothers. All you lads were."

"I'm not a lad," said Nooty.

"Sorry," said Dorcas. "Slip of the tongue. In my day girls stayed at home most of the time. Not that I've got anything at all against them getting out and about a bit now," he added hurriedly, not wanting another Grimma on his hands. "I'm not against that at all."

"I wish I'd been older on the Drive," said Nooty. "It must have been *amazing.*"

"It terrified the life out of me," said Dorcas.

The others wandered around the cab like tourists in a cathedral, gawking. Nooty tried to press a pedal.

"Amazing," she said, under her breath.

"Sacco, you get up there and take those keys out," said Dorcas. "The rest of you, no lollygagging. Those humans could be back any time. Nooty, stop making those *brrrm-brrrm* noises. I'm sure nice girls shouldn't make those kind of noises," he added lamely.

Sacco swarmed up the steering-wheel post and wrestled the keys out of the ignition while the rest of the boys poked around in the cab.

Grimma wasn't with them. She hadn't wanted to come up into the cab. She'd turned very quiet, in fact. She'd stayed down in the lane with a sullen look on her face.

But it had needed saying, Dorcas told himself.

He looked around the cab. Let's see, he thought . . . we've got the battery, we've got the fuel, was there anything else Big John needed?

"Come on, everyone," he called, "let's be getting out of here. Nooty, stop trying to *move* things all the time. It'd take all of you to shift the gear lever. Come on, before the humans come back."

He made his way to the door and heard a click behind him.

"I said come on—*What do you think you're doing?*"

The young nomes stared at him, wide-eyed.

"We're seeing if we can move the gear lever, Dorcas," said Nooty. "If you press this knob, you can—"

*"Don't press the knob! Don't press the knob!"*

The first inkling Grimma had that something was going wrong was a nasty little crunching sound and a change in the light.

The truck was moving. Not very fast, because the two front tires were flat. But the lane was steep. It was moving all right, and just because it had started off slowly didn't mean there wasn't something huge and unstoppable about it.

She stared at it in horror.

The lane ran between high banks all the way down to the big road—and the railway.

*"I said don't press it! Did I say press it? I said don't press it!"*

The terrified nomes stared at him, their open mouths a row of O's.

*"It's not the gear lever! It's the hand brake, you idiots!"*

Now they could all hear the crunching noise and feel the slight vibration.

"Er," said Sacco, his voice shaking, "what's a hand brake, Dorcas?"

"It keeps it stopped on hills and things! Don't just stand there! Help me push it back up!"

The cab was, very gently, beginning to sway from side to side. The truck was definitely moving. The hand brake wasn't. Dorcas heaved on it until blue and purple spots flashed in front of his eyes.

"I just gave the knob on the end a push!" Nooty babbled. "I only wanted to see what it did!"

"Yes, yes, all right . . ." Dorcas stared around. What he needed was a lever. What he needed was about fifty nomes. What he needed most of all was not to be here.

He staggered across the bouncing floor to the doorway and cautiously peered out. The hedge was moving past quite gently, as if it weren't in a particular hurry to get anywhere, but the surface of the lane already had a blurred look.

We could probably jump, he thought. And if we're lucky, we won't break anything. If we're even luckier, we'll avoid the wheels. How lucky do I feel, right at this minute?

Not very.

Sacco joined him.

"Perhaps if we took a good running jump—" he began.

There was a thump as the truck hit the bank, heeled over, and then bounced back onto the lane.

The nomes struggled to their feet.

"On the other hand, perhaps not a good idea," said Sacco. "What shall we do now, Dorcas?"

"Just hang on," said Dorcas. "I think the banks will keep it on the lane, and I suppose it'll just roll to a halt eventually." He sat down suddenly as the truck bounced off the bank again. "You wanted to know what a truck ride was like. Well, now you know."

There was another thump. The branch of a tree caught the door, swung it open, and then, with a terrible metallic noise, ripped it off.

"Was it like this?" shouted Nooty, above the noise. To Dorcas's amazement, now that the immediate danger was over, she seemed to be quite enjoying it. We're bringing up new nomes, he thought. They're not so scared of things as we were. They know about a bigger world.

He coughed.

"Well, apart from it being in the dark, and we could see where we were going, yes," he said. "I think we all ought to hang on to something. Just in case it gets bumpy."


The truck rolled down the lane and onto the main road. A car skidded into the hedge to avoid it; another truck managed to stop at the end of four long streaks of scorched rubber on the wet road.

None of the nomes in the cab noticed this at the time. All they felt was another thump as the truck bounced gently off the far side of the road and down the lane that ran toward the railway. Where, with red lights flashing, the barriers were coming down.

o   o   o

Sacco peered out of the stricken doorway.

"We've just crossed over a road," he said.

"Ah," said Dorcas.

"I just saw a car run into the back of another car, and a truck ended up going sideways," Sacco went on.

"Ah. Lucky we got over, then," said Dorcas. "There's some dangerous drivers around."

The gritty sound of the flat tires rolling over gravel gradually slowed down. There was the snap of something breaking behind the truck, a couple of bumps, and then another thump that brought them to a halt.

They heard a low, booming noise.

Nomes hear things differently from humans, and the shrill clanging of the grade crossing's warning alarms sounded, to them, like the mournful tolling of an ancient bell.

"We've stopped," said Dorcas. He thought: We could have pressed the brake pedal. We could have looked for something to press it with and pressed it. I must be getting too old. Oh, well. "Come on, no hanging around. We can jump out. You youngsters can, anyway."

"Why? What are you going to do?" said Sacco.

"I'm going to wait until you've all jumped out, and then I'm going to tell you to catch me," said Dorcas pleasantly. "I'm not as young as I was. Now, off you go."

They got down awkwardly, hanging on to the edge of the sill and dropping on to the road.

Dorcas lowered himself gingerly onto the brink and sat with his legs dangling over the drop.

It looked like a long way down.

Below him, Nooty prodded Sacco respectfully on the arm.

"Er. Sacco," she said, nervously.

"What is it?"

"Look at that metal rail thing over there."

"Well, what about it?"

"There's another one over *there*," said Nooty, pointing.

"Yes, I can see," said Sacco testily. "What about them? They're not doing anything."

"We're right in between them," said Nooty. "I just thought I should, you know, point it out. And there's that bell thing ringing."

"Yes, I can hear it," said Sacco irritably. "I wish it would stop."

"I just wondered why it was."

Sacco shrugged. "Who knows why anything happens?" he said. "Come *on*, Dorcas. *Please*. We haven't got all day."

"I'm just composing myself," said Dorcas quietly.

Nooty wandered miserably away from the group and looked down at one of the rails. It was bright and shiny.

And it seemed to be singing.

She bent closer. Yes, it was certainly making a faint humming sound. Which was odd. Bits of metal didn't normally make any noise at all. Not by themselves, anyway.

She looked up at the truck.

As she stared at the truck stuck between the flashing lights and the shiny rails, the world seemed to change slightly and a horrible idea formed in her head.

"Sacco!" she quavered. "Sacco, we're right on the railway line, Sacco!"

Something a long way off made a deep, mournful noise. *Two*

deep, mournful noises, one a little deeper and more mournful than the other.

*Dee*-dah.

*Dee*-dah.

From the gateway of the quarry, Grimma had a good view of the road all the way to the airport. She saw the train, and the truck.

The train had seen the truck too. It suddenly started to make the long-drawn-out screaming noise of bits of metal in distress. By the time it actually *hit* the thing, it seemed to be going quite slowly. It even managed to stay on the rails.

Bits of truck spun away in every direction, like a firework.

# 10

*I. Nisodemus said unto them, Do you doubt that I can
stop the power of Order?*
*II. And they said, Um . . .*

*From* The Book of Nome, Chases v. I–II

OTHER NOMES CAME running across the quarry floor, with Nisodemus
in the lead, and piled up in a crowd around the gate.

"What happened? What happened?"

"I saw everything," said a middle-aged nome. "I was on watch,
and I saw Dorcas and some of the boys go into the truck. And then
it rolled away down the hill and then it went over the road and then
it stopped right on the railway and then . . . and then . . ."

"I forbade all meddling with these infernal machines," said
Nisodemus. "And I said we were to stop, um, putting people on
watch, didn't I? The watch Arnold Bros (est. 1905) maintains should
be enough for humble nomes!"

"Yes . . . well . . . Dorcas said he thought it wouldn't do any harm
if we gave him a hand, sort of thing," said the nome nervously. "And
he said—"

"I gave *orders!*" screamed Nisodemus. "You will all obey me! Did
I not stop the truck by the power of Arnold Bros (est. 1905)?"

"No," said Grimma quietly. "No, you didn't. Dorcas did. He put nails down in the road."

There was a huge, horrified silence. In the middle of it Nisodemus went slowly white with rage.

"Liar!" he shouted.

"No," said Grimma, meekly. "He really did. He really did all sorts of things to help us, and we never said please or thank you and now he's dead."

There were sirens along the road below and a lot of excitement around the stationary train. Blue lights flashed.

The nomes shifted uneasily. One of them said, "He's not really dead, though, is he? Not *really*. I expect he jumped out at the last minute. A clever person like him."

Grimma looked helplessly at the crowd. She saw Nooty's parents in the crowd. They were a quiet, patient couple. She'd hardly ever spoken to them. Now their faces were gray and lined with worry. She gave in.

"Yes," she said. "Perhaps they got out."

"Bound to have done," muttered another nome, trying to look cheerful. "Dorcas isn't the type to go around dying all the time. Not when we need him."

Grimma nodded.

"And now," she went on, "I think even humans will be wondering what's happening here. They'll soon work out where the truck came from, and they'll be coming up here, and I think they might be very angry."

But Nisodemus licked his lips and said, "We won't be afraid. We will confront them and defy them. Um. We will treat them with scorn. We don't need Dorcas: We need nothing except faith in Arnold Bros (est. 1905). Nails, indeed!"

· 277 ·

"If you start out now," said Grimma, "you should all be able to get to the barn, even through what's left of the snow. I don't think the quarry will be a very safe place to be, quite soon."

There was something about the way she said it that made people nervous. Normally Grimma shouted or argued, but this time she spoke quite calmly. It wasn't like her at all.

"Go on," she said. "You'll have to start now. You'll have to take as much food and stuff as possible. Go on."

"No!" shouted Nisodemus. "No one is to move! Do you think Arnold Bros (est. 1905) will let you down? Um, I will protect you from the humans!"

Down below, a car with a flashing blue light on top of it pulled away from the excitement around the train, crossed the main road, and headed slowly up the lane.

"I will call upon the power of Arnold Bros (est. 1905) to *smite* the humans!" shouted Nisodemus.

The nomes looked unhappy. Arnold Bros (est. 1905) had never smitten anyone in the Store. He'd just founded it, and seen to it that nomes lived comfortable and not very strenuous lives in it, and apart from putting the signs on the walls hadn't really interfered very much. Now, suddenly, he was going around being angry and upset all the time, and smiting people. It was very bewildering.

"I will stand here and defy the dreadful minions of Order!" Nisodemus yelled. "I will teach them a lesson they won't forget."

The rest of the nomes said nothing. If Nisodemus wanted to stand in front of a car, then that was all right by them.

"We will *all* defy them!" he shouted.

"Er . . . what?" said a nome.

"Brothers, let us stand here resolute and show Order that we are united in opposition! Um. If you truly believe in Arnold Bros (est. 1905), no harm will come to you!"

The flashing light was well up the lane now. Soon it would be crossing the wide patch in front of the gates, where the great chain hung uselessly from the broken padlock.

Grimma opened her mouth to say: Don't be stupid, you idiots, Arnold Bros (est. 1905) doesn't want you to stand in front of cars. I've *seen* what happens to nomes who stand in front of cars. Your relatives have to bury you in an envelope.

She was about to say all that and decided not to. For months and months people had been telling nomes what to do. Perhaps it was time to stop.

She saw a number of worried faces in the crowd turn toward her, and someone said, "What shall we *do*, Grimma?"

"Yeah," said another nome, "she's a Driver, they always know what to do."

She smiled at them. It wasn't a very happy smile.

"Do whatever you think best," she said.

There was a chorus of indrawn breaths.

"Well, yeah," said a nome, "but, well, Nisodemus says we can stop this thing just by believing we can. Is that true, or what?"

"I don't know," said Grimma. "You might be able to. I know I can't."

She turned and walked off quickly toward the sheds.

"Stand firm," commanded Nisodemus. He hadn't been listening to the worried discussions behind him. Perhaps he wasn't able to listen to anything now, except for little voices deep inside his head.

"'Do whatever you think best,'" muttered a nome. "What sort of help is that?"

They stood in their hundreds, watching the car coming closer. Nisodemus stood slightly ahead of the crowd, holding his hands in the air.

The only sound was the crunch of tires on gravel.

If a bird had looked down on the quarry in the next few seconds, it would have been amazed.

Well, probably it wouldn't. Birds are somewhat stupid creatures and have a hard enough job even coming to terms with the ordinary, let alone the extraordinary. But if it had been an unusually intelligent bird—an escaped mynah bird, perhaps, or a parrot that had been blown several thousand miles off course by very strong winds—it would have thought:

Oh. There is a wide hole in the hill, with little old rusty sheds in it, and a fence in front of it.

And there is a car with a blue light on the top of it just going through a gate in the fence.

And there are little black dots on the ground ahead of it. One dot standing very still, right in the path of the thing, and the others, the others—

Breaking away and running. Running for their lives.

They never did find Nisodemus again, even though a party of strong-stomached nomes went back much later and searched through the ruts and the mud.

So a rumor grew up that perhaps, at the last minute, he had jumped up and caught hold of part of the car and had clambered onto it somehow. And then he'd waited there, too ashamed to face other nomes, until the car went back to wherever it came from, and had got off, and was living out the rest of his life quietly and without any fuss. He had been a good nome in his way, they said. Whatever else you might say about him, he believed in things, and he did what he thought was proper, so it was only right that he'd been spared and was still out there in the world, somewhere.

This was what they told one another, and what they wrote down in *The Book of Nome.*

What nomes might have thought in those private moments before they went to sleep . . . well, that was private.

Humans clomped slowly around the train and what remained of the truck. Lots of other vehicles had turned up at what was, for humans, great speed. Many of them had blue lights on top.

The nomes had learned to be worried by things with flashing blue lights on top.

The Land Rover belonging to the quarry men was there as well. One of the quarry men was pointing to the wrecked truck and shouting at the others. He'd opened the smashed engine compartment and was pointing to where the battery wasn't.

Beside the railway, the breeze rustled the long grass. And some of the long grass rustled without any wind at all.

Dorcas had been right. Where humans went once, they went again. The quarry belonged to them. Three trucks were parked outside the sheds, and humans were everywhere. Some were repairing the fence. Some were taking boxes and drums off the trucks. One was even in the manager's office, tidying up.

The nomes crouched where they could, listening fearfully to the sounds above them. There weren't many hiding places for two thousand nomes, small though they were.

It was a very long day. In the shadows under some of the sheds, in the darkness behind crates, in some cases even on the dusty rafters under the tin roofs, the nomes passed it as best they could.

There were escapes so narrow, a postcard couldn't have got through them. Old Munby Confectioneri and most of his family were left blinking in the light when a human moved the tatty old box they were cowering behind. Only a quick dash to the shelter of a stack of cans saved them. And, of course, the fact that humans never really looked hard at what they were doing.

That wasn't the worst bit, though.

The worst bit was much worse.

The nomes sat in the noisy darkness, not daring even to speak, and felt their world vanishing. Not because the humans hated nomes. *Because they didn't notice them.*

There was Dorcas's electricity, for example. He'd spent a long time twisting bits of wire together and finding a safe way to steal electricity from the fuse box. A human pulled them out without thinking, twiddled inside with a screwdriver, and put up a new box with a lock on it. Then it mended the telephone.

The Store nomes needed electricity. They couldn't remember a time when they had been without it. It was a natural thing, like air. And now theirs was a world of endless darkness.

And still the terror went on. The rough floorboards shook overhead, raining dust and splinters. Metal drums boomed like thunder. There was the continual sound of hammering. The humans were back, and they meant to stay.

They did go eventually, though. When the daylight drained from the winter sky, like steel growing cold, some of the humans got into their vehicles and drove off down the lane.

They did one puzzling thing before they left. Nomes had to scramble over one another to get out of the way when one of the floorboards in the manager's office was pulled up. A huge hand reached down and put a little tray on the packed earth under the floor. Then the darkness came back as the board was replaced.

The nomes sat in the gloom and wondered why on earth the humans, after a day like this, were giving them food.

The tray was piled with flour. It wasn't much, compared to Store food, but to nomes who had spent all day hungry and miserable, it smelled *good*.

A couple of younger ones crawled closer. It was the most tantalizing smell.

One of them took a handful of the stuff.

"Don't eat it!"

Grimma pushed her way through the packed bodies.

"But it smells so—" one of the nomes warbled.

"Have you ever smelled anything like it before?" she said.

"Well, no—"

"So you don't *know* it's good to eat, do you? Listen. I know about stuff like this. Where we—where I used to live, in the hole . . . there was a place along the road where humans came to eat, and sometimes we'd find stuff like this among the trash bins at the back. It kills you if you eat it!"

The nomes stared at the innocent little tray. Food that killed you? That didn't make sense.

"I remember there was some canned meat we had once in the Store," said an elderly nome. "Gave us all a nasty upset, I remember." He gave Grimma a hopeful look.

She shook her head. "This isn't like that," she said. "We used to find dead rats near it. They didn't die in a very nice way," she added, shuddering at the memory.

"Oh."

The nomes stared at the tray again. And there was a thump from overhead.

There was still a human in the quarry.

It was sitting in the old swivel chair in the manager's office, reading a paper.

From a knothole near the floor the nomes watched carefully. There were huge boots, great sweeps of trouser, a mountain range of jacket and, far above, the distant gleam of electric light on a bald head.

After a long while, the human put the paper down and reached over to the desk by its side. The watching nomes gazed at a pack of sandwiches bigger than they were, and a thermos flask that steamed when it was opened and filled the hut with the smell of coffee.

They climbed back down and reported to Grimma. She was sitting by the food tray and had ordered six of the older and more sensible nomes to stand guard around it to keep children away.

"He's not doing anything," she was told. "He's just sitting there. We saw him look out of the window once or twice."

"Then he'll be here all night," said Grimma. "I expect the humans are wondering who's causing all this trouble."

"What shall we *do?*"

Grimma sat with her chin on her hands.

"There's those big old tumbledown sheds across the quarry," she said, at last. "We could go there."

"Dorcas said—Dorcas used to say it was very dangerous in the old sheds," said a nome cautiously. "Because of all the old junk and stuff. Very dangerous, he said."

"More dangerous than here?" said Grimma, with just a trace of her old sarcasm.

"You've got a point."

"Please, m'm."

It was one of the younger female nomes. They held Grimma in awe because of the way she shouted at the men and read better than anyone. This one held a baby in her arms and kept curtseying every time she finished a sentence.

"What is it, Sorrit?" said Grimma.

"Please, m'm, some of the children are very hungry, m'm. There isn't anything wholesome to eat down here, you see." She gave Grimma a pleading look.

Grimma nodded. The stores were under the other sheds, what was left of them. The main potato store had been found by some of the humans, which was perhaps why the poison had been put down. Anyway, they couldn't light a fire and there was no meat. No one had been doing any proper hunting for *days*, because Arnold Bros (est. 1905) would provide, according to Nisodemus.

"As soon as it gets light, I think all the hunters we can spare should go out," said Grimma.

They considered this. The dawn was a long way away. To a nome, a night was as long as three whole days. . . .

"There's plenty of snow," said a nome. "That means we've got water."

"*We* might be able to manage without food, but the children won't," said Grimma.

"And the old people, too," said a nome. "It's going to freeze again tonight. We haven't got the electric and we can't light a fire outside."

They sat staring glumly at the dirt.

What Grimma was thinking was: They're not bickering. They're not grumbling. Things are so serious, they're actually not arguing and blaming each other.

"All right," she said, "and what do *you* all think we should do?"

# 11

*I. We will come out of the woodwork.*
*II. We will come out of the floor.*
*III. They will wish they had never seen us.*

*From* The Book of Nome, Humans v. I–III

THE HUMAN LOWERED its newspaper and listened.

There was a rustling in the walls. There was a scratching under the floor.

Its eyes swiveled to the table beside it.

A group of small creatures was dragging its packet of sandwiches across the tabletop. It blinked.

Then it roared and tried to stand up, and it wasn't until it was nearly upright that it found that its feet were tied very firmly to the legs of its chair.

It crashed forward. A crowd of tiny creatures, moving so fast that it could hardly see them, charged out from under the table and wrapped a length of old electrical wire around its outflung arms. Within seconds it was trussed awkwardly, but very firmly, between the furniture.

They saw its great eyes roll. It opened its mouth and mooed at them. Teeth like yellow plates clashed at them.

The wire held.

The sandwiches turned out to be cheese and chutney, and the thermos, once they got the top off, was full of coffee. "Store food," the nomes told one another. "Good Store food, like we used to know."

They poured into the room from every crack and mousehole. There was an electric heater by the table, and they sat in solemn rows in front of its glowing red bar, or wandered around the cramped office.

"We done it," they said, "just like that *Gullible Travels*. The bigger they come, the harder they fall!"

There was a school of thought that said they should kill the human, whose mad eyes followed them around the floor. This was when they found the box.

It was on one of the shelves. It was yellow. It had a picture of a very unhappy-looking rat on the front. It had the word SCRAMOFF in big red lettering, too. On the back . . .

Grimma's forehead wrinkled as she tried to read the smaller words on the back.

"It says, 'They Take A Bite, But They Don't Come Back For More!'" she said. "And apparently it contains Polydichloromethylinlon-4, whatever that is. 'Clears Outbuildings Of Troublesome . . .'" She paused.

"Troublesome what?" said the listening nomes. "Troublesome what?"

Grimma lowered her voice.

"It says, 'Clears Outbuildings Of Troublesome *Vermin* In A Trice!'" she said. "It's poison. It's the stuff they put under the floor."

The silence that followed this was black with rage. The nomes had raised quite a lot of children in the quarry. They had very firm views about poison.

"We should make the human eat it," said one of them. "Fill up its mouth with Polyputheketlon or whatever it is. Troublesome *vermin*."

"I think they think we're rats," said Grimma.

"And that would be all right, would it?" said a nome with withering sarcasm. "Rats are okay. We've never had any trouble with rats. No call to go around giving them poisoned food."

In fact the nomes got on rather well with the local rats, probably because their leader was Bobo, who had been a pet of Angalo's when they lived in the Store. The two species treated each other with the distant friendliness of creatures who could, at a pinch, eat one another but had decided not to.

"Yeah, the rats'd thank us for getting rid of a human," he went on.

"No," said Grimma. "No. I don't think we should do that. Masklin always said that they're nearly as intelligent as we are. You can't go around poisoning intelligent creatures."

"*They* tried."

"They're not nomes. They don't know how to behave," said Grimma. "Anyway, be sensible. More humans will come along in the morning. If they find a dead human, there'll be a lot of trouble."

That was a point. But they had shown themselves to a human. No nome could remember it ever being done before. They'd had to do it, or starve and freeze, but there was no knowing where it would end. *How* it would end was a bit more certain. It would probably end badly.

"Go and put it somewhere where the rats can't get it," said Grimma.

"I reckon we should just give it a taste—" said the nome.

"No! Just take the stuff away. We'll stay here the rest of the night and then move out before it's light."

"Well, all right. If you say so. I just hope we're not sorry about it later, that's all." The nomes carried the dreadful box away.

Grimma wandered over to where the human lay. It was well trussed up by now, and couldn't move a finger. It looked just like the picture of Gullible or whoever he was, except the nomes had got hold of what the nomes in those days had never heard of, which was lots of electric wire. It was a lot tougher than rope. And they were a lot angrier. Gullible hadn't been driving a great big truck around the place and putting down rat poison.

They'd gone through its pockets and piled up the contents in a heap. There'd been a big square of white cloth among them, which a group of nomes had managed to tie around the human's mouth after its mooing got on everyone's nerves.

Now they stood around eating fragments of sandwich and watching its eyes.

Humans can't understand nomes. Their voices are too fast and too high, like a bat squeak. It was probably just as well.

"*I* say we should find something sharp and stick it into it," said a nome. "In all the soft bits."

"There's things we could do with matches," said a lady nome, to Grimma's surprise.

"And nails," said a middle-aged nome.

The human growled behind its gag and strained at the wires.

"We could pull all its hair out," said the lady nome. "And then we could—"

"Do it, then," said Grimma, coming up behind them.

They turned.

"What?"

"Do it, if you want to," said Grimma. "There it is, right in front of you. Do what you like."

"What, *me*?" The lady nome drew back. "I didn't . . . not *me*. I didn't mean *me*. I meant . . . well, us. Nomekind."

"There you are, then," said Grimma. "And nomekind is only nomes. Besides, it's wrong to hurt prisoners. I read it in a book. It's called the *Geneva Convention*. When you've got people at your mercy, you shouldn't hurt them."

"Seems like the ideal time to me," said a nome. "Hit them when they can't hit back, that's what I say. Anyway, it's not as if humans are the same as real people." But he shuffled backward anyway.

"Funny, though, when you see their faces close to," said the lady nome, putting her head on one side. "They look a lot like us. Only bigger."

One of the nomes peered into the human's frightened eyes.

"Hasn't it got a hairy nose?" he said. "And ears, too."

"Quite gross," said the lady.

"You could almost feel sorry for them, with great big noses like that."

Grimma stared into the human's eyes. I wonder, she thought. They're bigger than us, so there must be room for brains. And they've got great big eyes. Surely they must have seen us once? Masklin said we've been here for thousands of years. In all that time, humans must have seen us.

They must have known we were real people. But in their minds they turned us into pixies. Perhaps they didn't want to have to share the world.

The human was definitely looking at her.

Could we share? she thought. They live in a big long slow world and we live in a small short fast one, and we can't understand each other. They can't even see us unless we stand still like I'm standing now. We move too quickly for them. They don't think we exist.

She stared up into the big frightened eyes.

We've never tried to—what was the word?—*communicate* with them before. Not properly. Not as though they were real people, thinking real thoughts. How can we tell them we're really real and really here?

But perhaps when you're lying down on the floor and tied up by little people you can hardly see and don't believe in, that's not the best time to start communicating. Perhaps we should try it another time. Not signs, not shouting, just trying to get them to understand us.

Wouldn't it be amazing if we could? They could do the big slow jobs for us and we could do—oh, little fast things. Fiddly things that those great fingers can't do . . . but not paint flowers or mend their shoes . . .

"Grimma? You ought to see this, Grimma," said a voice behind her.

The nomes were clustered around a white heap on the floor.

Oh, yes. The human had been looking at one of those big sheets of paper . . .

The nomes had spread it out flat on the floor. It looked a lot like the first one they'd seen, except this one was called READ IT FIRST IN YOUR SOARAWAY BLACKBURY EVENING POST & GAZETTE. It had more of the great blocky writing, some of the letters nearly as big as a nome's head.

Grimma shook her own head as she tried to make sense of it. She could understand the books quite well, she considered, but the papers seemed to use a different language. It was full of PROBES and

SHOCKS and fuzzy pictures of smiling humans shaking hands with other humans (TABLERS RAISE £455 FOR HOSPITAL APPEAL). It wasn't difficult to work out what each word meant, but when they were put together they either didn't mean anything at all or something quite unbelievable (CIVIC CENTER RATES RUMPUS).

"No, this is the bit," said one of the nomes, "this page here. Look, some of the words, they're the same as last time, look! *It's about Grandson Richard, 39!*"

Grimma ran the length of a story about somebody slamming somebody's plan for something.

There was indeed a fuzzy picture of Grandson Richard, 39, under the words: "TV-IN-THE-SKY HITCH."

She knelt down and stared at the smaller words below it.

"Read it aloud!" they said.

"'Richard Arnold, the Blackbury-based chairman of the Arnco Group, said in Florida today,'" she said, "'that scientists are still trying to r . . . r . . . regain control of Arnsat 1, the multimillion-pound com . . . communications sat . . . ellite—'"

The nomes looked at one another.

"Multimillion pound," they said. "That's really heavy."

"'Hopes were high after yesterday's s . . . s . . . successful l . . . lunch in Florida,'" Grimma read uncertainly, "'that Arnsat 1 would begin test tr . . . tr . . . transmissions today. Instead, it is s . . . sending a stream of strange sig . . . signals. 'It's like some sort of code,' said Richard, 39—'"

There was an appreciative murmur from the listeners.

"'It's as if it had a mind of its own,'" Grimma read.

There was more stuff about "teething troubles," whatever that meant, but Grimma didn't bother to read it.

She remembered the way Masklin had talked about the stars, and why they stayed up. And there was the Thing. He'd taken it with him. The Thing could talk to electricity, couldn't it? It could listen to the electricity in wires, and the stuff in the air that Dorcas called "radio." If anything could send strange signals, the Thing could. I may go even farther than the Long Drive, he'd said.

"They're alive," she said, to no one in particular. "Masklin and Gurder and Angalo. They got to the Florida place, and they're alive."

She remembered him trying to tell her, sometimes, about the sky and the Thing and where nomes first came from, and she'd never really understood, any more than he'd understood about the little frogs.

"They're alive," she repeated. "I know they are. I don't know exactly how or where, but they've got some sort of plan, and they're alive."

The nomes exchanged meaningful glances, and the kind of meaning they were full of was: She's fooling herself, but it'd take a braver nome than me to tell her.

Granny Morkie patted her gently on the shoulder.

"Yes, yes," she said soothingly. "And thank goodness they had a successful lunch. I bet they needed to get some food inside of them. And if I was you, my girl, I'd get some sleep."

Grimma dreamed.

It was a confused dream. Dreams nearly always are. They don't come neatly packaged. She dreamed of loud noises and flashing lights. And eyes.

Little, yellow eyes. And Masklin, standing on a branch, climbing through leaves, peering down at little yellow eyes.

*I'm seeing what he's doing now,* she thought. *He's alive. I always knew he was, of course. But Outer Space has got more leaves than I thought. Or perhaps none of it is real and I'm just dreaming. . . .*

Then someone woke her up.

It's never wise to speculate about the meaning of dreams, so she didn't.

It snowed again in the night, on an icy wind. Some of the nomes scouted around the sheds and came back with a few vegetables that had been missed, but it was a pitifully small amount. The tied-up human went to sleep after a while, and snored like someone sawing a thick log with a thin saw.

"The others will come looking for it in the morning," Grimma warned. "We mustn't be here then. Perhaps we should—"

She stopped. They all listened.

Something was moving around under the floorboards.

"Is anyone still down there?" Grimma whispered.

The nomes near her shook their heads. No one wanted to be in the chilly space under the floor when there was the warmth and light of the office for the having.

"And it can't be rats," she said.

Then someone called out, in that half-loud, half-soft way of someone who wants to make themselves heard while at the same time remaining as quiet as possible.

It turned out to be Sacco.

They dragged aside the floorboard the humans had loosened and helped him up. He was covered in mud and swaying with exhaustion.

"I couldn't find anyone!" he gasped. "I looked everywhere and couldn't find anyone and we saw the trucks come here and I saw the lights on and I thought the humans were still here and I came in and I heard your voices and you've got to come because it's Dorcas!"

"He's alive?" said Grimma.

"If he isn't, he can swear pretty well for a dead person," said Sacco, sagging to the floor.

"We thought you were all de—" Grimma began.

"We're all fine except for Dorcas. He hurt himself jumping out of the truck! Come on, *please!*"

"You don't look in any state to go anywhere," said Grimma. She stood up. "You just tell us where he is."

"We got him halfway up the lane, and we got so tired and I left them and came on ahead," Sacco blurted out. "They're under the hedge and—" His eyes fell on the snoring bulk of the human. He stared at Grimma.

"You've captured a *human?*" he said. He stumbled sideways. "Need a bit of a rest, so tired," he repeated, vaguely. Then he fell forward.

Grimma caught him and laid him down as gently as she could.

"Someone put him somewhere warm and see if there's any food left," she said to the nomes in general. "And I want some of you to help me look for the others. Come on. This isn't a night for being outside."

The expression on the faces of some of the nomes said that they definitely agreed with this point of view, and that among the people who shouldn't be out on a night like this was themselves.

"It's snowing quite a lot," said one of them, uncertainly. "We'll never find them in all the dark and snow."

Grimma glared at him.

"We might," she said. "We *might* find them in all the dark and snow. We *won't* find them by staying in the light and warm, I know that much."

Several nomes pushed their way forward. Grimma recognized Nooty's people, and the parents of some of the lads. Then there was a bit of a commotion from under the table, where the oldest nomes were clustering together to keep warm and have a good moan.

"I'm comin' too," said Granny Morkie. "Do me good to have a drop of fresh air. What you all lookin' at me like that for?"

"I think you ought to stay inside, Granny," said Grimma gently.

"Don't you try the bein'-tactful-to-old-people to me, my girl," said Granny, prodding her with her stick. "I bin out in deep snow before you was even thought of." She turned to the rest of the nomes. "Nothin' to it if you acts sensible and keeps yellin' out so's everyone knows where everyone is. I went out to help look for my Uncle Joe before I was a year old," she said proudly. "Dreadful snow, that was. It come down sudden like, when the men were out huntin'. We found nearly all of him, too."

"Yes, yes, all right, Granny," said Grimma quickly. She looked at the others. "Well, *we're* going," she said.

In the end fifteen of them went, many out of sheer embarrassment.

In the yellow light from the shed windows, the snowflakes looked beautiful. By the time they reached the ground, they were pretty unpleasant.

The Store nomes really *hated* the Outside snow. There had been snow in the Store, too, sprayed on merchandise around Christmas Fayre time. But it wasn't cold. And snowflakes were huge beautiful things that were hung from the ceilings on bits of thread. *Proper* snowflakes. Not ghastly things that looked all right in the air but turned into freezing wet stuff that was allowed to just lie around on the floor.

It was already as deep as their knees.

"What you do is," said Granny Morkie, "you lift your feet up really high and plonk them down. Nothin' to it."

The light from the shed shone out across the quarry, but the lane was a dark tunnel leading into the night.

"And spread out," said Grimma. "But keep together."

"Spread out and keep together," they muttered.

A senior nome put his hand up.

"You don't get *robins* at night, do you?" he asked cautiously.

"No, of course not," said Grimma.

"No, you don't get robins at night, dafty," said Granny Morkie. They looked relieved.

"No, you get foxes," Granny added in a self-satisfied way. "Great big foxes. They get good and hungry in the cold weather. And maybe you get owls." She scratched her chin. "Cunnin' devils, owls. You never hear 'em till they're almost on top o' you." She banged on the wall with her stick. "Look sharp, you lot. Best foot forward. Unless you're like my Uncle Joe—a fox got his best foot, 'e 'ad to have a wooden leg, 'e was livid."

There was something about Granny Morkie cheering people up that always got them moving. Anything was better than being cheered up some more.

The snowflakes were caking up on the dried grasses and ferns on either bank. Every now and again some of the snow fell off, sometimes onto the lane, often onto the nomes stumbling along it. They prodded the snowy tussocks and peered doubtfully into the gloomy holes under the hedge, while the flakes continued to fall in a soft, crackly silence. Robins, owls, and other terrors of the Outside lurked in every shadow.

Eventually the light was left behind, and they walked by the glow of the snow itself. Sometimes one of them would call out, softly, and then they'd all listen.

It was very cold.

Granny Morkie stopped suddenly.

"Fox," she announced. "I can smell it. Can't mistake a fox. *Rank*."

They huddled together and stared apprehensively into the darkness.

"Might not still be around, mind," said Granny. "Hangs about for a long time, that smell."

They relaxed a bit.

"Really, Granny," muttered Grimma.

"I was just tryin' to be a help," sniffed Granny Morkie. "You don't want my help, you've only got to say."

"We're doing this wrong," said Grimma. "It's *Dorcas* we're looking for. He wouldn't just be sitting out in the open, would he? He knows about foxes. He'd get the boys to find somewhere sheltered and as safe as possible."

Nooty's father stepped forward.

"If you look the way the snow falls," he said hesitantly, "you can see the air-conditioning is blowing it *this* way," he pointed, "so it piles up more on this side of things than that side. So they'd want to be as much away from the air-conditioning as possible, wouldn't they?"

"It's called the wind, when it's outside," said Grimma gently. "But you're right. That means . . ." She stared at the hedges. "They'd be on the other side of the hedge. In the field, up against the bank. Come on."

They scrambled up through the masses of dead leaves and dripping twigs and into the field beyond.

It was desolate. A few tufts of dead grass stuck above the endless wilderness of snow. Several of the nomes groaned.

It's the size, Grimma thought. They don't mind the quarry, or the thickets above it, or even the lane, because a lot of it is closed in and you can pretend there are sort of walls around you. It's too *big* for them here.

"Stick close to the hedge," she said, more cheerfully than she felt. "There's not so much snow there."

Oh, Arnold Bros (est. 1905), she thought. Dorcas doesn't believe in you, and I certainly don't believe in you, but if you could just see your way clear to existing just long enough for us to find them, we'd all appreciate it very much. And perhaps if you could stop the snow and see us all safely back to the quarry as well, that would be a big help.

That's daft, she thought. Masklin always said that if there was an Arnold Bros, he was sort of inside our heads, helping us think.

She realized that she was staring at the snow.

Why is there a hole in it? she thought.

# 12

*III. There is Nowhere to go, and we must Leave.*

*From* The Book of Nome, Exits Chap. 4, v. III

"Rabbits, I thought," she said.

Dorcas patted her hand.

"Well done," he said weakly.

"We were in the lane after Sacco left," said Nooty, "and it was getting really cold and Dorcas said to take him the other side of the hedge and, well, it was me who said you can see rabbits in this field sometimes, and *he* said find a rabbit hole. So we did. We thought we'd be here all night."

"Ow," moaned Dorcas.

"Don't make a fuss—I didn't hurt a bit," said Granny Morkie cheerfully as she examined his leg. "Nothin' broken, but it's a nasty sprain."

The Store nomes looked around the burrow with interest and a certain amount of approval. It was nicely closed in.

"Your ancestors probably lived in holes like this," said Grimma. "With shelves and things, of course."

"Very nice," said a nome. "Homely. Almost like being under the floor."

"Smells a bit, mind," said another.

"That'll be the rabbits," said Dorcas, nodding toward the deeper darkness. "We've heard them rustling about, but they're staying out of our way. Nooty said she thought there was a fox snuffling around a while ago."

"We'd better get you back as soon as possible," said Grimma. "I don't *think* any fox would bother the pack of us. After all, the local ones know who we are. Eat a nome and you die, that's what they've learned."

The nomes shuffled their feet. It was true, of course. The trouble *was*, they thought, that the person who'd really regret it the most would be the one nome who was eaten. Knowing that the fox might be given a bad time afterward wouldn't be a lot of consolation.

Besides, they were cold and wet, and the burrow—while it wouldn't have sounded a very comfortable proposition back at the quarry—was suddenly much better than the horrible night outside. They'd staggered past a dozen rabbit holes, calling down into the gloom, before they'd heard Nooty's voice answering them.

"I really don't think we need worry," said Grimma. "Foxes learn very quickly. Isn't that so, Granny?"

"Eh?" said Granny Morkie.

"I was telling everyone how foxes learn quickly," said Grimma desperately.

"Oh, yes. Right enough," said Granny. "He'll go a long way out of his way for something he likes to eat, will your average fox. Especially when it's cold weather."

"I didn't mean that! Why do you have to make everything sound so *bad*?"

"I'm sure I don't mean to," said Granny Morkie, and sniffed.

"We must get back," said Dorcas firmly. "This snow isn't just going to go away, is it? I can get along okay if I've got someone to lean on."

"We can make you a stretcher," said Grimma. "Though goodness knows there isn't much to get back *to*."

"We saw the humans go up the lane," said Nooty. "But we had to go all the way along to the badger tunnel and there were no proper tracks. Then we tried to cut across the fields at the bottom, and that was a mistake—they were all plowed up. We haven't had anything to eat," she added.

"Don't expect much, then," said Grimma. "The humans have taken most of our stores. They think we're rats."

"Well, that's not so bad," said Dorcas. "We used to encourage them to think we were, back in the Store. They used to put traps down. We used to hunt rats in the basement and put them in the traps, when I was a lad."

"Now they're using poisoned food," said Grimma.

"That's not good."

"Come on. Let's get you back."

The snow was still falling outside, but raggedy fashion, as if the last flakes in stock were being sold off cheaply. There was a line of red light in the east—not the dawn, but the promise of the dawn. It didn't look cheerful. When the sun did rise, it would find itself locked behind bars of cloud.

They broke off some pieces of dead cow parsley stalk to make a rough sort of chair for Dorcas, which four nomes could carry. He'd been right about the shelter of the hedge. The snow wasn't very deep there, but it made up for it by being littered with old leaves, twigs, and debris. It was slow going.

It must be great to be a human, Grimma thought, as thorns the length of her hand tore at her dress. Masklin was right, this really is their world. It's the right size for them. They go where they want and do whatever they like. We think we do things for ourselves, and all we do is live in odd corners of their world—under their floors, stealing things.

The other nomes trudged along in weary silence. The only sound, apart from the crunch of feet on snow and leaves, was of Granny Morkie eating. She'd found some hawthorn berries on a bush and was chewing her way through one with every sign of enjoyment. She'd offered them around, but the other nomes found them bitter and unpleasant.

"Prob'ly an acquired taste," she muttered, glaring at Grimma.

It's one we are all going to have to acquire, thought Grimma, ignoring Granny's hurt stare. The only hope we've got is to split up and leave the quarry in little groups, once we get back. Move out into the country, go back to living in old rabbit holes and eating whatever we can find. Some groups may survive the winter, once the old people have died off.

And it'll be good-bye electricity, good-bye reading, good-bye bananas . . .

*But I'll wait at the quarry until Masklin comes back.*

"Cheer up, my girl," said Granny Morkie, trying to be friendly. "Don't look so gloomy. It may never happen, that's what I always say."

Even Granny was shocked when Grimma looked at her with a face from which all the color had drained away. The girl's mouth opened and shut a few times.

Then she folded up, very gently, and collapsed to her knees and started to sob.

It was the most shocking sound they'd heard. Grimma yelled, complained, bullied, and commanded. Hearing her cry was *wrong*, as though the whole world had turned upside down.

"All I did was try and cheer her up," mumbled Granny Morkie.

The embarrassed nomes stood around in a circle. No one dared go near Grimma. Anything might happen. If you tried to pat her on the shoulder and say "There, there," anything might happen. She might bite your hand off, or anything.

Dorcas looked at the nomes on either side of him, sighed, and eased himself up off his makeshift carrier. He limped over to Grimma, catching hold of a thorn twig to steady himself.

"You've found us, we're going back to the quarry, everything's all right," he said soothingly.

"It isn't! We'll have to move on!" she sobbed. "You'd have been better off staying in the hole! It's all gone wrong!"

"Well, I would have said—" Dorcas began.

"We've got no food and we can't stop the humans and we're trapped in the quarry and I've tried to keep everyone together and now it's all gone wrong!"

"We ought to have gone up to that barn right at the start," said Nooty.

"You still could," said Grimma. "All the younger people could. Just get as far away from here as possible!"

"But children couldn't walk it, and old people certainly couldn't manage the snow," said Dorcas. "*You* know that. You're just despairing."

"We've tried everything! It's just got worse! We thought it would be a lovely life in the Outside, and now it's all falling to bits!"

Dorcas gave her a long, blank look.

"We might as well give up right now," she said. "We might as well give up and die right here."

There was a horrified silence.

It was broken by Dorcas.

"Er," he said. "Er. Are you sure? Are you *really* sure?"

The tone of his voice made Grimma look up.

All the nomes were staring.

There was a fox looking down at them.

It was one of those moments when Time itself freezes solid. Grimma could see the yellow-green glow in the fox's eyes and the cloud of its breath. Its tongue lolled out.

It looked surprised.

It was new to these parts and had never seen nomes before. Its not-very-complicated mind was trying to come to terms with the fact that the *shape* of the nomes—two arms, two legs, a head at the top— was a shape it associated with humans and had learned to avoid, but the size was the size it had always thought of as a mouthful.

The nomes stood rooted in terror. There was no sense in trying to run away. A fox had twice as many legs to run after you. You'd end up dead anyway, but at least you wouldn't end up dead and out of breath as well.

There was a growl.

To the nomes' astonishment, it had come from Grimma.

She snatched Granny Morkie's walking stick, strode forward, and whacked the fox across the nose before it could move. It yelped and blinked stupidly.

"Shove off!" she shouted. "How dare you come here!" She hit it again. It jerked its head away. Grimma took another step forward and caught it a backward thump across the muzzle.

The fox made up its mind. There were definitely rabbits farther down the hedge. Rabbits didn't hit back. It was a lot happier about rabbits.

It whined, backed away with its eyes fixed on Grimma, and then darted off into the darkness.

The nomes breathed out.

*"Well,"* said Dorcas.

"I'm sorry, but I just can't *stand* foxes," said Grimma. "And Masklin said we should let them know who's boss."

"I'm not arguing," said Dorcas.

Grimma looked vaguely at the stick.

"What was I saying before that?" she said.

"You were saying we might as well give up and die right here," said Granny Morkie helpfully.

Grimma glared at her. "No, I wasn't," she said. "I was just feeling a bit tired, that's all. Come on. We'll catch our death standing here."

"Or the other way round," said Nooty, staring into the fox-haunted darkness.

"That's not funny," snapped Grimma, striding off.

"I didn't mean it to be," said Nooty, shivering.

Overhead, quite unnoticed by the nomes, a rather strangely bright star zigzagged across the sky. It was small, or perhaps it was very big but a long way off. If you looked at it long enough, it might just have appeared disk shaped. It was causing a lot of messages to be sent through the air, all around the world.

It seemed to be looking for something.

There were flickering lights in the quarry by the time they got back. Another group of nomes was about to set out to look for them. Not with much enthusiasm, admittedly, but they were going to try.

The cheer that went up when it was realized that everyone was safely back almost made Grimma forget that they were safely back to a very unsafe place. She'd read something in the book of proverbs that summed it up perfectly. As far as she could remember, it was something about jumping out of the thing you cook in and into the thing you cooked on. Or something.

Grimma led the rescue party into the office and listened while Sacco, with many interruptions, recounted the adventure from the time Dorcas, out of sudden terror, had jumped out of the truck and had been carried off the rails just before the train arrived. It sounded brave and exciting. And pointless, Grimma thought, but she kept that to herself.

"It wasn't as bad as it looked," Sacco said. "I mean, the truck was smashed, but the train didn't even come off the rails. We saw it all," he finished. "I'm starving."

He gave them a bright smile, which faded like a sunset.

"There's no food?" he said.

"Even less than that," said a nome. "If you've got some bread, we could have a snow sandwich."

Sacco thought about this.

"There's the rabbits," he said. "There were rabbits in the field."

"And in the dark," said Dorcas, who appeared to have something on his mind.

"Well, yes," admitted Sacco.

"And with that fox hanging about," said Nooty.

Another proverb floated up in Grimma's mind.

"Needs must," she said, "when the Devil drives."

They looked at her in the flickering light of the matches.

"Who's he?" said Nooty.

"Some sort of horrible person who lives under the ground in a hot place, I think," said Grimma.

"Like the boiler room in the Store?"

"I suppose so."

"What sort of vehicle does he drive?" said Sacco, looking interested.

"It just means that sometimes you're forced to do things," said Grimma testily. "I don't think he actually *drives* anything."

"Well, no. There wouldn't be the room down there, for one thing."

Dorcas coughed. He seemed to be upset about something. Well, everyone was upset, but he was even more upset.

"All right," he said quietly.

Something about the way he said it made them pay attention.

"You'd all better come with me," he went on. "Believe me, I'd rather you didn't have to."

"Where to?" said Grimma.

"The old sheds. The ones by the cliff," said Dorcas.

"But they're all tumbled down. And you said they were very dangerous."

"Oh, they are. They are. There's piles of junk and stuff in cans the children shouldn't touch and stuff like that. . . ."

He twiddled his beard nervously.

"But," he said, "there's something else. Something I've been sort of working on, sort of."

He looked Grimma in the eye. "Something of mine," he said. "The most marvelous thing I've ever seen. Even better than frogs in a flower."

Then he coughed. "Anyway, there's plenty of room in there," he said. "The floors are just earth, er, but the sheds are big and there are lots of places, er, to hide."

A snore from the human shook the office.

"Besides, I don't like being so close to that thing," he added.

There was a general murmur of agreement about this.

"Had you thought about what you're going to do with it?" said Dorcas.

"Some people wanted to kill it, but I don't think that's a good idea," said Grimma. "I think the other humans would get really upset about it."

"Besides, it doesn't seem right," said Dorcas.

"I know what you mean."

"So . . . what shall we do with it?"

Grimma stared at the huge face. Every pore, every hair, was huge. It was strange to think that if there were creatures smaller than nomes, little people perhaps the size of ants, her own face might look like that. If you looked at it philosophically, the whole thing about big and small was just a matter of size.

"We'll leave it," she said. "But . . . is there any paper here?"

"Loads of it on the desk," said Nooty.

"Go and fetch some, please. Dorcas, you've always got something to write with, haven't you?"

Dorcas fumbled in his pockets until he found a stub of pencil lead.

"Don't waste it," he said. "Don't know if I'll ever get some more."

Eventually Nooty came back towing a yellowing sheet of paper. At the top of it, in heavy black lettering, were the words: Blackbury Sand & Gravel Ltd. Below that was the word: Invoice.

Grimma thought for a while, then licked the stub and, in big letters, started to write.

"What are you doing?" said Dorcas.

"Trying to communicate," said Grimma. She carefully traced another word, pressing quite hard.

"I've always thought it might be worth trying," said Dorcas, "but is this the right time?"

"Yes," said Grimma. She finished the last word.

"What do you think?" she said, handing Dorcas the pencil lead.

The writing was a bit jagged where she had pressed hard, and her grasp of grammar and writing wasn't as good as her skill at reading, but it was clear enough.

"I would have done it differently," said Dorcas, reading it.

"Perhaps you would, but this is the way *I've* done it."

"Yes." Dorcas put his head on one side. "Well, it's definitely a communication. You can't get much more communicating than that. Yes."

Grimma tried to sound cheerful. "And now," she said, "let's see this shed of yours."

Two minutes later the office shed was empty of nomes. The human snored on the floor, one hand outstretched.

There was a piece of paper in it now.

It said: Blackbury Sand & Gravel Ltd.

It said: Invoice.

It said: We Could Of Kiled You. LEAV US ALONE.

Now it was quite light outside, and the snow had stopped.

"They'll see our tracks," said Sacco. "Even humans will notice this many tracks."

"It doesn't matter," said Dorcas. "Just get everyone into the old sheds."

"Are you sure, Dorcas?" said Grimma. "Are you really *sure* this is a good idea?"

"No."

They joined the stream of nomes hurrying through a crack in the crumbling corrugated iron and entered the vast, echoing chamber of the shed.

Grimma looked around her. Rust and time had eaten large holes in the walls and ceiling. Old cans and coils of wire were stacked willy-nilly in the corners, along with odd-shaped bits of metal and jam jars with nails in them. Everything stank of oil.

"What's the bit we ought to know about?" she said.

Dorcas pointed to the shadows at the far end of the shed, where she could just make out something big and indistinct.

"It just looks like . . . some sort of big cloth . . ." she said.

"It's, um, underneath it. Is everyone in?" Dorcas cupped his hands around his mouth. "*Is everyone in?*" he shouted. He turned to Nooty.

"I need to know where everyone is," he said. "I don't want anyone to be frightened, but I don't want unnecessary people getting in the way."

"Unnecessary for what?" said Grimma, but he ignored her.

"Sacco, you take some of the lads and get those things we put in the hedge," said Dorcas. "We'll definitely need the battery, and I'm really not certain how much fuel there is."

"*Dorcas!* What is it?" said Grimma, tapping her foot.

Dorcas got like this sometimes, she knew. When he was thinking about machines or things he could do with his hands, he started to ignore people. His voice changed, too.

He gave her a long, slow look as if he were seeing her for the first time. Then he looked down at his feet.

"You'd better, er, come and see," he said. "I shall need you to explain things to everyone. You're so much better at that sort of thing."

Grimma followed him across the chilly floor as more nomes filed into the shed and huddled apprehensively along the walls.

He led her under the shadow of the tarpaulin, which formed a sort of big, dusty cave.

A tire like a truck's loomed up a little way away in the gloom, but it was far more knobbly than any she had seen.

"Oh. It's just a truck," she said uncertainly. "You've got a truck in here, have you?"

Dorcas said nothing. He just pointed upward.

Grimma looked up. And then looked up some more. Into the mouth of Big John.

# 13

*IV. Dorcas said, This is Big John, Great Beast with teeth.*
*V. Needs Must. If we are driven, let us Drive.*

*From* The Book of Nome, Big John Chap. 2,v. IV–V

SOMETIMES WORDS NEED music too. Sometimes the descriptions are not enough; books should be written with sound tracks, like films.

Something deep on an organ, perhaps.

Grimma stared.

*Dee-dah-DAH.*

It can't really be alive, she thought desperately. It's not really about to bite me. Dorcas wouldn't have brought me in here if he knew there was a monster about to bite me. I'm not going to be frightened. I'm not frightened at all. I am a thinking nome and I'm not *frightened!*

"I think the knobbly wheels are just to make it grip the ground better," said Dorcas, his voice sounding a long way off. "Now, I've had a good look around it and, you know, there's nothing really wrong with it, it's just very old—"

Grimma's gaze traveled along the huge yellow neck.

*Dee-dah-dee-dah-DUM.*

"Then I thought, I'm sure he could be started up. These diesel engines are quite easy really, and of course there were pictures in one of the books, although I'm not sure about these pipes, hydraulics I think it's called, but there was this book on one of the benches, *Workshop Manual*, and I've put grease on things and tidied it up," Dorcas gabbled.

*Dah-dah-dah-DUM.*

"I suppose the humans or whatever knew they would be coming back, and I've been up and looked at the controls and, you know, it's probably easier than the Truck was, only of course there's these extra levers for the hydraulics, but that shouldn't be a problem if there's enough fuel, which . . ."

He stopped, aware of her silence.

"Is there something the matter?" he said.

"What *is* it?" said Grimma.

"I was just telling you," said Dorcas. "It's fascinating. You see, these pipes pump some sort of stuff that makes those bits up there move, and those pistons are forced out, which makes the arm thing over there—"

"I didn't ask you what it does, I asked you what it *is*," said Grimma, impatiently.

"Didn't I say?" said Dorcas innocently. "Well, there's its name painted on it. Just up there, look."

She looked where he pointed. Grimma's brow wrinkled.

"John Deere?" she said.

"Well, I don't know him *that* well," said Dorcas. "I call him Big John. It's more respectful. And we should show respect. Come and see."

She followed him dreamily, and, once more, stared into the darkness under the tarpaulin.

"There," he said. "There's no mistaking what *they* are, I hope."

"Oh, my," said Grimma, and raised her hand to her mouth.

"Yes," said Dorcas. "That's what I thought. When I first found this I thought, Oh, it's a sort of truck, well, well, and then I walked up here and I found it was a truck with—"

"Teeth," said Grimma, softly. "Great big metal teeth."

"That's right," said Dorcas proudly. "Big John. A sort of truck. A truck with teeth."

*Dah-DUM.*

"Does it—does it work?" said Grimma.

"It should certainly. It should certainly. I've tested what I can. Basic principle *is* like a truck, but there's a lot of extra levers and things—"

"Why didn't you tell me about this before?" Grimma demanded.

"Dunno. Because I didn't have to, I suppose," said Dorcas.

"But it's *huge.* You can't keep something like this to yourself!"

"Everyone has to have something they can keep to themselves," said Dorcas vaguely. "Anyway, the size isn't important. It's just so, well, so perfect." Dorcas patted a knobbly tire. "You know you said humans think someone made the world in a week? When I saw Big John for the first time, I thought, Okay, this is what he used."

He stared up into the shadows.

"First thing we've got to do is get the tarpaulin off," he said. "It'll be very heavy, so we'll need lots of people. You'd better warn them. Big John can be a bit scary when you see him for the first time."

"Didn't frighten me a bit," said Grimma.

"I know," said Dorcas. "I was watching your face."

The nomes looked expectantly at Grimma.

"The thing to remember," she said, "is that it's just a machine. Just a sort of truck. But when you first see it, it can be rather frightening, so hold on to small children's hands. And run smartly backward when the tarpaulin comes down."

There was a chorus of nods.

"All right. Grab hold."

Six hundred nomes spat on their hands and grasped the edge of the heavy sheet.

"When I say pull, I want you to pull."

The nomes took the strain.

*"Pull!"*

The creases in the tarpaulin flattened out and disappeared.

*"Pull!"*

It began to move. Then, as it slid over Big John's angular shape, its own weight started to tug at it. . . .

*"Run!"*

It came down like an oily green avalanche, piling up into a mountain of folds, but no one bothered about it because the sun shone through the dusty, cobwebbed windows and made Big John glow.

Several nomes screamed. Mothers picked up their children. There was a movement toward the doors.

It *does* look like a head, Grimma thought. On a long neck. And he's got another one at the other end. What am I saying? *It* has got another one at the other end.

"I said it's all right!" she shouted, over the rising din. "Look! It's not even moving!"

"Hey!" shouted another voice. She looked up. Nooty and Sacco had climbed out along Big John's neck and were sitting there waving cheerfully.

That did it. The tide of nomes reached the wall and stopped. You always feel foolish, running away from something that isn't chasing you. They hesitated and then, slowly, inched their way back.

"Well, well," said Granny Morkie, hobbling forward. "So that's what they looked like. I always wondered."

Grimma stared at her.

"What what looked like?" she said.

"Oh, the big diggers," said Granny. "They'd all gone when I was born, but our dad saw 'em. Great big yellow things with teeth that et dirt, he said. I always thought he was just pulling my leg."

Big John was still not eating people. Some of the more adventurous nomes climbed on him.

"It was when the motorway was built," Granny went on, leaning on her stick. "They were all over the place, Dad said. Big yellow things with teeth and knobbly tires."

Grimma stared at her with the kind of expression reserved for people who turn out, against all expectation, to have interesting and secret histories.

"And there was others, too," the old woman went on. "Things that shoved dirt in heaps and everything. This would have been, oh, fifteen years ago now. Never thought I'd see one."

"You mean the roads were *made?*" said Grimma. Big John was covered with young nomes now. She could see Dorcas in the back of the cab, explaining what various levers did.

"That's what he said," said Granny. "You didn't think they was nat'ral, did you?"

"Oh. No. No. Of course not," said Grimma. "Don't be silly."

And she thought: I wonder if Dorcas is right. Perhaps everything was made. Some bits early, some bits later. You start with hills and clouds and things, and then you add roads and Stores. Perhaps the job of humans is to make the world, and they're still doing it. That's why the machines have to suit them.

Gurder would have understood this sort of thing. I wish he was back, she thought.

And then Masklin would be back, too.

She tried to think about something else.

Knobbly tires. That was a good start. Big John's back wheels were nearly as high as a human. It doesn't need roads. Of course it doesn't. It *makes* roads. So it has to be able to go where roads aren't.

She pushed her way through the crowds to the back of the cab, where another group of nomes was already nomehandling a plank into position, and scrambled up to where Dorcas was trying to make himself heard in the middle of an excited crowd.

"You're going to drive this out of here?" she demanded.

He looked up.

"Oh, yes," he said happily. "I think so. I hope so. I imagine we've got at least an hour before any more humans come, and it's not a lot different from a truck."

"We know how to do it!" shouted one of the younger nomes. "My dad told me all about the strings and stuff."

Grimma looked around the cab. It seemed to be full of levers.

It'd been almost a year since the Long Drive, and she'd never taken much notice of mechanical things, but she couldn't help thinking the old truck cab had been a lot less crowded. There had been some pedals and a lever and the steering wheel, and that had been about it.

She turned back to Dorcas.

"Are you sure?" she said doubtfully.

"No," he said. "You know I'm never sure. But a lot of the controls are for his mou . . . for the bucket. The thing with the teeth in it. At the end of his neck. I mean, the digging bits. We needn't bother with them. They're amazingly ingenious, though, and all you have to do—"

"Where's everyone going to sit? There isn't much room."

Dorcas shrugged. "I suppose the older people can travel in the cab. The youngsters will have to hang on where they can. We can wrap wires and things around the place. For handholds, I mean. Look, don't worry. We'll be driving in the light and we don't have to go fast."

"And then we'll get to the barn, won't we, Dorcas?" said Nooty. "Where it'll be warm and there's lots of food."

"I hope so," said Dorcas. "Now, let's get on with things. We haven't got much time. Where's Sacco with the battery?"

Grimma thought: Will there be lots of food at the barn? Where did we get that idea? Angalo said that turnips or something were stored up there, and there may be some potatoes. That's not exactly a feast.

Her stomach, thinking thoughts of its own, rumbled in disagreement. It had been a very long night to pass on a tiny piece of sandwich.

Anyway, we can't stay here now. Anywhere will be better than here.

"Dorcas," she said, "is there anything I can help with?"

He looked up. "You could read the instruction book," he said. "See if it says how to drive it."

"Don't you know?"

"Er. Not in so many words. Not *exactly*. I mean, I know how to do it, it's just that I don't know what to do."

The book was under the bench on one side of the shed. Grimma propped it up and tried to concentrate above the noise. I bet he does know, she thought. But this is his moment, and he doesn't want me getting in the way.

The nomes moved like people with a purpose. Things were far too bad to spend time grumbling. Funny thing, she thought as she turned the grubby pages, that people only seem to stop complaining when things get really bad. That's when they start using words like pulling together, shoulders to the wheel, and noses to the grindstone. She'd found "nose to the grindstone" in a book. Apparently it meant "to get on with things." She didn't see why people were supposed to work hard if you ground their noses; it seemed more likely that they'd work hard if you promised to grind their noses if they didn't.

It had been the same with *Road Works Ahead* on the Long Drive. The road ahead works. How could it mean anything else? But the road had been full of holes. Where was the sense in that? Words ought to mean what they meant.

She turned the page.

There was a big brown ring on this one, where a human had put down a cup.

Across the floor a group of nomes swarmed past around the slowly moving bulk of the battery. They were rolling it on rusty ball bearings.

The can of fuel wobbled past after it.

Grimma stared at the pictures of levers with numbers on them. Suddenly people were keen on the barn. Suddenly, when things were not just averagely awful but promising to be really dreadful, they seemed almost happy. Masklin had known about that. It's amazing what people would do, he said, if you found the right place to push.

She stared at the pages and tried to get interested in levers.

The clouds running before the sun were spreading across the pink of the sky. Red sky in the morning, Grimma had read once. It meant people who kept sheep were happy. Or not happy. Or perhaps it was cows.

In the dark office the human awoke, mooed for a while, and tried to jerk free of the cobweb of wires that held it down. After a lot of effort it wriggled most of one arm free.

What the human did next would have surprised most nomes. It caught hold of a chair and, with a great deal of grunting, managed to tip it over. It pulled it across the floor, manipulated the leg under a couple of strands of wire, and heaved.

A minute later it was sitting upright, pulling more wires free.

Its huge eyes fell on the scrap of paper on the floor.

It stared at it for a moment, rubbing its arms, and then it picked up the telephone.

Dorcas prodded vaguely at a wire.

"Are you sure the battery is connected the right way round, sir?" said Sacco.

"I can tell the difference between red wires and black wires, you know," said Dorcas mildly, prodding another wire.

"Then perhaps the battery doesn't have enough electricity," said Grimma helpfully, trying to see over their shoulders. "Perhaps it's all run to the bottom, or gone dry."

Dorcas and Sacco exchanged glances.

"Electricity doesn't sink," said Dorcas patiently. "Or dry up, as far as I know. It's either there or it isn't. Excuse me." He peered up into the mass of wires again and gave one a poke. There was a pop, and a fat blue spark.

"It's there all right," he added. "It's just that it isn't where it should be."

Grimma walked back across the greasy floor of the cab. Groups of nomes were standing around, waiting. Hundreds of them were clutching the strings lashed to the big steering wheel above them.

Other teams stood by with bits of wood pressing, like battering rams, on the pedals.

"Just a bit of a delay," she said. "All the electricity's got lost."

There were nomes everywhere. On the Long Drive there had been a whole truck for them. But Big John's cab was smaller, and people had to pack themselves in where they could.

What a ragged bunch, Grimma thought. And it was true. Even in the sudden rush from the Store, the nomes had been able to bring quite a lot of stuff. And they had been plump and well dressed.

Now they were thinner and leaner and much dirtier, and all they were taking with them was the torn and grubby clothes they stood up in. Even the books had been left behind. A dozen books took up the space of three dozen nomes, and while Grimma privately thought that some of the books were more useful than many of the nomes, she'd accepted Dorcas's promise that they would come back, one day, and try to retrieve them from their hiding place under the floor.

Well, thought Grimma. We tried. We really made an effort. We came to the quarry to dig in, look after ourselves, live proper lives. And we failed. We thought all we had to do was bring the right things from the Store, but we brought a lot of wrong things too. This time we'll need to go as far away from humans as possible, and I don't actually think anywhere is far enough.

She climbed up onto the rickety driving platform, which had been made by tying a plank across the cab. There were even nomes on this. They watched her expectantly.

At least driving Big John should be easier. The leaders of the teams on the controls could see her, so she wouldn't have to mess around with semaphore and bits of thread like they'd done when they left the Store. And a lot of the nomes had done this before, too. . . .

She heard Dorcas shout: "Try it this time!"

There was a click. There was a whirr. Then Big John roared.

The sound bounced around the cave of the shed. It was so loud and so deep, it wasn't really sound at all, just something that turned the air hard and then hit you with it. Nomes flung themselves flat on the trembling deck of the cab.

Grimma, clutching at her ears, saw Dorcas running across the floor, waving his hands. The team on the accelerator pedal gave him a "Who, us?" look and stopped pushing.

The sound died down to a deep rumbling, a *mummummummum* that still had a feel-it-in-the-bone quality. Dorcas hurried back and climbed, with a lot of stopping for breath, up to the plank. When he got there, he sat down and rubbed his brow.

"I'm getting too old for this sort of thing," he said. "When a nome gets to a certain age, it's time to stop stealing giant vehicles. Well-known fact. Anyway. It's ticking over nicely. You might as well take us out."

"What, all by myself?" said Grimma.

"Yes. Why not?"

"It's just that, well, I thought Sacco or someone would be up here." I thought a male nome would be driving, she thought.

"They'd *like* to," said Dorcas. "They'd *love* to. And we'd be zipping all over the place, I don't doubt it, with them crying, 'Yippee!' and whatnot. No. I want a nice peaceful drive across the fields, thank you very much. The gentle touch."

He leaned down.

"Everyone ready down there?" he yelled.

There was a chorus of nervous "yeses," and one or two cheerful ones.

"I wonder if putting Sacco in charge of the go-faster pedal is really a good idea," mused Dorcas. He straightened up. "Er. You're not *worried*, are you?" he said.

Grimma snorted. "What? Me? No. Of course not. It does not," she added, "present a problem."

"*O-kay*," he said. "Let's go."

There was silence, except for the deep thrumming of the engine. Grimma paused.

If Masklin were here, she thought, he'd do this better than me. No one mentions him anymore. Or Angalo. Or Gurder. They don't like thinking about them. That must be something nomes learned hundreds of years ago, in this place full of foxes and rushing things and a hundred nasty ways to die. If someone goes missing, you must stop thinking about them, you must put them out of your mind. But I think about him all the time.

I just went on about the frogs in the flowers, and I never thought about his dreams.

Dorcas gently put his arm around her. She was shaking.

"We should have sent some people to the airport," she muttered. "It would have showed that we cared, and—"

"We didn't have the time, and we didn't have the people," said Dorcas softly. "When he comes back, we can explain about that. He's bound to understand."

"Yes," she whispered.

"And now," said Dorcas, standing back, "let's go!"

Grimma took a deep breath.

"First gear," she bellowed, "and go forward verrrry slowly."

The teams pushed and pulled their way over the deck. There was a slight shudder and the engine noise dropped. Big John lurched forward and jolted to a stop. The engine coughed and died.

Dorcas looked thoughtfully at his fingernails.

"Hand brake, hand brake, hand brake," he hummed softly.

Grimma glared at him and cupped her hands round her mouth. "Take the hand brake off!" she shouted. "Right! *Now* get into first gear and go forward very slowly!"

There was a click, and silence.

"Starttheengine, starttheengine, starttheengine," murmured Dorcas, rocking back and forth on his heels.

Grimma sagged. "Put everything back where it was and start the engine," she screamed.

Nooty, in charge of the hand brake team, called up, "Do you want the hand brake on or off, miss?"

"What?"

"You haven't told us what to do with the hand brake, miss," said Sacco. The nomes with him started to grin.

Grimma shook a finger at him. "Listen," she snapped, "if I have to come down there and tell you what to do with the hand brake, you'll all be *extremely sorry*, all right? Now stop giggling like that and *get this thing moving! Quickly!*"

There was a click. Big John roared again and started to move. A cheer went up from the nomes.

"Right," said Grimma. "That's more like it."

"The doors, the doors, the doors, we didn't open the do-ors," hummed Dorcas.

"Of course we didn't open the doors," said Grimma, as the digger began to go faster. "What do we need to open the doors for? This is Big John!"

# 14

*V. There is nothing that can be in our way, for this is Big John, that Laughs at Barriers, and says brrm-brrm.*

*From* The Book of Nome, Big John Chap. 3, v. V

IT WAS A very old shed. It was a very rusty shed. It was a shed that wobbled in high winds. The only thing even vaguely new about it was the padlock on the door, which Big John hit at about six miles an hour. The rickety building rang like a gong, leaped off its foundations, and was dragged halfway across the quarry before it fell apart in a shower of rust and smoke. Big John emerged like a very angry chick from a very old egg and then rolled to a stop.

Grimma picked herself up from the plank and nervously started to pick bits of rust off herself.

"We've stopped," she said vaguely, her ears still ringing. "Why have we stopped, Dorcas?"

He didn't bother to try to get up. The thump of Big John hitting the door had knocked all the breath out of him.

"I think," he said, "that everyone might have been flung about a bit. Why did you want it to go so fast?"

"Sorry!" Sacco called up. "Bit of a misunderstanding there, I think!"

Grimma pulled herself together. "Well," she said, "I got us

out, anyway. I've got the hang of it now. We'll just . . . we'll just . . . we'll . . ."

Dorcas heard her voice fade into silence. He looked up.

There was a truck parked in front of the quarry. And three humans were running toward Big John in big, floating bounds.

"Oh dear," he said.

"Didn't it read my note?" wondered Grimma aloud.

"I'm afraid it did," said Dorcas. "Now, we shouldn't panic. We've got a choice. We can either—"

"Go forward," snapped Grimma. "Right now!"

"No, no," said Dorcas weakly, "I wasn't going to suggest that . . ."

"First gear!" Grimma commanded. "And lots of fast!"

"No, you don't want to do that," Dorcas murmured.

"Watch me," said Grimma. "I warned them! They can read, we know they can read! If they're really intelligent, they're intelligent enough to know better!"

Big John gathered speed.

"You mustn't do this," said Dorcas. "We've always kept away from humans!"

"They don't keep away from us!" shouted Grimma.

"But—"

"They demolished the Store, they tried to stop us escaping, now they're taking our quarry *and they don't even know what we are!*" said Grimma. "Remember the Gardening Department in the Store? Those horrible statues of garden ornaments? Well, I'm going to show them *real* nomes. . . ."

"You can't beat humans!" shouted Dorcas, above the roar of the engine. "They're too big! You're too small!"

"They may be big," said Grimma, "and I may be small. But *I'm* the one with the giant truck. With *teeth*." She leaned over the plank. "Everyone hang on down there," she shouted. "This may be rough."

It had dawned on the great slow creatures outside that something was wrong. They stopped their lumbering charge and, very slowly, tried to dodge out of the way. Two of them managed to leap into the empty office as Big John bowled past.

"I see," said Grimma. "They must think we're stupid. Take a big left turn. More. More. Now stop. Okay." She rubbed her hands together.

"What are you going to do?" whispered Dorcas, terrified.

Grimma leaned over the plank.

"Sacco," she said. "You see those other levers?"

The pale round blobs of the humans' faces appeared at the dusty windows of the shed.

Big John was twenty feet away, vibrating gently in the early-morning mist. Then the engine roared. The big front shovel came up, catching the sunlight. . . .

Big John leaped forward, bouncing across the quarry floor and taking out one wall of the shed like ripping the lid off a can. The other walls and the roof folded up gently, as if it were a house of cards with the ace of spades flipped away.

The digger careered around in a big circle, so that when the two humans crawled out of the wreckage, it was the first thing they saw. Throbbing, with the big metal mouth poised to bite.

They ran.

They ran almost as fast as nomes.

o　　o　　o

"I've always wanted to do that," said Grimma in a satisfied voice. "Now, where did the other human go?"

"Back to the truck, I think," said Dorcas.

"Fine," said Grimma. "Lots of right, Sacco. Stop. Now forward, slowly."

"Can we sort of stop this and just go, now? Please?" pleaded Dorcas.

"The humans' truck is in the way," said Grimma, reasonably enough. "They've stopped right in the entrance."

"Then we're trapped," said Dorcas.

Grimma laughed. It wasn't a very amusing sound. Dorcas suddenly felt almost as sorry for the humans as he was feeling for himself.

The humans must have been having similar thoughts, if humans had thoughts. He could see their pale faces watching Big John lurch toward them.

They're wondering why they can't see a human inside, he thought. They can't work it out. Here's this machine, moving all by itself. A bit of a puzzler, for humans.

They reached some sort of conclusion, though. He saw both truck doors fly open and the humans jumped out just as Big John—

There was a crunch, and the truck jerked as Big John hit it. The knobbly wheels spun for a moment, and then the truck rolled backward. Clouds of steam poured out.

"That's for Nisodemus," said Grimma.

"I thought you didn't like him," said Dorcas.

"Yes, but he was a nome."

Dorcas nodded. They were all, when you got right down to it, nomes. It was just as well to remember whose side you were on.

"May I suggest you change gear?" he said quietly.

·329·

"Why? What's wrong with the one we've got?"

"You'll be able to push better if you go down a gear. Trust me."

Humans were watching. They *were* watching, because a machine rolling around by itself is something that you do watch, even if you've just had to climb a tree or hide behind a hedge.

They saw Big John roll backward, change gear with a roar, and attack the truck again. The windows shattered.

Dorcas was really unhappy about this.

"You're killing a truck," he said.

"Don't be silly," said Grimma. "It's a machine. Just bits of metal."

"Yes, but someone made it," said Dorcas. "They must be very hard to make. I hate destroying things that are hard to make."

"They ran over Nisodemus," said Grimma. "And when we used to live in a hole, nomes were always being squashed by cars."

"Yes, but nomes aren't hard to make," said Dorcas. "You just need other nomes."

"You're weird."

Big John struck again. One of the truck's headlights exploded. Dorcas winced.

Then the truck was pushed clear. Smoke was billowing out from it now, where fuel had spilled over the hot engine. Big John backed off and rumbled around it. The nomes were really getting the hang of him now.

"Right," said Grimma. "Straight ahead." She nudged Dorcas. "We'll go and find this barn now, shall we?"

"Just go down the lane, and I think there's a gateway into the fields," Dorcas mumbled. "It had an actual gate in it," he added. "I suppose it would be too much to ask you to let us open it first?"

Behind them the truck burst into flames. Not spectacularly, but in a workmanlike way, as if it were going to go on burning all day. Dorcas saw a human take off its coat and flap uselessly at the fire. He felt quite sorry for it.

Big John rolled unopposed down the lane. Some of the nomes started to sing as they sweated over the ropes.

"Now, then," said Grimma, "where's this gateway? Through the gate and across the fields, you said, and—"

"It's just before you get to the car with the flashing lights on top," said Dorcas slowly. "The one that's just coming up the lane."

They stared at it.

"Cars with lights on the top are bad news," said Grimma.

"You're right there," said Dorcas. "They're often full of humans who very seriously want to know what's going on. There were lots of them down at the railway."

Grimma looked along the hedge.

"This is the gateway coming up, is it?" she said.

"Yes."

Grimma leaned down.

"Slow down and turn sharp right," she said.

The teams swung into action. Sacco even changed gear without being asked. Nomes hung like spiders from the steering wheel, hauling it around.

There *was* a gate in the gateway. But it was old and held to the post with bits of string in proper agricultural fashion. It wouldn't have stopped anything very determined, and it had no chance with Big John.

Dorcas winced again. He hated to see things broken.

The field on the other side was brown soil. Corrugated earth, the nomes called it, after the corrugated cardboard you sometimes got in the Packing Department in the Store. There was snow between the furrows. The big wheels churned it into mud.

Dorcas was half expecting the car to follow them. It stopped instead, and two humans in dark-blue suits got out and started to lumber across the field. There's no stopping humans, he thought glumly. They're like the weather.

The field ran gently uphill, around the quarry. Big John's engine thudded.

There was a wire fence ahead, with a grassy field beyond it. The wire parted with a twang. Dorcas watched it roll back and wondered whether Grimma would let him stop and collect a bit of it. You always knew where you were with wire.

The humans were still following. Out of the corner of his eye, because up here there was altogether too much outside to look at, Dorcas saw flashing lights on the main road, far away.

He pointed them out to Grimma.

"I know," she said. "I've seen them. But what else could we have done?" she added desperately. "Gone off and lived in the flowers like good little *pixies?*"

"I don't know," said Dorcas wearily. "I'm not sure about anything anymore."

Another wire fence twanged. There was shorter grass up here, and the ground curved—

And then there was nothing but sky, and Big John speeding up as the wheels bounced over the field at the top of the hill.

Dorcas had never seen so much sky. There was nothing around them, just a bit of scrub in the distance. And it was silent. Well, not silent at all, because of Big John's roar. But it looked the kind of place that *would* be silent if diggers full of desperate nomes weren't thundering across it.

Frantic sheep ran out of the way.

"There's the barn up ahead, that stone building on the horiz—" Grimma began. Then she said, "Are you all right, Dorcas?"

"If I keep my eyes shut," he whispered.

"You look dreadful."

"I *feel* worse."

"But you've been outside before."

"Grimma, we're the highest thing there is! There's nothing higher than us for miles, or whatever you call those things! If I open my eyes, I'll fall into the sky!"

Grimma leaned down to the perspiring drivers.

"Right just a bit!" she shouted. "That's it! Now all the fast you can!"

"Hold on to Big John!" she shouted to Dorcas, as the engine noise grew. "You know *he* can't fly!"

The machine bumped up on a stony track that led in the general direction of the distant barn. Dorcas risked opening one eye. He'd never been to the barn. Was anyone certain there was food there, or was it just a guess? Perhaps at least it'd be warm. . . .

But there was a flashing light near it, coming toward them.

"Why won't they leave us *alone?*" shouted Grimma. "Stop!"

Big John rolled to a halt. The engine idled in the chilly air.

"This must lead down to the road," said Dorcas.

"We can't go back," said Grimma.

"No."

"Or forward."

"No."

Grimma drummed her fingers on Big John's metal.

"Have you got any other ideas?"

"We could try going across the fields," said Dorcas.

"Where would that take us?" said Grimma.

"Away from here, for a start."

"But we wouldn't know where we were going!" said Grimma.

Dorcas shrugged. "It's either that or paint flowers."

Grimma tried to smile.

"And those little wings wouldn't suit me," she said.

"What's going on up there?" Sacco yelled up.

"We ought to tell people," Grimma whispered. "Everyone thinks we're going to the barn—"

She looked around. The car was closer, bumping heavily over the rough track. The two humans were still coming the other way. "Don't humans ever give up?" she said to herself.

She leaned over the edge of the plank.

"Some left, Sacco," she said. "And then just go steadily."

Big John bounced off the track and rolled over the cold grass. There was another wire fence in the far distance and a few more sheep.

We don't know where we're going, she thought. The only important thing is to *go*. Masklin was right. This isn't our world.

"Perhaps we should have talked to humans," she said aloud.

"No, you were right," said Dorcas. "In this world, everything belongs to humans, and we would belong to them, too. There wouldn't be any room for us to be *us*."

The fence came closer. There was a road on the other side. Not a track, but a proper road with black stone on it.

"Right or left?" said Grimma. "What do you think?"

"It doesn't matter," said Dorcas, as the digger twanged through the fence.

"We'll try going left, then," she said. "Slow down, Sacco! Left a bit. More. More. Steady at that. Oh, no!"

There was another car in the distance. It had a flashing light on the top.

Dorcas risked a look behind them.

There was another flashing light there.

"No," he said.

"What?" said Grimma.

"Just a little while ago you asked if humans ever gave up," he said. "They don't."

"Stop," said Grimma.

The teams trotted obediently across Big John's floor. The digger rolled gently to a halt again, engine idling.

"This is it," said Dorcas.

"Are we at the barn yet?" a nome called up.

"No," said Grimma. "Not yet. Nearly."

Dorcas made a face.

"We might as well accept it now," he said. "You'll end up waving a stick with a star on it. I just hope they don't force me to mend their shoes."

Grimma looked thoughtful. "If we drove as hard as we could at that car coming toward us—" she began.

"No," said Dorcas, firmly. "It really wouldn't solve anything."

"It'd make me feel a lot better," said Grimma.

She looked around at the fields.

"Why's it gone all dark?" she said. "We can't have been running all day. It was early morning when we started out."

"Doesn't time fly when you're enjoying yourselves?" said Dorcas gloomily. "And I don't like milk much. I don't mind doing their housework if I *don't* have to drink milk, but—"

"Just *look*, will you?"

Darkness was spreading across the fields.

"It might be an ellipse," said Dorcas. "I read about them: It all goes dark when the sun covers the moon. And possibly vice versa," he added doubtfully.

The car ahead of them squealed to a halt, crashed backward across the road into a stone wall, and came to an abrupt stop.

In the field by the road the sheep were running away. It wasn't the ordinary panic of sheep ordinarily disturbed. They had their heads down and were pounding across the ground with one aim in mind. They were sheep who had decided that this was no time to waste energy panicking when it could be used for galloping away as fast as possible.

A loud and unpleasant humming noise filled the air.

"My word," Dorcas said weakly. "They're pretty damn terrifying, these ellipses." Down below, the nomes *were* panicking. They weren't sheep, every nome could think for itself, and when you started to think hard about sudden darkness and mysterious humming noises, panicking seemed like a logical idea.

Little lines of crawling blue fire crackled over Big John's battered paintwork. Dorcas felt his hair standing on end.

Grimma stared upward.

The sky was totally black.

"It's . . . all . . . right," she said, slowly. "Do you know, I think it's all right!"

Dorcas looked at his hands. Sparks crackled off his fingertips.

"It is, is it?" was all he could think of to say.

"That isn't night, it's a shadow. There's something huge floating above us."

"And that's better than night, is it?" said Dorcas.

"I think so. Come on, let's get off."

She shinned down the rope to Big John's deck. She was smiling madly. That was almost as terrifying as everything else put together. They weren't used to Grimma smiling.

"Give me a hand," she said. "We've got to get down. So he can be sure it's us."

They looked at her in astonishment as she wrestled with the gangplank.

"Come *on*," she repeated. "Help me, can't you?"

They helped. Sometimes, when you're totally confused, you'll listen to anyone who seems to have any sort of aim in mind. They grabbed the plank and shoved it out of the back of the cab until it tilted and swung down toward the floor.

At least there wasn't so much sky now. The blue was a thin line around the edge of the solid darkness overhead.

Not entirely solid. When Dorcas's eyes grew used to it, he could make out squares and rectangles and circles.

Nomes scurried down the plank and milled around on the road below, uncertain whether to run or stay.

Above them one of the dark squares in the shadow moved aside. There was a clank, and then a rectangle of darkness whirred down very gently, like an elevator without wires, and landed softly on the road. It was quite big.

There was something on it. Something in a pot. Something red and yellow and green.

The nomes craned forward to see what it was.

# 15

*I. Thus ended the journey of Big John, and the nomes fled, looking not behind.*

*From* The Book of Nome, Strange Frogs Chap. VII, v. I.

DORCAS CLAMBERED DOWN awkwardly onto Big John's oily deck. It was empty now, except for the bits of string and wood that the nomes had used.

They've dropped things just any old how, he thought, listening to the distant chattering of the nomes. It's not right, leaving litter. Poor old Big John deserves more than this.

There was some sort of excitement going on outside, but he didn't pay it much attention.

He bumbled around for a bit, trying to coil up the string and push the wood into tidy heaps. He pulled down the wires that had let Big John taste the electricity. He got down on his hands and knees and tried to rub out the muddy footprints.

Big John made noises, even with the engine stopped. Little pops and sizzles, and the occasional ping.

Dorcas sat down and leaned against the yellow metal. He didn't know what was going on. It was so far outside anything he'd ever seen before that his mind wasn't letting him worry about it.

Perhaps it's just another machine, he thought wearily. A machine for making night come down suddenly.

He reached out and patted Big John.

"Well done," he said.

Sacco and Nooty found him sitting with his head against the cab wall, staring vacantly at his feet.

"Everyone's been looking for you!" Sacco said. "It's like an airplane without wings! It's just floating there in the air! So you must come and tell us what makes it go . . . I say, are you all right?"

"Hmm?"

"Are you all right?" said Nooty. "You look rather odd."

Dorcas nodded slowly. "Just a bit worn out," he said.

"Yes, but, you see, we need you," said Sacco insistently.

Dorcas groaned and allowed himself to be helped to his feet. He took a last look around the cab.

"It really went, didn't it?" he said. "It really went very well. All things considered. For his age."

He tried to give Sacco a cheerful look.

"What are you talking about?" said Sacco.

"All that time in that shed. Since the world was made, perhaps. And I just greased him and fueled him up and away he went," said Dorcas.

"The machine? Oh, yes. Well done," said Sacco.

"But—" Nooty pointed upward.

Dorcas shrugged.

"Oh, I'm not bothered about that," he said. "It's probably Masklin's doing. Perfectly simple explanation. Grimma is right. It's probably that flying thing he went off to get."

"But something's come out of it!" said Nooty.

"Not Masklin, you mean?"

"It's some kind of plant!"

Dorcas sighed. Always one thing after another. He patted Big John again.

"Well, *I* care," he said.

He straightened up and turned to the others. "All right," he said, "show me."


It was in a metal pot in the middle of the floating platform. The nomes craned and tried to climb on one another's shoulders to look at it, and none of them knew what it was except for Grimma, who was staring at it with a strange quiet smile on her face.

It was a branch from a tree. On the branch was a flower the size of a bucket.

If you climbed high enough, you could see that inside it, held with its glistening petals, was a pool of water. And from the depths of the pool, little yellow frogs stared up at the nomes.

"Have *you* any idea what it is?" said Sacco.

Dorcas smiled. "Masklin's found out that it's a good idea to send a girl flowers," he said. "And I think everything's all right." He glanced at Grimma.

"Yes, but *what* is it?"

"I seem to remember it's called a bromeliad," said Dorcas. "It grows on the top of very tall trees in wet forests a long way away, and little frogs spend their whole lives in it. Your whole life in one flower. Imagine that. Grimma once said she thought it was the most astonishing thing in the world."

Sacco bit his lip thoughtfully.

"Well, there's electricity," he said. "Electricity is quite astonishing."

"Or hydraulics," said Nooty, taking his hand. "You told me hydraulics was fascinating."

"Masklin must have got it for her," said Dorcas. "Very literal-minded lad, that lad. Very active imagination."

He stared from the flower to Big John looking small and old under the humming shadow of the Ship.

And felt, suddenly, quite cheerful. He was still tired enough to go to sleep standing up, but he felt his mind fizzing with ideas. Of course there were a lot of questions, but right now the answers didn't matter; it was enough just to enjoy the questions, and know that the world was full of astonishing things, and that he wasn't a frog.

Or at least he was the kind of frog who was interested in how flowers grew and whether you could get to other flowers if you jumped hard enough.

And, just when you'd got out of the flower, and were feeling really proud of yourself, you'd look at the new, big, wide endless world around you.

And eventually you'd notice that it had petals around the horizon.

Dorcas grinned.

"I'd very much like to know," he said, "what Masklin has been doing these past few weeks. . . ."

# WINGS

*The Third Book of the Nomes*

## AUTHOR'S NOTE

*No character in this book is intended to resemble any living creature of whatever size on any continent, especially if they've got lawyers.*

*I've also taken liberties with the Concorde itself, despite British Airways' kindness in letting me have a look around one. It really did look like shaped sky. But it didn't fly nonstop to Miami; it made a stop in Washington. But who wants to stop in Washington? Nomes couldn't do anything in Washington except cause trouble.*

*It's also just possible that people on the Concorde didn't have to eat special airline-food pink wobbly stuff. But everybody else has to.*

This is Masklin's story. . . .

*AIRPORT: A place where people hurry up and wait.*

> *From* A Scientific Encyclopedia
> for the Inquiring Young Nome
> *by Angalo de Haberdasheri*

LET THE EYE of your imagination be a camera. . . .

This is the universe, a glittering ball of galaxies like the ornament on some unimaginable Christmas tree.

Find a galaxy. . . .

*Focus*

This is a galaxy, swirled like the cream in a cup of coffee, every pinpoint of light a star.

Find a star. . . .

*Focus*

This is a solar system, where planets barrel through the darkness around the central fires of the sun. Some planets hug close, hot enough to melt lead. Some drift far out, where the comets are born.

Find a blue planet. . . .

*Focus*

This is a planet. Most of it is covered in water. It's called Earth.

Find a country. . . .

*Focus*

. . . blues and greens and browns under the sun, and here's a pale oblong which is . . .

*Focus*

. . . an airport, a concrete hive for silver bees, and there's a . . .

*Focus*

. . . building full of people and noise and . . .

*Focus*

. . . a hall of lights and bustle and . . .

*Focus*

. . . a bin full of rubbish and . . .

*Focus*

. . . a pair of tiny eyes . . .

*Focus*

*Focus*

*Focus*

Click!


Masklin slid cautiously down an old burger carton.

He'd been watching humans. Hundreds and hundreds of humans. It was beginning to dawn on him that getting on a jet plane wasn't like stealing a truck.

Angalo and Gurder had nestled deep into the rubbish and were gloomily eating the remains of a cold, greasy french fry.

This has come as a shock to all of us, Masklin thought.

I mean, take Gurder. Back in the Store he was the Abbot. He believed that Arnold Bros made the Store for nomes. And he still thinks there's some sort of Arnold Bros somewhere, watching over us, because we are important. And now we're out here, and all we've found is that nomes aren't important at all. . . .

And there's Angalo. He doesn't believe in Arnold Bros, but he likes to think Arnold Bros exists just so that he can go on not believing in him.

And there's me.

I never thought it would be this hard.

I thought jet planes were just trucks with more wings and less wheels.

There's more humans in this place than I've ever seen before. How can we find Grandson Richard, 39, in a place like this?

I hope they're going to save me some of that potato. . . .

Angalo looked up.

"Seen him?" he said, sarcastically.

Masklin shrugged. "There's lots of humans with beards," he said. "They all look the same to me."

"I *told* you," said Angalo. "Blind faith never works." He glared at Gurder.

"He could have gone already," said Masklin. "He could have walked right past me."

"So let's get back," said Angalo. "People will be missing us. We've made the effort, we've seen the airport, we've nearly got trodden on *dozens* of times. Now let's get back to the real world."

"What do you think, Gurder?" said Masklin.

The Abbot gave him a long, despairing look.

"I don't know," he said. "I really don't know. I'd hoped . . ."

His voice trailed off. He looked so downcast that even Angalo patted him on the shoulder.

"Don't take it so hard," he said. "You didn't *really* think some sort of Grandson Richard, 39, was going to swoop down out of the sky and carry us off to Florida, did you? Look, we've given it a try. It hasn't worked. Let's go home."

"Of course I didn't think *that*," said Gurder irritably. "I just thought that . . . maybe in some way . . . there'd be a way."

"The world belongs to humans. They built everything. They run everything. We might as well accept it," said Angalo.

Masklin looked at the Thing. He knew it was listening. Even though it was just a small black cube, it somehow always looked more alert when it was listening.

The trouble was, it spoke only when it felt like it. It'd always give you just enough help, and no more. It seemed to be testing him the whole time.

Somehow, asking the Thing for help was like admitting that you'd run out of ideas. But . . .

"Thing," he said, "I know you can hear me, because there must be loads of electricity in this building. We're at the airport. We can't find Grandson Richard, 39. We don't know how to *start* looking. Please help us."

The Thing stayed silent.

"If you *don't* help us," said Masklin quietly, "we'll go back to the quarry and face the humans, but that won't matter to you because we'll leave you here. We really will. And no nomes will ever find you again. There will never be another chance. We'll die out, there will be no more nomes anywhere, and it will be because of you. And in years and years to come you'll be all alone and useless and you'll think, Perhaps I should have helped Masklin when he asked me, and then you'll think, If I had my time all over again, I *would* have helped him. Well, Thing, imagine all that has happened and you've magically got your wish. Help us."

"It's a machine!" snapped Angalo. "You can't blackmail a machine—!"

One small red light lit up on the Thing's black surface.

"I know you can tell what other machines are thinking," said

Masklin. "But can you tell what nomes are thinking? Read my mind, Thing, if you don't think I'm serious. You want nomes to act intelligently. Well, I *am* acting intelligently. I'm intelligent enough to know when I need help. I need help now. And you can help. I know you can. If you don't help us, we'll leave right now and forget you ever existed."

A second light came on, very faintly.

Masklin stood up and nodded to the others.

"All right," he said. "Let's go."

The Thing made the little electronic noise that was the machine's equivalent of a nome clearing his throat.

*"How can I be of assistance?"* it said.

Angalo grinned at Gurder.

Masklin sat down again.

"Find Grandson Richard Arnold, 39," he said.

*"This will take a long time,"* said the Thing.

"Oh."

A few lights moved on the Thing's surface. Then it said, *"I have located a Richard Arnold, aged thirty-nine. He has just gone into the first-class departure lounge for flight 205 to Miami, Florida."*

"That didn't take a very long time," said Masklin.

*"It was three hundred microseconds,"* said the Thing. *"That's long."*

"I don't think I understood all of it, either," Masklin added.

*"Which parts didn't you understand?"*

"Nearly all of them," said Masklin. "All the bits after 'gone into.'"

*"Someone with the right name is here and waiting in a special room to get on a big silver bird that flies in the sky to go to a place called Florida,"* said the Thing.

"What big silver bird?" said Angalo.

"It means jet plane. It's being sarcastic," said Masklin.

"Yeah? How does it know all this stuff?" said Angalo suspiciously.

*"This building is full of computers,"* said the Thing.

"What, like you?"

The Thing managed to looked offended. *"They are very, very primitive,"* it said. *"But I can understand them. If I think slowly enough. Their job is to know where humans are going."*

"That's more than most humans do," said Angalo.

"Can you find out how we can get to him?" said Gurder, his face alight.

"Hold on, hold on," said Angalo, quickly. "Let's not rush into things here."

"We came here to find him, didn't we?" said Gurder.

"Yes! But what do we actually *do*?"

"Well, of course, we . . . we . . . that is, we'll . . ."

"We don't even know what a departure lounge is."

"The Thing said it's a room where humans wait to get on an airplane," said Masklin.

Gurder prodded Angalo with an accusing finger.

"You're frightened, aren't you," he said. "You're frightened that if we see Grandson Richard, 39, it'll mean there really *is* an Arnold Bros and you'll have been *wrong*! You're just like your father. He could never stand being wrong either!"

"I'm frightened about *you*," said Angalo. "Because you'll see that Grandson Richard is just a human. Arnold Bros was just a human, too. Or two humans. They just built the Store for humans. They didn't even know about nomes! And you can leave my father out of this, too."

The Thing opened a small hatch on its top. It did that sometimes. When the hatches were shut, you couldn't see where they were, but whenever the Thing was really interested in something, it opened up and extended a small silver dish on a pole, or a complicated arrangement of pipes.

This time it was a piece of wire mesh on a metal rod. It started to turn slowly.

Masklin picked up the box.

While the other two argued, he asked, quietly, "Do you know where this lounge thing is?"

*"Yes,"* said the Thing.

"Let's go, then."

Angalo looked round.

"Hey, what are you doing?" he said.

Masklin ignored him. He said to the Thing: "And do you know how much time we have before he starts going to Florida?"

*"About half an hour."*

Nomes live ten times faster than humans. They're harder to see than a high-speed mouse.

That's one reason why most humans hardly ever see them.

The other is that humans are very good at not seeing things they know aren't there. And since sensible humans know that there are no such things as people four inches high, a nome who doesn't want to be seen probably *won't* be seen.

So no one noticed three tiny blurs darting across the floor of the airport building. They dodged the rumbling wheels of luggage trolleys. They shot between the legs of slow-moving humans. They skidded around chairs. They became nearly invisible as they crossed a huge, echoing corridor.

And they disappeared behind a potted plant.

o     o     o

It has been said that everything everywhere affects everything else. This may be true.

Or perhaps the world is just full of patterns.

For example, in a tree nine thousand miles away from Masklin, high on a cloudy mountainside, was a plant that looked like one large flower. It grew wedged in a fork of the trees, its roots dangling in the air to trap what nourishment they could from the mists. Technically, it was an epiphytic bromeliad, although not knowing this made very little difference to the plant.

Water condensed into a tiny pool in the center of the bloom.

And there were the frogs.

Very, very small frogs.

They had such a tiny life cycle, it still had training wheels on it.

They hunted insects among the petals. They laid their eggs in the central pool. Tadpoles grew up and became more frogs. And made more tadpoles. Eventually they died and sank down and joined the compost at the base of the leaves, which, in fact, helped nourish the plant.

And this had been the way things were for as far back as the frogs could remember.*

Except that on this day, while it hunted for flies, one frog lost its way and crawled around the side of one of the outermost petals, or possibly leaves, and saw something it had never seen before.

It saw the universe.

More precisely, it saw the branch stretching away into the mists.

And several yards away, glistening with droplets of moisture in a solitary shaft of sunlight, was another flower.

The frog sat and stared.

---

*About three seconds. Frogs don't have good memories.

o o o

"Hngh! Hngh! Hngh!"

Gurder leaned against the wall and panted like a hot dog on a sunny day.

Angalo was almost as badly out of breath but was going red in the face trying not to show it.

"Why didn't you *tell* us!" he demanded.

"You were too busy arguing," said Masklin. "So I knew the only way to get you running was to start moving."

"Thank . . . you . . . very much," Gurder heaved.

"Why aren't you puffed out?" said Angalo.

"I'm used to running fast," said Masklin, peering around the plant. "Okay, Thing. Now what?"

*"Along this corridor,"* said the Thing.

"It's full of humans!" squeaked Gurder.

"Everywhere's full of humans. That's why we're doing this," said Masklin. He paused, and then added, "Look, Thing, isn't there any other way we can go? Gurder nearly got squashed just now."

Colored lights moved in complicated patterns across the Thing. Then it said, *"What is it you want to achieve?"*

"We must find Grandson Richard, 39," panted Gurder.

"No. Going to the Florida place is the important thing," said Masklin.

"It isn't!" said Gurder. "I don't want to go to any Florida!"

Masklin hesitated. Then he said, "This probably isn't the right time to say this, but I haven't been totally honest with you. . . ."

He told them about the Thing, and space, and the Ship in the sky. Around them there was the endless thundering noise of a building full of busy humans.

Eventually Gurder said, "You're not trying to find Grandson Richard at all?"

"I think he's probably very important," said Masklin hurriedly. "But you're right. At Florida there's a place where they have the sort of jet planes that go straight up to put kind of bleeping radio things in the sky."

"Oh, come *on*," said Angalo. "You can't just put things in the sky! They'd fall down."

"I don't really understand it myself," Masklin admitted. "But if you go up high enough, there is *no* down. I think. Anyway, all we have to do is to go to Florida and put the Thing on one of these going-up jets and it can do the rest, it says."

"All?" said Angalo.

"It can't be harder than stealing a truck," said Masklin.

"You're not suggesting we *steal* a plane?" said Gurder, by this time totally horrified.

"Wow!" said Angalo, his eyes lighting up as if by some internal power source. He loved vehicles of all sorts—especially when they were traveling fast.

"You would, too, wouldn't you," said Gurder accusingly.

"Wow!" said Angalo again. He seemed to be looking at a picture only he could see.

"You're crazy," said Gurder.

"No one said anything about stealing a plane," said Masklin quickly. "We aren't going to steal a plane. We're just going for a ride on one, I hope."

"Wow!"

"And we're *not* going to try to drive it, Angalo!"

Angalo shrugged.

"All right," he said. "But suppose I'm on it, and the driver becomes ill, then I expect I'll have to take over. I mean, I drove the Truck pretty well—"

"You kept running *into* things!" said Gurder.

"I was learning. Anyway, there's nothing to run into in the sky except clouds, and they look pretty soft," said Angalo.

"There's the *ground*!"

"Oh, the ground wouldn't be a problem. It'd be too far away."

Masklin tapped the Thing. "Do you know where the jet plane is that's going to Florida?"

"*Yes.*"

"Lead us there, then. Avoiding too many humans, if you can."


It was raining softly, and because it was early evening, lights were coming on around the airport.

Absolutely no one heard the faint tinkle as a little ventilation grille dropped off an outside wall.

Three blurred shapes lowered themselves down onto the concrete and sped away.

Toward the planes.


Angalo looked up. And up some more. And there was still more up to come. He ended up with his head craned all the way back.

He was nearly in tears. "Oh, wow!" he kept saying.

"It's too big," muttered Gurder, trying not to look. Like most of the nomes who had been born in the Store, he hated looking up and not seeing a ceiling. Angalo was the same, but more than being Outside he hated not going fast.

"I've seen them go up in the sky," said Masklin. "They really do fly. Honestly."

"Wow!"

It loomed over them, so big that you had to keep on stepping back and back to see how big it was. Rain glistened on it. The airport lights made smears of green and white bloom on its flanks. It wasn't a *thing*, it was a bit of shaped sky.

"Of course, they look smaller when they're a long way off," Masklin muttered.

He stared up at the plane. He'd never felt smaller in his life.

"I *want* one," moaned Angalo, clenching his fists. "*Look* at it. It looks as though it's going too fast even when it's standing still!"

"How do we get on it, then?" said Gurder.

"Can't you just see their faces back home if we turned up with this?" said Angalo.

"Yes. I can. Horribly clearly," said Gurder. "But how do we get on it?"

"We could—" Angalo began. He hesitated. "Why did you have to say that?" he snapped.

"There's the holes where the wheels stick through," said Masklin. "I think we could climb up there."

"*No,*" said the Thing, which was tucked under his arm. "*You would not be able to breathe. You must be properly inside. Where the planes go, the air is thin.*"

"I should hope so," said Gurder stoutly. "That's why it's air."

"*You would not be able to breathe,*" said the Thing patiently.

"Yes I would," said Gurder. "I've always been able to breathe."

"You get more air close to the ground," said Angalo. "I read that in a book. You get lots of air low down, and not much when you go up."

"Why not?" said Gurder.

"Dunno. It's frightened of heights, I guess."

Masklin waded through the puddles on the concrete so that he could see down the far side of the aircraft. Some way away a couple of humans were using some sort of machines to load boxes into a hole in the side of the plane. He walked back, around the huge tires, and squinted up at a long, high tube that stretched from the building.

He pointed.

"I think that's how humans are loaded onto it," he said.

"What, through a pipe? Like water?" said Angalo.

"It's better than standing out here getting wet, anyway," said Gurder. "I'm soaked through already."

"There's stairs and wires and things," said Masklin. "It shouldn't be too difficult to climb up there. There's bound to be a gap we can slip in by." He sniffed. "There always is," he added, "when humans build things."

"Let's do it!" said Angalo. "Oh, wow!"

"But you're not to try to steal it," said Masklin as they helped the slightly plump Gurder lumber into a run. "It's going where we want to go anyway—"

"Not where I want to go," moaned Gurder. "I want to go home!"

"—and you're not to try to drive it. There's not enough of us. Anyway, I expect it's a lot more complicated than a truck. It's a—do you know what it's called, Thing?"

*"A Concorde."*

"There," said Masklin. "It's a Concorde. Whatever that is. And you've got to promise not to steal it."

# 2

*CONCORDE: It goes twice as fast as a bullet and you get smoked salmon.*

*From* A Scientific Encyclopedia
for the Inquiring Young Nome
*by Angalo de Haberdasheri*

SQUEEZING THROUGH A gap in the humans-walking-onto-planes pipe wasn't as hard as coming to terms with what was on the other side.

The floors of the sheds in the quarry had been bare boards or stamped earth. In the airport building it was squares of a sort of shiny stone. But here—

Gurder flung himself facedown and buried his nose in it.

"Carpet!" he said, almost in tears. "Carpet! I never thought I'd see you again!"

"Oh, get up," said Angalo, embarrassed at the Abbot acting like that in front of someone who, however much of a friend he was, hadn't been born a Store nome.

Gurder stood up awkwardly. "Sorry," he mumbled, brushing himself off. "Don't know what possessed me there. It just took me back, that's all. Real carpet. Haven't seen real carpet for *months*."

He blew his nose noisily. "We had some beautiful carpets in the Store, you know. Beautiful. Some of them had patterns on them."

Masklin looked up the pipe. It was like one of the Store's corridors, and quite brightly lit.

"Let's move on," he said. "It's too exposed here. Where are all the humans, Thing?"

*"They will be arriving shortly."*

"How does it *know?*" Gurder complained.

"It listens to other machines," said Masklin.

*"There are also many computers on this plane,"* said the Thing.

"Well, that's nice," said Masklin vaguely. "You'll have someone to talk to, then."

*"They are quite stupid,"* said the Thing, and managed to express disdain without actually having anything to express it with.

A few feet away the corridor opened into a new space. Masklin could see a curtain, and what looked like the edge of a chair.

"All right, Angalo," he said. "Lead the way. I know you want to."

It was two minutes later.

The three of them were sitting under a seat.

Masklin had never really thought about the insides of aircraft. He'd spent days up on the cliff behind the quarry, watching them take off. Of course, he'd assumed there were humans inside. Humans got everywhere. But he'd never really thought about the insides. If ever there was anything that looked made up of outsides, it was a plane flying.

But it had been too much for Gurder. He was in tears.

"Electric light," he moaned. "And more carpets! And big soft seats! They've even got napkins on them! And there isn't any mud *anywhere*! There's even *signs*!"

"There, there," said Angalo helplessly, patting him on the shoulder. "It was a *good* Store, I know." He looked up at Masklin. "You've got to admit it's unsettling," he said. "I was expecting . . . well, wires and pipes and exciting levers and things. Not something like the Arnold Bros Furnishing Department!"

"We shouldn't stay here," said Masklin. "There'll be humans all over the place pretty soon. Remember what the Thing said."

They helped Gurder up and trotted under the rows of seats with him between them. But it wasn't like the Store in one important way, Masklin realized. There weren't many places to hide. In the Store there was always something to get behind or under or wriggle through. . . .

He could already hear distant sounds. In the end they found a gap behind a curtain, in a part of the aircraft where there were no seats. Masklin crawled inside, pushing the Thing in front of him.

They weren't distant sounds now. They were very close. He turned his head and saw a human foot a few inches away.

At the back of the gap there was a hole in the metal wall where some thick wires passed through. It was just big enough for Angalo and Masklin, and big enough for a terrified Gurder with the two of them pulling on his arms. There wasn't too much room, but at least they couldn't be seen.

They couldn't see, either. They lay packed together in the gloom, trying to make themselves comfortable on the wires.

After a while Gurder said, "I feel a bit better now."

Masklin nodded.

There were noises all around them. From somewhere far below came a series of metallic clonks. There was the mournful sound of human voices, and then a jolt.

"Thing?" he whispered.

*"Yes?"*

"What's happening?"

*"The plane is getting ready to become airborne."*

"Oh."

*"Do you know what that means?"*

"No. Not really."

*"It is going to fly in the air. Borne means to be carried, and air means air. To be borne in the air. Airborne."*

Masklin could hear Angalo's breathing.

He settled himself as best he could between the metal wall and a heavy bundle of wires, and stared into the darkness.

The nomes didn't speak. After a while there was a faint jerk and a sensation of movement.

Nothing else happened. It went on not happening.

Eventually Gurder, his voice trembling with terror, said, "Is it too late to get off, if we—?"

A sudden distant thundering noise finished the sentence for him. A dull rumbling shook everything around them very gently but very firmly.

Then there was a heavy pause, like the moment a ball must feel between the time it's thrown up and the time it starts to come down, and something picked up all three of them and slid them into a struggling heap. The floor tried to become the wall.

The nomes hung on to one another, stared into one another's faces, and screamed.

After a while, they stopped. There didn't seem much point in continuing. Besides, they were out of breath.

The floor, very gradually, became a proper floor again and didn't show any further ambitions to become a wall.

Masklin pushed Angalo's foot off his neck.

"I think we're flying," he said.

"Is that what it was?" said Angalo weakly. "It looks kind of more graceful when you see it from the ground."

"Is anyone hurt?"

Gurder pulled himself upright.

"I'm all bruises," he said. He brushed himself down. And then, because there is no changing nomish nature, he added, "Is there any food around?"

They hadn't thought about food.

Masklin stared behind him into the tunnel of wires.

"Maybe we won't need any," he said, uncertainly. "How long will it take to get to Florida, Thing?"

*"The captain has just said it will be six hours and forty-five minutes,"* said the Thing.*

"We'll starve to death!" said Gurder.

"Maybe there's something to hunt?" said Angalo hopefully.

"I shouldn't think so," Masklin said. "This doesn't look like a mouse kind of place."

"The humans'll have food," said Gurder. "Humans always have food."

"I *knew* you were going to say that," said Angalo.

"It's just common sense."

"I wonder if we can see out of a window?" said Angalo. "I'd like to see how fast we're going. All the trees and things whizzing past, and so on?"

"Look," said Masklin, before things got out of hand. "Let's just wait for a while, eh? Everyone calm down. Have a bit of a rest. *Then* maybe we can look for some food."

---

* About as long as two and a half days, to a nome.

They settled down again. At least it was warm and dry. Back in the days when he'd lived in a hole in a bank, Masklin had spent far too much time cold and wet to turn up his nose at a chance to sleep warm and dry.

He dozed. . . .

Airborne.

Air . . . born . . .

Perhaps there were hundreds of nomes who lived in the airplanes in the same way that nomes had lived in the Store. Perhaps they got on with their lives under the carpeted floor somewhere, while they were whisked to all the places Masklin had seen on the only map the nomes had ever found. It had been in a pocket diary, and the names of the faraway places written on it were like magic—Africa, Australia, China, Equator, Printed in Hong Kong, Iceland . . .

Perhaps they'd never looked out of the windows. Perhaps they'd never known that they were moving at all.

He wondered if this was what Grimma had meant by all the stuff about the frogs in the flower. She'd read it in a book. You could live your whole life in some tiny place and think it was the whole world. The trouble was, he'd been angry. He hadn't wanted to listen.

Well, he was out of the flower now, and no mistake. . . .

The frog had brought some other young frogs to its spot among the leaves at the edge of the world of the flower.

They stared at the branch. There wasn't just one flower out there, there were dozens, although the frogs weren't able to think like this because frogs can't count beyond one.

They saw lots of ones.

They stared at them. Staring is one of the few things frogs are good at.

Thinking isn't. It would be nice to say that the tiny frogs thought long and hard about the new flower, about life in the old flower, about the need to explore, about the possibility that the world was bigger than a pool with petals around the edge.

In fact, what they thought was: .–.–.mipmip.–.–.mipmip.–.–. mipmip.

But what they *felt* was too big for one flower to contain.

Carefully, slowly, not at all certain why, they plopped down onto the branch.

There was a polite beeping from the Thing.

*"You may be interested to know,"* it said, *"that we've broken the sound barrier."*

Masklin turned wearily to the others.

"All right, own up," he said. "Who broke it?"

"Don't look at me," said Angalo. "I didn't touch anything."

Masklin crawled to the edge of the hole and peered out.

There were human feet out there. Female human feet, by the look of it. They usually were the ones with the less practical shoes.

You could learn a lot about humans by looking at their shoes. It was about all a nome had to look at, most of the time. The rest of the human was normally little more than the wrong end of a pair of nostrils, a long way up.

Masklin sniffed.

"There's food somewhere," he said.

"What kind?" said Angalo.

"Never mind what kind," said Gurder, pushing him out of the way. "Whatever it is, I'm going to *eat* it."

"Get back!" Masklin snapped, pushing the Thing into Angalo's arms. "I'll go! Angalo, don't let him move!"

He darted out, ran for the curtain, and slid behind it. After a few seconds, he moved just enough to let one eye and a frowning eyebrow show.

The room was some sort of food place. The human females were taking trays of food out of the wall. Nomish sense of smell is sharper than a fox's; it was all Masklin could do not to drool. He had to admit it—it was all very well hunting and growing things, but what you got wasn't half as good as the food you found around humans.

One of the females put the last tray on a trolley and wheeled it past Masklin. The wheels were almost as tall as he was.

As it squeaked past, he darted out of his hiding place and leaped onto it, squeezing himself among the bottles. It was a stupid thing to do, he knew. It was just better than being stuck in a hole with a couple of idiots.

Rows and rows of shoes. Some black, some brown. Some with laces, some without. Quite a few of them without feet in them, because the humans had taken them off.

Masklin looked up as the trolley inched forward.

Rows and rows of legs. Some in skirts, but most in trousers.

Masklin looked up farther. Nomes rarely saw humans sitting down.

Rows and rows of bodies, topped with rows and rows of heads with faces at the front. Rows and rows of—

Masklin crouched back among the bottles.

Grandson Richard was watching him.

It was the face in the newspaper. It had to be. There was the little beard, and the smiling mouth with lots of teeth in it. And the hair that looked as though it had been dramatically carved out of something shiny rather than been grown in the normal way.

Grandson Richard, 39.

The face stared at him for a moment and then looked away.

He can't have seen me, Masklin told himself. I'm hidden away here.

What will Gurder say when I tell him?

He'll go mad, that's what.

I think I'll keep it to myself for a while. That might be an amazingly good idea. We've got enough to worry about as it is.

39. Either there've been thirty-eight other Grandson Richards, and I don't think that's what it means, or it's a newspaper human way of saying he's thirty-nine years old. Nearly half as old as the Store. And the Store nomes say the Store is as old as the world. I know that can't be true, but—

I wonder what it feels like to live nearly *forever*?

He burrowed farther into the things on the shelf. Mostly they were bottles, but there were a few bags containing knobbly things a bit smaller than Masklin's fist. He stabbed at the paper with his knife until he'd cut a hole big enough, and pulled one of them out.

It was a salted peanut. Well, it was a start.

He grabbed the packet just as a hand reached past.

It was close enough to touch.

It was close enough to touch *him*.

He could see the red of its fingernails as they slid by him, closed slowly over another packet of nuts, and withdrew.

It dawned on Masklin later that the giving-out-food woman wouldn't have been able to see him. She just reached down and into the tray for what she knew would be there, and this almost certainly didn't include Masklin.

That's what he decided later. At the time, with a human hand almost brushing his head, it all looked a lot different. He took a running dive off the trolley, rolled when he hit the carpet, and scurried under the nearest seat.

He didn't even wait to catch his breath. Experience had taught him that it was when you stopped to catch your breath that things caught you. He charged from seat to seat, dodging giant feet, discarded shoes, dropped newspapers and bags. By the time he crossed the bit of aisle to the food place, he was a blur even by nome standards. He didn't stop even when he reached the hole. He just leaped, and went through it without touching the sides.

"A peanut?" said Angalo. "Between three? That's not a mouthful each!"

"What do you suggest?" said Masklin, bitterly. "Do you want to go to the giving-out-food-woman and say there's three small hungry people down here?"

Angalo stared at him. Masklin had got his breath back now but was still very red in the face.

"You know, that could be worth a try," he said.

"What?"

"Well, if you were a human, would you expect to see nomes on a plane?" said Angalo.

"Of course I wouldn't—"

"I bet you'd be amazed if you *did* see one, eh?"

"Are you suggesting we deliberately show ourselves to a human?" Gurder said suspiciously. "We've never done that, you know."

"I nearly did just now," said Masklin. "I won't do it again in a hurry!"

"We've always preferred to starve to death on one peanut, you mean?"

Gurder looked longingly at the piece of nut in his hand. They'd eaten peanuts in the Store, of course. Around Christmas Fayre, when the Food Hall was crammed with food you didn't normally see in the other seasons, they made a nice end to a meal. Probably they made a nice start to a meal, too. What they didn't make was a meal.

"What's the plan?" he asked wearily.

One of the giving-out-food humans was pulling trays off a shelf when a movement made it look up. Its head turned very slowly.

Something small and black was being lowered down right by its ear.

It stuck tiny thumbs in small ears, wagged its fingers, and put out its tongue.

"Thrrrrrrrrp," said Gurder.

The tray in the human's hands crashed onto the floor in front of it. It made a long-drawn-out noise which sounded like a high-pitched foghorn and backed away, raising its hands to its mouth. Finally it turned, very slowly, like a tree about to fall, and fled between the curtains.

When it came back, with another human being, the little figure had gone.

So had most of the food.

"I don't know when I last had smoked salmon," said Gurder happily.

"Mmmph," said Angalo.

"You're not supposed to eat it like that," said Gurder severely. "You're not supposed to shove it all in your mouth and then cut off whatever won't fit. Whatever will people think?"

"'S no people here," said Angalo, but indistinctly. "'S just you an' Masklin."

Masklin cut the lid off a container of milk. It was practically nome-sized.

"This is more like it, eh?" said Gurder. "Proper food the natural way, out of tins and things. None of this having to clean the dirt off it, like in the quarry. And it's nice and warm in here, too. It's the only way to travel. Anyone want some of this"—he prodded a dish vaguely, not sure of what was in it—"stuff?"

The others shook their heads. The dish contained something shiny and wobbly and pink with a cherry on it, and in some strange way it managed to look like something you wouldn't eat even if it were pushed onto your plate after a week's starvation diet.

"What does it taste of?" said Masklin, after Gurder had chewed a mouthful.

"Tastes of pink," said Gurder.*

"Anyone fancy the peanut to finish with?" said Angalo. He grinned. "No? I'll chuck it away, shall I?"

"No!" said Masklin. They looked at him. "Sorry," he said. "I mean, you shouldn't. It's wrong to waste good food."

"It's *wicked*," said Gurder primly.

"Mmm. Don't know about wicked," said Masklin. "But it's stupid. Put it in your pack. You never know when you might need it."

Angalo stretched his arms and yawned.

"A wash would be nice," he said.

"Didn't see any water," Masklin said. "There's probably a sink or a lavatory somewhere, but I wouldn't know where to start looking."

---

* Little dishes of strange wobbly stuff tasting of pink turn up in nearly every meal on all airplanes. No one knows why. There's probably some sort of special religious reason.

"Talking of lavatories—" said Angalo.

"Right down the other end of the pipe, please," said Gurder.

*"And keep away from any wiring,"* volunteered the Thing. Angalo nodded in a puzzled fashion, and crawled away into the darkness.

Gurder yawned and stretched his arms.

"Won't the giving-out-food humans look for us?" he said.

"I don't think so," said Masklin. "Back when we used to live Outside, before we found the Store, I'm sure humans saw us sometimes. I don't think they really believe their eyes. They wouldn't make those weird garden ornaments if they'd ever seen a *real* nome."

Gurder reached into his robe and pulled out the picture of Grandson Richard. Even in the dim light of the pipe, Masklin recognized it as the human in the seat. He hadn't got creases on his face from being folded up, and he wasn't made up of hundreds of tiny dots, but apart from that . . .

"Do you think he's here somewhere?" said Gurder wistfully.

"Could be. Could be," said Masklin, feeling wretched. "But, look, Gurder . . . maybe Angalo goes a bit too far, but he could be right. Maybe Grandson Richard is just another human being, you know. Probably humans *did* build the Store just for humans. Your ancestors just moved in because, well, it was warm and dry. And—"

"I'm not listening, you know," said Gurder. "I'm not going to be told that we're just things like rats and mice. We're special."

"The Thing is quite definite about us coming from somewhere else, Gurder," said Masklin meekly.

The Abbot folded up the picture. "Maybe we did. Maybe we didn't," he said. "That doesn't matter."

"Angalo thinks it matters if it's true."

"Don't see why. There's more than one kind of truth." Gurder shrugged. "I might say: You're just a lot of dust and juices and bones and hair, and that's true. And I might say: You've got something inside your head that goes away when you die. That's true, too. Ask the Thing."

Colored lights flickered across the Thing's surface.

Masklin looked shocked. "I've *never* asked it that sort of question," he said.

"Why not? It's the first question *I'd* ask."

"It'll probably say something like 'Does not compute' or 'Inoperative parameters.' That's what it says when it doesn't know and doesn't want to admit it. Thing?"

The Thing didn't reply. Its lights changed their pattern.

"Thing?" Masklin repeated.

*"I am monitoring communications."*

"It often does that when it's feeling bored," said Masklin to Gurder. "It just sits there listening to invisible messages in the air. Pay attention, Thing. This is important. We want—"

The lights moved. A lot of them went red.

"Thing! We—"

The Thing made the little clicking noise that was its equivalent of clearing its throat.

*"A nome has been seen in the pilot's cabin."*

"Listen, Thing, we—what?"

*"I repeat: a nome has been seen in the pilot's cabin."*

Masklin looked around wildly.

"Angalo?"

*"That is an extreme probability,"* said the Thing.

# 3

*TRAVELING HUMANS: Large, nomelike creatures. Many humans spend a lot of time traveling from place to place, which is odd because there are usually too many humans at the place they're going to anyway. Also see under ANIMALS, INTELLIGENCE, EVOLUTION, and CUSTARD.*

*From* A Scientific Encyclopedia
for the Inquiring Young Nome
*by Angalo de Haberdasheri*

THE SOUND OF Masklin's and Gurder's voices echoed up and down the pipe as they scrambled over the wires.

"I *thought* he was taking too long!"

"You shouldn't have let him go off by himself! You know what he's like about driving things!"

"*I* shouldn't have let him?"

"He's just got no sense of—which way now?"

Angalo had said he thought the inside of a plane would be a mass of wires and pipes. He was nearly right. The nomes squeezed their way through a narrow, cable-hung world under the floor.

"I'm too old for this! There comes a time in a nome's life when he shouldn't crawl around the inside of terrible flying machines!"

"How many times have you done it?"

"Once too often!"

*"We are getting closer,"* said the Thing.

"This is what comes of showing ourselves! It's a Judgment," declared Gurder.

"Whose?" said Masklin grimly, helping him up.

"What do you mean?"

"There has to be someone to make a judgment!"

"I meant just a judgment in general!"

Masklin stopped.

"Where now, Thing?"

*"The message told the giving-out-food people that a strange little creature was on the flight deck,"* said the Thing. *"That is where we are. There are many computers here."*

"They're talking to you, are they?"

*"A little. They are like children. Mostly they listen,"* said the Thing smugly. *"They are not very intelligent."*

"What are we going to *do*?" said Gurder.

"We're going to—" Masklin hesitated. The word "rescue" was looming up somewhere in the sentence ahead.

It was a good, dramatic word. He longed to say it. The trouble was that there was another, simpler, nastier word a little further beyond.

It was "How?"

"I don't think they'd try to hurt him," he said, hoping it was true. "Maybe they'll put him somewhere. We ought to find a place where we can see what's happening." He looked helplessly at the wires and intricate bits of metal in front of them.

"You'd better let me lead, then," said Gurder in a matter-of-fact voice.

"Why?"

"You might be very good in wide-open spaces," said the Abbot, pushing past him. "But in the Store we knew all about getting around inside things."

He rubbed his hands together.

"Right," he said, then grabbed a cable and slid through a gap Masklin hadn't even noticed was there.

"Used to do this sort of thing when I was a boy," he said. "We used to get up to all sorts of tricks."

"Yes?" said Masklin.

"Down this way, I think. Mind the wires. Oh, yes. Up and down the lift shafts, in and out of the telephone switchboard . . ."

"I thought you always said kids spent far too much time running around and getting into mischief these days?"

"Ah. Yes. Well, *that's* juvenile delinquency," said Gurder sternly. "It's quite different from our youthful high spirits. Let's try up here."

They crawled between two warm metal walls. There was daylight ahead.

Masklin and Gurder lay down and pulled themselves forward.

There was an odd-shaped room, not a lot bigger than the cab of the truck itself. Like the cab, it was really just a space where the human drivers fitted into the machinery.

There was a *lot* of that.

It covered the walls and ceiling. Lights and switches, dials and levers. Masklin thought: If Dorcas were here, we'd never get him to leave. Angalo's here somewhere, and we want *him* to leave.

There were two humans kneeling on the floor. One of the giving-out-food females was standing by them. There was a lot of mooing and growling going on.

"Human talking," muttered Masklin. "I wish we could understand it."

*"Very well,"* said the Thing. *"Stand by."*

"You can understand human noises?"

*"Certainly. They're only nome noises slowed down."*

"What? *What?* You never told us that! You never told us that before!"

*"There are many billions of things I have not told you. Where would you like me to start?"*

"You can start by telling me what they're saying now," said Masklin. "Please?"

*"One of the humans has just said, 'It must have been a mouse or something,' and the other one said, 'You show me a mouse wearing clothes and I'll admit it was a mouse.' And the giving-out-food woman said, 'It was no mouse I saw. It blew a raspberry at me (exclamation).'"*

"What's a raspberry?"

*"The small red fruit of the plant* Rubus idaeus.*"*

Masklin turned to Gurder.

"Did you?"

"Me? What fruit? Listen, if there'd been any fruit around I'd have eaten it. I just went 'thrrrrp.'"

*"One of the humans has just said, 'I looked round and there it was, staring out of the window.'"*

"That's Angalo, all right," said Gurder.

*"Now the other kneeling-down human has said, 'Well, whatever it is, it's behind this panel and it can't go anywhere.'"*

"It's taking off a bit of the wall!" said Masklin. "Oh, no! It's reaching inside!"

The human mooed.

"*The human said, 'It bit me! The little devil bit me!'*" said the Thing, conversationally.

"Yep. That's Angalo," said Gurder. "His father was like that, too. A fighter in a tight corner."

"But they don't know what they've got!" said Masklin urgently. "They've seen him but he ran away! They're arguing about it! They don't really believe in nomes! If we can get him out before he's caught, they're bound to think it was a mouse or something!"

"I suppose we could get round there inside the walls," said Gurder. "But it'd take too long."

Masklin looked desperately around the cabin. Besides the three people trying to catch Angalo, there were two humans up at the front. They must be the drivers, he thought.

"I'm right out of ideas," he said. "Can you think of anything, Thing?"

"*There is practically no limit to what I can think of.*"

"I *mean*, is there anything you can do to help us rescue Gurder?"

"*Yes.*"

"You'd better do it, then."

"*Yes.*"

A moment later they heard the low clanging of alarms. Lights began to flash. The drivers shouted and leaned forward and started doing things to switches.

"What's going on?" said Masklin.

"*It is possible that the humans are startled that they are no longer flying this machine,*" said the Thing.

"They're not? Who is, then?"

The lights rippled smoothly across the Thing.

"*I am.*"

o    o    o

One of the frogs fell off the branch and disappeared quietly into the leafy canopy far below. Since very small, light animals can fall a long way without being hurt, it's quite likely that it survived in the forest world under the tree and had the second most interesting experience any tree frog has ever had.

The rest of them crawled onward.

Masklin helped Gurder along another metal channel full of wires. Overhead they could hear human feet and the growling of humans in trouble.

"I don't think they're very happy about it," said Gurder.

"But they haven't got time to look for something that was probably a mouse," said Masklin.

"It's not a mouse, it's Angalo!"

"But afterward they'll *think* it was a mouse. I don't think humans want to know things that disturb them."

"Sound just like nomes to me," said Gurder.

Masklin looked at the Thing under his arm.

"Are you really driving the Concorde?" he said.

"*Yes.*"

"I thought to drive things you had to turn wheels and change gears and things?" said Masklin.

"*That is all done by machines. The humans press buttons and turn wheels just to tell machines what to do.*"

"So what are you doing, then?"

"*I,*" said the Thing, "*am being in charge.*"

Masklin listened to the muted thunder of the engines.

"Is that hard?" he said.

*"Not in itself. However, the humans keep trying to interfere."*

"I think we'd better find Angalo quickly, then," said Gurder. "Come on."

They inched their way along another cable tunnel.

"They ought to thank us for letting our Thing do their job for them," said Gurder solemnly.

"I don't think they see it like that, exactly," said Masklin.

*"We are flying at a height of 55,000 feet at 1,352 miles per hour,"* said the Thing.

When they didn't comment, it added, *"That's very high and very fast."*

"That's good," said Masklin, who realized that some sort of remark was expected.

*"Very, very fast."*

The two nomes squeezed through the gap between a couple of metal plates.

*"Faster than a bullet, in fact."*

"Amazing," said Masklin.

*"Twice the speed of sound in this atmosphere,"* the Thing went on.

"Wow."

*"I wonder if I can put it another way,"* said the Thing, and it managed to sound slightly annoyed. *"It could get from the Store to the quarry in under fifteen seconds."*

"Good thing we didn't meet it coming the other way, then," said Masklin.

"Oh, stop teasing it," said Gurder. "It wants you to tell it it's a good boy . . . Thing," he corrected himself.

*"I do not,"* said the Thing, rather more quickly than usual. *"I was*

*merely pointing out that this is a very specialized machine and requires
skillful control."*

"Perhaps you shouldn't talk so much, then," said Masklin.

The Thing rippled its lights at him.

"That was nasty," said Gurder.

"Well, I've spent a year doing what the Thing's told me and I've
never had so much as a 'thank you,'" said Masklin. "How high are
fifty-five thousand feet, anyway?"

*"Ten point forty-two miles. Twice as far as the distance from the Store
to the quarry."*

Gurder stopped.

"Up?" he said. "We're that far *up?*"

He looked down at the floor.

"Oh," he said.

"Now don't *you* start," said Masklin quickly. "We've got enough
problems with Angalo. Stop holding on to the wall like that!"

Gurder had gone white.

"We must be as high as all those fluffy white cloud things," he
breathed.

*"No,"* said the Thing.

"That's some comfort, then," said Gurder.

*"They're all a long way below us."*

"Oh."

Masklin grabbed the Abbot's arm.

"Angalo, remember?" he said.

Gurder nodded slowly and inched his way forward, holding on
to things with his eyes closed.

"We mustn't lose our heads," said Masklin. "Even if we *are* up so
high." He looked down. The metal below him was quite solid. You

needed to use imagination to see through it to the ground below.

The trouble was that he had a very good imagination.

"Ugh," he said. "Come on, Gurder. Give me your hand."

"It's right in front of you."

"Sorry. Didn't see it with my eyes shut."

They spent ages cautiously moving up and down among the wiring, until eventually Gurder said, "It's no good. There isn't a hole big enough to get through. He'd have found it, if there was."

"Then we've got to find a way into the cab and get him out like that," said Masklin.

"With all those humans in there?"

"They'll be too busy to notice us. Right, Thing?"

*"Right."*

There is a place so far up there is no down.

A little lower, a white dart seared across the top of the sky, outrunning the night, overtaking the sun, crossing in a few hours an ocean that was once the edge of the world. . . .

Masklin lowered himself carefully to the floor and crept forward. The humans weren't even looking in his direction.

I hope the Thing really knows how to drive this plane, he thought.

He sidled along toward the panels where, with any luck, Angalo was hiding.

This wasn't right. He hated being exposed like this. Of course, it had probably been worse in the days when he used to have to hunt alone. If anything had caught him then, he would never have known it. He'd have been a mouthful. Whereas no one knew what humans would do to a nome if they caught one. . . .

He darted into the blessed shadows.

"Angalo!" he hissed.

After a while a voice from behind the wiring said, "Who is it?"

Masklin straightened up. "How many guesses do you want?" he said in his normal voice.

Angalo dropped down. "They chased me!" he said. "And one of them stuck its arm—"

"I know. Come on, while they're busy."

"What's happening?" said Angalo, as they hurried out into the light.

"The Thing is flying us."

"How? It's got no arms. It can't change gear or anything—"

"Apparently it's being bossy to the computers that do all that. Come on."

"I looked out of the window," bubbled Angalo. "There's sky all over the place!"

"Don't remind me," said Masklin.

"Let me just have one more look—" Angalo began.

"Listen, Gurder's waiting for us and we don't want any more trouble—"

"But this is better than any truck—"

There was a strangled kind of noise.

The nomes looked up.

One of the humans was watching them. Its mouth was open, and it had an expression on its face of someone who is going to have a lot of difficulty explaining what he has just seen, especially to himself.

The human was already getting to its feet.

Angalo and Masklin looked at each other.

"Run!" they shouted.

Gurder was lurking suspiciously in a patch of shadow by the door when they came past, arms and legs going like pistons. He caught up the skirts of his robe and scurried after them.

"What's happening? What's happening?"

"There's a human after us!"

"Don't leave me behind! Don't leave me behind!"

Masklin was just ahead of the other two as they raced up the aisle between the rows of humans, who paid no attention at all to three tiny blurs running between the seats.

"We shouldn't have . . . stood around . . . looking!" Masklin gasped.

"We might . . . never . . . have a chance . . . like that again!" panted Angalo.

"You're *right!*"

The floor tilted slightly.

"*Thing!* What are you doing!"

"*Creating a distraction.*"

"Don't! Everyone this way!"

Masklin darted between two seats, around a pair of giant shoes, and threw himself flat on the carpet. The others hurled themselves down behind him.

Two huge human feet were a few inches away from them.

Masklin pulled the Thing up close to his face.

"Let them have their airplane back!" he hissed.

"*I was hoping to be allowed to land it,*" said the Thing. Even though its voice was always flat and expressionless, Masklin still thought that it sounded wistful.

"Do you know how to land one of these things?" said Masklin.

*"I should like the opportunity to learn—"*

"Let them have it back right *now!*"

There was a faint lurch and a change in the pattern of the lights on the Thing's surface. Masklin breathed out.

"Now, will everyone act sensibly for five minutes?" he said.

"Sorry, Masklin," said Angalo. He tried to look apologetic, but it didn't work. Masklin recognized the wide-eyed, slightly mad smile of someone very nearly in his own personal heaven. "It was just that . . . do you know it's even blue below us? It's like there's no ground down there at all! And—"

"If the Thing tries any more flying lessons, we might all find out if that's true," said Masklin gloomily. "So let's just sit down and be quiet, shall we?"

They sat in silence for a while, under the seat.

Then Gurder said, "That human has got a hole in his sock."

"What about it?" said Angalo.

"Dunno, really. It's just that you never think of humans as having holes in their socks."

"Where you get socks, holes aren't far behind," said Masklin.

"They're good socks, though," said Angalo.

Masklin stared at them. They just looked like basic socks to him. Nomes in the Store used them as sleeping bags.

"How can you tell?" he said.

"They're Histyle Odorprufe," said Angalo. "Guaranteed eighty-five percent Polyputheketlon. We used to sell them in the Store. They cost a lot more than other socks. Look, you can see the label."

Gurder sighed.

"It was a good Store," he muttered.

"And those shoes," said Angalo, pointing to the great white shapes like beached boats a little way away. "See them? Crucial

Street Drifters with Real Rubber Sole Pat'd. Very expensive."

"Never approved of them, myself," said Gurder. "Too flashy. I preferred Men's, Brown, Laced. A nome could get a good night's sleep in one of those."

"Those Drifter things are Store shoes too, are they?" said Masklin, carefully.

"Oh, yes. Special Range."

"Hmm."

Masklin got up and walked over to a large leather bag half wedged under the seat. The others watched him scramble up it and then pull himself up until he could, very quickly, glance over the armrest. He slid back down.

"Well, well," he said, in a mad, cheerful voice. "That's a Store bag, isn't it?"

Gurder and Angalo gave it a critical look.

"Never spent much time in Travel Accessories," said Angalo. "But now that you mention it, it could be the Special Calf-Skin Carry-On Bag."

"For The Discerning Executive?" Gurder added. "Yes. Could be."

"Have you wondered how we're going to get off?" said Masklin.

"Same way as we got on?" said Angalo, who hadn't.

"I think that could be difficult. I think the humans might have other ideas," Masklin said. "I think, in fact, they might start look-ing for us. Even if they think we're mice. I wouldn't put up with mice on something like this if I was them. You know what mice are like for widdling on wires. Could be dangerous when you're ten miles high, a mouse going to the lavatory inside your computer. I think the humans will take it very seriously. So we ought to get off when the humans do."

"We'd get stamped on!" said Angalo.

"I was thinking maybe we could sort of . . . get in this bag, sort of thing," said Masklin.

"Ridiculous!" said Gurder.

Masklin took a deep breath.

"It belongs to Grandson Richard, you see," he said.

"I checked," he added, watching the expressions on their faces. "I saw him before, and he's in the seat up there. Grandson Richard," he went on, "39. He's up there right now. Reading a paper. Up there. Him."

Gurder had gone red. He prodded Masklin with a finger. "Do you expect me to believe," he said, "that Richard Arnold, the grandson of Arnold Bros (est. 1905), has *holes* in his *socks?*"

"That'd make them holy socks," said Angalo. "Sorry. Sorry. Just trying to lighten the mood a bit. You didn't have to glare at me like that."

"Climb up and see for yourself," said Masklin. "I'll help you. Only be careful."

They hoisted Gurder up.

He came down quietly.

"Well?" said Angalo.

"It's got 'R. A.' in gold letters on the bag, too," said Masklin.

He made frantic signs to Angalo. Gurder was looking as though he had seen a ghost.

"Yes, you can get that," said Angalo hurriedly. "*Gold Monogram at Only Five Ninety-Nine Extra*, it used to say on the sign."

"*Speak* to us, Gurder," said Masklin. "Don't just sit there looking like that."

"This is a very solemn moment for me," said Gurder.

"I thought I could cut through some of the stitching and we could get in at the bottom," said Masklin.

"I am not worthy," said Gurder.

"Probably not," said Angalo cheerfully. "But we won't tell anyone."

"And Grandson Richard will be helping us, you see," said Masklin, hoping that Gurder was in a state to take all this in. "He won't know it, but he'll be helping us. So it'll be all right. Probably it's *meant*."

Not meant *by* anyone, he told himself conscientiously. Just meant in general.

Gurder considered this.

"Well, all right," he said. "But no cutting the bag. We can get in through the zipper."

They did. It stuck a bit halfway, since zippers always do, but it didn't take long to get an opening big enough for the nomes to climb down inside.

"What shall we do if he looks in?" said Angalo.

"Nothing," said Masklin. "Just smile, I suppose."

The tree frogs were far out on the branch now. What had looked like a smooth expanse of gray-green wood was, close to, a maze of rough bark, roots, and clumps of moss. It was unbearably frightening for frogs who had spent their life in a world with petals round the edge.

But they crawled onward. They didn't know the meaning of the word "retreat." Or any other word.

# 4

*HOTEL: A place where TRAVELING HUMANS are parked at night. Other humans bring them food, including the famous BACON, LETTUCE, AND TOMATO SANDWICH. There are beds and towels and special things that rain on people to get them clean.*

*From* A Scientific Encyclopedia
for the Inquiring Young Nome
*by Angalo de Haberdasheri*

BLACKNESS.

"It's very dark in here, Masklin."

"Yes, and I can't get comfortable."

"Well, you'll have to make the best of it."

"A hairbrush! I've just sat down on a hairbrush!"

*"We will be landing shortly."*

"Good."

"And there's a tube of something—"

"I'm hungry. Isn't there anything to eat?"

"I've still got that peanut."

"Where? Where?"

"Now you've made me drop it."

"Gurder?"

"Yes?"

"*What* are you *doing*? Are you cutting something?"

"He's cutting a hole in his sock."

Silence.

"Well? What of it? I can if I want to. It's my sock."

More silence.

"I shall just feel better for doing it."

Still more silence.

"It's just a human, Gurder. There's nothing special about it."

"We're in its bag, aren't we?"

"Yes, but you said yourself that Arnold Bros is something in our heads. Didn't you?"

"Yes."

"Well, then?"

"This just makes me feel better, that's all. Subject closed."

"*We're about to land.*"

"How will we know when—"

"*I am sure I could have done it better. Eventually.*"

"Is this the Florida place? Angalo, get your foot out of my face."

"*Yes. This country traditionally welcomes immigrants.*"

"Is that what we are?"

"*Technically you are en route to another destination.*"

"Which?"

"*The stars.*"

"Oh. Thing?"

"*Yes?*"

"Is there any record of nomes being here before?"

"What do you mean? *We're* the nomes!"

"Yes, but there may have been others."

"We're all that there is! Aren't we?"

Tiny colored lights flickered in the darkness of the bag.

"Thing?" Masklin repeated.

*"I am searching available data. Conclusion: no reliable sighting of nomes. All recorded immigrants have been in excess of four inches high."*

"Oh. I just wondered. I wondered if we were all that there was."

"You heard the Thing. No reliable sightings, it said."

"No one saw *us* until today."

"Thing, do you know what happens next?"

*"We will pass through Immigration and Customs. Are you now, or have you ever been, a member of a subversive organization?"*

Silence.

"What, us? Why are you asking us that?"

*"It is the sort of question that gets asked. I am monitoring communications."*

"Oh. Well, I don't think we have. Have we?"

"No."

"No."

"No. I didn't think we had been. What does subversive mean?"

*"The question seeks to establish whether you've come here to overthrow the government of the United States."*

"I don't think we want to do that. Do we?"

"No."

"No."

"No, we don't. They don't have to worry about us."

"Very clever idea, though."

"What is?"

"Asking the questions when people arrive. If anyone was coming here to do some subversive overthrowing, everyone'd be down on him like a pound of bricks as soon as he answered 'Yes.'"

"It's a sneaky trick, isn't it," said Angalo, in an admiring tone of voice.

"No, we don't want to do any overthrowing," said Masklin to the Thing. "We just want to steal one of their going-straight-up jets. What are they called again?"

*"Space shuttles."*

"Right. And then we'll be off. We don't want to cause any trouble."

The bag bumped around and was put down.

There was a tiny sawing noise, totally unheard amid the noise of the airport. A very small hole appeared in the leather.

"What's he doing?" said Gurder.

"Stop pushing," said Masklin. "I can't concentrate. Now . . . it looks like we're in a line of humans."

"We've been waiting for *ages*," said Angalo.

"I expect everyone's being asked if they're going to do any over-throwing," said Gurder wisely.

"I hardly like to bring this up," said Angalo, "but how are we going to find this Shuttle?"

"We'll sort that out when the time comes," said Masklin uncer-tainly.

"The time's come," said Angalo. "Hasn't it?"

Masklin shrugged helplessly.

"You didn't think we'd arrive in this Florida place and there'd be signs up saying *This Way To Space*, did you?" said Angalo sarcastically.

Masklin hoped his thoughts didn't show up on his face. "Of course not," he said.

"Well, what do we do next?" Angalo insisted.

"We . . . we . . . we ask the Thing," said Masklin. He looked relieved. "That's what we'll do. Thing?"

*"Yes?"*

Masklin shrugged. "What do we do next?"

"Now that," said Angalo, "is what I call planning."

The bag shifted. Grandson Richard, 39, was moving up the line.

"Thing? I said, what do we do—"

*"Nothing."*

"How can we do nothing?"

*"By performing an absence of activity."*

"What good is that?"

*"The paper said Richard Arnold was going to Florida for the launch of the communications satellite. Therefore, he is now going to the place where the satellite is. Ergo, we will go with him."*

"Who's Ergo?" said Gurder, looking around.

The Thing flickered its lights at him.

*"It means 'Therefore,'"* it said.

Masklin looked doubtful. "Do you think he'll take this bag with him?"

*"Uncertain."*

There wasn't a lot in the bag, Masklin had to admit. It contained mainly socks, papers, a few odds and ends like hairbrushes, and a book called *The Spy With No Trousers*. This last item had caused them some concern when the bag had been unzipped just after the plane landed, but Grandson Richard had thrust the book among the papers without glancing inside. Now that there was a little light to see by, Angalo was trying to read it. Occasionally he'd mutter under his breath.

"It seems to me," Masklin said eventually, "that Grandson Richard isn't going to go straight off to watch the satellite fly away. I'm sure he'll go somewhere and sleep first. Do you know when this Shuttle jet flies, Thing?"

"*Uncertain. I can only talk to other computers when they are within my range. The computers here know only about airport matters.*"

"He's going to have to go to sleep soon, anyway," said Masklin. "Humans sleep through most of the night. I think that's when we'd better leave the bag."

"And then we can talk to him," said Gurder.

The others stared at him.

"Well, that's why we came, isn't it?" said the Abbot.

"Originally? To ask him to save the quarry?"

"He's a *human*!" snapped Angalo. "Even you must realize that by now! He's not going to help us! Why should he help us? He's just a human whose ancestors built a store! Why do you go on believing he's some sort of great big nome in the sky?"

"Because I haven't got anything else to believe in!" shouted Gurder. "And if you don't believe in Grandson Richard, why are you in his bag?"

"That's just a coincidence—"

"You *always* say that! You always say it's just a coincidence!"

The bag moved, so they lost their balance again and fell over.

"We're moving," said Masklin, still peering out of the hole and almost glad of anything that would stop the argument. "We're walking across the floor. There's a lot of humans out there. A *lot* of humans."

"There always are," sighed Gurder.

"Some of them are holding up signs with names on them."

"That's just like humans," Gurder added.

The nomes were used to humans with signs. Some of the humans in the Store used to wear their names all the time. Humans had strange long names, like "Mrs. J. E. Williams, Supervisor" and "Hello, My Name Is Tracy." No one knew why humans had to wear their names. Perhaps they'd forget them otherwise.

"Hang on," said Masklin, "this can't be right. One of them is holding up a sign saying 'Richard Arnold.' We're walking toward it! We're talking to it!"

The deep muffled rumble of the human voice rolled above the nomes like thunder.

Hoom-voom-boom?

Foom-hoom-zoom-boom.

Hoom-zoom-*boom*-foom?

Boom!

"Can you understand it, Thing?" said Masklin.

*"Yes. The man with the sign is here to take our human to a hotel. It's a place where humans sleep and are fed. All the rest of it was just the things humans say to each other to make sure that they're still alive."*

"What do you mean?" said Masklin.

*"They say things like 'How are you?' and 'Have a nice day' and 'What do you think of this weather, then?' What these sounds mean is: I am alive and so are you."*

"Yes, but nomes say the same sort of things, Thing. It's called 'getting along with people.' You might find it worth a try."

The bag swung sideways and hit something. The nomes clung desperately to the insides. Angalo clung with one hand. He was trying to keep his place in the book.

"I'm getting hungry again," said Gurder. "Isn't there anything to eat in this bag?"

"There's some toothpaste in this tube."

"I'll pass on the toothpaste, thanks."

Now there was a rumbling noise. Angalo looked up. "I know *that* sound," he said. "Infernal combustion engine. We're in a vehicle."

*"Again?"* said Gurder.

"We'll get out as soon as we can," said Masklin.

"What kind of truck is it, Thing?" said Gurder.

*"It is a helicopter."*

"It's certainly noisy," said Gurder, who had never come across the word.

"It is a 'plane without wings,'" said Angalo, who had.

Gurder gave this a few moments' careful and terrified thought.

"Thing?" he said, slowly.

*"Yes?"*

"What keeps it up in the—" Gurder began.

*"Science."*

"Oh. Well. Science? Good. That's all right, then."

The noise went on for a long time. After a while it became part of the nomes' world, so when it stopped, the silence came as a shock.

They lay in the bottom of the bag, too discouraged even to talk. They felt the bag being carried, put down, picked up, carried again, put down, picked up one more time, and then thrown onto something soft.

And then there was blessed stillness.

Eventually Gurder's voice said: "All right. What *flavor* toothpaste?"

Masklin found the Thing among the heap of paper clips, dust, and twisted bits of paper at the bottom of the bag.

"Any idea where we are, Thing?" he said.

"*Room 103, Cocoa Beach New Horizons Hotel,*" said the Thing. "*I am monitoring communications.*"

Gurder pushed past Masklin. "I've got to get out," he said. "I can't stand it in here anymore. Give me a leg up, Angalo. I reckon I can just reach the top of the bag—"

There was the long-drawn-out rumble of the zipper. Light flooded in as the bag was opened. The nomes dived for whatever cover was available.

Masklin watched a hand taller than he was reach down, close around a smaller bag with the toothpaste and washcloth in it, and pull it out.

The nomes didn't move.

After a while there came the distant sound of rushing water.

The nomes still didn't move.

Boom-boom foom zoom-hoom-hoom, choom zoom hoooom . . .

The human noise rose above the gushing. It echoed even more than normal.

"It . . . sounds like it's . . . singing?" whispered Angalo.

. . . Hoom . . . hoom-boom-boom hoom . . . zoom-hoom-boom *HOOOooooOOO*mmm Boom.

"What's happening, Thing?" Masklin hissed.

"*It has gone into a room to have water showering on it,*" said the Thing.

"What does it want to do that for?"

"*I assume it wants to keep clean.*"

"So is it safe to get out of the bag now?"

*"'Safe' is a relative word."*

"What? What? Like 'uncle,' you mean?"

*"I mean that nothing is totally safe. But I suggest that the human will be wetting itself for some time."*

"Yeah. There's a lot of human to clean," said Angalo. "Come on. Let's do it."

The bag was lying on a bed. It was easy enough to climb down the covers onto the floor.

. . . Hoom-hoom booOOOOM boom . . .

"What do we do now?" said Angalo.

"After we've eaten, that is," said Gurder firmly.

Masklin trotted across the thick carpet. There was a tall glass door in the nearest wall. It was slightly open, letting in a warm breeze and the sounds of the night.

A human would have heard the click and buzz of crickets and other small mysterious creatures whose role in life is to sit in bushes all night and make noises that are a lot bigger than they are. But nomes hear sounds slowed down and stretched out and deeper, like a cassette player with dying batteries. The dark was full of the thud and growl of the wilderness.

Gurder joined Masklin and squinted anxiously into the blackness.

"Could you go out and see if there is something to eat?" he said.

"I've a horrible feeling," said Masklin, "that if I go out there now, there *will* be something to eat, and it'll be me."

Behind them the human voice sang on.

. . . Boom-hoom-hoom-BOOOooooMMM womp womp . . .

"What's the human singing about, Thing?" said Masklin.

*"It is a little difficult to follow. However, it appears that the singer wishes it to be known that he did something his way."*

"Did what?"

*"Insufficient data at this point. But whatever it was, he did it at a) each step along life's highway and b) not in a shy way. . . ."*

There was a knock at the door. The singing stopped. So did the gushing of the water. The nomes ran for the shadows.

"Sounds a bit dangerous," Angalo whispered. "Walking along highways, I mean. Each step along life's sidewalk would be better—"

Grandson Richard came out of the shower room with a towel around its waist. It opened the door. Another human, with all its clothes on, came in with a tray. There was a brief exchange of hoots, and the clothed human put down the tray and went out again. Grandson Richard disappeared into the shower room again.

. . . Buh-buh buh-buh hoom hoOOOmm . . .

"Food!" Gurder whispered. "I can smell it! There's food on that tray!"

*"A bacon, lettuce, and tomato sandwich with coleslaw,"* said the Thing. *"And coffee."*

"How did you know?" said all three nomes in unison.

*"He ordered it when he checked in."*

"Coleslaw!" moaned Gurder ecstatically. "Bacon! *Coffee!*"

Masklin stared upward. The tray had been left on the edge of a table.

There was a lamp near it. Masklin had lived in the Store long enough to know that where there was a lamp, there was a wire.

He'd never found a wire he couldn't climb.

Regular meals, that was the problem. He'd never been used to them. When he'd lived Outside, before the Store, he'd got accustomed to going for days without food and then, when food *did* turn up, eating until he was greasy to the eyebrows. But the Store nomes expected something to eat several times an hour. The Store nomes ate all the time. They only had to miss half a dozen meals and they started to complain.

"I think I could get up there," he said.

"Yes. Yes," said Gurder.

"But is it all right to eat Grandson Richard's sandwich?" Masklin added.

Gurder opened his eyes. He blinked.

"That's an important theological point," he muttered. "But I'm too hungry to think about it, so let's eat it first, and then if it turns out to be wrong to eat it, I promise to be very sorry."

. . . Boom-hoom whop whop, foom hoom . . .

*"The human says that the end is now near and he is facing a curtain,"* the Thing translated. *"This may be a shower curtain."*

Masklin pulled himself up the wire and onto the table, feeling very exposed.

It was obvious that the Floridians had a different idea about sandwiches. Sandwiches had been sold back in the Store's Food Hall. The word meant something thin between two slices of damp bread. Floridian sandwiches, on the other hand, filled up an entire tray, and if there *was* any bread, it lurked deep in a jungle of cress and lettuce.

He looked down.

"Hurry up!" hissed Angalo. "The water's stopped again!"

. . . Boom-hoom hoom whop hoom whop . . .

Masklin pushed aside a drift of green stuff, grabbed the sandwich, hauled it to the edge of the tray and pushed it down onto the floor.

. . . foom hoom hoom HOOOOooooOOOOmmmmm-WHOP.

The shower room door opened.

"Come on! Come *on!*" Angalo yelled.

Grandson Richard came out. He took a few steps, and stopped.

He looked at Masklin.

Masklin looked at him.

There are times when Time itself pauses.

Masklin realized that he was standing at one of those points where History takes a deep breath and decides what to do next.

I can stay here, he thought. I can use the Thing to translate, and I can try to explain everything to him. I can tell him how important it is for us to have a home of our own. I can ask him if he can do something to help the nomes in the quarry. I can tell him how the Store nomes thought that his grandfather created the world. He'll probably enjoy knowing that. He looks friendly, for a human.

He *might* help us.

Or he'll trap us somehow, and call other humans, and they'll all start milling around and mooing, and we'll be put in a cage or something, and prodded. It'll be just like the Concorde drivers. They probably didn't want to hurt us, they just didn't understand what we were. And we haven't got time to let them find out.

It's their world, not ours.

It's too risky. No. I never realized it before, but we've got to do it *our* way. . . .

Grandson Richard slowly reached out a hand and said: "Whoomp?"

Masklin took a running jump.

Nomes can fall quite a long way without being hurt, and in any case a bacon, lettuce, and tomato sandwich broke his fall.

There was a blur of activity, and the sandwich rose on three pairs of legs. It raced across the floor, leaking mayonnaise.

Grandson Richard threw a towel at it. It missed.

The sandwich leaped over the doorsill and vanished into the chirping, velvety, dangerous night.

There were other dangers besides falling off the branch. One of the frogs was eaten by a lizard. Several others turned back as soon as they were out of the shade of their flower because, as they pointed out, ".–.–.mipmip.–.–.mipmip.–.–."

The frog in the lead looked back at his dwindling group. There was one . . . and one . . . and one . . . and one . . . and one, which added up to—it wrinkled its forehead in the effort of calculation—yes, one.

Some of the one were getting frightened. The leading frog realized that if they were ever going to get to the new flower and survive there, there'd need to be a lot more than one frog. They'd need at least one, or possibly even one. He gave them a croak of encouragement.

"Mipmip," he said.

# 5

*FLORIDA (or FLORIDIA): A place where may be found ALLIGATORS, LONG-NECKED TURTLES, and SPACE SHUTTLES. An interesting place that is warm and wet and there are geese. BACON, LETTUCE, AND TOMATO SANDWICHES may be found here also. A lot more interesting than many other places. The shape when seen from the air is like a bit stuck on a bigger bit.*

*From* A Scientific Encyclopedia
for the Inquiring Young Nome
*by Angalo de Haberdasheri*

LET THE EYE of your imagination be a camera . . .

This is the globe of the world, a glittering blue-and-white ball like the ornament on some unimaginable Christmas tree.

Find a continent. . . .

*Focus*

This is a continent, a jigsaw of yellows, greens, and browns.

Find a place. . . .

*Focus*

This is a bit of the continent, sticking out into the warmer sea to the southeast. Most of its inhabitants call it Florida.

Actually, they don't. Most of its inhabitants don't call it anything. They don't even know it exists. Most of them have six legs, and buzz. A lot of them have eight legs and spend a lot of time in webs waiting for six-legged inhabitants to arrive for lunch. Many of the rest have four legs, and bark or moo or even lie in swamps pretending to be logs. In fact, only a tiny proportion of the inhabitants of Florida have two legs, and even most of *them* don't call it Florida. They just go tweet, and fly around a lot.

Mathematically, an almost insignificant number of living things in Florida call it Florida. But they're the ones who matter. At least, in their opinion. And their opinion is the one that matters. In their opinion.

*Focus*

Find a highway . . .

*Focus*

. . . traffic swishing quietly through the soft warm rain . . .

*Focus*

. . . high weeds on the bank . . .

*Focus*

. . . grass moving in a way that isn't quite like grass moving in the wind . . .

*Focus*

. . . a pair of tiny eyes . . .

*Focus*

*Focus*

*Focus*

Click!

Masklin crept back through the grass to the nomes' camp, if that's what you could call a tiny dry space under a scrap of thrown-away plastic.

It has been hours since they'd *run away* from Grandson Richard, as Gurder kept on putting it. The sun was rising behind the rain-clouds.

They'd crossed a highway while there was no traffic, they'd blundered around in damp undergrowth, scurrying away from every chirp and mysterious croak, and finally they'd found the plastic. And they'd slept. Masklin had stayed on guard for a while, but he wasn't certain what he was guarding against.

There was a positive side. The Thing had been listening to radio and television and had found the place the going-straight-up shuttles went from. It was only eighteen miles away. And they'd definitely made progress. They'd gone—oh, call it half a mile. And at last it was warm. Even the rain was warm. And the bacon, lettuce, and tomato sandwich was holding up.

But there were still almost eighteen miles to go.

"When did you say the launch is?" said Masklin.

*"Four hours' time,"* said the Thing.

"That means we'll have to travel at more than four miles an hour," said Angalo gloomily.

Masklin nodded. A nome, trying hard, could probably cover a mile and a half in an hour over open ground.

He hadn't given much thought to how they could get the Thing into space. If he'd thought about it at all, he'd imagined that they could find the Shuttle plane and wedge the Thing on it somewhere. If possible maybe they could go too, although he wasn't too sure about that. The Thing said it was cold in space, and there was no air.

"You could have asked Grandson Richard to help us!" said Gurder. "Why did you run away?"

"I don't know," said Masklin. "I suppose I thought we ought to be able to help ourselves."

*"But you used the Truck. Nomes lived in the Store. You used the Concorde. You're eating human food."*

Masklin was surprised. The Thing didn't often argue like that.

"That's different," he said.

*"How?"*

"They didn't know about us. We took what we wanted. We weren't given it. They think it's their world, Thing! They think everything in it belongs to them! They name everything and own everything! I looked up at him and I thought, Here's a human in a human's room, doing human things. How can he ever understand about nomes? How can he ever think tiny people are real people with real thoughts? I can't just let a human take over. Not just like that!"

The Thing blinked a few lights at him.

"We've come too far not to finish it ourselves," Masklin mumbled. He looked up at Gurder.

"Anyway, when it came to it, I didn't exactly see you rushing up ready to shake him by the finger," he said.

"I was embarrassed. It's always embarrassing, meeting deities," said Gurder.

They hadn't been able to light a fire. Everything was too wet. Not that they needed a fire, it was just that a fire was more civilized. Someone had managed to light a fire there at some time, though, because there were still a few damp ashes.

"I wonder how things are back home," said Angalo after a while.

"All right, I expect," said Masklin.

"Do you really?"

"Well, more *hope* than expect, to tell the truth."

"I expect your Grimma's got everyone organized," said Angalo, trying to grin.

"She's not *my* Grimma," snapped Masklin.

"Isn't she? Whose is she, then?"

"She's—" Masklin hesitated. "Hers, I suppose," he said lamely.

"Oh. I thought the two of you were set to—" Angalo began.

"We're not. I told her we were going to get married, and all she could talk about was frogs," said Masklin.

"That's females for you," said Gurder. "Didn't I say that letting them learn to read was a bad idea? It overheats their brains."

"She said the most important thing in the world was little frogs living in a flower," Masklin went on, trying to listen to the voice of his own memory. He hadn't been listening very hard at the time. He'd been too angry.

"Sounds like you could boil a *kettle* on her head," said Angalo.

"It was something she'd read in a book, she said."

"My point exactly," said Gurder. "You know I never really agreed with letting everyone learn to read. It unsettles people."

Masklin looked gloomily at the rain.

"Come to think of it," he said, "it wasn't frogs exactly. It was the *idea* of frogs. She said there's these hills where it's hot and rains all the time, and in the rainforests there are these very tall trees and right in the top branches of the trees there are these like great big flowers called . . . bromeliads, I think, and water gets into the flowers and makes little pools and there's a type of frog that lays eggs in the pools and tadpoles hatch and grow into new frogs and these little frogs live their whole lives in the flowers right at the top of the trees and don't even know about the ground, and once you know the world is full of things like that your life is never the same."

He took a deep breath.

"Something like that, anyway," he said.

Gurder looked at Angalo.

"Didn't understand *any* of it," he said.

*"It's a metaphor,"* said the Thing. No one paid it any attention.

Masklin scratched his ear. "It seemed to mean a lot to her," he said.

*"It's a metaphor,"* said the Thing.

"Women always want something," said Angalo. "My wife is always carrying on about dresses."

"I'm sure he would have helped," said Gurder. "If we'd talked to him. He'd probably have given us a proper meal and, and—"

"—given us a home in a shoebox," said Masklin.

"—and given us a home in a shoebox," said Gurder automatically. "No! I mean, maybe. I mean, why not? A decent hour's sleep for a change. And then we—"

"—we'd be carried around in his pocket," said Masklin.

"Not necessarily. Not necessarily."

"We would. Because he's big and we're small."

*"Launch in three hours and fifty-seven minutes,"* said the Thing.

Their temporary camp overlooked a ditch. There didn't seem to be any winter in Florida, and the banks were thick with greenery.

Something like a flat plate with a spoon on the front sculled slowly past. The spoon stuck out of the water for a moment, looked at the nomes vaguely, and then dropped down again.

"What was that thing, Thing?" said Masklin.

The Thing extended one of its sensors.

*"A long-necked turtle."*

"Oh."

The turtle swam peacefully away.

"Lucky, really," said Gurder.

"What?" said Angalo.

"It having a long neck like that *and* being called a long-necked turtle. It'd be really awkward having a name like that if it had a short neck."

*"Launch in three hours and fifty-six minutes."*

Masklin stood up.

"You know," said Angalo, "I really wish I could have read more of *The Spy With No Trousers*. It was getting exciting."

"Come on," Masklin said. "Let's see if we can find a way."

Angalo, who had been sitting with his chin in his hands, gave him an odd look.

"What, now?"

"We've come too far to just stop, haven't we?"

They pushed their way through the weeds. After a while a fallen log helped them across the ditch.

"Much greener here than at home, isn't it," said Angalo.

Masklin pushed through a thick stand of leaves.

"Warmer, too," said Gurder. "They've got the heating fixed here." *

"No one fixes heating Outside, it just happens," said Angalo.

"If I get old, this is the kind of place I'd like to live, if I had to live Outside," Gurder went on, ignoring him.

*"It's a wildlife preserve,"* said the Thing.

Gurder looked shocked. "What? Like jam? Made of *animals*?"

*"No. It is a place where animals can live unmolested."*

"You're not allowed to hunt them, you mean?"

---

* For generations the Store nomes had known that temperature was caused by air conditioning and the heating system; like many of them, Gurder never quite gave up certain habits of thinking.

*"Yes."*

"You're not allowed to hunt anything, Masklin," said Gurder. Masklin grunted.

There was something nagging at him. He couldn't quite put his finger on it. Probably it was to do with the animals after all.

"Apart from turtles with long necks," he said, "what other animals are there here, Thing?"

The Thing didn't answer for a moment. Then it said, *"I find mention of sea cows and alligators."*

Masklin tried to imagine what a sea cow looked like. But they didn't sound too bad. He'd met cows before. They were big and slow and didn't eat nomes, except by accident.

"What's an alligator?" he said.

The Thing told him.

"What?" said Masklin.

"What?" said Angalo.

*"What?"* said Gurder. He pulled his robe tightly around his legs.

"You idiot!" shouted Angalo.

"Me?" said Masklin hotly. "How should I know? Is it my fault? Did I miss a sign at the airport saying *Welcome To Floridia, Home Of Large Meat-Eating Reptiles Up To Twelve Feet Long?*"

They watched the grasses. A damp warm world inhabited by insects and turtles was suddenly a disguise for horrible terrors with huge teeth.

Something's watching us, Masklin thought. I can feel it.

The three nomes stood back to back. Masklin crouched down, slowly, and picked up a large stone.

The grass moved.

"The Thing did say they don't all grow to twelve feet," said Angalo, in the silence.

"We were blundering around in the darkness!" said Gurder. "With things like that around!"

The grass moved again. It wasn't the wind that was moving it.

"Pull yourself together," muttered Angalo.

"If it *is* alligators," said Gurder, trying to look noble, "I shall show them how a nome can die with dignity."

"Please yourself," said Angalo, his eyes scanning the undergrowth. "I'm planning to show them how a nome can run away with speed."

The grasses parted.

A nome stepped out.

There was a crackle behind Masklin. His head spun around. Another nome stepped out.

And another.

And another.

Fifteen of them.

The three travelers swiveled like an animal with six legs and three heads.

It was the fire that I saw, Masklin told himself. We sat right down by the ashes of a fire, and I looked at them, and I didn't wonder who could have made them.

The strangers wore gray. They seemed to be all sizes. And every single one of them had a spear.

I wish I had mine, Masklin thought, trying to keep as many of the strangers as possible in his line of sight.

They weren't pointing their spears at him. The trouble was, they weren't exactly *not* pointing them, either.

Masklin told himself that it was very rare for a nome to kill another nome. In the Store it was considered bad manners, while Outside . . . well, there were so many other things that killed nomes in any case. Besides, it was wrong. There didn't have to be any other reasons.

He just had to hope that these nomes felt the same way.

"Do you know these people?" asked Angalo.

"Me?" said Masklin. "Of course not. How could I?"

"They're Outsiders. I dunno, I suppose I thought all Outsiders would know each other."

"Never seen them before in my life," said Masklin.

"I *think*," said Angalo, slowly and deliberately, "that the leader is that old guy with the big nose and the topknot with a feather in it. What do you think?"

Masklin looked at the tall, thin, old nome who was scowling at the three of them.

"He doesn't look as if he likes us very much."

"I don't like the look of him at *all*," said Angalo.

"Have you got any suggestions, Thing?" said Masklin.

"*They are probably as frightened of you as you are of them.*"

"I doubt it," said Angalo.

"*Tell them you will not harm them.*"

"I'd much rather they told me they're not going to harm *us*."

Masklin stepped forward and raised his hands.

"We are peaceful," he said. "We don't want anyone to be hurt."

"Including us," said Angalo. "We really mean it."

Several of the strangers backed away and raised their spears.

"I've got my hands raised," said Masklin over his shoulder. "Why should they be so upset?"

"Because you're holding a large rock," said Angalo flatly. "I don't know about them, but if you walked toward me holding something like that, *I'd* be pretty scared."

"I'm not sure I want to let go of it," said Masklin.

"Perhaps they don't understand us—"

Gurder moved.

The Abbot hadn't said a word since the arrival of the new nomes. He'd just gone very pale.

Now some sort of internal timer had gone off. He gave a snort, leaped forward, and bore down on Topknot like an enraged balloon.

"How *dare* you accost us, you—you Outsider!" he screamed.

Angalo put his hands over his eyes. Masklin got a firm hold on his rock.

"Er, Gurder—" he began.

Topknot backed away. The other nomes seemed puzzled by the small explosive figure that was suddenly among them. Gurder was in the grip of the kind of anger that is almost as good as armor.

Topknot screeched something back at Gurder.

"Don't you harangue me, you grubby heathen," said Gurder. "Do you think all these spears really frighten us?"

"Yes," whispered Angalo. He sidled closer to Masklin. "What's got into him?" he said.

Topknot shouted something at his nomes. A couple of them raised their spears, uncertainly. Several of the others appeared to argue.

"This is getting worse," said Angalo.

"Yes," said Masklin. "I think we should—"

A voice behind them snapped out a command. All the Floridians turned. So did Masklin.

Two nomes had come out of the grass. One was a boy. The other was a small, dumpy woman, the sort you'd cheerfully accept an apple pie from. Her hair was tied in a bun, and like Topknot's, it had a long gray feather stuck through it.

The Floridians looked sheepish. Topknot spoke at length. The woman said a couple of words. Topknot spread his arms above him and muttered something at the sky.

The woman walked around Masklin and Angalo as if they were items on display. When she looked Masklin up and down, he caught her eye and thought: She looks like a little old lady, but she's in charge. If she doesn't like us, we're in a lot of trouble.

She reached up and took the stone out of his hand. He didn't resist.

Then she touched the Thing.

It spoke. What it said sounded very much like the words the woman had just used. She pulled her hand away sharply and looked at the Thing with her head on one side. Then she stood back.

At another command the Floridians formed, not a line, but a sort of V shape with the woman at the tip of it and the travelers inside it.

"Are we prisoners?" said Gurder, who had cooled off a bit.

"I don't think so," said Masklin. "Not exactly prisoners, yet."

The meal was some sort of a lizard. Masklin quite enjoyed it; it reminded him of his days as an Outsider, before they found the Store. The other two ate it only because not eating it would be impolite, and it probably wasn't a good idea to be impolite to people who had spears when you didn't.

The Floridians watched them solemnly.

There were at least thirty of them, all wearing identical gray clothes. They looked quite like the Store nomes, except for being slightly darker and much skinnier. Many of them had large, impressive noses, which the Thing said was perfectly okay and all because of genetics.

The Thing was talking to them. Occasionally it would extend one of its sensors and use it to draw shapes in the dirt.

"Thing's probably telling 'em we-come-from-place-belong-far-on-big-bird-that-doesn't-go-flap," said Angalo.

A lot of the time the Thing was simply repeating the woman's own words back at her.

Eventually Angalo couldn't stand it anymore.

"What's *happening*, Thing?" he said. "Why's the woman doing all the talking?"

*"She is the leader of this group,"* said the Thing.

"A woman? Are you serious?"

*"I am always serious. It's built in."*

"Oh."

Angalo nudged Masklin. "If Grimma ever finds out, we're in *real* trouble," he said.

*"Her name is Very-small-tree, or Shrub,"* the Thing went on.

"And you can understand her?" said Masklin.

*"Gradually. Their language is very close to original Nomish."*

"What do you mean, original Nomish?"

*"The language your ancestors spoke."*

Masklin shrugged. There was no point in trying to understand that now.

"Have you told her about us?" he said.

*"Yes. She says—"*

Topknot, who had been muttering to himself, stood up suddenly and spoke very sharply at great length, with a lot of pointing to the ground and to the sky.

The Thing flashed a few lights.

*"He says you are trespassing on the land belonging to the Maker of*

Clouds. *He says that is very bad. He says the Maker of Clouds will be very angry.*"

There was a general murmur of agreement from many of the nomes. Shrub spoke to them sharply. Masklin stuck out a hand to stop Gurder from getting up.

"What does, er, Shrub think?" he said.

"*I don't think she is very sympathetic to the topknot person. His name is Person-who-knows-what-the-Maker-of-Clouds-is-thinking.*"

"And what is the Maker of Clouds?"

"*It's bad luck to say its true name. It made the ground and it is still making the sky. It—*"

Topknot spoke again. He sounded angry.

We need to be friends with these people, Masklin thought. There has to be a way.

"The Maker of Clouds is . . ." Masklin thought hard. ". . . a sort of Arnold Bros (est. 1905)?"

"*Yes,*" said the Thing.

"A real thing?"

"*I think so. Are you prepared to take a risk?*"

"What?"

"*I think I know the identity of the Maker of Clouds. I think I know when it will make some more sky.*"

"What? When?" said Masklin.

"*In three hours and ten minutes.*"

Masklin hesitated.

"Hold on a moment," he said, slowly. "That sounds like the same sort of time that—"

"*Yes. All three of you, please get ready to run. I will now write the name of the Maker of Clouds.*"

"Why will we have to run?"

*"They might get very angry. But we haven't time to waste."*

The Thing waved the sensor. It wasn't intended as a writing implement, and the shapes it drew were angular and hard to read.

It scrawled four shapes in the dust.

The effect was instantaneous.

Topknot started to shout again. Some of the Floridians leaped to their feet. Masklin grabbed the other two travelers.

"I'm really going to thump that old nome in a minute," said Gurder. "How can anyone be so narrow-minded?"

Shrub sat silently while the row went on around her. Then she spoke, very loudly but very calmly.

*"She is telling them,"* said the Thing, *"that it is not wrong to write the name of the Maker of Clouds. It is often written by the Maker of Clouds itself. How famous the Maker of Clouds must be, that even these strangers know its name, she says."*

That seemed to satisfy most of the nomes. Topknot started to grumble to himself.

Masklin relaxed a bit and looked down at the figures in the sand. "N . . . A . . . 8 . . . A?" he said.

*"It's an 'S,'"* said the Thing, *"not an '8.'"*

"But you've only been talking to them for a little while!" said Angalo. "How can you know something like this?"

*"Because I know how nomes think,"* said the Thing. *"You always believe what you read, and you've all got very literal minds. Very literal minds indeed."*

# 6

*GEESE: A type of bird that is slower than, e.g., CON-CORDE, and you don't get anything to eat. According to nomes who know them well, a goose is the most stupid bird there is, except for a duck. Geese spend a lot of time flying to other places. As a form of transport, the goose leaves a lot to be desired.*

*From* A Scientific Encyclopedia
for the Inquiring Young Nome
*by Angalo de Haberdasheri*

IN THE BEGINNING, said Shrub, there was nothing but ground. NASA saw the emptiness above the ground and decided to fill it with sky. It built a place in the middle of the world and sent up towers full of clouds. Sometimes they also carried stars, because at night, after one of the cloud towers had gone up, the nomes could sometimes see new stars moving across the sky.

The land around the cloud towers was NASA's special country. There were more animals there, and fewer humans. It was a pretty good place for nomes. Some of them believed that NASA had arranged it all for precisely that reason.

Shrub sat back.

"And does *she* believe that?" said Masklin. He looked across the clearing to where Gurder and Topknot were arguing. Neither could understand what the other was saying, but they were still arguing.

The Thing translated.

Shrub laughed.

*"She says, days come, days go, who needs to believe anything? She sees things happen with her own eyes, and these are things she knows happen. Belief is a wonderful thing for those who need it, she says. But she knows this place belongs to NASA, because its name is on signs."*

Angalo grinned. He was so excited, he was nearly in tears.

"They live right by the place the going-up jets go from and they think it's some sort of magic place!" he said.

"Isn't it?" said Masklin, almost to himself. "Anyway, it's no more strange than thinking the Store was the whole world. Thing, how do they watch the going-up jets? They're a long way away."

*"Not far at all. Eighteen miles is not far at all, she says. She says they can be there in little more than an hour."*

Shrub nodded at their astonishment and then, without another word, stood up and walked away through the bushes. She signaled the nomes to follow her. Half a dozen Floridians trailed after their leader, making the shape of a V with her at the point.

After a few yards the greenery opened out again beside a small lake.

The nomes were used to large bodies of water. There were reservoirs near the airport. They were even used to ducks. But the things paddling enthusiastically toward them were a lot bigger than ducks. Besides, ducks were like a lot of other animals and recognized in nomes the shape, if not the size, of humans and kept a safe distance away from them. They didn't come tearing toward them as if the mere sight of them were the best thing that had happened all day.

Some of these creatures were almost flying in their desire to get to the nomes.

Masklin looked around automatically for a weapon. Shrub grabbed his arm, shook her head, and said a couple of words.

*"They're friendly,"* the Thing translated.

"They don't look it!"

*"They're geese,"* said the Thing. *"Quite harmless, except to grass and minor organisms. They fly here for the winter."*

The geese arrived with a bow wave that surged over the nomes' feet, and arched their necks down toward Shrub. She patted a couple of fearsome-looking beaks.

Masklin tried hard not to look like a minor organism.

*"They migrate here from colder climates,"* the Thing went on. *"They rely on the Floridians to pick the right course for them."*

"Oh, good. That's . . ." Masklin stopped while his brain caught up with his mouth. "You're going to tell me these nomes fly on them, right?"

*"Certainly. They travel with the geese. Incidentally, you have two hours and forty-one minutes to launch."*

"I want to make it absolutely clear," said Angalo slowly, as a great feathery head dabbled in the water a few inches away, "that if you're suggesting that we ride on a geese—"

*"A goose. One geese is a goose."*

"—you can think again. Or compute, or whatever it is you do."

*"You have a better suggestion, of course,"* said the Thing. If it had had a face, it would have been sneering.

"Suggesting we don't ride on them strikes me as a whole lot better, yes," said Angalo.

"I dunno," said Masklin, who had been watching the geese speculatively. "I might be prepared to give it a try."

*"The Floridians have developed a very interesting relationship with the geese,"* said the Thing. *"The geese provide the nomes with wings, and the nomes provide the geese with brains. They fly north to Canada in the summer, and back here for the winter. It's almost a symbiotic relationship, although of course they're not familiar with the term."*

"Aren't they? Silly old them," Angalo muttered.

"I don't understand you, Angalo," said Masklin. "You're mad for riding in machines with whirring bits of metal pushing them along, yet you're worried about sitting on a perfectly natural bird."

"That's because I don't understand how birds work," said Angalo. "I've never seen an exploded working diagram of a goose."

*"The geese are the reason the Floridians have never had much to do with humans,"* the Thing continued. *"As I said, their language is almost original Nomish."*

Shrub was watching them carefully. There was something about the way she was treating them that still seemed odd to Masklin. It wasn't that she was afraid of them, or aggressive, or unpleasant.

"She's not surprised," he said aloud. "She's interested, but she's not surprised. They were upset because we were *here*, not because we existed. *How many other nomes has she met?*"

The Thing had to translate.

It was a word that Masklin had known for only a year.

Thousands.


The leading tree frog was trying to wrestle with a new idea. It was very dimly aware that it needed a new type of thought.

There had been the world, with the pool in the middle and the petals round the edge. One.

But farther along the branch was another world. From here it looked tantalizingly like the flower they had left. One.

The leading frog sat in a clump of moss and swiveled each eye so that it could see both worlds at the same time. One there. And one *there.*

One. And one.

The frog's forehead bulged as it tried to get its mind around a new idea. One and one were one. But if you had one *here* and one *there* . . .

The other frogs watched in bewilderment as their leader's eyes whizzed round and round.

One here and one there couldn't be one. They were too far apart. You needed a word that meant both ones. You needed to say . . . you needed to say . . .

The frog's mouth widened. It grinned so broadly that both ends almost met behind its head.

It had worked it out.

".–.–.mipmip.–.–!" it said.

It meant: one. And one *more* one.

Gurder was still arguing with Topknot when they got back.

"How do they manage to keep it up? They don't understand what each other's saying!" said Angalo.

"Best way," said Masklin. "Gurder? We're ready to go. Come on."

Gurder looked up. He was very red in the face. He and Topknot were crouched on either side of a mass of scrawled diagrams in the dirt.

"I need the Thing!" he said. "This idiot refuses to understand anything!"

"You won't win any arguments with him," said Masklin. "Shrub says he argues with all other nomes they meet. He likes to."

"What other nomes?" said Gurder.

"There's nomes everywhere, Gurder. That's what Shrub says.

There's other groups even in Floridia. And—and—and in Canadia, where the Floridians go in the summer. There were probably even other nomes back home! We just never found them!"

He pulled the Abbot to his feet.

"And we haven't got a lot of time left," he added.

"I'm not going up on one of those things!"

The geese gave Gurder a puzzled look, as if he were an unexpected frog in their waterweed.

"I'm not very happy about it either," said Masklin, "but Shrub's people do it all the time. You just snuggle down in the feathers and hang on."

*"Snuggle?"* shouted Gurder. "I've never snuggled in my life!"

"You rode on the Concorde," Angalo pointed out. "And that was built and driven by humans."

Gurder glared like someone who wasn't going to give in easily.

"Well, who built the geese?" he demanded.

Angalo grinned at Masklin, who said: "What? Dunno. Other geese, I expect."

"Geese? *Geese?* And what do *they* know about designing for air safety?"

"Listen," said Masklin. "They can take us all the way across this place. The Floridians fly thousands of miles on them. Thousands of miles, without even any smoked salmon or pink wobbly stuff. It's worth trying it for eighteen miles, isn't it?"

Gurder hesitated. Topknot muttered something.

Gurder cleared his throat.

"Very well," he said haughtily. "I'm sure if this misguided individual is in the habit of flying on these things, I should have no difficulty whatsoever." He stared up at the gray shapes bobbing out in the lagoon. "Do the Floridians talk to the creatures?"

The Thing tried this on Shrub. She shook her head. No, she said, geese were quite stupid. Friendly but stupid. Why talk to something that couldn't talk back?

"Have you told her what we're doing?" said Masklin.

*"No. She hasn't asked."*

"How do we get on?"

Shrub stuck her fingers in her mouth and whistled.

Half a dozen geese waddled up the bank. Close to, they didn't look any smaller.

"I remember reading something about geese once," said Gurder, in a sort of dreamy terror. "It said they could break a human's arm with a blow of their nose."

"Wing," said Angalo, looking up at the feathery gray bodies looming over him. "It was their wing."

"And it was swans that do that," said Masklin weakly. "Geese are the ones you mustn't say boo to."

Gurder watched a long neck weave back and forth above him.

"Wouldn't dream of it," he said.

A long time after, when Masklin came to write the story of his life, he described the flight of the geese as the fastest, highest, and most terrifying of all.

People said, Hold on, that's not right. You said, Masklin, that the plane went so fast it left its sound behind, and so high up there was blue all around it.

And he said, That's the point. It went so fast you didn't know how fast it was going; it went so high you couldn't see how high it was. It was just something that happened. And the Concorde looked as though it was *meant* to fly. When it was on the ground, it looked kind of lost.

The geese, on the other hand, looked as aerodynamic as a pillow. They didn't roll into the sky and sneer at the clouds like the plane did. No, they ran across the top of the water and hammered desperately at the air with their wings and then, just when it was obvious they weren't going to achieve anything, they suddenly did; the water dropped away and there was just the slow creak of wings pulling the goose up into the sky.

Masklin would be the first to admit that he didn't understand about jets and engines and machines, so maybe that was why he didn't worry about traveling in them. But he thought he knew a thing or two about muscles, and the knowledge that it was only a couple of big muscles that were keeping him alive was not comforting.

Each traveler shared a goose with one of the Floridians. They didn't do any steering, as far as Masklin could see. That was all done by Shrub, who sat far out on the neck of the leading goose.

The ones behind it followed their leader in a perfect V shape.

Masklin buried himself in the feathers. It was comfortable, if a bit cold. Floridians, he learned later, had no difficulty sleeping on a flying goose. The mere thought gave Masklin nightmares.

He peered out just long enough to see distant trees sweeping by much too fast, and stuck his head down again.

"How long have we got, Thing?" he said.

*"I estimate arrival in the vicinity of the launch pad one hour from launch."*

"I suppose there's absolutely no possibility that launches have anything to do with lunches?" said Masklin wistfully.

"No."

"Pity. Well—have you any suggestions about how we get on the machine?"

*"That is almost impossible."*

"I thought you'd say that."

*"But you could put ME on,"* the Thing added.

"Yes, but how? Tie you to the outside?"

*"No. Get me close enough and I will do the rest."*

"What rest?"

*"Call the Ship."*

"Yes, where is the Ship? I'm amazed satellites and things haven't bumped into it."

*"It is waiting."*

"You're a great help, sometimes."

*"Thank you."*

"That was meant to be sarcastic."

*"I know."*

There was a rustling beside Masklin, and his Floridian co-rider pushed aside a feather. It was the boy he had seen with Shrub. He'd said nothing but had just stared at Masklin and the Thing. Now he grinned and said a few words.

*"He wants to know if you feel sick."*

"I feel fine," Masklin lied. "What's his name?"

*"His name is Pion. He is Shrub's oldest son."*

Pion gave Masklin another encouraging grin.

*"He wants to know what it is like in a jet,"* said the Thing. *"He says it sounds exciting. They see them sometimes, but they keep away from them."*

The goose canted sideways. Masklin tried to hang on with his toes as well as his feet.

*"It must be much more exciting than geese, he says,"* said the Thing.

"Oh, I don't know," said Masklin weakly.

Landing was much worse than flying. It would have been better on water, Masklin was told later, but Shrub had brought them down on land. The geese didn't like that much. It meant that they had to almost stand on the air, flapping furiously, and then drop the last few inches.

Pion helped Masklin down onto the ground, which seemed to him to be moving from side to side. The other travelers tottered toward him through the throng of birds.

"The ground!" panted Angalo. "It was so close! No one seemed to mind!"

He sagged to his knees.

"And they make honking noises!" he said. "And keep swinging from side to side! And they're all knobbly under the feathers!"

Masklin flexed his arms to let the tension out.

The land around them didn't seem a lot different from the place they'd left, except that the vegetation was lower and Masklin couldn't see any water.

*"Shrub says that this is as close as the geese can go,"* the Thing said. *"It is too dangerous to go any farther."*

Shrub nodded and pointed to the horizon.

There was a white shape on it.

"That?" said Masklin.

"That's it?" said Angalo.

*"Yes."*

"Doesn't look very big," said Gurder quietly.

"It's still quite a long way off," said Masklin.

"I can see helicopters," said Angalo. "No wonder Shrub didn't want to take the geese any closer."

"We must be going," said Masklin. "We've got an hour, and I reckon that's barely enough. Er. We'd better say good-bye to Shrub. Can you explain, Thing? Tell her that—that we'll try and find her again. Afterward. If everything's all right. I suppose."

"If there *is* any afterward," Gurder added. He looked like a badly washed dishcloth.

Shrub nodded when the Thing had finished translating, and then pushed Pion forward.

The Thing told Masklin what she wanted.

"What? We can't take him with us!" said Masklin.

*"Young nomes in Shrub's people are encouraged to travel,"* said the Thing. *"Pion is only fourteen months old and already he has been to Alaska."*

"Try and explain that we're not going to a Laska," said Masklin. "Try and make her understand that all sorts of things could happen to him!"

The Thing translated.

*"She says that is good. A growing boy should always seek out new experiences."*

"What? Are you translating me properly?" said Masklin suspiciously.

*"Yes."*

"Well, have you told her it's dangerous?"

*"Yes. She says that danger is what being alive is all about."*

"But he could be killed!" Masklin shrieked.

*"Then he will go up into the sky and become a star."*

"Is that what they believe?"

*"Yes. They believe that the operating system of a nome starts off as a goose. If it is a good goose, it becomes a nome. When a good nome*

*dies, NASA takes it up into the sky and it becomes a star."*

"What's an operating system?" said Masklin. This was religion. He always felt out of his depth with religion.

*"The thing inside you that tells you what you are,"* said the Thing.

"It means a soul," said Gurder wearily.

"Never heard such a lot of nonsense," said Angalo cheerfully. "At least, not since we were in the Store and believed we came back as garden ornaments, eh?" He nudged Gurder in the ribs.

Instead of getting angry about this, Gurder just looked even more despondent.

"Let the lad come if he likes," Angalo went on. "He shows the right spirit. He reminds me of me when I was like him."

"His mother says that if he gets homesick, he can always find a goose to bring him back," said the Thing.

Masklin opened his mouth to speak.

But there were times when you couldn't say anything because there was nothing to say. If you had to explain anything to someone else, then there had to be something you were both sure of, some place to start, and Masklin wasn't sure that there was any place like that around Shrub. He wondered how big the world was to her. Probably bigger than he could imagine. But it stopped at the sky.

"Oh, all right," he said. "But we have to go right away. No time for long tearful—"

Pion nodded to his mother and came and stood by Masklin, who couldn't think of anything to say. Even later on, when he understood the geese nomes better, he never quite got used to the way they cheerfully parted from one another. Distances didn't seem to mean much to them.

"Come on then," he managed.

Gurder glowered at Topknot, who had insisted on coming this far. "I really wish I could talk to that nome," he said.

"Shrub told me he's quite a decent nome, really," said Masklin. "He's just a bit set in his ways."

"Just like you, Gurder," said Angalo.

"Me? I'm not—" Gurder began.

"Of course you're not," said Masklin soothingly. "Now, let's go."

They jogged through scrub two or three times as high as they were.

"We'll never have time," Gurder panted.

"Save your breath for running," said Angalo.

"Do they have smoked salmon on Shuttles?" said Gurder.

"Dunno," said Masklin, pushing his way through a particularly tough clump of grass.

"No, they don't," said Angalo authoritatively. "I remember reading about it in a book. They eat out of tubes."

The nomes ran in silence while they thought about this.

"What, toothpaste?" said Gurder after a while.

"No, not toothpaste. Of course not toothpaste. I'm *sure* not toothpaste."

"Well, what else do you know that comes in tubes?"

Angalo thought about this.

"Glue?" he said, uncertainly.

"Doesn't sound a good meal to me. Toothpaste and glue?"

"The people who drive the space jets must like it. They were all smiling in the picture I saw," said Angalo.

"That wasn't smiling, that was probably just them trying to get their teeth apart," said Gurder.

"No, you've got it all wrong," Angalo decided, thinking fast. "They have to have their food in tubes because of gravity."

"What about gravity?"

"There isn't any."

"Any what?"

"Gravity. So everything floats around."

"What, in water?" said Gurder.

"No, in air. Because there's nothing to hold it on the plate, you see."

"Oh." Gurder nodded. "Is that where the glue comes in?"

Masklin knew that they could go on like this for hours. What these sounds mean, he thought, is: I am alive and so are you. And we're all very worried that we might not be alive for much longer, so we'll just keep talking, because that's better than thinking.

It had all looked better when it was days or weeks away, but now when it was—

"How long, Thing?"

*"Forty minutes."*

"We've got to have another rest! Gurder isn't running, he's just falling upright."

They collapsed in the shade of a bush. The Shuttle didn't look much closer, but they could see plenty of other activity. There were more helicopters. According to frantic signs from Pion, who climbed up the bush, there were humans, much farther off.

"I need to sleep," said Angalo.

"Didn't you sleep on the goose?" said Masklin.

"Did *you?*"

Angalo stretched out in the shade.

"How are we going to get on the Shuttle?" he said.

Masklin shrugged. "Well, the Thing says we don't have to get on it, we just have to put the Thing on it."

Angalo pushed himself up on his elbows. "You mean we don't get to ride on it? I was looking forward to that!"

"I don't think it's like the Truck, Angalo. I don't think they leave a window open for anyone to sneak in," said Masklin. "I think it'd take more than a lot of nomes and some string to fly it, anyway."

"You know, that was the best time of my life, when I drove the Truck," said Angalo dreamily. "When I think of all those months I lived in the Store, not even knowing about the Outside . . ."

Masklin waited politely. His head felt heavy.

"Well?" he said.

"Well what?"

"What happens when you think of all those months in the Store not knowing about the Outside?"

"It just seems like a waste. Do you know what I'm going to do if—I mean, when we get home? I'm going to write down everything we've learned. We should be doing that, you know. Making lots of our own books. Not just reading human books, which are full of made-up things. And not just making books like Gurder's *Book of Nome*. Books of *proper* stuff, like Science. . . ."

Masklin glanced at Gurder. The Abbot wasn't making any comment. He was asleep already.

Pion curled up and started to snore. Angalo's voice trailed off. He yawned.

They hadn't slept for hours. Nomes slept mainly at night but needed catnaps to get through the long day. Even Masklin was nodding.

"Thing?" he remembered to say, "wake me up in ten minutes, will you?"

# 7

*SATELLITES: They are in SPACE and stay there by going so fast that they never stay in one place long enough to fall down. TELEVISIONS are bounced off them. They are part of SCIENCE.*

*From* A Scientific Encyclopedia
for the Inquiring Young Nome
*by Angalo de Haberdasheri*

IT WASN'T THE Thing that woke Masklin up. It was Gurder.

Masklin lay with his eyes half closed, listening. Gurder was talking to the Thing in a low voice.

"I believed in the Store," he said, "and then it was just a, a sort of thing built by humans. And I thought Grandson Richard, 39, was some special person, and he turned out to be a human who sings when he wets himself—"

"*—takes a shower—*"

"—and now there's thousands of nomes in the world! Thousands! Believing all sorts of things! That stupid Topknot person believes that the going-up shuttles make the sky. Do you know what I thought when I heard that? I thought, If he'd been the one arriving in my world instead of the other way around, he'd have thought I was just as stupid! I *am* just as stupid! Thing?"

*"I was maintaining a tactful silence."*

"Angalo believes in silly machinery and Masklin believes in, oh, I don't know. Space. Or not believing in things. And it all works for them. I try and believe in *important* things and they don't last for five minutes. Where's the fairness in that?"

*"Only another tactful and understanding silence suffices at this point."*

"I just wanted to make some sense out of life."

*"This is a commendable aim."*

"I mean, what is the truth of everything?"

There was a pause. Then the Thing said: *"I recall your conversation with Masklin about the origin of nomes. You wanted to ask me. I can answer now. I was made. I know this is true. I know that I am a thing made of metal and plastic, but also that I am something that lives inside that metal and plastic. It is impossible for me not to be absolutely certain of it. This is a great comfort. As to nomes, I have data that says nomes originated on another world and came here thousands of years ago. This may be true. It may not be true. I am not in a position to judge."*

"I knew where I was, back in the Store," said Gurder, half to himself. "And even in the quarry it wasn't too bad. I had a proper job. I was important to people. How can I go back now, knowing that everything I believed about the Store and Arnold Bros and Grandson Richard is just . . . is just an *opinion?*"

*"I cannot advise. I am sorry."*

Masklin decided it was a diplomatic time to wake up. He made a grunting noise just to be sure that Gurder heard him.

The Abbot was very red in the face.

"I couldn't sleep," he said shortly.

Masklin stood up.

"How long, Thing?"

*"Twenty-seven minutes."*

"Why didn't you wake me up!"

*"I wished you to be refreshed."*

"But it's still a long way off. We'll never get you onto it in time. Wake up, you." Masklin prodded Angalo with his foot. "Come on, we'll have to run. Where's Pion? Oh, there you are. Come *on*, Gurder."

They jogged on through the scrub. In the distance, there was the low mournful howl of sirens.

"You're cutting it really fine, Masklin," said Angalo.

"Faster! Run faster!"

Now that they were closer, Masklin could see the Shuttle. It was quite high up. There didn't seem to be anything useful at ground level.

"I hope you've got a good plan, Thing," he panted, as the four of them dodged between the bushes, "because I'll never be able to get you all the way up there."

*"Do not worry. We are nearly close enough."*

"What do you mean? It's still a long way off!"

*"It is close enough for me to get on."*

"What is it going to do? Take a flying leap?" said Angalo.

*"Put me down."*

Masklin obediently put the black box on the ground. It extended a few of its probes, which swung around slowly for a while and then pointed toward the going-up jet.

"What are you playing at?" said Masklin. "This is wasting *time!*"

Gurder laughed, although not in a very happy way.

"I know what it's doing," he said. "It's sending itself onto the Shuttle. Right, Thing?"

*"I am transmitting an instruction subset to the computer on the communications satellite,"* said the Thing.

The nomes said nothing.

*"Or, to put it another way . . . yes, I am turning the satellite computer into a part of me. Although not a very intelligent one."*

"Can you really do that?" said Angalo.

*"Certainly."*

"Wow. And you won't miss the bit you're sending?"

*"No. Because it will not leave me."*

"You're sending it and keeping it at the same time?"

*"Yes."*

Angalo looked at Masklin.

"Did you understand any of that?" he demanded.

"I did," said Gurder. "The Thing's saying it's not just a machine, it's a sort of . . . a sort of collection of electric thoughts that live in a machine. I think."

Lights flickered around on top of the Thing.

"Does it take a long time to do?" said Masklin.

*"Yes. Please do not take up vital communication power at this point."*

"I think he means he doesn't want us to talk to him," said Gurder. "He's concentrating."

"It," said Angalo. "It's an it. And it made us run all the way here just so's we can hurry up and wait."

"It probably has to be close up to do . . . whatever it is it's doing," said Masklin.

"How long's it going to take?" said Angalo. "It seems ages since it was twenty-seven minutes to go."

"Twenty-seven minutes at least," said Gurder.

"Yeah. Maybe more."

Pion pulled at Masklin's arm, pointed to the looming white shape with his other hand, and rattled off a long sentence in Floridian or, if the Thing was right, nearly original Nomish.

"I can't understand you without the Thing," said Masklin. "Sorry."

"No speaka da goose-oh," said Angalo.

A look of panic spread across the boy's face. He shouted this time, and tugged harder.

"I think he doesn't want to be near the going-up jets when they start up," said Angalo. "He's probably afraid of the noise. Don't—like—the—noise, right?" he said.

Pion nodded furiously.

"They didn't sound too bad at the airport," said Angalo. "More of a rumble. I expect they might frighten unsophisticated people."

"I don't think Shrub's people are particularly unsophisticated," said Masklin thoughtfully. He looked up at the white tower. It had seemed a long way away, but in some ways it might be quite close.

Really very close.

"How safe do you think it is here?" he said. "When it goes up, I mean."

"Oh, come *on*," said Angalo. "The Thing wouldn't have let us come right here if it wasn't safe for nomes."

"Sure, sure," said Masklin. "Right. You're right. Silly to dwell on it, really."

Pion turned and ran.

The other three looked back at the Shuttle. Lights moved in complicated patterns on the top of the Thing.

Somewhere another siren sounded. There was a sensation of power, as though the biggest spring in the world were being wound up.

When Masklin spoke, the other two seemed to hear him speak their own thoughts.

"Exactly how good," he said, very slowly, "do you think the Thing is at judging how close nomes can stand to a going-up jet when it goes up? I mean, how much experience has it got, do you think?"

They looked at one another.

"Maybe we should back off a little bit . . . ?" Gurder began.

They turned and walked away.

Then each one of them couldn't help noticing that the others seemed to be walking faster and faster.

Faster and faster.

Then, as one nome, they gave up and ran for it, fighting their way through the scrub and grass, skidding on stones, elbows going up and down like pistons. Gurder, who was normally out of breath at anything above walking pace, bounded along like a balloon.

"Have . . . *you* . . . any . . . any . . . idea . . . how . . . how . . . close . . . ?" Angalo panted.

The sound behind them started like a hiss, like the whole world taking a deep breath. Then it turned into . . .

. . . not noise, but something more like an invisible hammer that smacked into both ears at once.

# 8

*SPACE: There are two types of space: a) something con-taining nothing and b) nothing containing everything. It is what you have left when you haven't got anything else. There is no air or gravity, which is what holds people on to things. If there wasn't space, everything would be in one place. It is designed to be a place for SATELLITES, SHUTTLES, PLANETS, and THE SHIP.*

From A Scientific Encyclopedia
for the Inquiring Young Nome
*by Angalo de Haberdasheri*

AFTER SOME TIME, when the ground had stopped shaking, the nomes picked themselves up and stared blearily at one another.

"          !" said Gurder.

"What?" said Masklin. His own voice sounded a long way away, and muffled.

"          ?" said Gurder.

"                    ?" said Angalo.

"                    ?"

"What? I can't hear you! Can you hear *me*?"

"          ?"

Masklin saw Gurder's lips move. He pointed to his own ears and shook his head.

"We've gone deaf!"

"                                        ?"

"                                                    ?"

"Deaf, I said." Masklin looked up.

Smoke billowed overhead, and out of it, rising fast even to a nome's high-speed senses, was a long, growing cloud tipped with fire. The noise dropped to something merely very loud and then, very quickly, disappeared.

Masklin stuck a finger in his ear and wiggled it around.

The absence of sound was replaced by the terrible hiss of silence.

"Anyone listening?" he ventured. "Anyone hearing me?"

"That," said Angalo, his voice sounding blurred and unnaturally calm, "was pretty loud. I don't reckon many things come much louder."

Masklin nodded. He felt as though he'd been pounded hard by something.

"You know about these things, Angalo," he said weakly. "Humans ride on them, do they?"

"Oh, yes. Right at the top."

"No one makes them do it?"

"Er. I don't think so," said Angalo. "I think the book said a lot of them want to do it."

"They *want* to do it?"

Angalo shrugged. "That's what it said."

There was only a distant dot now, at the end of a widening white cloud of smoke.

Masklin watched it.

We must be *insane*, he thought. We're tiny and it's a big world, and we never stop to learn enough about where we are before we go somewhere else. At least back when I lived in a hole, I knew everything there was to know about living in a hole, and now it's a year later and I'm at a place so far away, I don't even know how far away it is, watching something I don't understand go to a place so far up there is no down. And I can't go back. I've got to go right on to the end of whatever all this is, because I can't go back. I can't even stop.

So *that's* what Grimma meant about the frogs. Once you know things, you're a different person. You can't help it.

He looked back down. Something was missing.

The Thing . . .

He ran back the way they'd come.

The little black box was where he'd left it. The rods had withdrawn into it, and there weren't any lights.

"Thing?" he said uncertainly.

One red light came on faintly. Masklin suddenly felt cold, despite the heat around him.

"Are you all right?" he said.

The light flickered.

*"Too quick. Used too much pow . . ."* it said.

"Pow?" said Masklin. He tried hard not to wonder why the word hadn't been much more than a growl.

The light dimmed.

"Thing? Thing?" He tapped gently on the box. "Did it work? Is the Ship coming? What do we do now? Wake up! *Thing?*"

The light went out.

Masklin picked the Thing up and turned it over and over in his hands.

"Thing?"

Masklin and Gurder hurried up, with Pion behind them.

"Did it work?" said Angalo. "Can't see any Ship yet."

Masklin turned his face toward them.

"The Thing's stopped," he said.

"Stopped?"

"All the lights have gone out!"

"Well, what does that mean?" Angalo started to look panicky.

"I don't know!"

"Is it dead?" said Gurder.

"It *can't* die! It's existed for thousands of years!"

Gurder shook his head. "Sounds like a good reason for dying," he said.

"But it's a, a *thing*."

Angalo sat down with his arms around his knees.

"Did it say if it got everything sorted out? When's the Ship coming?"

"Listen, don't you care? It's run out of pow!"

"Pow?"

"It must mean electricity. It kind of sucks it out of wires and stuff. I think it can store it for a while, too. And now it must have run out."

They looked at the black box. It had spent thousands of years being handed down from nome to nome without ever saying a word or lighting a light. It had woken up again only when it had been brought into the Store, near electricity.

"It looks creepy, sitting there doing nothing," said Angalo.

"Can't we find it some electricity?" said Gurder.

"Around here? There isn't any!" Angalo snapped. "We're in the middle of nowhere!"

Masklin stood up and gazed around. It was just possible to see some buildings in the distance. There was a movement of vehicles around them.

"What about the Ship?" said Angalo. "Is it on its way?"

"I don't know!"

"How will it find us?"

"I don't know!"

"Who's driving it?"

"I don't—" Masklin stopped in horror. "No one! I mean, who *could* be driving it? There hasn't been anyone on it for thousands of years!"

"Who was going to bring it here, then?"

"I don't know! The Thing, maybe?"

"You mean it's on its way and no one's driving it?"

"Yes! No! I don't know!"

Angalo squinted up at the blue sky.

"Oh, wow," he said, glumly.

"We need to find some electricity for the Thing," said Masklin. "Even if it's managed to summon the Ship, the Ship will still need to be told where we are."

"*If* it summoned the Ship," said Gurder. "It might have run out of pow before it had time."

"We can't be sure," said Masklin. "Anyway, we must help the Thing. I hate to see it like that."

Pion, who had disappeared into the scrub, came back dragging a lizard.

"Ah," said Gurder without any enthusiasm. "Here comes lunch."

"If the Thing was talking, we could tell Pion you can get awfully tired of lizard, in time," said Angalo.

"In about two seconds," said Gurder.

"Come on," said Masklin, wearily. "Let's go and find some shade and think up another plan."

"Oh, a plan," Gurder said, as if that were worse than lizard. "I like plans."

They ate—not very well—and lay back watching the sky. The brief sleep on the way hadn't been enough. It was easy to doze.

"I must say, these Floridians have got it all worked out," said Gurder lazily. "It's cold back home, and here they've got the heating turned up just right."

"I keep telling you, it's not the heating," said Angalo, straining his eyes for any sign of a descending ship. "And the wind isn't the air conditioning, either. It's the sun that makes you warm."

"I thought that was just for lighting," said Gurder.

"And it's where all the heat comes from," said Angalo. "I read it in a book. It's a great ball of fire bigger than the world."

Gurder eyed the sun suspiciously.

"Oh, yes?" he said. "What keeps it up?"

"Nothing. It's just kind of *there*."

Gurder squinted at the sun again.

"Is this generally known?" he said.

"I suppose so. It was in the book."

"For anyone to read? I call that irresponsible. That's the sort of thing that can really upset people."

"There's thousands of suns up there, Masklin says."

Gurder sniffed. "Yes, he's told me. It's called the glaxie, or something. Personally, I'm against it."

Angalo chuckled.

"I don't see what's so funny," said Gurder coldly.

"Tell him, Masklin," said Angalo.

"It's all very well for you," Gurder muttered. "You just want to drive things fast. *I* want to make sense of them. Maybe there *are* thousands of suns, but *why?*"

"Can't see that it matters," said Angalo lazily.

"It's the only thing that *does* matter. Tell him, Masklin."

They both looked at Masklin.

At least, where Masklin had been sitting.

He'd gone.

Beyond the top of the sky was the place the Thing had called the universe. It contained—according to the Thing—everything and nothing. And there was very little everything and more nothing than anyone could imagine.

For example, it was often said that the sky was full of stars. It was untrue. The sky was full of sky. There were unlimited amounts of sky and really, by comparison, very few stars.

It was amazing, therefore, that they made such an impression. . . .

Thousands of them looked down now as something round and shiny drifted around the Earth.

It had *Arnsat 1* painted on its side, which was a bit of a waste of paint since stars can't read.

It unfolded a silver dish.

It should then have turned to face the planet below it, ready to beam down old movies and new news.

It didn't. It had new orders.

Little puffs of gas jetted out as it turned around and searched the sky for a new target.

By the time it had found it, a lot of people in the old movies and new news business were shouting very angrily at one another down telephone lines, and some of them were feverishly trying to give it new instructions.

But that didn't matter, because it wasn't listening anymore.

Masklin galloped through the scrub. They'll argue and bicker, he thought. I've got to do this quickly. I don't think we've got a lot of time.

It was the first time he'd been really alone since the days when he'd lived in a hole and had to go out hunting by himself because there was no one else.

Had it been better then? At least it had been simpler. You just had to try to eat without being eaten. Just getting through the day was a triumph. Everything had been bad, but at least it had been a kind of understandable, nome-sized badness.

In those days the world had ended at the highway on one side and the woods beyond the field on the other side. Now it had no kind of boundaries at all, and more problems than he knew what to do with.

But at least he knew where to find electricity. You found it near buildings with humans in them.

The scrub ahead of Masklin opened out onto a track. He turned onto it and ran faster. Go along any track and you'd find humans on it somewhere. . . .

There were footsteps behind him. He turned around and saw Pion. The young Floridian gave him a worried smile.

"Go away!" Masklin said. "Go on! Go! Go back! Why are you following me? Go away!"

Pion looked hurt. He pointed up the track and said something.

"I don't understand!" shouted Masklin.

Pion stuck a hand high above his head, palm downward.

"Humans?" Masklin guessed. "Yes. I know. I know what I'm doing. Go back!"

Pion said something else.

Masklin lifted up the Thing. "Talking box no go," he said helplessly. "Good grief, why should I have to speak like this? You must be at least as intelligent as me. Go on, go away. Go back to the others."

He turned and ran. He looked back briefly and saw Pion watching him.

How *much* time have I got? he wondered. Thing once told me the Ship flies very fast. Maybe it could be here any minute. Maybe it's not coming at all. . . .

He saw figures loom over the scrub. Yes, follow any track and sooner or later you find humans. They get everywhere.

Yes, maybe the Ship isn't coming at all.

If it isn't, he thought, then what I'm going to do now is probably the most stupid thing any nome has ever done anywhere in the total history of nomekind.

He stepped out into a circle of gravel. A small truck was parked in it, with the name of the Floridian god NASA painted on the side. Close by, a couple of humans were bent over a piece of machinery on a tripod.

They didn't notice Masklin. He walked closer, his heart thumping.

He put down the Thing.

He cupped his hands around his mouth.

He tried to shout as clearly and as slowly as possible.

"Hey, there! You! Hum-mans!"

"He did *what?*" shouted Angalo.

Pion ran through his pantomime of gestures again.

*"Talked* to *humans?"* said Angalo. "Went in a thing with *wheels?"*

"I thought I heard a truck engine," said Gurder.

Angalo pounded a fist into his palm.

"He was worried about the Thing," he said. "He wanted to find it some electricity!"

"But we must be miles from any buildings!" said Gurder.

"Not the way Masklin's going!" Angalo snarled.

"I *knew* it would come to this!" Gurder moaned. "Showing ourselves to humans! We never used to do that sort of thing in the Store! What are we going to *do?"*


Masklin thought: Up to now, it's not too bad.

The humans hadn't really known what to do about him. They'd even backed away! And then one of them had rushed to the truck and talked into a machine on a string. Probably some sort of telephone, Masklin thought knowledgeably.

When he hadn't moved, one of the humans had fetched a box out of the back of the truck and crept toward him as if expecting Masklin to explode. In fact, when he waved, the human jumped back clumsily.

The other humans said something, and the box was cautiously put down on the gravel a few feet from Masklin.

Then both humans watched him expectantly.

He kept smiling, to put them at their ease, and climbed into the box. Then he gave them another wave.

One of the humans reached down gingerly and picked up the box, lifting it up in the air as though Masklin were something very rare and delicate. He was carried to the truck. The human got in and, still holding the box with exaggerated care, placed it on its knees. A radio crackled with deep human voices.

Well, no going back now. Knowing that, Masklin very nearly relaxed. Perhaps it was best to look at it as just another step along life's sidewalk.

They kept staring at him, as if they didn't believe what they were seeing.

The truck lurched off. After a while it turned onto a concrete road, where another truck was waiting. A human got out, spoke to the driver of Masklin's truck, laughed in a slow human way, looked down at Masklin, and stopped laughing very suddenly.

It almost ran back to its own truck and started speaking into another telephone.

I knew this would happen, Masklin thought. They don't know what to do with a real nome. Amazing.

But just so long as they take me somewhere where there's the right kind of electricity . . .

Dorcas, the engineer, had once tried to explain electricity to Masklin, but without much success because Dorcas wasn't too certain about it either. There seemed to be two kinds, straight and wiggly. The straight kind was very boring and stayed in batteries. The wiggly kind was found in wires in the walls and things, and somehow the Thing could steal some of it if it was close enough. Dorcas used to talk about wiggly electricity in the same tone of voice Gurder used for talking about Arnold Bros (est. 1905). He'd tried to study it back in the Store. If it was put into freezers it made things cold, but if the same electricity went into an oven it made things hot, so how did it *know*?

Dorcas used to talk, Masklin thought. I said "used to." I hope he *still* does.

He felt light-headed and oddly optimistic. Part of him was saying: That's because if you for one second think seriously about the position you've put yourself in, you'll panic.

Keep smiling.

The truck purred along the road, with the other truck following it. Masklin saw a third truck rattle down a side road and pull in behind them. There were a lot of humans on it, and most of them were watching the skies.

They didn't stop at the nearest building but drove on to a bigger one with many more vehicles outside. More humans were waiting for them.

One of them opened the truck door, doing it very slowly even for a human.

The human carrying Masklin got out of the truck.

Masklin looked up at dozens of staring faces. He could see every eyeball, every nostril. Every one of them looked worried. At least, every eyeball did. The nostrils just looked like nostrils.

They were worried about *him.*

Keep smiling.

He stared back up at them and, still almost giggling with repressed panic, said, "Can I help you, gentlemen?"

*SCIENCE: A way of finding things out and then making them work. Science explains what is happening around us the whole time. So does RELIGION, but science is better because it comes up with more understandable excuses when it's wrong. There is a lot more Science than you think.*

*From* A Scientific Encyclopedia
for the Inquiring Young Nome
*by Angalo de Haberdasheri*

GURDER, ANGALO, AND Pion sat under a bush. It gave them a bit of shade. The cloud of gloom over them was almost as big.

"We'll never even get home without the Thing," said Gurder.

"Then we'll get Masklin out," said Angalo.

"That'll take forever!"

"Yeah? Well, that's nearly as long as we've got here, if we can't get home." Angalo had found a pebble that was almost the right shape to attach to a twig with strips torn off his coat; he'd never seen a stone axe in his life, but he had a definite feeling that there were useful things that could be done with a stone tied to the end of a stick.

"I wish you'd stop fiddling with that thing," Gurder said. "What's the big plan, then? Us against the whole of Floridia?"

"Not necessarily. You needn't come."

"Calm down, Mr. To-the-Rescue. One idiot's enough."

"I don't hear you coming up with any better ideas." Angalo swished the axe through the air once or twice.

"I haven't got any."

A small red light started to flash on the Thing.

After a while, a small square hole opened up and there was a tiny whirring sound as the Thing extended a little lens on a stick. This turned around slowly.

Then the Thing spoke.

*"Where,"* it asked, *"is this place?"*

It tilted the lens up and there was a pause while it surveyed the face of the human looking down at it.

*"And why?"* it added.

"I'm not sure," said Masklin. "We're in a room in a big building. The humans haven't hurt me. I think one of them has been trying to talk to me."

*"We appear to be in some sort of glass box,"* said the Thing.

"They even gave me a little bed," said Masklin. "And I think the thing over there is some kind of lavatory—but *look*, what about the Ship?"

*"I expect it is on its way,"* said the Thing calmly.

"Expect? *Expect?* You mean you don't know?"

*"Many things can go wrong. If they have gone right, the Ship will be here soon."*

"If they don't, I'm stuck here for life!" said Masklin bitterly. "I came here because of you, you know."

*"Yes, I know. Thank you."*

Masklin relaxed a bit.

"They're being quite kind," he said. He thought about this. "At least I think so," he added. "It's hard to tell."

He looked through the transparent wall. A lot of humans had been in to look at him in the last few minutes. He wasn't quite certain whether he was an honored visitor or a prisoner or maybe something in between.

"It seemed the only hope at the time," he said lamely.

*"I am monitoring communications."*

"You're always doing that."

*"A lot of them are about you. All kinds of experts are rushing here to have a look at you."*

"What kind of experts? Experts in nomes?"

*"Experts in talking to creatures from other worlds. Humans haven't met anyone from another world, but they've still got experts in talking to them."*

"All this had better work," said Masklin soberly. "Humans really know about nomes now."

*"But not what nomes are. They think you have just arrived."*

"Well, that's true."

*"Not arrived here. Arrived on the planet. Arrived from the stars."*

"But we've been here for thousands of years! We *live* here!"

*"Humans find it a lot easier to really believe in little people from the sky than little people from the Earth. They would rather think of little green men than leprechauns."*

Masklin's brow wrinkled. "I didn't understand any of that," he said.

*"Don't worry about it. It doesn't matter."* The Thing let its lens swivel around to see more of the room.

*"Very nice. Very scientific,"* it said.

Then it focused on a wide plastic tray by Masklin.

"*What is that?*"

"Oh, fruit and nuts and meat and stuff," said Masklin. "I think they've been watching me to see what I eat. I think these are quite bright humans, Thing. I pointed to my mouth and they understood I was hungry."

"*Ah,*" said the Thing. "*Take me to your larder.*"

"Pardon?"

"*I will explain. I have told you that I monitor communications?*"

"All the time."

"*There is a joke. That is, a humorous anecdote or story, known to humans. It concerns a ship from another world landing on this planet, and strange creatures get out and say to a gas pump, trash can, slot machine, or similar mechanical device, 'Take me to your leader.' I surmise this is because they are unaware of the shape of humans. I have substituted the similar word larder, referring to a place where food is stored. This is a humorous pun, or play on words for hilarious effect.*"

It paused.

"Oh," said Masklin. He thought about it. "These would be the little green men you mentioned?"

"*Very . . . Wait a moment. Wait a moment.*"

"What? What?" said Masklin urgently.

"*I can hear the Ship.*"

Masklin listened as hard as he could.

"I can't hear a thing," he said.

"*Not sound. Radio.*"

"Where is it? Where is it, Thing? You've always said the Ship's up there, but *where?*"

o     o     o

The remaining tree frogs crouched amid the moss to escape the heat of the afternoon sun.

Low in the eastern sky was a sliver of white.

It would be nice to think that the tree frogs had legends about it. It would be nice to think that they thought the sun and moon were distant flowers—a yellow one by day, a white one by night. It would be nice to think they had legends about them, and said that when a good frog died, its soul would go to be big flowers in the sky. . . .

The trouble is that it's *frogs* we're talking about here. Their name for the sun was ".–.–mipmip.–.–." Their name for the moon was ".–.–mipmip.–.–." Their name for *everything* was ".–.–mipmip.–.–." And when you're stuck with a vocabulary of one word, it's pretty hard to have legends about anything at all.

The leading frog, however, was dimly aware that there was something wrong with the moon.

It was growing brighter.

"We left the Ship on the moon?" said Masklin. "Why?"

*"That's what your ancestors decided to do,"* said the Thing. *"So they could keep an eye on it, I assume."*

Masklin's face lit up slowly, like clouds at sunrise.

"You know," he said, excitedly, "right back before all this, right back when we used to live in the old hole, I used to sit out at nights and watch the moon. Perhaps in my blood I really knew that up there—"

*"No, what you were experiencing was probably primitive superstition,"* said the Thing.

Masklin deflated. "Oh. Sorry."

*"And now, please be quiet. The Ship is feeling lost and wants to be told what to do. It has just woken up after fifteen thousand years."*

"I'm not very good at mornings myself," Masklin said.

There is no sound on the moon, but this doesn't matter because there is no one to hear anything. Sound would just be a waste.

But there is light.

Fine moondust billowed high across the ancient plains of the moon's dark crescent, expanding in boiling clouds that went high enough to catch the rays of the sun. They glittered.

Down below, something was digging itself out.

"We left it in a *hole?*" said Masklin.

Lights rippled back and forth across all the surfaces of the Thing.

*"Don't say that's why you always lived in holes,"* it said. *"Other nomes don't live in holes."*

"No, that's true," said Masklin. "I ought to stop thinking only about the—"

He suddenly went quiet. He stared out of the glass tank, where a human was trying to interest him in marks on a blackboard.

"You've got to stop it," he said. "Right now. Stop the Ship. We've got it all wrong. Thing, we can't go! It doesn't belong to just us! We can't take the Ship!"

The three nomes lurking near the Shuttle launching place watched the sky. As the sun neared the horizon, the moon sparkled like a Christmas decoration.

"It must be caused by the Ship!" said Angalo. "It must be!" He beamed at the others. "That's it, then. It's on its way!"

"I never thought it would work . . ." Gurder began.

Angalo slapped Pion on the back, and pointed.

"See that, my lad?" he said. "That's the Ship, that is! Ours!"

Gurder rubbed his chin and nodded thoughtfully at Pion.

"Yes," he said. "That's right. Ours."

"Masklin says there's all kinds of stuff up there," said Angalo dreamily. "And masses of space. That's what space is well known for, lots of space. Masklin said the Ship goes faster than light goes, which is probably wrong, otherwise how'd you see anything? You'd turn the lights on, and all the light would drop backward out of the room. But it's pretty fast—"

Gurder looked back at the sky again. Something at the back of his mind was pushing its way to the front and giving him a curious gray feeling.

"Our Ship," he said. "The one that brought nomes here."

"Yeah, that's right," said Angalo, hardly hearing him.

"And it'll take us all back," Gurder went on.

"That's what Masklin said, and—"

"All nomes," said Gurder. His voice was as flat and heavy as a sheet of lead.

"Sure. Why not? I expect I'll soon work out how to drive it back to the quarry, and we can pick them all up. And Pion here, of course."

"What about Pion's people?" said Gurder.

"Oh, they can come too," said Angalo expansively. "There's probably even room for their geese!"

"And the others?"

Angalo looked surprised. "What others?"

"Shrub said there were lots of other groups of nomes. Everywhere."

Angalo looked blank. "Oh, them. Well, I don't know about them. But we *need* the Ship. You know what it's been like ever since we left the Store."

"But if we take the Ship away, what will *they* have if they need it?"

Masklin had just asked the same question.

The Thing said, *"010011010101011101010100101101011100010."*

"What did you say?"

The Thing sounded tetchy. *"If I lose concentration, there might not be a Ship for anyone,"* it said. *"I am sending fifteen thousand instructions per second."*

Masklin said nothing.

*"That's a lot of instructions,"* the Thing added.

"By rights the Ship must belong to all the nomes in the world," said Masklin.

*"010011001010010010 . . ."*

"Oh, shut up and tell me when the Ship is going to get here."

*"0101011001 . . . Which do you want me to do? . . . 01001100 . . ."*

"What?"

*"I can shut up OR I can tell you when the Ship is going to arrive. I can't do both."*

"Please tell me when the Ship is going to arrive," said Masklin patiently, "and then shut up."

*"Four minutes."*

"Four minutes!"

*"I could be three seconds off,"* said the Thing. *"But I calculate it as four minutes. Only now it's three minutes thirty-eight seconds. It'll be three minutes and thirty-seven seconds any second now. . . ."*

"I can't hang around in here if it's coming that soon!" said Masklin, all thoughts of his duty to the nomes of the world temporarily forgotten. "How can I get out? This thing's got a lid on it."

*"Do you want me to shut up first, or get you out and then shut up?"* said the Thing.

"Please!"

*"Have the humans seen you move?"* said the Thing.

"What do you mean?"

*"Do they know how fast you can run?"*

"I don't know," said Masklin. "I suppose not."

*"Get ready to run, then. But first put your hands over your ears."*

Masklin thought it would be best to obey. The Thing could be deliberately infuriating at times, but it didn't pay to ignore its advice.

Lights on the Thing made a brief star-shaped pattern.

It started to wail. The sound went up and then went beyond Masklin's hearing. He could feel it even with his hands over his ears; it seemed to be making unpleasant bubbles in his head.

He opened his mouth to shout at the Thing, and the walls exploded. One moment there was glass, and the next there were bits of glass, drifting out like a jigsaw puzzle where every piece had suddenly decided it wanted some personal space. The lid slid down, almost hitting him.

*"Now pick me up and run,"* ordered the Thing, before the shards had spilled across the table.

Humans around the room were turning to look in that slow, clumsy way humans had.

Masklin grabbed the Thing and took off across the polished surface.

"Down!" he said. "We're high up, how do we get down?" He looked around desperately. There was some sort of machine at the other end of the table, covered with little dials and lights. He'd watched one of the humans using it.

"Wires," he said. "There's always wires!"

He skidded around, dodged easily around a giant hand as it tried to grab him, and sped along the table.

"I'll have to throw you over," he panted. "I can't carry you down!"

*"I'll be all right."*

Masklin slid to a stop by the table edge and threw the Thing down. There *were* wires running down toward the floor. He leaped for one, swung around madly, and then half fell and half slid down it.

Humans were lurching toward him from everywhere. He picked up the Thing again, hugging it to his chest, and darted forward. There was a foot—brown shoe, dark blue sock. He zigged. There were two more feet—black shoes, black socks. And they were about to trip over the first foot . . .

He zagged.

There were more feet, and hands reaching vainly down. Masklin was a blur, dodging and weaving between feet that could flatten him.

And then there was nothing but open floor.

Somewhere an alarm sounded, its shrill note sounding deep and awesome to Masklin.

*"Head for the door,"* suggested the Thing.

"But more humans'll be coming in," hissed Masklin.

*"That's good, because we're going out."*

Masklin reached the door just as it opened. A gap of a few inches appeared, with more feet behind it.

There wasn't any time to think. Masklin ran over the shoe, jumped down on the other side, and ran on.

"Where now? Where now?"

*"Outside."*

"Which way is that?"

*"Every way."*

"Thank you very much!"

Doors were opening all along the corridor. Humans were coming out. The problem was not evading capture—it would take a very alert human even to see a nome running at full speed, let alone catch one—but simply avoiding being trodden on by accident.

"Why don't they have mouseholes? Every building should have mouseholes!" Masklin moaned.

A boot stamped down an inch away. He jumped.

The corridor was filling with humans. Another alarm started to sound.

"Why's all this happening? I can't be causing all this? There can't be all this trouble over just one nome!"

*"It's the Ship. They have seen the Ship."*

A shoe almost awarded Masklin the prize for the most perfectly flattened nome in Florida. As it was, he almost ran into it.

Unlike most shoes, it had a name on it. It was a Crucial Street Drifter with Real Rubber Sole, Pat'd. The sock above it looked as though it could be a Histyle Odorprufe, made of Guaranteed eighty-five percent Polyputheketlon, the most expensive sock in the world.

Masklin looked farther up. Beyond the great sweep of blue trouser and the distant clouds of sweater was a beard.

It was Grandson Richard, 39.

Just when you thought there was no one watching over nomes, the universe went and tried to prove you wrong. . . .

Masklin took a standing jump and landed on the trouser leg, just as the foot moved. It was the safest place. Humans didn't often tread on other humans.

The foot took a step and came down again. Masklin swung backward and forward, trying to pull himself up the rough cloth. There was a seam an inch away. He managed to grab it; the stitches gave a better handhold.

Grandson Richard, 39, was in a crush of people all heading the same way. Several other humans banged into him, almost jarring Masklin loose. He kicked his boots off and tried to grip with his toes.

There was a slow thumping as Grandson Richard's feet hit the ground.

Masklin reached a pocket, got a decent foothold, and climbed on. A bulky label helped him up to the belt. Masklin was used to labels in the Store, but this was pretty big even by big label standards. It was covered in lettering and had been riveted to the trousers, as if Grandson Richard were some sort of machine.

"'Grossbergers Hagglers, the First Name in Jeans,'" he read. "And there's lots of stuff about how good they are, and pictures of cows and things. Why d'you think he wants labels all over him?"

*"Perhaps if he hasn't got labels, he doesn't know what his clothes are,"* said the Thing.

"Good point. He'd probably put his shoes on his head."

Masklin glanced back at the label as he grabbed the sweater.

"It says here that these jeans won a gold medal in the Chicago Exhibition in 1910," he said. "They've certainly lasted well."

Humans were streaming out of the building.

The sweater was much easier to climb. Masklin hauled himself up quickly. Grandson Richard had quite long hair, which also helped when it was time to climb up onto the shoulder.

A doorframe passed briefly overhead, and then the deep blue of the sky.

"How long, Thing?" Masklin hissed. Grandson Richard's ear was only a few inches away.

*"Forty-three seconds."*

The humans spilled out onto the wide concrete space in front of the building. Some more hurried out of the building, carrying machinery. They kept running into one another because they were all staring at the sky.

Another group was clustered around one human, who was looking very worried.

"What's going on, Thing?" Masklin whispered.

*"The human in the middle of the group is the most important one here. It came to watch the Shuttle launch. Now all the others are telling it that it's got to be the one to welcome the Ship."*

"That's a bit of a nerve. It's not *their* Ship."

*"Yes, but they think it's coming to talk to them."*

"Why should they think that?"

*"Because they think they're the most important creatures on the planet."*

"Hah!"

*"Amazing, isn't it?"* said the Thing.

"Everyone knows nomes are more important," said Masklin. "At least . . . every nome does." He thought about this for a moment and shook his head. "So that's the head human, is it? Is it some sort of extra-wise one, or something?"

*"I don't think so. The other humans around it are trying to explain to it what a planet is."*

"Doesn't it know?"

*"Many humans don't. Mistervicepresident is one of them. 001010011000."*

"You're talking to the Ship again?"

*"Yes. Six seconds."*

"It's really coming. . . ."

*"Yes."*

# 10

*GRAVITY: This is not properly understood, but it is what makes small things, like nomes, stick to big things, like planets. Because of SCIENCE, this happens whether you know about gravity or not. Which goes to show that Science is happening all the time.*

*From* A Scientific Encyclopedia
for the Inquiring Young Nome
*by Angalo de Haberdasheri*

ANGALO LOOKED AROUND.

"Gurder, come *on.*"

Gurder leaned against a tuft of grass and fought to get his breath back.

"It's no good," he wheezed. "What are you thinking of? We can't fight humans alone!"

"We've got Pion. And this is a pretty good axe."

"Oh, that's really going to scare them. A stone axe. If you had two axes, I expect they'd give in right away."

Angalo swung it backward and forward. It had a comforting feel.

"You've got to try," he said simply. "Come on, Pion. What are you watching? Geese?"

Pion was staring at the sky.

"There's a dot up there," said Gurder, squinting.

"It's probably a bird," said Angalo.

"Doesn't look like a bird."

"Then it's a plane."

"Doesn't look like a plane."

Now all three of them were staring upward, their upturned faces forming a triangle.

There was a black dot up there.

"You don't think he actually *managed* it, do you?" said Angalo uncertainly.

What had been a dot was now a small dark circle.

"It's not moving, though," said Gurder.

"It's not moving sideways, anyway," said Angalo, still speaking very slowly. "It's moving more sort of down."

What had been a small dark circle was a larger dark circle, with just a suspicion of smoke or steam around its edges.

"It might be some sort of weather," said Angalo. "You know. Special Floridian weather?"

"Oh, yeah? One great big hailstone, right? It's the Ship! Coming for us!"

It was a lot bigger now and yet, and yet . . . still a very long way off.

"If it could come for us just a little way away, I wouldn't mind," Gurder quavered. "I wouldn't mind walking a little way."

"Yeah," said Angalo, beginning to look desperate. "It's not so much coming as, as . . ."

". . . *dropping,*" said Gurder.

He looked at Angalo.

"Shall we run?" he said.

"It's got to be worth a try," said Angalo.

"Where shall we run to?"

"Let's just follow Pion, shall we? He started running a while ago."

Masklin would be the first to admit that he wasn't too familiar with forms of transport, but what they all seemed to have in common was a front, which was in front, and a back, which wasn't. The whole point was that the front was where they went forward from.

The thing dropping out of the sky was a disk—just a top connected to a bottom, with edges round the sides. It didn't make any noise, but it seemed to be impressing the humans no end.

"That's it?" he said.

"*Yes.*"

"Oh."

And then things seemed to come into focus.

The Ship wasn't big. It needed a new word. It wasn't *dropping* through the thin wisps of cloud up there, it was simply pushing them aside. Just when you thought you'd got some idea of the size, a cloud would stream past and the perspective would wind back. There had to be a special word for something as big as that.

"Is it going to crash?" he whispered.

"*I shall land it on the scrub,*" said the Thing. "*I don't want to frighten the humans.*"

"Run!"

"What do you think I'm doing?"

"It's still right above us!"

"I'm running! I'm running! I can't run any faster!"

A shadow fell across the three running nomes.

"All the way to Floridia to be squashed under our own Ship," moaned Angalo. "You never really believed in it, did you? Well, now you're going to believe in it really hard!"

The shadow deepened. They could see it racing across the ground ahead of them—gray around the edges, spreading into the darkness of night. Their own private night.

"The others are still out there somewhere," said Masklin.

*"Ah,"* said the Thing. *"I forgot."*

"You're not supposed to forget things like that!"

*"I've been very busy lately. I can't think of everything. Just nearly everything."*

"Well don't squash anyone!"

*"I shall stop it before it lands. Don't worry."*

The humans were all talking at once. Some of them had started to run toward the falling ship. Some were running away from it.

Masklin risked a glance at Grandson Richard's face. It was watching the ship with a strange, rapt expression.

As Masklin stared, the big eyes swiveled slowly sideways. The head turned around. Grandson Richard stared down at the nome on his shoulder.

For the second time, the human saw him. And this time, there was nowhere to run.

Masklin rapped the Thing on its lid.

"Can you slow my voice down?" he said quickly. An amazed expression was forming on the human's face.

*"What do you mean?"*

"I mean you just repeat what I say, but slowed down. And louder. So it—so he can understand it?"

*"You want to communicate? With a human?"*

"Yes! Can you do it?"

*"I strongly advise against it! It could be very dangerous!"*

Masklin clenched his fists. "Compared to what, Thing? Compared to what? How much more dangerous than not communicating, Thing? Do it! Right now! Tell him . . . tell him we're *not* trying to hurt any humans! Right now! I can see his hand moving already! Do it!" He held the box right up to Grandson Richard's ear.

The Thing started to speak in the low, slow tones of human speech.

It seemed to go on for a long time.

The human's expression froze.

"What did you say? What did you say?" said Masklin.

*"I said, if he harms you in any way I shall explode and blow his head off,"* said the Thing.

"You didn't!"

*"I did."*

"You call that communicating?"

*"Yes. I call it very effective communicating."*

"But it's a dreadful thing to say! Anyway . . . you never told me you could explode!"

*"I can't. But it doesn't know that. It's only human,"* said the Thing.

The Ship slowed its fall and drifted down across the scrublands until it met its own shadow. Beside it, the tower where the Shuttle had been launched looked like a pin alongside a very large black plate.

"You landed it on the ground! You said you wouldn't!" said Masklin.

*"It's not on the ground. It is floating just above the ground."*

"It looks as though it's on the ground to me!"

*"It is floating just above it,"* repeated the Thing patiently.

Grandson Richard was looking at Masklin down the length of his nose. He looked puzzled.

"What makes it float?" Masklin demanded.

The Thing told him.

"Auntie who? Who's she? There's relatives on board?"

*"Not Auntie. Anti. Antigravity."*

"But there's no flames or smoke!"

*"Flames and smoke are not essential."*

Vehicles were screaming toward the bulk of the Ship.

"Um. Exactly *how* far off the ground did you stop it?" Masklin inquired.

*"Four inches seemed adequate—"*

Angalo lay with his face pressed into the sandy soil.

To his amazement, he was still alive. Or at least, if he *was* dead, then he was still able to think. Perhaps he was dead, and this was wherever you went afterward.

It seemed pretty much like where he'd been before.

Let's see, now. He'd looked up at the great thing dropping out of the sky right toward his head, and had flung himself down, expecting at any second to become just a little greasy mark in a great big hole.

No, he probably hadn't died. He'd have remembered something important like that.

"Gurder?" he ventured.

"Is that you?" said Gurder's voice.

"I hope so. Pion?"

"Pion!" said Pion, somewhere in the darkness.

Angalo pushed himself up onto his hands and knees.

"Any idea where we are?" he said.

"In the Ship?" suggested Gurder.

"Don't think so," said Angalo. "There's soil here, and grass and stuff."

"Then where did the Ship go? Why's it all dark?"

Angalo brushed the dirt off his coat. "Dunno. Maybe . . . maybe it missed us. Maybe we were knocked out, and now it's nighttime?"

"I can see a bit of light around the horizon," said Gurder. "That's not right, is it? That's not how nights are supposed to be."

Angalo looked around. There *was* a line of light in the distance. And there was also a strange sound, so quiet that you could miss it but which, once you had noticed it, also seemed to fill up the world.

He stood up to get a better view.

There was a faint thump.

"Ouch!"

Angalo reached up to rub his head. His hand touched metal. Crouching a little, he risked turning his head to see what it was he'd hit.

He went very thoughtful for a while.

Then he said, "Gurder, you're going to find this amazingly hard to believe. . . ."

"*This* time," said Masklin to the Thing, "I want you to translate *exactly*, do you understand? Don't try to frighten him!"

Humans had surrounded the Ship. At least, they were trying to surround it, but you'd need an awful lot of humans to surround something the size of the Ship. So they were just surrounding it in places.

More trucks were arriving, many of them with sirens blaring. Grandson Richard had been left standing by himself, watching his own shoulder nervously.

"Besides, we owe him something," said Masklin. "We used his satellite. And we stole things."

*"You said you wanted to do it your way. No help from humans, you said,"* said the Thing.

"It's different now. There is the Ship," said Masklin. "We've made it. We're not begging anymore."

*"May I point out that you're sitting on his shoulder, not him on yours,"* said the Thing.

"Never mind that," said Masklin. "Tell it—I mean, ask him to walk toward the Ship. And say please. And say that we don't want anyone to get hurt. Including me," he added.

Grandson Richard's reply seemed to take a long time. But he did start to walk toward the crowds around the Ship.

"What did he say?" said Masklin, hanging on tightly to the sweater.

*"I don't believe it,"* said the Thing.

"He doesn't believe me?"

*"He said his grandfather always talked about the little people, but he never believed it until now. He said: Are you like the ones in the old Store?"*

Masklin's mouth dropped open. Grandson Richard was watching him intently.

"Tell him yes," Masklin croaked.

*"Very well. But I do not think it'll be a good idea."*

The Thing boomed. Grandson Richard rumbled a reply.

*"He says his grandfather made jokes about little people in the Store,"* said the Thing. *"He used to say they brought him luck."*

Masklin felt the horrible sensation in his stomach that meant the world was changing again, just when he thought he understood it.

"Did his grandfather ever see a nome?" he said.

*"He says no. But he says that when his grandfather and his grandfather's brother were starting the Store and stayed late every night to do the office work, they used to hear sounds in the walls, and they used to tell each other there were little Store people. It was a sort of joke. He says that when he was small, his grandfather used to tell him about little people who came out at night to play with the toys."*

"But the Store nomes never did things like that!" said Masklin.

*"I didn't say the stories were true."*

The Ship was a lot closer now. There didn't seem to be any doors or windows anywhere. It was as featureless as an egg.

Masklin's mind was in turmoil. He'd always believed that humans were quite intelligent. After all, nomes were very intelligent. Rats were quite intelligent. And foxes were intelligent, more or less. There ought to be enough intelligence sloshing around in the world for humans to have some too. But this was something more than intelligence.

He remembered the book called *Gulliver's Travels*. It had been a big surprise to the nomes. There had never been an island of small people. He was certain of that. It was a, a, a made-up thing. There had been lots of books in the Store that were like that. They'd caused no end of problems for the nomes. For some reason, humans needed things that weren't true.

They never really thought nomes existed, he thought, but they wanted to believe that we did.

"Tell him," he said, "tell him I must get into the Ship."

Grandson Richard whispered. It was like listening to a gale.

*"He says there are too many people."*

"Why are all the humans around it?" said Masklin, bewildered. "Why aren't they frightened?"

Grandson Richard's reply was another gale.

*"He says they think some creatures from another world will come out and talk to them."*

"Why?"

*"I don't know,"* said the Thing. *"Perhaps they don't want to be alone."*

"But there's no one in it! It's *our* Ship—" Masklin began.

There was a wail. The crowd put their hands over their ears.

Lights appeared on the darkness of the Ship. They twinkled all over the hull in patterns that raced backward and forward and disappeared. There was another wail.

"There *isn't* anyone in it, is there?" said Masklin. "No nomes were left on it in hibernation or anything?"

High up on the Ship a square hole opened. There was a whiffling noise, and a beam of red light shot out and set fire to a patch of scrub several hundred yards away.

People started to run.

The Ship rose a few feet, wobbling alarmingly. It drifted sideways a little. Then it went straight up so fast that it was just a blur and jerked to a halt high over the crowd. And then it turned over. And then it went on its edge for a while.

It floated back down again and landed, more or less. That is, one side touched the ground and the other rested on the air, on nothing.

The Ship spoke, loudly.

To the humans it must have sounded like a high-pitched chattering.

What it actually said was: "Sorry! Sorry! Is this a microphone? Can't find the button that opens the door . . . let's try this one. . . ."

Another square hole opened. Brilliant blue light flooded out.

The voice boomed out across the country again.

"Got it!" There was the distorted *thud-thud* of someone who isn't certain if their microphone is working and who is tapping it experimentally. "Masklin, are you out there?"

"That's Angalo!" said Masklin. "No one else drives like that! Thing, tell Grandson Richard I must get on the Ship! Please!"

The human nodded.

Humans were milling around the base of the Ship. The doorway was too high up for them to reach.

With Masklin hanging on grimly, Grandson Richard pushed his way through the throng.

The Ship wailed again.

"Er," came Angalo's hugely amplified voice, apparently talking to someone else. "I'm not sure about this switch, but maybe it's . . . Certainly I'm going to press it, why shouldn't I press it? It's next to the door one—it must be safe. Look, shut up. . . ."

A silver ramp wound out of the doorway. It looked big enough for humans.

"See? See?" said Angalo's voice.

"Thing, can you speak to Angalo?" said Masklin. "Tell him I'm out here, trying to get to the Ship?"

"*No. He appears to be randomly pressing buttons. It is to be hoped that he does not press the wrong ones.*"

"I thought you could tell the Ship what to do!" said Masklin.

The Thing managed to sound shocked. "*Not when a nome is in it,*" it said. "*I can't tell it not to do what a nome tells it to do. That's what being a machine is all about.*"

Grandson Richard was shoving his way through the pushing, shouting mass of humans, but it was hard going.

Masklin sighed.

"Ask Grandson Richard to put me down," he said. Then he

added, "And say thank you. Say it . . . it would have been nice to talk more."

The Thing did the translation.

Grandson Richard looked surprised. The Thing spoke again. Then he reached up a hand toward Masklin.

If he had to make that list of horrible moments, Masklin would have put this one at the top. He'd faced foxes, he'd helped to drive the Truck, he'd flown on a goose—but none of them was half so bad as letting a human being actually touch him. The huge whorled fingers uncurled and passed on either side of his waist. He shut his eyes.

Angalo's booming voice said, "Masklin? Masklin? If anything bad's happened to you, there's going to be *trouble*."

Grandson Richard's fingers gripped Masklin lightly, as though the human were holding something very fragile. Masklin felt himself being slowly lowered toward the ground. He opened his eyes. There was a forest of human legs around him.

He looked up into Grandson Richard's huge face and, trying to make his voice as deep and slow as possible, said the only word any nome had said directly to a human in fifteen thousand years.

"Good-bye."

Then he ran through the maze of feet.

Several humans with official-looking trousers and big boots were standing at the bottom of the ramp. Masklin scurried between them and ran on upward.

Ahead of him blue light shone out of the open hatchway. As he ran, he saw two dots appear on the lip of the entrance.

The ramp was long. Masklin hadn't slept for hours. He wished he'd got some sleep on the bed when the humans were studying him; it had looked quite comfortable.

Suddenly, all his legs wanted to do was go somewhere close and lie down.

He staggered to the top of the ramp, and the dots became the heads of Gurder and Pion. They reached out and pulled him into the Ship.

He turned around and looked down into a sea of human faces below him. He'd never looked down on a human face before.

They probably couldn't even see him. They're waiting for the little green men, he thought.

"Are you all right?" said Gurder urgently. "Did they do anything to you?"

"I'm fine, I'm fine," murmured Masklin. "No one hurt me."

"You look dreadful."

"We should have talked to them, Gurder," said Masklin. "They *need* us."

"Are you *sure* you're all right?" said Gurder, peering anxiously at him.

Masklin's head felt full of cotton. "You know you believed in Arnold Bros (est. 1905)?" he managed to say.

"Yes," said Gurder.

Masklin gave him a mad, triumphant grin.

"Well, he believed in you, too! How about that?"

And Masklin folded up, very gently.

# 11

*THE SHIP: The machine used by nomes to leave Earth. We don't yet know everything about it, but since it was built by nomes using SCIENCE, we will.*

*From* A Scientific Encyclopedia
for the Inquiring Young Nome
*by Angalo de Haberdasheri*

THE RAMP WOUND in. The doorway shut. The Ship rose in the air until it was high above the buildings.

And it stayed there while the sun set.

The humans below tried shining colored lights at it, and playing tunes at it, and eventually just speaking to it in every language known to humans.

It didn't seem to take any notice.

Masklin woke up.

He was on a very uncomfortable bed. It was all soft. He hated lying on anything softer than the ground. The Store nomes liked sleeping on fancy bits of carpet, but Masklin's bed had been a bit of wood. He'd used a piece of rag for a cover and thought that was luxury.

He sat up and looked around the room. It was fairly empty. There was just the bed, a table, and a chair.

A table and a chair.

In the Store, the nomes had made their furniture out of matchboxes and cotton reels; the nomes living Outside didn't even know what furniture *was*.

This looked rather like human furniture, but it was nome sized.

Masklin got up and padded across the metal floor to the door. Nome sized, again. A doorway made by nomes for nomes to walk through.

It led into a corridor lined with doors. There was an old feel about it. It wasn't dirty or dusty. It just felt like somewhere that had been absolutely clean for a very, very long time.

Something purred toward him. It was a small black box, rather like the Thing, mounted on little treads. A small revolving brush on the front was sweeping dust into a slot. At least, if there had been any dust it would have been sweeping it. Masklin wondered how many times it had industriously cleaned this corridor, while it waited for nomes to come back. . . .

It bumped into his foot, beeped at him, and then bustled off in the opposite direction. Masklin followed it.

After a while he passed another one. It was moving along the ceiling with a faint clicking noise, cleaning it.

He turned the corner and almost walked into Gurder.

"You're up!"

"Yes," said Masklin. "Er. We're on the Ship, right?"

"It's amazing—!" Gurder began. He was wild-eyed, and his hair was sticking up at all angles.

"I'm sure it is," said Masklin reassuringly.

"But there's all these . . . and there's great big . . . and there's these *huge* . . . and you'd never believe how wide . . . and there's so much . . ." Gurder's voice trailed off. He looked like a nome who would have to learn new words before he could describe things.

"It's too big!" he blurted out. He grabbed Masklin's arm. "Come on," he said, and half ran along the corridor.

"How did you get on?" said Masklin, trying to keep up.

"It was amazing! Angalo touched this panel thing and it just moved aside and then we were inside and there was an elevator thing and then we were in this great big room with a seat and Angalo sat down and all these lights came on and he started pressing buttons and moving things!"

"Didn't you try to stop him?"

Gurder rolled his eyes. "You know Angalo and machines," he said. "But the Thing is trying to get him to be sensible. Otherwise we'd be crashing into stars by now," he added gloomily.

He led the way through another arch into—

Well, it had to be a room. It was inside the Ship. It was just as well he knew that, Masklin thought, because otherwise he'd think it was Outside. It stretched away, as big as one of the departments in the Store.

Vast screens and complicated-looking panels covered the walls. Most of them were dark. Shadowy gloom stretched away in every direction, except for a little puddle of light in the very center of the room.

It illuminated Angalo, almost lost in a big padded chair. He had the Thing in front of him, on a sloping metal board studded with switches. He had obviously been arguing with it—when Masklin walked up, Angalo glared at him and said, "It won't do what I tell it!"

The Thing looked as small and black and square as it could.

*"He wants to drive the Ship,"* it said.

"You're a machine! You *have* to do what you're told!" snapped Angalo.

*"I'm an* intelligent *machine, and I don't want to end up very flat at the bottom of a deep hole,"* said the Thing. *"You can't pilot the Ship yet."*

"How do you know? You won't let me try! I drove the Truck, didn't I? It wasn't my fault all those trees and streetlights and things got in the way," he added, after catching Masklin's eye.

"I expect the Ship is more difficult," said Masklin diplomatically.

"But I'm learning about it all the time," said Angalo. "It's easy. All the buttons have got little pictures on them. Look . . ."

He pressed a button.

One of the big screens lit up, showing the crowds outside the ship.

"They've been waiting there for ages," said Gurder.

"What do they want?" said Angalo.

"Search me," said Gurder. "Who knows what humans want?"

Masklin stared at the throng below the Ship.

"They've been trying all sorts of stuff," said Angalo. "Flashing lights and music and stuff like that. And radio too, the Thing says."

"Haven't you tried talking back to them?" said Masklin.

"No. Haven't got anything to say," said Angalo. He rapped on the Thing with his knuckles. "Right, Mr. Clever—if I'm not going to do the driving, who is?"

*"Me."*

"How?"

*"There is a slot by the seat."*

"I see it. It's the same size as you."

*"Put me in it."*

Angalo shrugged and picked up the Thing. It slid smoothly into the floor until only the top of it was showing.

"Look, er," said Angalo, "can't I do something? Operate the windshield wipers or something? I'd feel like a twerp sitting here doing nothing."

The Thing didn't seem to hear him. Its light flickered on and off for a moment, as if it were making itself comfortable in a mechanical kind of way. Then it said, in a much deeper voice than it had ever used before: *"RIGHT."*

Lights came on all over the Ship. They spread out from the Thing like a tide; panels lit up like little skies full of stars, big lights in the ceiling flickered on, there was a distant banging and fizzing as electricity was woken up, and the air began to smell of thunderstorms.

"It's like the Store at Christmas Fayre," said Gurder.

*"ALL SYSTEMS IN WORKING ORDER,"* boomed the Thing. *"NAME OUR DESTINATION."*

"What?" said Masklin. "And don't shout."

*"Where are we going?"* said the Thing. *"You have to name our destination."*

"It's got a name already. It's called the quarry, isn't it?" said Masklin.

*"Where is it?"* said the Thing.

"It's—" Masklin waved an arm vaguely. "Well, it's over that way somewhere."

*"Which way?"*

"How should I know? How many ways are there?"

"Thing, are you telling us you don't know the way back to the quarry?" said Gurder.

*"That is correct."*

"We're lost?"

*"No. I know exactly what planet we're on,"* said the Thing.

"We can't be lost," said Gurder. "We're here. We know where we are. We just don't know where we aren't."

"Can't you find the quarry if you go up high enough?" said Angalo. "You ought to be able to see it, if you go up high enough."

*"Very well."*

"Can I do it?" said Angalo. "Please?"

*"Press down with your left foot and pull back on the green lever, then,"* said the Thing.

There wasn't so much a noise as a change in the type of silence. Masklin thought he felt heavy for a moment, but then the sensation passed.

The picture in the screen got smaller.

"Now, this is what I call proper flying," said Angalo, happily. "No noise and none of that stupid flapping."

"Yes, where's Pion?" said Masklin.

"He wandered off," said Gurder. "I think he was going to get something to eat."

"On a machine that no nome has been on for fifteen thousand years?" said Masklin.

Gurder shrugged. "Well, maybe there's something at the back of a cupboard somewhere," he said. "I want a word with you, Masklin."

"Yes?"

Gurder moved closer and glanced over his shoulder at Angalo, who was lying back in the control seat with a look of dreamy contentment on his face.

He lowered his voice.

"We shouldn't be doing this," he said. "I know it's a dreadful thing to say, after all we've been through. But this isn't just *our* Ship. It belongs to all nomes, everywhere."

He looked relieved when Masklin nodded.

"A year ago you didn't even believe there *were* any other nomes anywhere," Masklin said.

Gurder looked sheepish. "Yes. Well. That was then. This is now. I don't know what I believe in anymore, except that there must be thousands of nomes out there we don't know about. There might even be other nomes living in Stores! We're just the lucky ones who had the Thing. So if we take the Ship away, there won't be any hope for them."

"I know, I know," said Masklin wretchedly. "But what can we do? *We* need the Ship right now. Anyway, how could we find these other nomes?"

"We've got the Ship!" said Gurder.

Masklin waved a hand at the screen, where the landscape was spreading out and becoming misty.

"It'd take forever to find nomes down there. You couldn't do it even with the Ship. You'd have to be on the ground. Nomes keep hidden! You nomes in the Store didn't know about my people, and we lived a few miles away. We'd never have found Pion's people except by accident. Besides"—he couldn't resist prodding Gurder gently—"there's a bigger problem, too. You know what we nomes are like. Those other nomes probably wouldn't even *believe* in the Ship."

He was immediately sorry he'd said that. Gurder looked more unhappy than he'd ever seen him.

"That's true," the Abbot said. "I wouldn't have believed it. I'm not sure I believe it now, and I'm *on* it."

"Maybe, when we've found somewhere to live, we can send the

Ship back and collect any other nomes we can find," Masklin hazarded. "I'm sure Angalo would enjoy that."

Gurder's shoulders began to shake. For a moment Masklin thought the nome was laughing, and then he saw the tears rolling down the Abbot's face.

"Um," he said, not knowing what else to say.

Gurder turned away. "I'm sorry," he muttered. "It's just that there's so much . . . changing. Why can't things stay the same for five minutes? Every time I get the hang of an idea, it suddenly turns into something different and *I* turn into a fool! All I want is something real to believe in! Where's the harm in that?"

"I think you just have to have a flexible mind," said Masklin, knowing even as he said the words that this probably wasn't going to be a lot of help.

"Flexible? Flexible? My mind's got so flexible I could pull it out of my ears and tie it under my chin!" snapped Gurder. "And it hasn't done me a whole lot of good, let me tell you! I'd have done better just believing everything I was taught when I was young! At least I'd only have been wrong once! This way I'm wrong all the time!"

He stamped away down one of the corridors.

Masklin watched him go. Not for the first time he wished he believed in something as much as Gurder did so he could complain to it about his life. He wished he was back—yes, even back in the hole. It hadn't been too bad, apart from people being cold and wet and getting eaten all the time. But at least he had been with Grimma. They would have been cold and wet and hungry together. He wouldn't have been so lonely. . . .

There was a movement by him. It turned out to be Pion, holding a tray of what had to be . . . fruit, Masklin decided. He put aside being lonely for a moment and realized that hunger had been waiting for an opportunity to make itself felt. He'd never seen fruit that shape and color.

He took a slice from the proffered tray. It tasted like a nutty lemon.

"It's kept well, considering," he said, weakly. "Where did you get it?"

It turned out to have come from a machine in a nearby corridor. It looked fairly simple. There were hundreds of pictures of different sorts of food. If you touched a picture, there was a brief humming noise and then the food dropped onto a tray in a slot. Masklin tried pictures at random and got several different sorts of fruit, a squeaky green vegetable thing, and a piece of meat that tasted rather like smoked salmon.

"I wonder how it does it," he said aloud.

A voice from the wall beside him said: *"Would you understand if I told you about molecular breakdown and reassembly from a wide range of raw materials?"*

"No," said Masklin truthfully.

*"Then it's all done by Science."*

"Oh. Well, that's all right, then. That *is* you, Thing, isn't it?"

*"Yes."*

Chewing on the fish meat, Masklin wandered back to the control room and offered some of the food to Angalo. The big screen was showing nothing but clouds.

"Won't see any quarry in all this," he said.

Angalo pulled one of the levers back a bit. There was that brief feeling of extra weight again.

They stared at the screen.

"Wow," said Angalo.

"That looks familiar," said Masklin. He patted his clothes until he found the folded, crumpled map they'd brought all the way from the Store.

He spread it out, and glanced from it to the screen.

The screen showed a disk, made up mainly of different shades of blue and wispy bits of cloud.

"Any idea what it is?" said Angalo.

"No, but I know what some of the bits are called," said Masklin. "That one that's thick at the top and thin at the bottom is called South America. Look, it's just like it is on the map. Only it should have the words 'South America' written on it."

"Still can't see the quarry, though," said Angalo.

Masklin looked at the image in front of them. South America. Grimma had talked about South America, hadn't she? That's where the frogs lived in flowers. She'd said that once you knew about things like frogs living in flowers, you weren't the same person.

He was beginning to see what she meant.

"Never mind about the quarry for now," he said. "The quarry can wait."

*"We should get there as soon as possible, for everybody's sake,"* said the Thing.

Masklin thought about this for a while. It was true, he had to admit. All kinds of things might be happening back home. He had to get the Ship back quickly, for everybody's sake.

And then he thought: I've spent a long time doing things for everybody's sake. Just for once, I'm going to do something for me. I don't think we can find other nomes with this Ship, but at least I know where to look for frogs.

"Thing," he said, "take us to South America. And don't argue."

## 12

*FROGS: Some people think that knowing about frogs is important. They are small and green, or yellow, and have four legs. They croak. Young frogs are tadpoles. In my opinion, this is all there is to know about frogs.*

*From* A Scientific Encyclopedia
for the Inquiring Young Nome
*by Angalo de Haberdasheri*

FIND A BLUE planet. . . .

*Focus*

This is a planet. Most of it is covered in water, but it's still called Earth.

Find a country . . .

*Focus*

. . . blues and greens and browns under the sun, and long wisps of rain cloud being torn by the mountains . . .

*Focus*

. . . on a mountain, green and dripping, and there's a . . .

*Focus*

. . . tree, hung with moss and covered with flowers and . . .

*Focus*

. . . on a flower with a little pool in it. It's an epiphytic bromeliad.

Its leaves, although they might be petals, hardly quiver at all as three very small and very golden frogs pull themselves up and gaze in astonishment at the fresh clear water. Two of them look at their leader, waiting for it to say something suitable for this historic occasion.

It's going to be ".–.–.mipmip.–.–."

And then they slide down the leaf and into the water.

Although the frogs can spot the difference between day and night, they're a bit hazy on the whole idea of Time. They know that some things happen after other things. Really intelligent frogs might wonder if there is something that prevents everything happening all at once, but that's about as close as they can get to it.

So how long it was before a strange night came in the middle of the day is hard to tell, from a frog's point of view. . . .

A wide black shadow drifted over the treetops and came to a halt. After a while there were voices. The frogs could hear them, although they didn't know what they meant or even what they were. They didn't sound like the kind of voices frogs were used to.

What they heard went like this: "How many mountains are there, anyway? I mean, it's ridiculous! Who needs this many mountains? I call it inefficient. One would have done. I'll go mad if I see another mountain. How many more have we got to search?"

"I like them."

"And some of the trees are the wrong height."

"I like them too, Gurder."

"And I don't trust Angalo doing the driving."

"I think he's getting better, Gurder."

"Well, I just hope no more airplanes come flying around, that's all."

Gurder and Masklin swung in a crude basket made out of bits of metal and wire. It hung from a square hatchway under the Ship.

There were still huge rooms in the Ship that they hadn't explored yet. Odd machines were everywhere. The Thing had said the Ship had been used for exploring.

Masklin hadn't quite trusted any of it. There were probably machines that could have lowered and pulled up the basket easily, but he'd preferred to loop the wire around a pillar inside the Ship and, with Pion helping inside, to pull themselves up and down by sheer nomish effort.

The basket bumped gently on the tree branch.

The trouble was that humans wouldn't leave them alone. No sooner had they found a likely-looking mountain than airplanes or helicopters would buzz around, like insects around an eagle. It was distracting.

Masklin looked along the branch. Gurder was right. This would have to be the last mountain.

But there were certainly flowers here.

He crawled along the branch until he reached the nearest flower. It was three times as high as he was. He found a foothold and pulled himself up.

There was a pool in there. Six little yellow eyes peered up at him. Masklin stared back.

So it was true, after all. . . .

He wondered if there was anything he should say to them, if there was anything they could possibly understand.

It was quite a long branch, and quite thick. But there were tools and things in the Ship. They could let down extra wires to hold the branch and winch it up when it was cut free. It would take some time, but that didn't matter. It was important.

The Thing had said there were ways of growing plants under lights the same color as the sun, in pots full of a sort of weak soup that helped plants grow. It should be the easiest thing to keep a branch alive. The easiest thing in . . . the world.

If they did everything carefully and gently, the frogs would never know.

If the world was a bathtub, the progress of the Ship through it would be like the soap, shooting backward and forward and never being where anyone was expecting it to be. You could spot where it had just been by airplanes and helicopters taking off in a hurry.

Or maybe it was like the ball in a roulette wheel, bouncing around and looking for the right number. . . .

Or maybe it was just lost.

They searched all night. If there *was* a night. It was hard to tell. The Thing tried to explain that the Ship went faster than the sun, although the sun actually stood still. Some parts of the world had night while other parts had day. This, Gurder said, was bad organization.

"In the Store," he said, "it was always dark when it should be. Even if it was *just* somewhere built by humans." It was the first time they'd heard him admit the Store was built by humans.

There didn't seem to be anywhere familiar.

Masklin scratched his chin.

"The Store was in a place called Blackbury," he said. "I know that much. So the quarry couldn't have been far away."

Angalo waved his hand irritably at the screens.

"Yes, but it's not like the map," he said. "They don't stick names on places! It's ridiculous! How's anyone supposed to know where anywhere is?"

"All right," said Masklin. "But you're *not* to fly down low again to try to read the signposts. Every time you do that, humans rush into the streets and we get lots of shouting on the radio."

*"That's right,"* said the Thing. *"People are bound to get excited when they see a ten-million-ton starship trying to fly down the street."*

"I was very careful last time," said Angalo stoutly. "I even stopped when the traffic lights went red. I don't see why there was such a fuss. All the trucks and cars started crashing into one another, too. And you call *me* a bad driver."

Gurder turned to Pion, who was learning the language fast. The geese nomes had a knack for that. They were used to meeting nomes who spoke other languages.

"Your geese never got lost," he said. "How did they manage it?"

"They just did not get lost," said Pion. "They knew always where they going."

"It can be like that with animals," said Masklin. "They've got instincts. It's like knowing things without knowing you know them."

"Why doesn't the Thing know where to go?" said Gurder. "It could find Floridia, so somewhere important like Blackbury ought to be *no* trouble."

*"I can find no radio messages about Blackbury. There are plenty about Florida,"* said the Thing.

"At least land somewhere," said Gurder. Angalo pressed a couple of buttons.

"There's just sea under us right now," he said. "And—what's that?"

Below the Ship and a long way off, something tiny and white skimmed over the clouds.

"Could be goose," said Pion.

"I . . . don't . . . think . . . so," said Angalo carefully. He twiddled a knob. "I'm really learning about this stuff," he said.

The picture on the screen flickered a bit, and then expanded.

There was a white dart sliding across the sky.

"Is it the Concorde?" said Gurder.

"Yes," said Angalo.

"It's going a bit slow, isn't it?"

"Only compared to us," said Angalo.

"Follow it," said Masklin.

"We don't know where it's going," said Angalo in a reasonable tone of voice.

"I do," said Masklin. "You looked out of the window when we were on the Concorde. We were going toward the sun."

"Yes. It was setting," said Angalo. "Well?"

"It's morning now. It's going toward the sun again," Masklin pointed out.

"Well? What about it?"

"It means it's going home."

Angalo bit his lip while he worked this out.

"I don't see why the sun has to rise and set in different places," said Gurder, who refused to even try to understand basic astronomy.

"Going home," said Angalo, ignoring him. "Right. I see it. So we go with it, yes?"

"Yes."

Angalo ran his hands over the Ship's controls.

"Right," he said. "Here we go. I expect the Concorde drivers will probably be quite pleased to have some company up here."

o     o     o

The Ship drew level with the plane.

"It's moving around a lot," said Angalo. "And it's starting to go faster, too."

"I think they may be worried about the Ship," said Masklin.

"Can't see why," said Angalo. "Can't see why at all. We're not doing anything except following 'em."

"I wish we had some proper windows," said Gurder, wistfully. "We could wave."

"Have humans ever seen a ship like this before?" Angalo asked the Thing.

*"No. But they've made up stories about ships coming from other worlds."*

"Yes, they'd do that," said Masklin, half to himself. "That's just the sort of thing they'd do."

*"Sometimes they say the ships will contain friendly people—"*

"That's us," said Angalo.

*"—and sometimes they say they will contain monsters with wavy tentacles and big teeth."*

The nomes looked at one another.

Gurder cast an apprehensive eye over his shoulder. Then they all stared at the passages that radiated off the control room.

"Like alligators?" said Masklin.

*"Worse."*

"Er," Gurder said, "we *did* look in all the rooms, didn't we?"

"It's something they make up, Gurder. It's not real," said Masklin.

"Whoever would want to make up something like that?"

"Humans would," said Masklin.

"Huh," said Angalo, nonchalantly trying to swivel around in the chair in case any tentacled things with teeth were trying to creep up on him. "I can't see why."

"I think I can. I've been thinking about humans a lot."

"Can't the Thing send a message to the Concorde drivers?" said Gurder. "Something like 'Don't worry, we haven't got any teeth and tentacles, guaranteed'?"

"They probably wouldn't believe us," said Angalo. "If *I* had teeth and tentacles all over the place, that's just the sort of message I'd send. Cunning."

The Concorde screamed across the top of the sky, breaking the transatlantic record. The Ship drifted along behind it.

"I reckon," said Angalo, looking down, "that humans are just about intelligent enough to be crazy."

"I think," said Masklin, "that maybe they're intelligent enough to be lonely."

The plane touched down with its tires screaming. Fire engines raced across the airport, and there were other vehicles behind them.

The great black Ship shot over them, turned across the sky like a Frisbee, and slowed.

"There's the reservoir!" said Gurder. "Right under us! And that's the railway line! And that's the quarry! It's still there!"

"Of course it's still there, idiot," muttered Angalo, as he headed the ship toward the hills, which were patchy with melting snow.

"Some of it," said Masklin.

A pall of black smoke hung over the quarry. As they got closer, they saw it was rising from a burning truck. There were more trucks around it, and also several humans who started to run when they saw the shadow of the Ship.

"Lonely, eh?" snarled Angalo. "If they've hurt a single nome, they'll wish they'd never been born!"

"If they've hurt a single nome, they'll wish *I'd* never been born," said Masklin. "But I don't think anyone's down there. They wouldn't hang around if the humans came. And who set fire to the truck?"

"Yay!" said Angalo, waving a fist in the air.

Masklin scanned the landscape below them. Somehow he couldn't imagine people like Grimma and Dorcas sitting in holes, waiting for humans to take over. Trucks didn't just set fire to themselves. A couple of buildings looked damaged, too. Humans wouldn't have done that, would they?

He stared at the field by the quarry. The gate had been smashed, and a pair of wide tracks led through the slush and mud.

"I think they got away in another truck," he said.

"What do you mean, *yay*?" said Gurder, lagging a bit behind the conversation.

"Across the fields?" said Angalo. "It'd get stuck, wouldn't it?"

Masklin shook his head. Perhaps even a nome could have instincts. "Follow the tracks," he said urgently. "And quickly!"

"Quickly? *Quickly?* Do you know know difficult it is to make this thing go *slowly?*" Angalo nudged a lever. The ship lurched up the hillside, straining at the indignity of restraint.

They'd been up here before, on foot, months ago. It was hard to believe.

The hills were quite flat on the top, forming a kind of plateau overlooking the airport. There was the field where there had been potatoes. There was the thicket where they'd hunted, and the wood where they'd killed a fox for eating nomes.

And there . . . there was something small and yellow, rolling across the fields.

Angalo craned forward.

"Looks like some kind of a machine," he admitted, fumbling for levers without taking his eyes off the screen. "Weird kind of one, though."

There were other things moving on the roads down there. They had flashing lights on top.

"Those cars are chasing it, do you think?" said Angalo.

"Maybe they want to talk to it about a burning truck," said Masklin. "Can you get to it before they do?"

Angalo narrowed his eyes. "Listen, I think we can get to it before they do even if we go via Floridia." He found another lever and gave it a nudge.

There was the briefest flicker in the landscape, and the truck was now right in front of them.

"See?" he said.

"Move in more," said Masklin.

Angalo pressed a button. "See, the screen can show you below—" he began.

"There's nomes!" said Gurder.

"Yeah, and those cars are running away!" shouted Angalo. "That's it, run away! Otherwise it's teeth-and-tentacles time!"

"So long as the nomes don't think that too," said Gurder. "Masklin, do you think—"

Once again, Masklin wasn't there.

I should have thought about this before, he thought.

The piece of branch was thirty times longer than a nome. They'd been keeping it under lights, and it seemed to be growing quite happily with one end in a pot of special plant water. The nomes who had once flown in the Ship had obviously grown lots of plants that way.

Pion helped him drag the pot toward the hatch. The frogs watched Masklin with interest.

When it was positioned as well as the two of them could manage, Masklin let the hatch open. It wasn't one that slid aside. The ancient nomes had used it as a kind of elevator, but it didn't have wires—it went up and down by some force as mysterious as auntie's gravy or whatever it was.

It dropped away. Masklin looked down and saw the yellow truck roll to a halt. When he straightened up, Pion was giving him a puzzled look.

"Flower is a message?" said the boy.

"Yes. Kind of."

"Not using words?"

"No," said Masklin.

"Why not?"

Masklin shrugged.

"Don't know how to say them."

It nearly ends there. . . .

But it shouldn't end there.

Nomes swarmed all over the Ship. If there *were* any monsters with tentacles and teeth, they'd have been overwhelmed by sheer force of nome.

Young nomes filled the control room, where they were industriously trying to press buttons. Dorcas and his trainee engineers had disappeared in search of the Ship's engines. Voices and laughter echoed along the gray corridors.

Masklin and Grimma sat by themselves, watching the frogs in their flower.

"I had to see if it was true," said Masklin.

"The most wonderful thing in the world," said Grimma.

"No. I think there are probably much more wonderful things in the world," said Masklin. "But it's pretty good, all the same."

Grimma told him about events in the quarry—the fight with the humans, and the stealing of Big John the earthmover to escape. Her eyes gleamed when she talked about fighting humans. Masklin looked at her with his mouth open in admiration. She was muddy, her dress torn; her hair looked like it had been combed with a hedge, but she crackled with so much internal power that she was nearly throwing off sparks. It's a good thing we got here in time, he thought. Humans ought to thank me.

"What are we going to do now?" she said.

"I don't know," said Masklin. "According to the Thing, there's worlds out there with nomes on them. Just nomes, I mean. Or we can find one all to ourselves."

"You know," said Grimma, "I think the Store nomes would be happier just staying on the Ship. That's why they like it so much. It's like being in the Store. All the Outside is outside."

"Then I'd better go along to make sure they remember that there *is* an Outside. It's sort of my job, I suppose," said Masklin. "And when we've found somewhere, I want to bring the Ship back."

"Why? What'll be here?" said Grimma.

"Humans," said Masklin. "We should talk to them."

"Huh!"

"They really want to believe in . . . I mean, they spend all their time making up stories about things that don't exist. They think it's just themselves in the world. We never thought like that. We always *knew* there were humans. They're terribly lonely and don't know it."

He waved his hands vaguely. "It's just that I think we might get along with them," he finished.

"They'd turn us into pixies!"

"Not if we come back in the Ship. If there's one thing even humans can tell, it's that the Ship isn't very pixieish."

Grimma reached out and took his hand.

"Well . . . if that's what you really want to do . . ."

"It is."

"I'll come back with you."

There was a sound behind them. It was Gurder. The Abbot had a bag slung around his neck and had the drawn, determined look of someone who is going to See It Through no matter what.

"Er. I've come to say good-bye," he said.

"What do you mean?" said Masklin.

"I heard you say you're coming back in the Ship?"

"Yes, but—"

"Please don't argue." Gurder looked around. "I've been thinking about this ever since we got the Ship. There *are* other nomes out there. *Someone* ought to tell them about the Ship coming back. We can't take them now, but someone ought to find all the other nomes in the world and make sure that they know about the Ship. Someone ought to be telling them about what's really true. It should be me, don't you think? I've got to be useful for *something*."

"All by yourself?" said Masklin.

Gurder rummaged in the bag.

"No, I'm taking the Thing," he said, producing the black cube.

"Er—" Masklin began.

*"Don't worry,"* said the Thing. *"I have copied myself into the Ship's own computers. I can be here and there at the same time."*

"It's something I really want to do," said Gurder helplessly.

Masklin thought about arguing and then thought, Why? Gurder will probably be happier like this. Anyway, it's true, this Ship belongs to all nomes. We're just borrowing it for a while. So Gurder's right. Maybe someone ought to find the rest of them, wherever they are in the world, and tell them the truth about nomes. I can't think of anyone better for the job than Gurder. It's a big world. You need someone really ready to *believe*.

"Do you want anyone to go with you?" he said.

"No. Maybe I can find some nomes out there to help me." He leaned closer. "To tell the truth," he said, "I'm looking forward to it."

"Er. Yes. There's a lot of world, though," said Masklin.

"I've taken that into consideration. I've been talking to Pion."

"Oh? Well . . . if you're sure . . ."

"Yes. More than I've ever been about anything, now," said Gurder. "And I've been pretty sure of a lot of things in my time, as you know."

"We'd better find somewhere suitable to set you down."

"That's right," said Gurder. He tried to look brave. "Somewhere with a lot of geese," he said.


They left him at sunset, by a lake. It was a brief parting. If the Ship stayed anywhere for more than a few minutes now, humans would flock toward it.

The last Masklin saw of him was a small waving figure on the shore. And then there was just a lake, turning into a green dot on a dwindling landscape. A world unfolded, with one invisible nome in the middle of it.

And then there was nothing.

The control room was full of nomes watching the landscape unroll as the Ship rose.

Grimma stared at it.

"I never realized it looked like that," she said. "There's so much of it!"

"It's pretty big," said Masklin.

"You'd think one world would be big enough for all of us," said Grimma.

"Oh, I don't know," said Masklin. "Maybe one world isn't big enough for anyone. Where are we heading, Angalo?"

Angalo rubbed his hands and pulled every lever all the way back.

"So far up," he said, with satisfaction, "that there is no down."

The Ship curved up, toward the stars. Below, the world stopped unrolling because it had reached its edges, and became a black disk against the sun.

Nomes and frogs looked down on it.

And the sunlight caught it and made it glow around the rim, sending rays up into the darkness, so that it looked exactly like a flower.